# STATE OF GRACE

## FIRST FAMILY SERIES, BOOK 2

## MARIE FORCE

**State of Grace**
**First Family Series, Book 2**
**By: Marie Force**

Published by HTJB, Inc.
Copyright 2021. HTJB, Inc.
Cover design by Kristina Brinton
Cover photography by Regina Wamba
Models: Robert John and Ellie Dulac
Print Layout: E-book Formatting Fairies
ISBN: 978-1952793318

# CHAPTER ONE

D C Metro Police Lieutenant Sam Holland rushed through the doors to NBC4 at a quarter after eight on a Monday morning, twelve days before Christmas. Her Secret Service agents, Vernon and Jimmy, followed close behind her. For this TV appearance, she was also Samantha Cappuano, first lady of the United States. The only reason the *Today* show was interested in this interview was *because* she was first lady, a title she was still getting used to two and a half weeks after her husband had suddenly been promoted from vice president to president.

The department's psychiatrist, Dr. Trulo, was waiting in the lobby along with a staffer from the TV station and Lilia Van Nostrand, Sam's White House chief of staff.

"I'm glad to see you," Dr. Trulo said. "I was afraid you were standing me up."

"Sorry I'm late," Sam said. "Aubrey was having a rough morning, and I needed a few extra minutes with her."

"Is she okay?" Lilia asked as they followed a young woman who seemed to know where she was going.

"She will be."

Everyone they encountered stopped what they were doing to watch Sam go by. She hated that, but it came with the territory she and Nick now found themselves in as the nation's first couple. If their profile had been uncomfortably high as the second couple, it was a thousand times higher now, and she was working on making the transition. However, after a seismic shift such as the one that had occurred in their lives, she would need more than a couple of weeks to fully process their change in status.

"Right this way," the young woman said as she led them into a green room. "We're so excited to have you here, Mrs. Cappuano."

Even though she was in full uniform with the name HOLLAND on her chest, the woman still referred to her as Mrs. Cappuano. She was coming around to also understanding that *everyone* thought of her as Mrs. Cappuano, except her colleagues with the MPD. "I'm sorry. I didn't catch your name."

"It's Yvonne, ma'am."

Sam shook her hand. "Very nice to meet you, Yvonne."

"Likewise, ma'am. You have no idea how exciting it is for us to have you here."

"Thanks for having us."

"Please make yourselves comfortable and have some refreshments. We'll come for you in about twenty minutes."

"Thank you." Sam glanced with yearning at the table containing bagels, muffins and pastries. Carbs went straight to her ass, but she hadn't gotten to eat breakfast before leaving the White House because she'd been tending to Aubrey. "Screw it. I'm hungry." She helped herself to a cup of coffee and a cinnamon roll. "Have something, you guys. We wouldn't want to be rude."

While Dr. Trulo and Lilia checked out the offerings, Sam took a bite of the pastry and had to hold back a moan of pleasure. Dear God, that was good. She usually avoided such things, especially these days, when she found herself on the business end of a TV camera far too often. It was true what they said—the camera added ten pounds.

The BlackBerry she carried to keep in touch with her husband buzzed with a text from the man himself. *Aubrey is off to school and is all smiles. Whatever happened this morning seems to have passed. For now, anyway.*

Sam wrote right back. *Thanks for letting me know. I hated to leave her upset. Do you think they're picking up on the tension?*

*Possibly.*

Their maternal grandparents had recently filed for custody of the six-year-old twins who'd been living with Sam and Nick since their parents were murdered more than two months ago.

*We just need to make sure we're not bringing that tension around them. They pick up on everything.*

*Very true. I'll be watching you on TV. Break a leg (not really).*

Sam laughed. With her propensity for accidents, it was important to add that last part. *I hope I don't make a fool of myself (and you) on national TV.*

*Even if you do, I'll still love you.*

*Thank goodness for that.*

Yvonne returned exactly when she said she would, and they were shown to a studio, outfitted with microphones, told how the remote interview would be conducted and checked by hair and makeup people.

She and Dr. Trulo had met the previous afternoon to go over their notes for the interview, and Sam felt as ready as she ever did to speak in front of millions of people. They'd been asked to talk about the grief group she and the doctor had recently founded within the Metropolitan Police Department that provided an outlet for victims of violent crime.

Now that she was the first lady, the effort had gained greater exposure, and she hoped to make the program part of her platform in her new role.

Both Hoda and Savannah would be interviewing them, and before they went live, the two anchors came on to say hello and thank them for coming on the show.

"It's so nice to meet you after hearing so much about you," Hoda said.

"Thank you," Sam said. "You as well."

"How's life in the White House?" Savannah asked.

"It's different," Sam said with a laugh. "We're still getting used to it and finding a new routine there."

"Do you mind if we ask you about the adjustment during the interview?"

"No, that's fine. I just won't speak about my husband or his administration. Since I'm not briefed on any of that, I'd rather not be asked those questions, especially when we're here to talk about the grief group."

"Understood," Hoda said. "We'll be back from commercial in a few and will bring you right in."

"Sounds good." She glanced at Dr. Trulo, who was looking at her with amusement. His wiry gray hair had been combed into submission for the occasion. "What?"

"'I'm not briefed on any of that.'"

"Well, I'm not."

He laughed. "It's a good way to say, 'Stay in the lane we agreed to.'"

"Exactly. If you knew how many times reporters asked me questions about Nick, you'd know why I said that."

"I get it. I just thought it was funny that you're speaking the lingo now."

"I'm really not. That's about the extent of my political-wife lingo."

"Stand by," the producer said. "We're back in three, two, one."

"We have two very special guests with us this morning," Hoda said, smiling. "Our new first lady, Samantha Cappuano, also known at the Metropolitan Police Department in Washington, DC, as Lieutenant Sam Holland, and Metro PD psychiatrist Dr. Anthony Trulo are here to talk about an exciting new initiative they've founded within the MPD and one they hope will become a national project. Welcome to both of you."

"Thanks for having us," Sam said.

"Thank you for the invitation to talk about a project that's near and dear to both of us," Dr. Trulo said.

"Before we get to that," Savannah said, "we're all curious about how you and your family are adapting to your new home."

"Everyone is doing well," Sam said. "It's been two days since the last time I got lost trying to find the residence inside the White House, so I take that as progress. The kids are doing much better than I am with finding their way around."

"This is the first time in more than a decade that young children have lived at the White House," Hoda said. "What're they enjoying the most?"

"Scotty, who just turned fourteen, loves the movie theater, and the twins, who are six, are partial to the pool. They want to swim every night after dinner."

"Who's on lifeguard duty?" Hoda asked. "You or the president?"

"Mostly him, but I've done a few shifts."

"We asked you to come on today to discuss the grief group for victims of violent crime that you've initiated within the MPD," Savannah said. "Can you tell us about that?"

Sam looked to Dr. Trulo, who signaled for her to take the lead.

She'd get him for that later. "As you may have heard," she said with a laugh, "I'm a homicide detective. In the course of my work, I encounter family members and others deeply affected by the violent loss of loved ones. For some time, I've wished there was a mechanism in place to better support the secondary victims of violent crime. When I mentioned the idea to Dr. Trulo, he suggested a grief group."

"And you've formed the group within your department?" Hoda asked.

"We have," Dr. Trulo said. "We've had the first meeting and feel it was a big success. People who've lost spouses, children, parents and friends attended the meeting, and we've heard from several of them that they've met up again outside the meeting."

"That's amazing," Hoda said, "that they're making friends and finding additional support."

"That was our hope," Dr. Trulo said, "and we also hope our model might be adopted by other police departments across the country. Grief groups are a source of tremendous support to people suffering from loss. We wanted to provide an extra level of support to those grappling with violent loss, which often involves a protracted criminal proceeding that adds to the agony. The justice system moves slowly, and the families need support sometimes for years."

"There's such a huge need," Savannah said. "How do you narrow down who's invited?"

"It's open to anyone who feels they need it," Sam said, "but we do ask that the people attending have been touched by violent crime."

"You've had experience with that in your family as well," Hoda said.

"That's right," Sam said. "My father, Skip Holland, who was the MPD deputy chief at the time, was shot on the job and left a quadriplegic for nearly four years before he succumbed to his injuries in October."

"We're so sorry for your loss," Savannah said.

A picture of Sam with her dad from before the shooting came on the screen, triggering a tidal wave of grief that caught her off guard and unprepared to manage it while on national television. It took a huge effort not to let the pain show. "Thank you. We miss him."

"If other departments are interested in finding out more about your grief program, how can they get in touch?" Hoda asked.

Dr. Trulo gave his email address. "Or they can call the MPD and ask for me. I'd be happy to talk to anyone about what we've done so far and what we hope to do in the future."

"Definitely call him," Sam said. "You're more likely to get a reply."

"What she said," Dr. Trulo added, smiling.

The hosts laughed, thanked them for coming on the show and wished them luck with the grief group and with her new role as the first lady.

"Thank you so much for having us," Sam said, breathing a sigh of relief that she'd gotten through the interview without embarrassing herself or Nick.

"That was great, guys," Savannah said after the show went to commercial. "I'm sure you're going to hear from departments all over the country who are interested in your program."

"We appreciate the chance to talk about it," Sam said.

"And we appreciate the first national interview with the new first lady," Savannah said, smiling.

"I do what I can for the people," Sam said, trotting out her trademarked saying, which the hosts found amusing.

After they said their goodbyes, another young woman appeared to help remove Sam's microphone. She couldn't get free fast enough. Even though it was for a good cause, seeking publicity would never fall into her comfort zone.

Sam had shit to do and no time for delays. Starting today, she and her squad were reexamining unsolved cases overseen by disgraced officers Stahl, a former lieutenant, and Conklin, former deputy chief, to make sure they'd been handled properly. After recently solving the fifteen-year-old murder case of Calvin Worthington in a single afternoon, Sam was afraid of what they might find.

"You did good, kiddo," Dr. Trulo said as they followed Yvonne through the winding hallways that hopefully would lead them out of there.

"Thanks, you did, too. I hope you're ready to be inundated with requests for info."

"I'm ready. I typed up a program description and a list of

suggestions for getting started that I can send to anyone who requests it."

"Of course you did. I keep hoping I'm going to wake up one day as the kind of person who comes prepared, but so far it hasn't happened."

Dr. Trulo cracked up. "Good thing you're surrounded by others who can handle the prep work for you."

"Thank God for that, especially lately." She never would've survived the last couple of weeks without a cadre of dedicated family, friends and colleagues who'd helped her, Nick and the kids through the biggest transition of their lives. Everything would be going as well as could be expected if it hadn't been for the custody battle that loomed over every breath she took.

"Do you have time for a brief parking-lot consult?" she asked.

"I've always got time for you."

"In case I've never told you, you're one of the people I'm thankful for."

"Aw, thanks. It's a pleasure to work with you and to be your friend." In a whisper, he added, "*My friend* is the *first lady* of the whole United States!"

"Hush with that nonsense."

His laughter made her smile as they walked out together with Vernon leading and Jimmy bringing up the rear.

Sam would never get used to the Secret Service detail, but had compromised by agreeing to have two agents with her at all times. Mostly, she tried to ignore them and pretend they weren't there.

"Now, what can I do for you this fine morning?"

Sam glanced up at the dark clouds that hung over the nation's capital and shivered in the late autumn chill. With Christmas right around the corner, the days were getting shorter, and every day seemed colder than the last. "Are you one of those people who loves the winter?"

"I love all four seasons for different reasons."

Sam leaned against the black BMW Nick had outfitted to protect her from just about anything that could happen over the course of an average workday. "The twins' maternal grandparents have filed for custody of them."

"Oh damn. I hadn't heard that."

"We've kept it quiet so it won't turn into a three-ring circus.

That's the last thing they need. The twins don't even know about it, and if I have my way, they never will."

"What're the lawyers saying?"

"That they have no case. Jameson and Cleo were very clear who they wanted making decisions for Aubrey and Alden, and that's Elijah." Their older brother was a junior at Princeton and had designated Sam and Nick as the children's legal guardians while he was still in school. The three of them made all the big decisions about the kids together, and Elijah had become part of their family, too.

"Then it should be okay, right?"

"'Should be' are the key words there. They're making a BFD about custody now that Nick is president. They don't want the kids in the spotlight or in danger because of their proximity to him."

"They say that as if the twins aren't protected by the finest security in the world."

"Exactly, and the ultimate irony is they wanted nothing to do with the kids before their parents' killers were caught. The minute we solved the case, they tried pulling the concerned-family act. Elijah thinks they're far more interested in the billions in inheritance that come with the kids than they are in the kids themselves."

"He may be right about that. I know it's hard not to go to the worst-case scenario with this situation, but you have the parents' wishes working in your favor. The courts take that very seriously and would have to find fault with Elijah to even consider overturning the parents' request. The grandparents' case is a huge long shot, and they know that as well as you do."

"Still, the stress is real."

"I'm sure it is. You and Nick have invested a lot of yourself in those kids and their brother."

"It was the strangest thing, Doc. It took all of a day for them to feel like *ours*."

"Amazing how that happens, huh? All those years of fertility struggles, and now you're the mom of three and a half kids."

"I know. Nothing happened the way we thought it would, but we wouldn't trade this family for anything." Sam's cell phone rang, and when she checked the caller ID, she didn't recognize the number. "I probably ought to grab this."

"Go ahead. I'll see you back at the house. Reminder that my door is always open to you, Lieutenant."

"Thanks, Doc." Sam squeezed his arm and then opened her flip phone. "Lieutenant Holland."

"Um, hello, this is Marlene Peters. I'm a friend of Cameron Green's. We spoke during the Armstrong investigation."

"Oh right. What's up?"

"I heard something through the PTA grapevine that I thought might be of interest to you." Her children attended the exclusive Northwest Academy on Connecticut Avenue, where Aubrey and Alden were kindergarten students.

"What's that?"

"The name of the person who leaked the photos of the president at Aubrey and Alden's birthday party." Those photos had caused a shitstorm for Nick, who'd taken advantage of a break between meetings during a tense standoff with Iran to come to their former home on Ninth Street to celebrate the twins' birthday. One of the other parents had violated the nondisclosure agreement everyone had signed by leaking pictures of Nick with the kids while the secretary of State was being detained by the Iranians.

"You're right. That's info I'd very much like to have."

"It won't come back to me, will it?"

"Absolutely not. Your name will never be mentioned."

"His name is Bryson Thorn. His son Sebastian is in class with Alden and Aubrey."

"How do you know it came from him?"

"Multiple reliable sources. That's all I can say, or it'll come around to bite me in the ass."

"Any idea why he'd do it?"

"I don't know him, but one of the people who told me it was him said he'd do it for the attention and to stir the pot."

"Who'd want that kind of negative attention with everyone pissed at him, not to mention potential legal exposure for violating the NDA?"

"You know that saying about how some people will take any attention, even bad attention? I think that applies here."

"I'll never understand people."

"Right there with you. I've also heard that he's spouted off about your husband's youth, inexperience and reluctance to be president."

"Do you know where he lives?"

She provided an address in the swanky Spring Valley neighborhood.

"What does he do for a living?"

"Stockbroker. The wife is a piece of work. None of the other mothers like her."

"I appreciate this info, Marlene."

"I think it's egregious that he leaked those photos. Just about everyone I've spoken to agrees. Your husband wasn't doing anything wrong, and Bryson did it with the sole purpose of causing trouble for him. He may not align with him politically, but he was a guest in the man's home."

"It's good to know others see it the same way we do."

"Many others do. People are pissed, and the word's getting out that he was the leaker."

"Thanks again for letting me know."

"You got it."

Sam ended the call and thought about how she wanted to handle the info Marlene had given her. She'd planned to go right to HQ and change out of the uniform that had gotten a little snug since she'd worn it at her dad's funeral. She needed to quit with the comfort eating.

However, the uniform might come in handy on this mission. Opening her phone, she put through a call to her friend Lieutenant Archelotta, who ran the department's IT division.

"Hey, Sam. Saw you on TV this morning. The place is buzzing about it."

"In a good way, I hope."

"Mostly. People love the grief group and think it's a great idea. Well, Ramsey doesn't, but no one listens to him."

"I wish he'd find someone else to obsess about. But I didn't call to talk about that jackass. I need a personal favor."

"Um, okay, but I thought we weren't doing that anymore?"

Sam laughed at the unexpected comeback from the only fellow officer she'd ever fooled around with when she was between marriages. "Shut up."

Archie sputtered with laughter. "What can I do for you?"

"I found out who leaked the photos of Nick at the twins'

birthday party, and I could use some proof that they came from his IP address."

"I'd have to investigate something like that after hours."

"Understood, and I'd be happy to pay for your time."

"No charge. I'd love to help you nail the guy who did that."

"You're the best. I'll send you his info."

"I'll get on it tonight and let you know what I find."

"Thanks, Archie. It means a lot to have friends watching our backs in this new situation."

"*Situation,*" he said, snorting with laughter. "You mean the *situation* with you guys being the first couple?"

"Yeah, that's the one."

"We got you covered. I'll text you later."

Thankful to have him in her corner, she ended that call and put through another to her partner, Detective Freddie Cruz.

"You looked good on TV," he said when he picked up.

"I always look good."

She could "hear" his eyes rolling through the phone. "Whatever you say, rock star. What's up?"

"We need to take a trip to Spring Valley."

"What's way the hell up there?"

"The guy who leaked the photos of Nick at the twins' birthday party."

"Oh snap, a revenge mission. I'm always up for that, even if it means a trip to the outer reaches of Northwest."

Sam gave him the address. "Meet me there?"

"On my way."

# CHAPTER TWO

As Sam sat outside the Thorns' mansion—there was no other word for the massive contemporary home—and waited for Freddie, she thought about the differences between rich people and everyone else. Rich people needed huge houses with doorbells that sounded like air-raid sirens. At what point did things get so good for a person that they needed a doorbell that would scare the shit out of them every time someone rang it? Although, those doorbells probably got used only when the cops came to visit.

That thought made Sam laugh to herself. By some people's standards, she was probably rich now. Nick had told her his salary as president would be four hundred thousand dollars, which was a king's ransom to her as a public servant. After his presidency, he'd command millions in fees to speak and write books and generally be his awesome self. But one thing Sam knew for sure was no matter how much money her sugar daddy brought home, she'd never live in a mansion with an air-raid-siren doorbell.

She was still cracking up at the direction her thoughts had taken when Freddie knocked on her window.

Sam got out of the car.

"What's so funny?"

"If I told you, you'd have me committed."

"I'm already building a detailed case, so be careful what you tell me."

"Good to know."

"What's the deal with the leaker?"

"His name is Bryson Thorn. His son Sebastian is in class with the twins."

"Bryson and Sebastian Thorn. They sound like romance novel names."

Sam chuckled. "Yeah, I guess they do. You wanna bet what kind of doorbell this place has?"

"I'm sure it'll be one that sends you into fits."

"Let's find out, shall we?"

"I'm with you, LT, and P.S., you're freaking me out with the uniform."

"It's freaking me out, too, especially since it doesn't fit like it did at my dad's funeral. I've been stress eating."

"You're allowed."

"Not if my uniform doesn't fit!"

"You'll get back on track."

Sam went through the wrought-iron gate ahead of him. "My poor, delusional Freddie. That's not how it works for women. Once the fat arrives, it never, ever, *ever* goes away. Like, *ever*."

"That is not true."

"Yes, it is! Ask any woman. A nuclear bomb can't get rid of fat once it's gotten comfy on an ass or hips or arms or thighs or stomach. Fat *loves* the stomach."

He cringed. "Whatever you say."

Sam positioned her hand over the huge doorbell button. The bigger the button, the louder the commotion. "Ready for this?"

"Bring it."

Sam pushed the button and stood back to listen to what could only be called a symphony orchestra of sounds. "Are you kidding me right now?"

"You might need to press it again so I can fully experience it a second time."

Sam pushed the button.

"Wow, that's got to be the craziest one we've ever heard."

"Takes the gold medal for crazy doorbells. I couldn't deal with it." She peeked through the beveled glass on the side of the door and saw a man coming to the door wearing headphones and a scowl on his face. Sam remembered him from the party. He'd checked out their home like a Realtor hosting an open house.

When he saw cops on his front stairs, he recoiled as he opened the door.

"Mr. Thorn?"

"Yeah."

"I'm Lieutenant Holland, and this is my partner, Detective Cruz. We met when you and your son came to a birthday party at my house." Tall with dark hair and wearing a wrinkled Oxford shirt, he reminded her of the actor Vince Vaughn.

"I remember."

"You got a second?"

"I'm, ah, kind of busy working," he said, seeming suddenly flustered.

"This'll only take a minute."

"Uh, sure." He stepped aside to allow them to enter the house.

The foyer ceiling was easily thirty feet tall. Sam wondered if all the heat ended up at the top, but she wasn't there to ask that question. "How's Sebastian doing?"

Taken aback by the question, he said, "He's fine. He's at school."

"Alden and Aubrey enjoyed having him at their party."

"Oh, well, that's good. He had fun. It's nice of you to step up for them. What happened to their parents was horrific."

"Indeed it was, which was why we wanted them to have a great party. They'd been through so much, losing their parents shortly before their birthday." Sam made a clucking sound as she shook her head. "Poor babies."

"They're sweet kids. The parents were nice people."

"Yes, they are and were, which is why I wonder why someone would want to harm the people who are caring for them after their terrible loss."

His brows came together in an expression of confusion. "I'm not sure what you mean."

"Don't you?" Sam unleashed her unblinking stare on him. As a kid, no one had been able to beat her in a staring contest. That skill had come in handy many times on the job, and now was no exception.

Thorn blinked first. "I, ah, have to get back to work."

"I know you're the one who leaked the photos of my husband at the party."

"*What?* I didn't do that!"

"Yes, you did. I have several witnesses willing to testify that it was you, not to mention my IT people are tracing the IP address as we speak."

He sputtered with outrage. "I have no idea what you're talking about."

"Yes, you do. I figured I'd stop by to let you know my husband and I intend to fully enforce the legal terms of the NDA you signed when the Secret Service vetted you ahead of the party. You'll be hearing from our attorneys. I hope the stock market is good to you, because we plan to sue your pants off."

"You can't just come into someone's home and start accusing them of things."

"Detective Cruz, can I do that?"

"Yes, ma'am. That's actually a big part of our jobs. We visit people's homes and accuse them of things almost every day."

Sam *loved* him and the way he rolled with her so, *so* much.

"Here's the deal, Mr. Thorn. By uploading those photos, you violated the airtight NDA you signed before you entered my home. My husband and I will be filing suit against you imminently, and we plan to make it a doozy." She looked around him into one of those formal living rooms no one actually used—except when cops came to call. "Detective Cruz, how do you think my sofa is going to look in that living room? Nick and I will need a bigger place after we leave the White House. This would do, don't you think?"

"The sofa would look great there, for sure."

"You've made your point," Thorn said on a low growl.

"Have I?" Sam leaned in a little closer. "It was a dick move to try to hurt the people providing love and shelter to two children whose parents were murdered in the most horrific way imaginable. Their murders were among the worst we've ever encountered, and we've seen it all. Did it make you feel like a big man to get that scoop and make trouble for my husband?"

His mulish look spoke volumes. "I've said all I'm going to say."

"Excellent. We'll see you in court. Let's go, Detective. I'll take the measurements the next time I'm here."

They walked out of the house, leaving the door open. It slammed shut behind them, making Sam laugh.

"Holy shit, that was fun," Freddie said.

"I wish I'd recorded it as a training video. You were on *fire*."

"So were you."

"Come for my family, and I'm coming for you."

"Are you really going to sue him?"

"You bet your ass I am. We need to send a message that we're not putting up with this shit. He signed the NDA, and now he's going to feel our wrath."

"Do you have Archie tracking the IP address—and P.S., I'm shocked that you even know what that is."

"I know stuff," she said indignantly, "and yes, he's doing it for me on his own time as a personal favor."

"That's awesome. I'm so glad you're sticking it to Thorn. The stuff about your sofa fitting in his living room was a nice touch."

"I'm glad you thought so, even though you know I'd never live in a place like that. Nick and I would get lost trying to find each other."

"If you can find each other in the White House, you can find each other in there."

"I guess that's true. Lately, our biggest challenge is chasing Skippy. That dog keeps escaping from the residence."

"She's so cute. The whole country is following her Instagram account. She has, like, twenty million followers already."

"That's all Scotty's doing. Do you know she gets more than five hundred letters a week at the White House, and we only just got her!"

"That's crazy."

"We're working on a form letter from Skippy to send to the people who write to her. Scotty thinks the whole thing is awesome, and he loves having her, but we're training him to keep better tabs on her. They found her eating daisies in the floral shop in the basement last week."

Freddie rocked with laughter. "She's going to be on the front page of the papers at this rate."

"Only we could end up with the wildest puppy in the pound." When they reached their cars, she said, "Thanks for driving all the way out here to have my back on a personal matter. I've learned the hard way not to go into any house by myself." She shuddered, thinking of the day former lieutenant Stahl had taken her hostage in the Springer house.

"Don't think about that," Freddie said, tuned into her as always. "He's in prison where he belongs."

"Thank goodness for that. Let's get back to HQ and dive into Stahl's files to figure out what other cases of his got the shaft."

"I'm a little afraid of what we're going to find in those files."

"Me, too." As Sam drove back to headquarters in heavy traffic, she juggled the secure BlackBerry. Nick picked up on the second ring. "I can never believe you actually take my calls when you're presiding over the fate of the free world."

"The fate of the free world has nothing on my lovely wife," he said, sounding amused. "What's going on?"

"I found out who leaked the photos from the birthday party and paid him a little visit."

"Not by yourself, I hope." He was forever concerned about her safety, and with good reason after the crazy shit that regularly happened to her on the job.

"Of course not. I had Freddie with me. The guy lives in a McMansion in Spring Valley with thirty-foot ceilings and a doorbell that sounds like the Boston Pops on the Fourth of July. I put him on notice that we'll be fully enforcing the NDA and filing a big fat lawsuit against him."

"What'd he say to that?"

"He denies it was him, but he's lying. He broke out in a sweat when I told him I knew it was him."

"That's my love. Making men sweat on a daily basis."

"It's one of my superpowers. Anyway, I wanted to tell you I'm going to call Andy and ask him to file a lawsuit against him ASAP."

"Go for it."

"It's apt to make the news." She hated to worry about such things, but she didn't want to cause any more grief for him than he already had to deal with as president. His opponents had been relentless, calling him the "reluctant president" because of his announcement that he wouldn't be running for the Democratic nomination in the next election—days before President Nelson's untimely death elevated Nick to the top job.

"I hope it does so other people we cross paths with in the next three years will know we take our privacy and that of our family quite seriously."

"It's very sexy when you go into protector mode."

"I'd say the same about you, and by the way, we're probably giving the people at the NSA something to talk about."

"Wait! Are they listening to us?"

He laughed so hard, he went silent.

"Nick! This isn't funny!"

"Yes, it is," he said, wheezing from laughter. "No one is listening."

"You'll pay for that later."

"I'll look forward to that. By the way, you were great on the *Today* show. We're getting bombed with calls and emails and comments on the social media posts about your appearance. People think the idea for the grief group for victims of violent crime is fantastic."

"That's good. Doesn't bring our people back, but it helps to know we're not alone." The loss of her father was still a raw wound two months after he succumbed to injuries sustained in an on-the-job shooting almost four years ago.

"You, my love, are never alone."

"That helps. I'll see you at home?"

"I'll be here. Feels like I never leave these days."

Sam vowed to remedy that by working with Brant, his lead Secret Service agent, to plan a date night soon. "We'll have to do something about that, but for now, I need to get back to it."

"Be careful out there, love. You're my everything."

"I'm always careful. Later."

She ended the call, smiling the way she always did when she got to talk to him during her workday.

Digging through her contacts on the flip phone, she found the number for their attorney friend Andy Simone.

"Mr. Simone's office."

"Hi, this is Sam Cappuano calling for Mr. Simone. Is he free?" For a full ten seconds, there was dead silence. "Hello?"

"Yes, of course, Mrs. Cappuano. I'll put you right through to him, and if I may say, I just love you and your husband."

In the background, Sam heard Andy say, "Put the call through, Janice."

"Sorry," Janice said.

Sam held back laughter. "Thank you for your support, Janice."

"Please hold for Mr. Simone."

"Sorry about that, Sam," Andy said when he came on the line. "She's got a bad case of starstruck-itis."

"It's going around lately. Believe it or not, that very thing happens several times a day."

"I believe it," Andy said. "How're things at 1600 Pennsylvania Avenue?"

"Not bad, all things considering. The butlers make for easy living, and the kids love the extras, like the pool and the movie theater."

"I'm glad you're settling in. If you're calling about the custody situation, I'm still waiting to hear back from the grandparents' attorney. I sent him the documentation proving Elijah is the guardian his parents appointed. I suspect they're trying to find a way around that, but there isn't one."

"Well, that's a relief."

"It's not over yet, but I feel good about where we are."

"I'm very glad to hear that, but that wasn't the reason for my call. I wanted to tell you I've figured out who leaked the photos of Nick at the twins' birthday party, and we're interested in suing him for the breach of the NDA. We feel like we need to send a message to people on the periphery of our lives that we'll stridently protect our privacy in this crazy new situation we're in."

"I've already got something drafted because I figured you'd find out who it was. I'll take care of that for you today. What kind of damages are you thinking?"

"The guy is loaded, so we want to make it hurt."

"So, a million?"

"That'd work."

"It'll cost him a bundle to defend against the suit, too."

"Good. I want it to *really* hurt."

"Oh, it will. Not to mention the publicity it'll generate. What do you have in the way of proof?"

"Apparently, it's somewhat common knowledge among the parents that he was the one who did it, and I've got a friend in IT working on connecting the leak to his IP address."

"If we have that, we won't need the parents."

"Good, because I don't think they'd want to be involved."

Sam gave him the man's name and address. "His son Sebastian is in school with the twins."

"How do you feel about a potential suit causing trouble for the kids at school?"

"You think that'd happen in kindergarten?"

"I think it's possible at all ages."

"Huh, well, Nick and I feel strongly that we need to send this message so we won't be dealing with this crap the whole time he's in office. We can explain to the kids what's happening so they're prepared if Sebastian says anything."

"All right, sounds good. Send me a copy of the NDA he signed and the IT evidence when you have it."

"Will do. Thanks for taking care of all this crap for us, Andy."

"Are you kidding? Having you guys as clients is great for business, not to mention my ego."

Sam laughed. "Glad to help boost both those things."

"Elsa is so excited about the Christmas Eve party, I think she may spontaneously combust."

"We're looking forward to it."

"I call the Lincoln Bedroom."

"Nick suggested we do some sort of game to determine who gets that room."

"That'd be fun—and funny."

"We figure we need to enjoy the hell out of the place if we're required to live there."

"I couldn't agree more. Will be in touch on all things."

"Thanks, Andy."

Sam felt better knowing they were doing something to deal with the egregious violation of their privacy from the twins' birthday party. The opposition media was still going on about Nick having the time to attend a party while the secretary of State was being detained in Iran. He'd taken an hour to run home to see the kids between meetings, but no one wanted to hear that. Apparently, he was expected to work twenty-four hours a day while president or else.

Before he'd become president, they'd had a couple of "close calls," with the Nelson administration twice engulfed in scandals serious enough that Nick was put on notice that he needed to be ready should the president be forced to resign. The endless scrutiny was the part Sam had feared the most, and it had started almost right away with the media and Nick's detractors picking apart everything he said and did.

Firing the secretary of State had caused another uproar, especially when the sacked secretary went on TV to vent his outrage at the "young, inexperienced" president who'd shown him the door after getting more information about what'd really happened in Iran. Nick needed to be surrounded by people he could trust, and he no longer trusted Martin Ruskin after the incident in Iran.

Over the last few weeks, Sam had done her best to stay sort of "sealed off" from the drama that surrounded the presidency and the White House, but she wanted to be there to support Nick, so she had to stay somewhat plugged in. She walked a fine line between needing to know and not wanting to know who was coming for him now.

Her anxiety had been a challenge lately, but she did her best to keep that hidden from him because he had enough of his own anxiety to deal with. He didn't need hers, too, especially when he struggled so horribly with insomnia.

While stopped at a red light, she gave Nick a call to update him on what Andy had had to say about the lawsuit—and the custody battle—and was preparing her message when he surprised her by picking up again.

"What's up?"

Sam filled him in on the latest from Andy on the custody situation and told him what they'd decided about the lawsuit. "The first couple suing someone for a million dollars is going to make the news."

"Yes, I suppose it will, but isn't that the point?"

"Before we do anything more, run it by your people to make sure we aren't causing more trouble than we're solving with this."

"I will, but I'm determined to send a message to this guy and anyone else who'd stab us in the back in our own home."

"You know I agree, but I'm not the one who's going to have to fend off the media attention when the word gets out. You need to be prepared for that."

"I'm meeting with Terry, Christina and Trevor in a few minutes," he said of his top aides. "I'll run it by them."

"Sounds good. And I'm hoping the grandparents can't find a way around Cleo and Jameson's airtight guardianship provision for Elijah."

"There is no way around it. The parents have spoken and so has the guardian."

Sam wished she could be so certain. "I guess we'll see."

"Try not to worry. We've got the advantage in this situation, and they know it."

"What? Me worry?" She pulled into the lot at HQ, which was

surrounded by media trucks these days. "HQ is overrun with news trucks. Do they think I'm suddenly going to get chatty about you and your administration?"

"Hope springs eternal."

Her colleagues must hate the intrusion, Sam thought, not that most of them would ever say so. A few would, but most wouldn't even if they thought it. "Gotta go to work. Love you."

"Love you, too."

# CHAPTER THREE

Nick ended the call with Sam and dwelled for a second on the tension he felt coming from her as they continued to adjust to the massive changes in their lives since he'd suddenly ascended to the presidency. He looked around the Oval Office, still amazed that he got to work in the most famous office on earth, that his family lived upstairs in the residence and people called him Mr. President.

Terry knocked on the door and stuck his head in. "Are you free, Mr. President?"

"I am," Nick said. "Come in." He brought his briefing book with him to the collection of chairs and sofas in the middle of the room and settled in his usual chair. When had he decided what his "usual chair" in the Oval Office was going to be? The thought amused him, as many things did in this new surreal existence.

Terry, Trevor and Christina took seats on the sofas as one of the butlers brought in afternoon refreshments, which were one of the best perks of his new job.

"Help yourselves, friends," Nick said, gesturing to the tray of cookies, coffee and tea.

"Don't mind if I do," Terry said, taking a cookie and pouring himself a coffee.

Nick tried to eat only one of the delicious cookies per day, and he'd already had his allotment in the morning meeting with his cabinet. "What's on the docket?"

"Brandon Halliwell called," Terry said, referring to the chair of the Democratic National Committee. "He wants to discuss your choice for vice president before you announce anything. He said he has some thoughts about how Senator Sanford could be better used as the new secretary of State."

"She's my top choice to be vice president."

"He's aware of that and is asking you to reconsider. He and others believe she'd be better suited to the secretary of State role and that she'd be more interested in that. They want Henderson for VP."

Nick held back a groan. "You gotta be kidding me. After everything we went through to narrow the field, he's throwing this at me?"

"He is, and I have to say, sir, I tend to agree that Sanford would be a better fit for State," Terry said.

"Whose side are you on, anyway?"

"Yours, sir. Always. But Sanford has deep diplomatic experience on the Foreign Relations Committee, and you do, in fact, need a new secretary of State."

Since he'd fired the other guy, that was. He had zero regrets about that decision, even if Ruskin was trashing him all over town. "I guess we need to bring Gretchen Henderson back in, then," Nick said with a twinge of unease. Sam had had one of her "feelings" about Henderson, and he'd learned to take those things seriously, but with the DNC pushing for Henderson, he was running up against a strong headwind. "Who else is there besides her?"

"You're set on appointing a woman, right?" Christina asked.

"Absolutely."

"Then I'd say she's the best you're going to get. We've done the vetting on every other high-profile female in the national spotlight and we're down to her."

"How's that possible?" Nick asked.

Christina gave him a lengthy rundown of the top female operatives, all of whom had declined to be considered for a wide variety of reasons ranging from family concerns that required their involvement to vital committee assignments or governorships that would be useful in other ways.

"In short," Christina concluded, "Henderson is the one the DNC wants. They like the idea of a young, dynamic pair as the face of the party going forward. Henderson has made a lot of friends with her get-out-the-vote efforts on behalf of candidates around the country. She has a ton of support at the grass-roots level."

Nick debated whether he should mention that Sam had gotten an unsettling vibe from Gretchen, but she'd had only a passing encounter with the woman as Sam was leaving and Gretchen was arriving. Even though he'd learned to trust his wife's gut feelings, it'd be foolish to make a decision of this magnitude based on a thirty-second interaction. "Have her come back in for another meeting. I want to talk to her again before I decide for sure."

"Will do," Christina said.

"Speaking of Ruskin," Trevor said, "we're getting bombed with requests for details about why he was fired and whether it was related to what happened in Iran. We've got multiple networks and news outlets threatening to file Freedom of Information requests if we don't come clean."

"Well, I did promise that we'd tell the people what happened once we reviewed the events in Tehran. What do you guys recommend?"

Terry spoke up first. "I say you tell your side of the story—that he was less than forthcoming about the events in Iran, and you no longer have confidence in his abilities to represent the United States on the world stage. You could say that you need to feel you can trust the people working within your administration, and while many of your cabinet secretaries are holdovers from the Nelson administration, you value trust and loyalty above all other things. And you could add that former secretary Ruskin knows exactly why his tenure was terminated."

Trevor had been taking frantic notes the entire time Terry was speaking.

"Did you get that?" Nick asked him.

Trevor nodded.

"Let's release that as a statement—exactly what Terry said." He glanced at Christina. "Do you approve?"

"My only worry is that you'll further infuriate Ruskin with the statement, which will add fuel to his fire."

"I honestly don't care what he says about me," Nick said. "I know the truth, and so does he. I'm comfortable with the statement. Go ahead and release it at the daily briefing, Christina."

Nick checked the silver TAG Heuer watch Sam had given him.

He had twenty minutes until a meeting with the Joint Chiefs of Staff and the secretary of Defense about some issues in the South China Sea that had been mentioned in the morning briefing documents over the last couple of days.

The meetings never ended and ran the gamut from deadly boring to truly terrifying, with almost nothing in the middle. Not to mention the decisions he was forced to make on a daily basis—everything from sending troops into a hot spot in the Middle East to proposed cuts to programs that benefited the country's neediest citizens to conversations with world leaders about issues such as climate change, immigration and cyberattacks.

There was no shortage of problems, needs and ideas, but at the end of every meeting, everyone in the room looked to him because his take was the only one that mattered.

If he allowed himself to think too much about the responsibility that sat on his shoulders, he might buckle under the weight of it. Since buckling wasn't an option, he tried to take things one minute—and one meeting—at a time, while still trying to determine who among Nelson's secretaries he could trust and who he couldn't.

A knock on the door of the Oval Office interrupted his musings and the conversation that had gone on without him among his top aides. "Come in," Nick called.

"Pardon the interruption, Mr. President," said Derek Kavanaugh, Nick's longtime personal friend as well as his deputy chief of staff.

"Come on in, Derek," Nick said.

"I wanted to make you aware of a situation in Des Moines. Gunfire has broken out at a Meet with Santa event being held at an elementary school. We have reports of multiple fatalities, including children."

"Ah, God," Nick said, aching for families who'd lost children right before Christmas.

"The FBI and ATF have deployed resources to the scene, and we're expecting more information in about thirty minutes," Derek added.

"Thank you, Derek."

"Sorry to be the bearer of such awful news, sir."

"It is awful, and right before Christmas." Nick felt sick to his stomach. Gun violence had become such an enormous challenge for the country, and one with no easy solutions. The deaths of innocent children would bring the issue back to the forefront once again.

Terry, Christina and Trevor looked as shocked and saddened as Nick felt as they followed him into the study off the Oval Office to watch the TV coverage of the unfolding tragedy.

"You'll need to make a statement in the next few hours," Trevor said. "I'll work on that."

"What does one say about such a horrific thing?" Nick asked.

"You speak from your heart," Terry said.

His heart was broken, and whatever he said about this latest instance of unspeakable violence would certainly need to reflect that.

SAM WALKED into a silent pit and realized her entire team was gathered around the TV in the conference room. "What's going on?" she asked when she joined them.

"Shooting at an elementary school in Des Moines," Gonzo said. "During a Santa event for kids."

"Oh no," Sam said on a long exhale. "How bad?"

"Horrific," Jeannie McBride said. "At least thirty dead, and they expect the death toll to rise."

"Oh my God," Sam said, her legs wanting to buckle under her as she imagined the horror of families taking their children to see Santa only to be attacked by a madman with a gun.

The TV anchors announced that the president would be making a statement in the seconds before the scene shifted to the White House briefing room. Nick walked into the room, looking visibly shaken and paler than usual, which made Sam hurt for him. He stepped up to the podium to face a silent press corps.

"At approximately eleven thirty this morning in Des Moines, Iowa, a lone gunman entered an elementary school where older children had invited their younger siblings to meet Santa. The gunman opened fire on a group of more than two hundred parents, children and volunteers. More than thirty people are dead, many of them children. The gunman was killed in a shootout with police." His voice broke as he battled his emotions. "As a father of young children, I ache for the horror that's been perpetrated in Des Moines today and for the pain the community is experiencing so close to Christmas. I've deployed the full resources of the federal government to assist in the investigation and to provide comfort to the grieving families and community. My wife and I are heartbroken for those who suffered unimaginable losses today and for the people of Des Moines as they cope with this horrific tragedy."

He left the podium without taking any of the questions that were fired at him by reporters who wanted to know what he planned to do about gun violence in the United States and whether he'd be traveling to Des Moines.

"You should go to him," Freddie said quietly so he wouldn't be overheard. "Go there, Sam."

His words jolted her out of the shocked state she'd slipped into. "Yeah. You're right. I, uh, I'll be back when I can."

"We'll cover for you," Freddie said.

Sam squeezed his arm as she left the conference room and headed for the ladies' room to change out of her uniform into the clothes she'd brought for after the TV interview. As she worked on removing the uniform, she realized her hands were shaking. All she could think about was Alden and Aubrey, and how excited they'd been to meet Santa at an event they'd held at the White House over the weekend. Tears filled her eyes at the thought of such a horror befalling the precious children in Des Moines.

She folded her uniform and stuffed it into the bag and was leaving the restroom when she ran straight into SVU Detective Ramsey, her sworn enemy.

"Well, look who it is. Little Miss Mary TV star. You're such an attention whore."

She tried to push past him with the goal of ignoring him, but he wouldn't yield. After getting the news about the shooting in Des Moines, the last thing on her mind was Ramsey and his nonsense.

"Better than being an actual whore," she said when he gave her no choice but to engage. "How's the little missus taking the news about your affair?"

His expression turned thunderous in an instant. "I know it was you who dug up that shit about me."

"I had nothing to do with it, but here's a pro tip—if there's no shit to find, then it's not possible to dig anything up. You have a good day, Detective."

"Your day is coming, you bitch."

Sam turned to face him. "Are you threatening a superior officer by any chance, Detective?"

"Fuck you."

"Nah, I'll pass."

Ramsey stormed off as Captain Malone approached her from the other end of the corridor. "What was that about?"

"The usual pleasantries," Sam said, "but he did warn me that my day is coming. And that's a direct quote. Perhaps you could pretend to have overheard that part of the conversation?"

"Perhaps I could, and that of course would lead to yet another suspension for the detective. They're starting to add up."

"At what point will there be enough to get rid of him?"

"Not soon enough. He has 'rights,' you know."

Sam rolled her eyes. "I was going to come find you. I assume you heard what's going on in Des Moines."

"I did. It's horrifying."

"I was thinking I should go to be with Nick. I know I'm on duty, but..."

"No, you should go. We'll take care of things here today."

"Thank you for understanding. I'll make up the time."

"We owe you more time than you could make up in a lifetime."

"I guess that's a good thing, since I've got this other part-time gig going on."

Malone snorted with laughter. "Is that what you're calling it? A part-time gig?"

"I'm still not sure what to call it. I'm figuring it out on a day-to-day basis."

"You're doing fine. Go support your husband and the country during this horrific tragedy. We've got things covered here."

"Thank you for the support, Captain. It's appreciated. I know this is a unique situation—"

His bark of laughter cut her off. "Unique. That's one word for having the first lady of the United States heading up our Homicide division simultaneously. Public Affairs is being bombed with requests for interviews about how you're handling the dual roles, how we're managing it, etc."

Sam was appalled to hear that. "Tell them I'm sorry for the added workload and to deny all interviews on my behalf. I'll never understand why the media thinks they should have unfettered access to my every move."

"You don't understand that? Really?"

"Well, I do, but I hate it. Right now, I need to go be with Nick as he handles a massive tragedy."

"Go do that. We'll hold down the fort here."

"Thanks, Cap." Sam headed for the morgue exit and ran into Chief Medical Examiner Dr. Lindsey McNamara, who was in tears.

"It's the most awful thing," Lindsey said, hugging Sam.

"It is."

"Are you going to the White House?"

"I am. I figured Nick could use the support."

"Terry texted me that everyone there is a mess." Lindsey's fiancé, Terry O'Connor, was Nick's chief of staff. "And right before Christmas. I just can't handle it."

"I know. It's horrific. I'll catch up with you later."

"I'll be here, and I'll be praying for you both as you lead the country through this."

"We need all the prayers we can get."

"You'll do it beautifully. I have no doubt."

"Thank you." Sam left her friend with a sad smile as she headed out into the blustery cold, wishing she had as much confidence in herself as Lindsey did. The eyes of the entire world would be on Nick, and her by extension, as they tried to console a grieving city and nation. No life experience or education could prepare anyone to deal with something like this.

Vernon and Jimmy were in the black SUV that accompanied Sam everywhere she went these days. When Vernon saw her coming, he rolled down the driver's side window. "I assume you've heard the news about the shooting."

"Yes, I have, and I'm heading to the White House to be with Nick."

"We'll be right behind you."

When she'd agreed to have a detail trailing her, she'd insisted on continuing to drive herself. As she navigated the short distance "home" to the White House, she tried to muster the courage it would take to get through the next few hours and days. People would be looking to them for solace and compassion, and they'd do their best to provide whatever was needed even as their own hearts ached for the victims and their families.

*This is what it will be like,* she thought. For the next three years, anytime something awful or tragic happened in the country or the world, people would look to Nick—and her—for guidance on how to handle it.

She swallowed hard, hoping she, and they, had the fortitude to provide the kind of leadership that would be needed to guide the country through such a senseless tragedy.

When she arrived at the White House and was waved through the gate, she parked at the door to the East Wing, where her offices were located. She went right to the office of her chief of staff, Lilia Van Nostrand, who dabbed at tears with a tissue as she watched the coverage from Des Moines.

"Hey," Sam said, startling the other woman.

"Oh, you're here." She stood and came around the desk.

Sam hugged her. "I'm here."

"It's so awful."

"Yes, it is. I'm going to find my husband."

Lilia nodded. "It'll be good for him to have you here."

"That's what I figured. I'll see you in a bit."

"I'll be here."

Sam headed from the East Wing to the West, realizing at some point over the last few weeks that the massive White House campus had become more familiar and less daunting.

Nick's vice presidential reception team had moved to the lobby of the Oval Office and waved her right through when she arrived. They, too, looked as if they'd been crying. Hell, the whole country was probably crying today.

Nick was seated at the Resolute desk, surrounded by aides, all of whom seemed to be talking as he kept half an eye on a television that had been brought in. Only when he glanced away from the TV did he see her in the doorway, a faint smile lighting up his weary face.

"Excuse me," he said to the others as he stood and came to greet her with the kind of hug he specialized in. "Thanks for coming."

"I figured you might need this," she said, holding on even tighter, her arms around his waist inside his suit coat.

"You figured absolutely right."

"What's the latest?"

"Forty-two confirmed dead, thirty of them children under the age of ten. The gunman, who is among the dead, was a disgruntled former employee of one of the families attending the event. The five of them are among the dead."

"Dear God," she said, blinking back tears. She saw and heard a lot of horrible things in the course of her work, but this was on a whole other level. "What can I do?"

"It helps that you're here. How long can you stay?"

"As long as you need me."

He linked her hand with his and brought her with him to rejoin his team as they worked to manage the unfolding crisis.

Sam stood by his side later that afternoon as he again addressed the nation to express their profound sorrow and disbelief at the nightmare unfolding in Iowa.

"These were babies," he said, his voice breaking, "going to see Santa, full of excitement for Christmas. The person who perpetrated this cowardly act did so out of vengeance toward a former employer. He was known to have had significant mental health challenges, but had refused any form of treatment. I took an oath to preserve and protect the Constitution of the United States, and I shall do so with every fiber of my being, including protecting the right to bear arms afforded by the Second Amendment. But we must find a way to keep assault weapons out of the hands of people who shouldn't have them. I promise you here and now that finding a way to make that happen will be a cornerstone of my administration. I ask people of goodwill who have watched this tragedy unfold today to join me in this effort to come together as a nation to work toward solutions that would make this country safer for all of us, especially our children. Sam and I send our deepest condolences to the families whose lives were shattered today and to the people of Des Moines and Iowa who are coping with this unspeakable tragedy. We will keep you in our prayers during the difficult days and weeks to come."

He didn't take any questions because he didn't want to debate sensible gun control measures. Not tonight. There'd be time for that later.

"I need to see my own kids," Nick said after he and Sam left the press room.

"Me, too."

# CHAPTER FOUR

They climbed the stairs to the residence where they found the kids in the kitchen under the supervision of Sam's stepmother, Celia, who'd moved into the White House to help with the children. After the recent loss of her husband, Skip, Celia had welcomed the distraction that came with being part of their chaotic life. As she hugged Sam and Nick, she, too, looked as if she'd been crying.

Their fourteen-year-old son, Scotty, was subdued as he stroked Skippy's soft fur while the twins chattered on, blissfully unaware of the tragedy that had occurred in Des Moines. Sam hoped to keep them unaware. Her phone rang, and she stepped out of the kitchen to take the call from Archie. "Hey," she said. "What's up?"

"I was able to tie the IP address to the post your guy made under an anonymous account. We've got him."

"That's great, Archie. Thank you for this. Let me know what I owe you."

"No charge. What he did was lame. He deserves whatever you have planned for him."

"We have a massive lawsuit planned, and you've provided the final piece we needed."

"I sent the info to your personal email."

"Appreciate this, my friend."

"Anytime. How're you guys holding up over there? It's just the most horrible thing."

"It really is, and we're taking it a minute at a time."

"I saw Nick just now. He said all the right things."

"It's hard to know what the right things are during something like this."

"He got it right. People are fed up with this shit."

"It's a very difficult issue, but one that needs some sensible solutions."

"If anyone can get this done, Nick can."

"I guess we'll see. Thank you again for using your superpowers to help me."

Laughing, he said, "Happy to do it. See you tomorrow."

Sam ended that call and put through another to Andy.

"Hey," he said. "Saw you guys on TV just now. It's so awful."

"Yes, it is."

"Nick did a good job of setting the right tone."

"I think so, too. In other news, I heard from my IT guy, and he was able to connect the dots to our friend Mr. Thorn. I'll forward his info to you the next time I'm on a computer."

"That's great news. I've got the suit ready to be filed and served as soon as you give the green light."

"Hang on a second." She gestured for Nick to join her in the hallway. "Andy has what he needs to file the suit against Thorn. Just confirming you're still on board."

"I'm on board, but will we be crucified for the timing after the shooting?"

"We could say it was already in the works when the shooting happened, which is true."

He thought about that for a second. "Tell Andy to go ahead, then."

"Did you hear that?" Sam asked Andy.

"I did. We'll take care of it tomorrow. I'll let you know when he's been served."

"Thanks again, Andy."

"Happy to help. Could I speak to Nick for a second?"

"Sure, hang on." Sam handed her phone to Nick. "He wants to talk to you."

Leaving Nick to speak to his friend in private, Sam went back to the kitchen and found Shelby Hill and her son, Noah, had joined the group. Shelby had agreed to be the White House social secretary and had hired a nanny to help with Noah during work hours. They'd set up a playroom on the third floor of the residence that Noah, Alden and Aubrey were enjoying.

"How was your day, Mrs. Hill?" Sam asked her close friend, whose face was red and puffy from crying.

"Wonderful and awful. The news of the shooting has broken my heart."

They kept their voices down so the children wouldn't overhear them.

"I know. Mine, too. I worry about people going numb to the violence because it's so much a part of our everyday lives."

"It's unbearable. Babies going to see Santa." Tears ran down Shelby's cheeks that Noah adorably wiped away. "Thank you, sweet boy. Mama is sad tonight."

"Go home and snuggle with your husband," Sam said, hugging her friend.

"That's the plan, but I wanted to see my other babies before I left. How cute is Scotty with that dog?"

"Adorable." Skippy was glued to Scotty at all times, and when he wasn't home, the dog came looking for Sam, which everyone found hilarious. Now that Scotty had finished eating, the dog had moved to his lap. Before long, she'd be too big for anyone's lap, but Sam suspected that wouldn't matter to Scotty, who was madly in love with the puppy.

Usually, this was Sam's favorite time of the day—home with her husband and children, even if the home was new to them. But tonight, she couldn't escape the dark cloud of despair that hung over everything after the day's events. They went through the motions with the Littles, overseeing baths and pajamas and story time, all the while protecting them from the heartbreak that had seized the country. Alden and Aubrey had already been through enough heartbreak recently. They didn't need any more.

After the twins were settled in the bed they still shared despite having their own rooms at the White House, Sam and Nick went to check on Scotty and found him snuggled up to Skippy in his bed.

"I thought we agreed she's not allowed in the bed," Nick said, seemingly trying to be stern and failing miserably. They could both see how happy the dog made their son.

"I tried telling her she's not allowed, but she keeps ending up here."

"You're supposed to be in charge," Nick said.

"She has a mind of her own."

"Typical woman," Nick muttered with a wink and smile for his wife.

"Easy, mister," Sam said. "Push over and let me in."

Scotty rolled his eyes but made room for her to sit next to him, her back against his pillows.

"How're you doing?"

He shrugged. "It's hard to make sense of someone shooting kids who were there to see Santa."

"Sure is," Nick said, sighing as he stretched out across the foot of the bed.

"Why would someone do that?" Scotty asked.

"We're fairly certain there was a mental health component, as there often is when these things happen."

"How does someone with mental health problems end up with a gun so they can do that to so many people?"

"That's a very good question and one the FBI and ATF will be investigating."

"What's the ATF?"

"The Bureau of Alcohol, Tobacco, Firearms and Explosives."

"That's an odd combination of things."

Nick pulled his phone from his pocket. "Here's what the website says. 'ATF is a law enforcement agency in the United States' Department of Justice that protects our communities from violent criminals, criminal organizations, the illegal use and trafficking of firearms, the illegal use and storage of explosives, acts of arson and bombings, acts of terrorism, and the illegal diversion of alcohol and tobacco products. We partner with communities, industries, law enforcement, and public safety agencies to safeguard the public we serve through information sharing, training, research, and use of technology.'"

"That's interesting," Scotty said. "So it's their job to figure out where and how the guy got the gun, then?"

"Both them and the FBI, among other law enforcement. We've deployed the full resources of the federal government to assist local law enforcement as needed."

"It's cool that you can do that," Scotty said.

"That's what the government is here to do—to help people

who need it. We don't always succeed in that mission, but in cases like this, our role is pretty clear-cut."

"Will you have to go there?"

"I suppose we will, but not right away. Taking me anywhere requires a massive security presence at the federal, state and local levels, and they have their hands full right now with the situation they're dealing with. They don't need me coming in to make their jobs harder. But we'll go when the time is right."

"It's nice of you to think of that stuff."

"If it was just me and Mom, we'd be on a plane tonight, but nothing is ever that simple for us anymore."

"I saw what you said earlier about guns and stuff, and I hope you can get something done."

"Personally, I think we've been approaching it all wrong by making it about the guns," Sam said. "We need to make it about the people who shouldn't have access to guns. We need a vastly expanded mental health network in this country, a central reporting site where people can anonymously report people showing concerning or violent behavior, and then have mental health professionals intervene rather than law enforcement."

Nick tipped his head as he studied her. "How'd you like to head up my Mental Health and Violence Task Force?"

Sam rolled her eyes. "As if."

"Your approach is exactly what's needed. Less reactiveness and more proactiveness. We need people who understand the issue, who see the results of our failings in this regard every day. You'd be the perfect person to head up this effort."

"You're serious," Sam said, stunned.

"Dead serious. I bet the department would even be willing to make this role an official part of your duties, since it dovetails so perfectly with your day job."

"Which requires most of my waking hours. When do you see me having time to fit in something else?"

"Gonzo is back to full duty and could take on a little more responsibility to give you time to work on this important issue. Think about it. Nothing has to be decided today."

"I think you should do it, Mom. You'd be really good at it."

"I appreciate the votes of confidence."

"Will you think about it?" Nick asked.

"I will."

Nick smiled widely.

"I didn't say I'd do it!"

"Just getting you to think about something is a big win," Scotty said.

"You hush," she said, elbowing him playfully.

He grunted and then laughed.

"If you need to talk about any of this, you know where we are, right?" Nick asked Scotty.

"I know where you are. The whole world knows where you are." He ran his fingers through Skippy's silky hair as she slept next to him. "Are we still having our Christmas party?"

"I suppose we will, but we'll keep it low-key out of respect for the victims and their families," Nick said.

"You're good at this being-president thing," Scotty said.

"I'm glad you think so."

"Duh, everyone thinks so."

"Well, no, not everyone," Nick said. "I have plenty of people who are picking apart everything I do and say."

Scotty shrugged. "That's politics for you. Most people think you're awesome, and by the way, I was thinking about that bet we made about you being president in four years and have decided you owe me a hundred bucks, because it happened even sooner than I said."

Sam lost it laughing, appreciating the levity Scotty brought to their lives at times like this when they badly needed it. "He's got you there, Dad."

"You're supposed to be on my side at all times," Nick reminded her.

"I am, except for when I'm on his."

"Best mom ever," Scotty said.

Hearing him say those words, Sam felt like she'd been hit straight in the heart with the sharpest of arrows. "Surely that can't possibly be true."

"It's true. You're tied for first with my other mom."

"I'm very honored to be tied for first with her and to get to be your mom." Sam kissed the top of his head and stood before she made a fool of herself sobbing all over him. She'd yearned for so long to be a mother. Although it hadn't happened the way she'd thought it would, she wouldn't trade being this boy's mother for anything in the world. "Sleep tight. I love you, and I'll make sure you get your C-note from Dad." Standing in the doorway, she waited for Nick.

"Love you, too."

"We'll see you in the morning," Nick said, giving Scotty a fist bump.

"Dad?"

"Yeah?"

"Do you think I could go with you guys when you go to see the families of the people who died?"

"That might be a lot for you to handle," he said.

"I'd be okay. I've been through some stuff of my own. I understand what they're going through."

"I suppose you do, but I honestly think this might be too much for you," Nick said. "Hell, it'll be too much for us."

"It's very nice of you to offer to go, though," Sam said, dreading that trip with every fiber of her being even though she knew they had to do it. After recently losing her father, her emotions were still raw, but she'd never let Nick do that trip alone. "We'll see you in the morning."

"Don't stay up too late," Nick added. "Love you."

"Love you guys, too."

When they went into their suite of rooms at the end of the same hallway that housed the Lincoln Bedroom and closed the door, Sam retrieved the monitor that kept tabs on the twins in their bedroom and put it on the table in the sitting room. "I need a drink so badly after this day."

"Right there with you."

"Can we turn on the TV to see the latest?"

"Yeah, I suppose we should be keeping an eye on it."

"I wish we didn't have to."

"Me, too."

The butlers kept them well stocked in everything they could want or need. Sam went to the elegant bar cart in the corner of the room and fixed a white wine for herself and bourbon for Nick. She brought their drinks to the sofa and sat next to him, curling her feet under her as they tuned into CNN's coverage of the horror in Des Moines.

Anderson Cooper was interviewing grief-stricken parents who'd lost all three of their children along with the husband's mother, who'd taken them to the event. Pictures of the adorable kids and their grandmother were shown on the screen as their parents talked about each of them through gut-wrenching sobs.

"How do they go on after this?" Nick asked softly.

"I have no idea. It's unbearable."

Sam's cell phone rang with a call from Dispatch, which made her groan as she put down her still-full glass of wine. "Holland."

"Lieutenant, Patrol is reporting that a body has been found in an abandoned vehicle on Second Avenue Southeast. Are you able to respond?"

The word *no* was on the tip of her tongue. She'd checked out of work to be available for Nick, but for now, he'd done what he could to address the tragedy, and duty was calling her back to work. "I'm on my way," she said. "Please contact Detective Carlucci as well."

"Yes, ma'am."

Carlucci's partner, Detective Dominguez, was still on medical leave after a recent domestic altercation with her now-ex-boyfriend that had resulted in a ruptured spleen.

Sam ended the call and turned to Nick. "I'm sorry I have to go into work."

"It's okay. I appreciate you being here earlier."

"I wish I could do more."

"Can you come to Iowa with me sometime in the next few days?"

"I'll make that happen." Somehow. She drew him into a kiss. "Try to get some rest tonight. It's going to be a long week."

"I'll try," he said.

"Do you think we ought to cancel the holiday festivities?"

"Not yet." Their plan was to have Christmas Eve and Christmas morning at the White House with all their closest friends and family in attendance. "After we tend to the needs of the people of Des Moines and the country, we can have a private holiday that'll belong only to us."

"Are you sure that's possible?"

"Nope, but I'm sure we're going to try."

His smile lit up his lovely hazel eyes. "I'm looking forward to it."

"Me, too. We need it." Ten days off to spend together with their kids was the closest thing to heaven either of them could imagine, even if he'd still have to work part of every day. Three days after

Christmas, they were due to head to Camp David for the first time and were looking forward to that as well.

He gave her a tight hug before he released her. "Take care of my beautiful wife out there. She's my whole world."

"I will. Don't worry."

"What? Me worry?" He gave her one last quick kiss. "Love you."

"Love you, too."

In the hallway, Sam approached Nate, one of their favorite Secret Service agents. "I need to go into work."

"If you can give me five minutes, I'll get a detail together for you."

"Thank you." It went against everything Sam believed in to cool her heels for even five minutes when someone had been murdered in her city, but she'd promised Nick she'd allow for a detail on the job.

So she waited.

# CHAPTER FIVE

Ten long minutes later, she drove out of the White House gates and headed for the southeastern quadrant of the city with two agents trailing her in a black SUV. The detail was a small price to pay to keep from adding to Nick's already considerable stress level. He'd told her he couldn't and wouldn't be president unless she agreed to a minimal detail when she was on the job.

Vernon and Jimmy were the agents who trailed her during the regular workday. She had no idea who was in the car behind her now and didn't need to know. They had their job to do, and she had hers. With traffic light that time of day, she arrived at the crime scene fifteen minutes after she left the White House and thirty minutes after receiving the phone call from Dispatch. That was thirty minutes too long, but sadly, her victim wasn't going anywhere until she arrived.

After double-parking a block away, she approached the yellow crime scene tape and flashed her badge to the Patrol officer who'd been put in charge of keeping people away from the Honda minivan that housed their victim.

He raised the tape to allow Sam to duck underneath it.

"Thank you. What've we got?"

"I'm Officer Smyth, and this is my partner, Officer Linton." Smyth, who was tall, Black and muscular, was the older of the two. Linton was a dark-haired woman with brown eyes and a curvy body.

"An honor to meet you, ma'am," Linton said while Smyth tried not to roll his eyes.

"Give me the gist," Sam said.

"From what the neighbors tell us," Linton said, "the Honda Odyssey van was parked here several days ago, and it's received some parking tickets. Earlier today, one of the neighbors noticed a smell coming from the vehicle, and when she looked inside, she saw a foot sticking out from under a blanket."

Sam wanted to gag at the thought of what a dead body enclosed inside a car for several days would smell like. "I assume the car is locked?"

"It is," Smyth said. "We took the liberty of calling a locksmith. He'll be here any minute."

"Good thinking," Sam said, appreciative of anyone who saved her time on the job. She peered in the window, saw the same foot the neighbors had seen and wondered why the cops who'd ticketed the car—repeatedly—hadn't bothered to look inside. At the front of the car, she retrieved the tickets and tucked them into her coat pocket for further investigation later. "Did you call in the plate?"

"We did," Linton said. "It's registered to a Robert Tappen of M Street Northeast in Brentwood."

"Has it been reported stolen or missing?"

"We've had no reports involving this vehicle," Smyth said.

"Appreciate the good work," Sam said. "You were very thorough. I'd like to speak to the neighbor who called it in."

"Right this way, Lieutenant." Linton led Sam to a woman sitting on stairs. "This is Marcie Crossman. She lives here and had noticed the van parked here for a few days before she decided to look inside. Mrs. Crossman, this is Lieutenant Holland."

"The first lady," Marcie said with a small smile. "I'd say it's nice to meet you, but..." She gestured to the car. "I couldn't believe what I was seeing when I saw the foot."

"How long has the van been parked there?" Sam asked, making a note of the woman's name in the notebook she carried with her.

"A couple of days. I can't say for sure when it first showed up."

"That helps. Is there anything else you can tell me about it?"

"Only that it started to smell today, which is when I looked inside."

"Do you know anyone by the name of Tappen?"

"No, I don't."

"Will you please write down your name and number for me, just in case I have follow-up questions?"

Marcie took the pad from Sam, wrote down the information and handed it back to her.

"Thank you for your help and for calling it in."

"I hope you figure out who's in there and what happened to them."

"Oh, we will. Don't worry."

When Sam walked around the van, she found Detective Dani Carlucci peering inside the window. Tall, blonde and curvy, Dani had recently scared the crap out of Sam by going unresponsive. When they'd gone to check on her, they'd found her seriously ill from food poisoning. Sam hadn't seen her since she'd come back to work. "Hey," she said. "How you feeling?"

"Better. Not one hundred percent yet, but good enough to come back to work."

"Salmonella is the worst, from what I've heard."

"I wouldn't wish it on anyone, except Detective Ramsey."

Sam laughed at the mention of their nemesis. "We wish all forms of dysentery on him."

"Indeed. What've we got?"

Sam brought her up to speed on what she'd learned so far, waving to the Crime Scene Unit commander, Lieutenant Haggerty, as he arrived, going through the details again with him.

"Lieutenant," Smyth said, "the locksmith is here."

"Thank you, Officer Smyth. Let's get the onlookers moved out of here before we open the doors."

"Yes, ma'am."

The locksmith recognized Sam but didn't make a big deal out of it, which earned him points with her. He went right to work and had them inside the van five minutes later. When the doors opened, the foul odor came rushing out, making Sam and the others gag.

"Gnarly," the locksmith said, summing it up with one well-chosen word.

Inside the van, the bound, gagged body of a blonde female had been placed on the floor of the second row of seats and covered with a blanket. If not for the smell, she might never have been noticed.

Carlucci took photos with her phone while Sam leaned in for a closer look at the victim. With the duct tape on the woman's face, Sam couldn't see much. However, she noted the woman's purse, computer bag and suitcase were all still in the car, which more or less ruled out any sort of robbery motive. The only thing that she didn't see were the car keys. After donning latex gloves, she found the woman's wallet in her purse and found her license. Holding it up under the car's dome light, she noted the woman's smiling face. Her name was Pamela Tappen.

"Let's bag up her possessions and get them to the lab for processing." After they'd done that and sent the items to the lab via a Patrol officer, Sam said, "Let's wait for the ME, and then we can head to the Tappens's house to see what we can find out about Pamela."

"I'm with you, LT," Carlucci said.


THE TAPPEN FAMILY lived in a three-story townhome that was connected to a dozen others. The façade was white with black shutters, and the stairs had been sanded for ice.

"What I want to know," Dani said, "is how she got so stinky when it's so cold. Wouldn't the cold act almost like a fridge?"

"Bodily fluids," Sam said bluntly.

"Ugh, so she was alive in there for a while?"

"It's a theory."

Sam rang the doorbell and noted it was a regular, average doorbell and not the ridiculous symphony orchestra she'd encountered at the Thorn mausoleum. A fiftysomething man came to the door wearing an apron that said Kiss the Chef. He had a towel thrown over his shoulder, and the aromas of garlic and basil he brought with him made Sam's mouth water.

The man did a double take when he saw who was on his front porch.

"Mr. Tappen, I'm Lieutenant Holland, and this is Detective Carlucci. We wondered if we could speak to you for a moment."

"Of course, but what's this about?" he asked as he stepped aside to admit them into the nicely kept home.

"Do you own a white Honda Odyssey minivan?" Sam asked.

"I do. That's my wife's car."

"What's your wife's name?"

"Pam." All at once, he seemed to realize that police being at his door could mean only one thing. "Is something wrong with her?"

Sam gestured to a sofa in a nearby living room. "Could we sit for a second?"

"Um, sure." He led the way and sat on the love seat while Sam and Dani sat together on the sofa.

"When was the last time you spoke to your wife?"

"Friday. She was traveling for work this past weekend, and she's so busy that it's not unusual that we don't hear from her while she's gone. She's due home tonight."

Sam couldn't for the life of her imagine not speaking to Nick for four days. She'd go mad. "What does she do for work?"

"She owns a business that provides conference services to a wide array of clients, everything from registration support to publications, signage, etc. She does it all, and when she's on-site at a show, she puts in sixteen-hour days."

"So you don't text with her or anything during the shows?"

"Hardly ever. Now that our kids are older, she doesn't check in like she did when they were little. Wh-what is this about?"

"Mr. Tappen, I'm sorry to have to tell you that your van was found in Southeast with the body of a blonde female inside it. Your wife's purse and other belongings were in the car. We're working under the assumption that the body is that of your wife."

His face seemed to go completely lax with shock. "Oh my God."

"The medical examiner would like you to come in to identify her, if possible."

"You... My Pam is dead?" he asked, his eyes filling as his hands began to tremble.

"I'm afraid so."

"Oh God," he whispered, dropping his head into his hands. "How can this be happening?"

"Are you home alone?"

"Yes, my sons are at football practice, and my daughter is away at college in Massachusetts."

"Were you here when Pam left for her work trip on Friday?"

"No, I went from work to Delaware for a tournament for my sons' AAU football team. Pam was so bummed to miss it."

"Are you able to come with us to identify the body?"

"I, ah, yeah. I just need to, uh, deal with the stove."

Sam nodded to Dani to go with him. They needed to ensure he didn't make any phone calls or do anything other than shut off the stove and grab a coat. A few minutes later, Sam was driving Tappen to HQ, while Dani stayed behind to speak to the neighbors about whether they'd witnessed anything unusual involving the Tappens's van the previous weekend. It was a long shot, but worth asking.

"Was your wife having any problems with anyone in her life?" Sam asked Mr. Tappen, who sat in the front seat with her. She'd debated whether to allow him that privilege, but since he wasn't a suspect—at the moment, anyway—she'd had no reason to cuff him or treat him like a criminal.

"Not that I know of. I mean, we have teenagers, so we have issues with them, but it's just the usual stuff that everyone deals with."

"What kind of issues?" Sam asked, glancing at him.

The man looked shell-shocked, but who could blame him? He'd been making dinner when the police came to tell him his wife had probably been murdered.

"Staying out past curfew, drinking, smoking pot, slacking off in school. The same stuff everyone deals with."

"How many children do you have?"

"Three. My boys are fifteen and seventeen, and my daughter is nineteen."

Sam also couldn't imagine not speaking to Scotty for four days, no matter how busy she was at work. "And you say it wasn't unusual for her to go completely dark while working a show?"

"Not at all. We all understood that when she was working, we wouldn't hear from her. She knew I could handle things at home and that I'd text if I needed her for something."

What was perfectly routine for this family would've been unthinkable for hers, Sam thought, but hey, different strokes for different folks. When they arrived at HQ, Sam drove around to the morgue entrance and parked. "I want to prepare you before we go in. The body we found had suffered some decomposition. She'd been bound and gagged with duct tape, and we believe she'd been there for a couple of days by the time she was discovered."

"Christ have mercy," he whispered.

Sam made a call to let Lindsey know she was bringing Mr. Tappen in.

"We're ready," Lindsey said.

Sam shut off the car, got out and waited for him to walk around the car.

He hesitated. "I don't know if I can do this."

"I'm sorry to ask it of you, but we need to know for sure who our victim is."

After taking a deep breath of frigid air, he released it and nodded for her to lead the way inside. They stepped into the cold, antiseptic-smelling morgue, where Dr. Lindsey McNamara greeted them. Sam was glad her friend was there to walk Mr. Tappen through the dreadful process of identifying his wife.

Sam introduced him to Lindsey, whose green eyes were full of the compassion she gave to all the victims who landed in her morgue and their families.

"If you'd follow me, we can get this over with," Lindsey said.

Sam brought up the rear as they walked into the exam room where the body had been laid out on a table and covered by a sheet.

"Are you ready?" Lindsey asked him.

"I... I guess so."

When Lindsey drew the sheet back from her face, Sam noticed the duct tape had been removed from the woman's mouth, but some of the sticky residue remained on her face.

Tappen's knees buckled, and Sam moved quickly to grab him before he could fall to the floor. His anguished wail confirmed the woman's identity.

"Pammy! *Oh my God.* Who could've done this to her? Everyone loved her!"

With the shock still fresh, Sam knew this wasn't the time to grill him about every aspect of his wife's life, but who knew how much time they'd already lost while she was dead inside a parked car? "Mr. Tappen, is there someone I could call for you? A friend or family member?"

He covered his mouth with his hand as tears ran down his face, his gaze fixed on the decomposing face of his wife. "My, uh... My kids. I should call my kids."

"I'd like to be with you when you inform them of their mother's death."

"Uh, sure. That's fine, I guess." He glanced at her, looking shocked and confused. "How do we do this? My daughter is away at school."

"Can you text your sons and ask them to come here after practice?"

"Y-yes, I can do that." He withdrew the phone from his pocket with a shaking hand and sent the text. "My older son is asking why. What do I tell him?"

"Say you'll explain when they get here."

He sent the text. "They should be here in about fifteen minutes. What about my daughter in college?"

"We'll call her after we talk to the boys." Sam dreaded those conversations, even though they were a necessary part of any homicide investigation. Watching the reactions of the people closest to a victim while hearing that he or she had been murdered could be informative.

Lindsey handed him her business card. "I'll be performing an autopsy before we release her to the funeral home of your choosing. You can call me at your convenience to let me know which one you'd like to use."

Tappen took the card and put it in his pocket. "Thank you." After another long look at his late wife, he said, "Are we done in here?"

"Yes," Sam said. "Right this way." She led him out of the morgue and through the corridors that led to the pit where her detectives worked. The pit that was a beehive of activity during the day was now dark and quiet. They went into the conference room. Sam turned on the lights. "Can I get you a water or anything?"

"A water would be good, thanks."

"I'll get that for you, but I'd ask you not to contact anyone until I'm back in the room."

"Why?"

"It's standard procedure."

He nodded as if he understood when she'd bet that none of this made sense to him. How could it?

"I'll be right back."

She went to the vending area and bought two bottles of water, and when she turned away from the machine, Detective Ramsey was there.

He took two steps to close the distance between them so he

was staring into her face with fire in his eyes. "I hope you're happy. My wife filed for divorce."

"Why would that make me happy?"

"Because that's what you wanted when you sent your dogs to dig for shit on me."

"I don't know what you're talking about. We didn't dig for anything on you, but of course, if there's nothing to be found..." She shrugged. "Can you move? I'm working."

"I'm going to tell you something right now," he said on a low growl. "You'd better watch your back. I don't care who you're married to. You're nothing special, and before long, the whole world is going to know that."

"Did you eat garlic for lunch?" She made a distasteful face while delighting in his hateful expression. "While I have you, let me ask you... What is it about me that you hate so much? Is it my last name? The fact that I'm a lieutenant, and you're... not? Or is it that I'm a woman, and you're not? That might be it. Of course, it could be just that I'm fucking awesome at my job, and you're not. Hmmm, you know what? I find that I don't care. I've got the husband of a victim in my conference room. I care about him. You? I don't care about you, so if you'd just step aside, I can get back to doing important stuff."

He didn't move.

Sam sighed, hating that he was wasting her time. "Do I need to get physical with you? We've already done that once, and as I recall, you ended up in the hospital. But hey, it's your funeral."

Ramsey started to raise his hand as if he was going to strike her.

She placed her hand on the butt of her weapon. "Move your ass, *now*, *Sergeant*, or I'll take whatever measures needed to protect myself."

"That won't be necessary, Lieutenant."

Sam would never admit to being relieved to hear Captain Malone's voice coming from behind Ramsey.

"Detective Ramsey will be getting the fuck out of here right now if he knows what's good for him," Malone said.

"I think he was just about to move along," Sam said.

Ramsey gave her a filthy look before turning and storming off.

"Are you all right?" Malone asked.

"I'm better than fine. I got off a few good comments, the kind you usually think of long after the opportunity has passed."

"In other words, you made a bad situation worse?"

"Define 'worse.' Apparently, his wife is divorcing him. I can't imagine why anyone wouldn't want to be married to a prize like him."

Malone rolled his eyes. "What've you got with the woman in the van?"

"Not sure yet. I've got the husband in the conference room and the two teenage sons on the way here so he can tell them about their mother. The daughter is in college in Massachusetts, so we'll be calling her."

"Are you leaning in any directions?"

"Nothing yet. We're an hour in and have identified the victim as Pam Tappen. According to her husband, Robert, it wasn't uncommon for his wife to punch out completely for days at a time when she was working at a conference. She ran a business providing conference services to a wide range of organizations. She'd been gone all weekend working at an event, or so he believed."

"The woman had children, and she didn't check in while she was away?"

"I found that odd, too." She didn't mention that she could barely stand to go an hour without speaking to her husband, let alone four days. That information was probably common knowledge to everyone who knew them as well as Malone did.

The captain followed her back to the pit.

Sam dropped off the water for Mr. Tappen in the conference room and told him she'd be back in a minute. She pulled the tickets she'd taken off the van out of her coat pocket and handed them to Malone. "These were on the van where Mrs. Tappen's body was found. If you look at the dates, you'll see that over the course of the weekend, Patrol officers left two tickets, but apparently, neither of them looked inside the van. She might've been found sooner if they'd bothered to look."

Frowning, he took the tickets from her. "I'll take care of it."

A young Patrol officer came into the pit. "Lieutenant, we have Justin and Lucas Tappen here to see you and their father."

"Please bring them to the conference room."

Sam took off her coat, intending to stash it in her office, but stopped short when she realized the door was open. "Someone's been in here. I locked it when I left earlier, and no one else has a key but you."

"Step back." Malone went to Freddie's cubicle, found a ruler and used it to push the door open. With his flashlight, he revealed that the office had been tossed. Paper, files, framed photos and awards she'd received on the job were scattered on the floor. Glass had been broken, and the awards were in pieces. "Motherfucker."

Her heart ached at the sight of the photo of her and her dad on the floor, shattered, as if someone had slammed it to the floor. "Do you think it was a coincidence that Ramsey was here late on a Monday night, and then we discover this?"

"We don't believe in coincidences."

# CHAPTER SIX

W hile Malone waited for Crime Scene detectives to comb through the carnage in her office, Sam returned to the conference room to check on Mr. Tappen.

"My sons should be here soon."

"They're here. One of our officers is bringing them in. Please allow me to tell them about their mother."

He nodded, and judging from the puffiness of his eyes and face, he'd been weeping while he was alone in the room.

Her heart went out to him as he absorbed the terrible shock that came with a loved one's murder. One minute, he'd been making dinner at home, and the next, his entire life—and his children's—had been turned upside down.

Two handsome, dark-haired young men were brought into the room by a patrolman.

"Justin and Lucas, this is Lieutenant Holland," Mr. Tappen said.

"You're the first lady, right?" Justin, the younger of the two boys, asked.

"That's right. Can you come in and have a seat?"

"Why are we here, Dad?" Lucas asked, eyeing her with curiosity.

"It's about Mom," Bob said when the two boys were seated next to each other.

"What about her?" Justin asked, his gaze moving between his father and Sam.

"I'm sorry to have to tell you that your mother was found dead today," Sam said, having learned getting right to the point was the best strategy in these cases.

Justin's eyes filled as he looked to his father for confirmation. "Is it true, Dad? She... She's dead?"

Bob nodded and reached for his younger son, who broke down into sobs.

Lucas looked down at the table while his brother's heartbroken sobs filled the room. "What happened to her?" Lucas asked, glancing up at Sam with torment in his expression.

"She was found bound and gagged in the back of her van, which was parked in Southeast."

Hearing that, Lucas dropped his head into his hands. "Do you know who did it?"

"Not yet," Sam said. "We're in the earliest stages of the investigation."

"Does Molly know?" Justin asked.

"Not yet," his dad replied. "We're going to call her."

"You should have Aunt Amy go there and tell her," Justin said. "She shouldn't be alone when she hears this."

"That's a good idea," Bob said.

"Who's Amy?" Sam asked.

"My wife's best friend from college. She lives an hour from where Molly goes to school. The kids have always been close to her."

"I think it's a good idea to have her there when you tell Molly," Sam said. "Why don't you make that call now? Please put it on speaker."

Sam had to listen as Bob told his wife's best friend that Pam had been murdered. Her friend's heartbroken screams of disbelief echoed through the conference room.

When the woman had finally calmed to the point of soft sobs, Bob said, "Is Tom home, Amy?"

"He's right here."

"Can the two of you go to be with Molly when we tell her the news?"

"Yes, of course. We'll go now."

"Call me when you're close."

"I will. You're sure it's her, right?"

"Yes, we're sure."

"God, who could've done such a thing to Pam? She was the best person I ever knew."

Sam wished she had a dollar for every time she heard a murder victim described that way. There were, of course, exceptions, such as recent homicide victim Ginny McLeod, who'd alienated nearly everyone in her life by stealing from them before she was murdered by her husband. "We'll do our best to get you some answers," Sam said.

The people who loved Pam were in the earliest stages of realizing that the answers they craved wouldn't bring back the person they'd loved.

While they waited for Amy and her husband to get to Molly Tappen, Sam asked the most pressing question she had for them. "Was she having problems with anyone in her life? Personal, work, neighbors, friends?"

All three were shaking their heads before she finished asking the question.

"Everyone loves her," Justin said. "My friends like to hang out at our house because she makes us cookies and listens to their problems."

His use of the present tense to describe his mother gutted her, as it always did. It would be a while before he spoke of her in the past tense.

"She avoided drama like the plague," Bob said. "She'd dropped friends who'd brought drama to her life."

*Sounds like a girl after my own heart*, Sam thought. "Would any of them have been angry enough about being dropped to do something like this to her?"

Bob shook his head. "That happened years ago. We haven't seen any of them in ages."

"We're going to need a list of her closest friends, work colleagues and others she interacted with on a daily or weekly basis, with their contact information and addresses if you have them. Can you work on that while we wait for Amy to get to Molly's?" Sam pushed a yellow pad and pen across the table to Bob. "Also, who else has keys to the van?"

"Just Pam and I did. The boys have another vehicle they share."

"Okay, work on that list, and I'll be back."

·  ·  ·

SAM STEPPED out of the conference room into the chaos of a Crime Scene investigation unfolding in her office. Looking to avoid that, she went to the cubicle belonging to Detective Dominguez and called Nick on the BlackBerry.

"Hey, babe. How's it going?"

"Another rough one. A beloved wife and mother found bound and gagged in her own minivan. She'd apparently been there for days by the time she was found."

"She wasn't reported missing?"

"No, she wasn't. I guess it wasn't unusual for her to go silent when she was working at a conference, which was what she did for a living. Her company supported conference events."

"And she didn't talk to her family at all?"

"Nope."

"That's weird."

"See, I thought so, too. I can't for the life of me picture going a whole weekend without talking to you or Scotty or the twins. Or even my sisters and my dad, when he was still here."

"I'd hunt you down before I'd go a weekend without talking to you. I'd be twitching after twelve hours."

"Same, but we're strange that way."

"I like our kind of strange. It works for me."

"Me, too. How are things there?"

"I just checked the kids, and everyone is asleep. In other news, I'm already getting serious pushback on my comments from earlier, but I'm not backing down from them. We absolutely must attack the mental health element behind the violence in this country."

"I couldn't agree more."

"It hasn't been made public yet, but the gunman had a history of violent episodes that had led his family on more than one occasion to ask to have him held for psych evals. He was never held for longer than seventy-two hours because he refused treatment every time. And then he managed to get his hands on a gun and do what he did today. The people closest to him believe his goal was to be killed by the police, which is what happened."

"The thing I never understand is if he's looking to end his own life, why does he have to take innocent people with him?"

"I don't understand that either. If he wanted to kill himself, as horrible as that is, I suppose that's his right, but he certainly didn't have the right to take others with him."

"No, he didn't. My heart is hurting for all the families that were forever broken by his selfish actions."

"Are you going to head up my mental health task force?" Nick asked.

"I've been thinking about that, and I'd like to be involved, but I don't think I can be the chair. Maybe we should ask Dr. Trulo? As the department psychiatrist for close to thirty years, he's seen it all and would be better positioned to oversee it."

"That's a brilliant idea. If you text me his number, I'll give him a call."

"You'll give him a heart attack if you call him. At least let me warn him."

Nick's soft laughter made her smile as only he could. "Go ahead and give him a heads-up that he's going to hear from me."

"I'll do that, and I'll send you his number."

"Thank you. Are you there all night?"

"Probably not, but for a while longer. Oh, and get this... We think Ramsey tossed my office."

"How did he get into your office?"

"He must've picked the lock somehow. Everything is on the floor. A total mess. Malone has Crime Scene processing it."

"Why do you think it was him?"

"Because he was skulking around and cornered me in the vending area."

"Cornered you. What does that mean?"

Sam immediately regretted sharing that detail. "He tried to start something with me, but I definitely got the upper hand, and then Malone came along and told him to fuck off."

"Jeez, Sam, that's the stuff that gives me nightmares."

"I was never in any danger."

"Sure, you weren't. That guy can't stand you."

"He might've stepped into it big-time by being in the building when my office was trashed. I'm just hoping he was sloppy about it, and CSU can tie him to it." Even if that would mean another of her colleagues had ended up in trouble that somehow involved her. It wasn't her fault that Stahl had wrapped her in razor wire and threatened to set her on fire, or that Conklin had sat on info relevant to her dad's unsolved shooting for four years, or that

Detective Offenbach had been off having an affair when he was supposed to be at a conference.

"I hate to think of you having enemies within the department."

"I suppose it goes with the territory, especially if a woman is good at a job that's traditionally done by men."

Lindsey came into the pit and stopped short at the sight of CSU working in Sam's office.

"I need to run, babe. I'll be home as soon as I can."

"Be careful. Your husband loves you."

"Love you, too."

Sam ended the call and stood, waving Lindsey over to the cubicle.

"What. The. *Hell*. Sam?"

"Someone trashed my office. I discovered it about ten minutes after Ramsey cornered me in the vending area to tell me his wife is divorcing him and somehow that's my fault."

"Holy crap. How in the hell is that your fault?"

"Someone sent him anonymous proof of an affair through interoffice mail. I guess the word has gotten out and back to his wife somehow. He blames me for that."

"But it never occurs to him that if he hadn't had the affair in the first place, no one could've uncovered it."

"Exactly. Anyway, did you need me for something?"

"Yeah, I wanted to tell you that Pam Tappen died inside that van from a combination of asphyxia and hypothermia."

"So she was alive when someone left her there to suffocate and freeze to death?"

"Yes."

"Horrifying."

"Indeed. I place the time of death around Sunday evening."

"So if they grabbed her on Friday, that means it took two full days for her to die. Christ have mercy." Sam thought about that for a second, recalling that Pam's things had been left in the car. "This was personal. Someone wanted her to suffer."

"I agree. I was able to get some prints from the duct tape and CSU pulled a bunch from inside the van, but none of them were in the system."

Sam processed that news as she glanced at the conference room. "According to the family, everyone loved her."

"Not everyone."

"What kind of monster does something like this to another human being?"

Lindsey raised an eyebrow. "After all these years on this job, you still have to ask that?"

"I guess I've never received a satisfactory answer to the question."

"And you never will. I'll send you my full report when I have it."

"Thanks, Doc."

Sam took a deep breath and blew it out before returning to the conference room to check on the Tappens.

"We've made a list of the people she's closest to," Bob said.

"Here's a question for you. If she was so critical to the conference she was attending, wouldn't they have reached out to you when she didn't show up?"

"Not necessarily. She was a sole proprietor. I'm not sure they would've known to contact me if she wasn't there."

"I'm going to be honest with you, Mr. Tappen. I find it odd that she would take off for a weekend and have absolutely no contact with her husband or three children or not have an emergency contact on file with the organizations she worked for."

"I know it must sound strange to you, but that's been our routine for years. She has a very intense job when she's at the conferences, and we leave her alone to do it."

"And you never contact her?"

"You did that once when Justin had appendicitis, and she flew home, remember, Dad?" Lucas asked.

"Yes, that was an exception, but for the most part, when she's working, we carry on without her. It's only a week or so out of every month, and we've been doing it for so long that it's routine to us."

"Could I have a minute alone with you, Mr. Tappen?" It would be up to him to decide how many of the details of their mother's death he would share with his kids.

He glanced at the boys, who got up and left the room.

After the door closed behind them, Sam said, "I'm a mother, Mr. Tappen. I wouldn't go a single day without talking to my children."

"With all due respect, Lieutenant, I believe you're a relatively new mother, so of course it seems strange to you not to talk to your son."

"In forty years, I'm still going to want to talk to him every day."

For the first time, Tappen's expression became angry. "My wife adored her children, and they adored her. Her company provided a large chunk of our family's annual income, and we relied upon it, thus we stepped aside and allowed her to do her job when she needed us to. I'd appreciate it if you wouldn't judge us—or especially her—for the choices we made in the best interests of our family."

"Fair enough, and I don't mean to judge you or her. I'm asking the questions necessary to figure out who'd want to kill her."

"We have no idea who'd want to kill her," Tappen said.

"I need to tell you some additional details that you're going to find difficult to hear."

"More difficult than hearing she was found murdered?"

"Perhaps, yes."

He seemed to brace himself.

"She died of asphyxia and hypothermia, which means she was alive when she was bound and gagged, probably on Friday, and left in the van to suffocate and freeze to death. The medical examiner has put the time of death sometime on Sunday evening." Sam waited a beat to give him a second to process that it took two days for her to die. "This was personal. Whoever did this wanted her to suffer."

"We don't know of anyone who'd want her to suffer like that." Bob seemed truly baffled as he fought tears. "She did so much for others. Our neighbor has been fighting breast cancer for the last two years. Pam made dinner for her family every week since she was diagnosed. She takes that same woman's kids to practices and picks them up. She volunteers at a homeless shelter and does fundraising for them. She's all about giving of herself to others, especially to our family."

"What about through her work? Did she have problems with any clients or colleagues?"

"Not that I know of," Bob said. "Most of her clients were longtime accounts, except for the one this week. That was a new one."

Which gave her a thread to pull, Sam thought. "Do you have the name of the organization?"

"I can look it up in her office at home."

"I'd like to have our people go through her office, computer and phone, if we can locate it, to see if she was having any issues with anyone that you might not have been aware of. We've requested a warrant, but I wanted to make you aware of what we'll need to do."

"Yes, of course. We'll do whatever we can to aid in the investigation."

"We have officers at your home to ensure the crime scene, if there is one, won't be compromised. We've also requested a warrant to examine your phone."

"Why?"

"It's routine."

"I have nothing to hide."

Bob's phone chimed with a text. "Amy is in Cambridge and is asking if she can call me before she goes up to Molly's place."

"Yes, have her call," Sam said, getting up to let the boys back into the room.

Over the next ten minutes, she got to listen to Molly answer her door to her tearful Aunt Amy and Uncle Tom. She asked why they were there, and Amy said, "Your dad needs to speak to you."

"Um, okay..."

After Amy handed the phone to Molly, she said, "Dad? What's wrong?"

Listening to Bob tell his daughter that her mother had been found murdered was yet another horrific moment in a day full of them. Molly's anguished screams brought everyone in the conference room to tears, including Sam.

"Who could've done this?" she asked between sobs.

"We don't know, honey," Bob said, "but Lieutenant Holland is helping us to figure that out."

"I want to come home," Molly said, choking on a sob.

"Yes, of course."

"We'll drive her," Amy said. "We'll leave tonight."

After they ended the call with Amy and Molly, Sam asked for Bob's phone, which she turned over to IT detectives for a thorough examination after he'd signed a release form permitting the investigation. When she returned to the conference room, she continued the questioning of Bob and his sons. "Have any of you noticed anything out of place or unusual in the house this week?"

She'd wondered if Pam had been abducted at home or somewhere else.

"Not that I can think of," Bob said.

"Me either," Lucas said as Justin shook his head.

"We're going to put you up in a hotel while Crime Scene processes your home," Sam said.

"Why is that necessary?" Bob asked. "She hasn't been there in four days."

"A crime could've occurred there, and you might not realize it."

He wanted to argue with her, and she couldn't blame him. In addition to the shock of his wife's murder, now he was being barred from his own home.

"We'll move as quickly as we can to get you back in your home as soon as possible."

Bob seemed to understand that there was no point in arguing.

Sam got up to arrange for a hotel. She went to speak to Lieutenant Haggerty, who was standing outside her office, overseeing the detectives sifting for evidence among the wreckage.

"Nothing yet," he said when he saw her coming.

"I was going to ask for your help with something else. I have a possible crime scene at the M Street home of Bob and Pam Tappen."

"Possible?"

"I'm not sure if anything happened there, and if it did, it would've been as long as four days ago."

He winced. "So if there is a crime scene, it's thoroughly compromised."

"Yes."

"Sure, that sounds fun. We can get there in the morning."

"Thanks. I'm putting the family up at a hotel in the meantime." She returned to Dominguez's cubicle to use the phone to call the Patrol commander. "I could use the assistance of one of your people. I'm in the Homicide pit."

"I'll send someone to you."

"Thanks."

Sam was still watching the detectives working in her office when Officer Charles came into the pit. She was delighted to see the officer who'd done such an amazing job handling the details of her father's police funeral. The young, Black officer was going to be a star within the department, and Sam was looking forward to watching that happen. "Fancy meeting you here on a Monday night."

Her pretty face lit up with a big smile. "I picked up an extra shift."

"Have you heard that I'm trying to poach you from the chief?" Sam asked.

"I did hear a rumor to that effect, and I'd be honored to help you with anything you need."

"Do you have time to help me? I understand the chief keeps you pretty busy."

"I have the time, and I'd love to work with you and learn from you."

Sam gave her a side-eyed look. "Have you been taking suck-up advice from Detective Cruz by any chance?"

Officer Charles laughed. "I haven't, but I'll keep in mind that he's got some expertise in that area."

"He's the master when it comes to sucking up."

"Lieutenant Dawkins said you needed help with something tonight?"

"I do, and I'm thrilled she sent you." Sam used her chin to gesture toward the conference room. "Pam Tappen was found murdered in her minivan earlier tonight."

"I heard about that. She'd been there a few days?"

Sam nodded. "I've got Bob Tappen and his sons, Justin and Lucas here. His daughter, Molly, is on the way from the Boston area with close family friends. We need to get them set up in a hotel for at least a day or two while Crime Scene goes through their house."

"I can take care of that for you."

"Make sure they have whatever they need. The disruption is only making a difficult time worse for them."

"Will do."

"Thank you, and touch base with me again soon."

"I'll do that, too."

Sam took Officer Charles into the conference room to introduce her to the Tappens. "You'll be in very good hands with her," Sam told them. "I'll check in with you in the morning and will keep you posted of any developments."

"Thank you," Bob said.

With the Tappens in the capable hands of Officer Charles, Sam called Dani Carlucci. "Anything new?"

"Not yet. Still talking to the neighbors, but so far, no one saw anything suspicious over the last few days."

"We're working with a time line that could go back as far as Friday. It's going to be tough to find anyone who remembers anything from that far back."

"I'll keep trying."

"Request backup if you feel you need it."

"I'm good."

"Before I let you go, what're you hearing from Gigi?"

"An occasional text. She's feeling better, dying to get back to work and sick of sitting around at home."

"She's got a few more weeks to go before she'll be cleared to return."

"I'm afraid she'll go mad before then."

"I'd feel the same way. I'm going to head home and start fresh in the morning with the company Pam was due to support at their event this past weekend. Shoot me a text if anything pops."

"Will do."

# CHAPTER SEVEN

Detective Gigi Dominguez was, in fact, going crazy being sidelined from work and life as she recovered from injuries sustained in an altercation with her now-former boyfriend, Ezra, who was receiving in-patient treatment for bipolar disorder. After he'd taken her mother, sister and nephews hostage in her mother's home, Gigi was done making excuses for the man who'd been part of her life since high school.

It'd been bad enough that he'd given her a concussion and ruptured her spleen, which had to be removed in an emergency surgery, but when he'd involved her family... That was the end of the line for her. Yes, she'd promised she would check on him while he was in treatment, but she'd agreed to that only to get him to release her family.

She would keep her promise to check on him.

But she would never see him again.

She shivered, reliving the night when she'd tried to get him to a hospital and how he'd exploded with outrage that she'd suggested anything might be wrong. No, she couldn't think about that, because when she did, her entire body trembled with the bone-deep fear she'd experienced at realizing he'd become a threat to her personal safety.

And she'd missed that.

*How* had she missed that? She was trained to spot those things and hadn't with him until it was too late to stop him from seriously injuring her.

Weeks later, she was still trying to unpack the emotions from that night and the one a few days later when he'd held her family at gunpoint, demanding to be allowed to see her.

Tears burned in her eyes as she relived the horror of her beloved family members being in mortal danger because of her. She refused to give in to the tears, fearing that if she let herself fall apart, she might never recover. Between battling her own difficult memories and the relentless coverage of the shooting in Des Moines, her emotions were all over the place.

A soft knock on her apartment door drew her out of the dark place her thoughts had gone.

"Just a sec."

She was still moving slowly, uncertain which was worse—abdominal surgery or a severe concussion. At the moment, they were tied for first place. Before she opened the door, she looked through the peephole and saw her colleague Detective Cameron Green.

*What's he doing here—again?*

Gigi took half a second to tighten the belt on her robe and to run her fingers through her hair to straighten wild curls.

After disengaging the new locks that Cam had installed for her after she came home from the hospital, she opened the door to her handsome blond colleague.

Smiling, he held up a brown bag with handles. "I got some more of that Mexican you liked last week."

He was too sweet and too kind and too everything, including sexy. She'd noticed that long before her life had exploded in her face. But she'd been with Ezra since high school, and thus Cameron Green had remained firmly in the friend-and-colleague category.

"Come in." She stepped back to admit him, reminding herself for the umpteenth time since the incident with Ezra that she had nothing to fear from this man, or the others she worked with who'd been by to check on her. Her squad had made it their personal responsibility to keep her fed and entertained, but no one had been more faithful than Cameron.

"I can drop and go if you're not up for company," he said.

"Did you get food for yourself, too?"

"Yep, but I can take it home if you're tired."

"That's okay. We can eat together."

"Great," he said, flashing a smile that belonged in a commercial for perfect teeth.

Gigi couldn't understand why this colleague was different from the others. When he smiled at her, her belly fluttered and her heart did this weird skipping thing that made her feel light-headed. Or maybe that was just the concussion.

But she didn't think that was it. She suspected it was *him*, and that was unnerving for a number of reasons.

"What did the doctor say today?" Cameron asked as he unloaded enough food onto her coffee table to feed ten people. He always brought extra to get her through the next day, too.

"He said everything is healing the way it should be, which isn't fast enough for me."

Cameron refilled her water glass and sat next to her on the sofa, cracking open a beer for himself. "It's going to take the time it takes, and you can't try to rush it."

Dipping a chip into the queso he always brought after learning she loved it, she said, "Sitting around all day is making me crazy."

"It's what your body needs to heal, Gigi."

"I know," she said, sighing. "But I'll be fat as a house if you keep feeding me such yummy food."

He seemed annoyed that she'd say such a thing about herself. "No, you won't."

Gigi tipped her head and decided to ask the question that'd been foremost on her mind when it came to him. "What're you doing here, Cam?"

"Huh? I thought we were eating dinner."

"We are, but what are you *doing*?"

He put down his fork and wiped his face with a paper napkin that had the restaurant's logo on it. "I'm helping out a friend and colleague."

"That's all it is?"

"What else would it be?"

"I don't know. That's what I'm asking you."

He picked up his fork and poked at the chicken enchiladas he usually inhaled. "Can't it just be a friend helping another friend? Can't it just be that I hate what he did to you, and helping you keeps me from killing him for daring to lay a hand on you?"

The ferocity in his words startled her, as she'd never seen that side of him, except for at work when his intensity was directed at the scumbags they hunted as Homicide detectives. He was one of the best detectives she'd ever worked with. The entire squad thought so. But what did it mean that he wanted to kill the man who'd harmed her?

"You're confusing me, Cameron."

"I don't mean to," he said with a sigh. "You're dealing with a lot right now. You don't need any more."

"What more would you be adding to the pile?"

"I don't think we should talk about this now. Later, when you're feeling better, we can talk more."

"You're still confusing me. What is there to talk about?"

He closed his eyes and took a deep breath. "I broke up with Jaycee."

"What? When?"

"Two weeks ago."

"I thought you really liked her."

"I did. I mean... I do, but..."

Gigi put her hand on his arm. "What's going on, Cameron? I hope you know you can talk to me, and I'll want to hear anything you have to say."

He made a sound that was a cross between a groan and a laugh. "I'm not so sure you'd want to hear this."

"Try me."

After taking another drink from his beer bottle, he put it down on the table. Another long moment passed before he turned so he was facing her. "I broke up with Jaycee because I have feelings for someone else."

"Oh, well, then I suppose that was the right thing to do."

"Yeah, I guess, but the thing is, this person I like, she's going through a rough time right now, and the last thing she needs is me adding to it by telling her something she may or may not want to hear."

Gigi blamed the concussion for the thirty seconds it took her to figure out he was talking about her. Cameron Green was telling her that he liked her, that he'd broken up with his girlfriend because he had feelings for *her*. All at once, she couldn't seem to breathe or think or do anything other than stare at him.

She'd been ashamed of the crush she'd had on him while technically still dating Ezra. For some time, she'd wanted to end things with her high school boyfriend, but had hesitated due to the instability of his mental health. Turned out she'd been right to be hesitant, because when she'd broached the subject of taking some time apart, she'd ended up in the hospital.

"I know this isn't the right time, Gigi," he said softly. "I don't expect you to say or do anything now, or ever, if you don't feel the same way."

"Cameron."

"What?"

She crooked her finger at him, asking him to come closer.

At first, he seemed too surprised to move.

"Cam."

He blinked and moved to close the distance that stood between them on her sofa.

Gigi summoned all the courage she possessed to make a move that would change everything for them both. But after hearing he had feelings for her—and seeing proof of that in the way he'd cared for her over the last couple of weeks—she found it didn't take courage to lightly touch her lips to his.

An urgent sound came from the back of his throat in the second before he raised his hands to her face and tipped her chin to improve the angle.

Gigi shivered with the thrill of kissing the man she'd admired from the day he'd first joined their squad. Not only was he handsome, sexy and super professional, but he was smart, clever, thoughtful and caring.

He broke the kiss and leaned his forehead against hers, seeming to collect himself.

"What's wrong?" she asked.

"Absolutely nothing."

"Why'd you stop?"

He curled a length of her hair around his index finger. "Because you're still recovering, and the last thing you need is further complications."

"Is that what this will be? Complicated?"

"I sure as hell hope so." He caressed her face with the lightest of touches that set her entire body on fire with desire.

"What about work?"

"We're on different shifts, and neither of us supervises the other. It should be fine. We'd have to disclose it to Sam, though."

"And this is what you want? I'm what you want?"

"If you had any idea how much I want you, Gigi, you'd tell me to leave."

"No, I wouldn't."

"Yes, you would."

She shook her head.

He nodded.

She smiled. "Why didn't you say something sooner?"

"You weren't ready to hear it. You still aren't."

"Yes, I am. I'm much better than I was at first."

"What about in here?" he asked, tapping a finger lightly over the vicinity of her heart.

She took a second to get her thoughts in order. "I loved Ezra for a long time, but over the last year or so, things had gotten really difficult. It's been obvious for a while that he was battling something, but he refused to get help or get treatment. It was hard for me to continue being supportive of someone who wouldn't do the bare minimum to care for himself. I decided a while ago that I needed to end our relationship, but because of his problems, I had to choose the time wisely. I thought I'd caught him on a good night, but…" She exhaled a deep breath before she looked up at him. "In truth, I'd left him quite some time before everything happened."

"It absolutely *kills* me that he hurt you."

"That was the illness, not him. The Ezra I knew and loved would've never done this to me or taken my family hostage." She cringed, remembering the horror of that night. "He was the sweetest guy you'd ever meet until the illness took hold when he was in his early twenties. Since then, it's been a struggle for him and everyone who loves him."

"Hopefully, now he'll get the treatment he needs."

"I hope so."

"Is it over with him for you?"

"Has been for a while. What about you with Jaycee?"

"Has been for a while, although she didn't take it well when I told her that."

"What happened?"

"She was really angry. She thought we were going to get married. I'm not sure why she thought that. We never talked about it. At least I never did. She said I'd embarrassed her in front of her family and friends."

"How did you embarrass her? By telling her you wanted out of the relationship?"

"I guess. Apparently, she'd told people we were getting married. I mean, why would she do that when she and I had never once talked about getting married?"

"She embarrassed herself. I have no doubt you were always honest and forthright with her."

"I was. I enjoyed spending time with her, but I never thought she was *it*, you know?"

"I do. As much as I loved Ezra, I couldn't picture forever with him. After a while, I think we stayed together out of habit more than anything. We'd been together for thirteen years, since we were *sixteen*."

"That's a long time."

She looked up at him, feeling madly vulnerable. "I've never dated anyone else. I'm not sure I'd even know how."

His green eyes twinkled with amusement. "You want to find out?"

"I think I would."

He kissed her again, softly, gently, and then pulled back. "I ought to go."

"You didn't finish eating."

"I can take it with me."

"Don't go."

"You're dealing with a lot, Gigi. Maybe we should wait, you know..."

"I don't want to wait. I've had the biggest crush on you from the second you first stepped foot into our squad." Hearing how he felt about her made it easy to speak the truth to him.

His expression quickly shifted to total shock, which made her laugh.

"Don't tell me you didn't know," she said.

"I didn't! I had no clue. If I'd known that, I never would've dated Jaycee, or anyone else, because I've had the same crush on you for all this time."

He reached for her, and she sighed as he wrapped his arms around her.

"The timing might be terrible," she said as she rested her head against his chest, "but I want this. I want you."

"I want you, too, but more than anything, I want to do this right. You need time to heal and recover from what's happened."

"Will you help me do that the way you have been since the beginning?"

"There's nothing I'd rather do than help you with anything you need."

"I need more of this," she said, tightening her arms around him.

"You can have as much of this as you want."

"I'm going to want a lot of it."

"Me, too." He drew back to look down at her with the intensity that made him so good at his job now focused exclusively on her.

"Thank you for the way you've been so there for me through all this."

"I wish I could've done more."

"You did just enough."

"Anything you want or need, sweet Gigi, you tell me, and I'll get it for you."

"For right now, all I need is you."

"You've got me, sweetheart."

# CHAPTER EIGHT

Nick poured a glass of bourbon from the bar cart the butlers kept stocked in the sitting room off their bedroom and took it with him to the third-floor conservatory, which had become a favorite spot for the family. From up there, he had a bird's-eye view of the capital city and the monuments, which were lit up for the night.

The White House was decorated to the nines for Christmas, with every square inch decked out with trees and greenery and items pertaining to the "Made in America" theme Gloria Nelson had chosen months before her husband's sudden death. Nick had invited Gloria to come back to view the end result of her hard work, but she'd gracefully declined the invitation, saying it was too soon for her to return.

After a day of tragic news, Nick was heartsick for the people whose lives had been shattered and for the country that couldn't seem to solve the problem associated with guns, violence and mental health. Surely a country as vast and resourceful as the United States could come up with a way to protect the Second Amendment right to bear arms while ensuring that people who shouldn't have guns couldn't get them.

It sounded so simple on paper, but in reality, it was one of the most vexing challenges of their time.

His personal BlackBerry rang, and he drew it out of his pocket, expecting the call to be from Sam. But it was from Elijah.

"Hey," Nick said to the twins' older brother, who'd become like

an extra son to him and Sam since the twins came into their lives
in early October. "How's it going?"

"Okay, I guess."

"What's wrong?" Nick asked, immediately on alert. He hadn't
known Elijah for long, but he'd developed a strong bond with the
young man and knew something wasn't right.

"I've been thinking about the custody thing with Cleo's
family."

"What about it?" Nick could barely breathe as he waited to hear
what Elijah had to say. As the twins' legal guardian, it was up to Elijah
to decide where they lived and what was best for them. He'd decided
that since they had made such a smooth transition to living with Sam,
Nick and Scotty, they should stay with them until they came of age.

"I was just thinking that maybe we should consider letting
them have the kids."

If Nick had been struck by lightning, he wouldn't have been
any more shocked than he was to hear that. "What happened,
Elijah?" He'd been there when Cleo's sister and her husband had
tried to strong-arm their way into the twins' lives and had been as
appalled by their behavior as Sam and Nick had been.

"Nothing happened."

"Elijah, I'd like to think you and I have reached the point
where we trust each other."

"We have. Of course we have."

"Then you need to talk to me and tell me why you're thinking
the kids might belong with people we've already agreed wouldn't
be good for them."

"I can't tell you. You'll never look at me the same way again if
I do."

"I'm going to come there."

"What? You can't just come here. You need a motorcade and
planning and... You can't."

"I'll be there in a couple of hours."

"Nick... Don't."

"What time do you have class tomorrow?"

"Not until one."

"Then you come here. Tell your detail you need to come down
right now."

"Will they do that?"

"I'll talk to the Secret Service and make it happen."

"Okay."

"Whatever is wrong, Eli, we'll figure it out together. And for the record, there's nothing you could tell me that would change how Sam and I feel about you or the kids."

"Don't be so sure about that."

Nick hadn't heard Elijah sound so despondent since his dad and stepmother had been murdered. "I am sure about that. Go tell your detail what you need."

"Okay."

As he ended the call, all Nick could think was, *What now?* What had happened that had upset Elijah to the point that he was considering surrendering custody of the twins to people who hadn't wanted anything to do with them until their parents' killer had been caught? When Sam had called them during the course of the investigation, they'd never even asked how the children were or where they were.

Those people would get custody of those beautiful kids over Nick's cold, dead body. He went downstairs to speak to Nate, the agent positioned at the top of the stairs that led to the residence.

"Good evening, Mr. President," Nate said. "Is there something I can help you with?"

"Yes, Nate. Elijah needs to come here from Princeton right away. He's speaking to his detail about transport, but I was hoping to add my request for urgency."

"Of course, sir. We'll see to that right away."

Even with the Secret Service motorcade to cut through any traffic, it would still be close to three hours before Eli arrived. Until then, Nick was left to wonder what the hell was going on.

He was about to return to his bedroom when Sam appeared at the bottom of the stairs, looking tired after being called back to work. Nick waited for her as she trudged up the red-carpeted stairs and took the hand he held out to her.

"I just heard from Eli's detail, Mr. President," Nate said. "We're all set."

"Thank you very much, Nate."

"No problem, sir."

"What's that about?" Sam asked as they walked into their private rooms.

"Eli called me. He's upset about something and said maybe we ought to let Cleo's family have custody of the twins."

"*What?* No way."

"He said we'll never look at him the same way after hearing whatever has him so upset. I told him nothing could change the way we feel about him or the kids. His detail is driving him down right now."

"Oh God. What's this going to be?"

"I don't know, but I told him whatever it is, we'll figure it out together."

Sam rested a hand over her abdomen. "My stomach hurts."

Nick put an arm around her and kissed the top of her head. "Try not to worry until we hear what's going on. He knows the kids are better off with us."

"This has been one hell of a day."

"And it's not over yet."

ELIJAH ARRIVED at the White House shortly after midnight, coming up the stairs to the residence with a backpack slung over his shoulder.

Sam greeted him with a hug. "Are you hungry?"

He shook his head. "I don't think I could eat, but thank you."

"Come on in." Nick shut the door to give them the privacy they needed. "You want a drink?"

Eli looked up at him, seeming surprised by the offer since he was only twenty. "Yeah, that'd be good."

Nick poured bourbon for the two of them and wine for Sam. He sat next to Sam on the sofa while Eli sat across from them. "Talk to us. Tell us what's wrong."

Sam had never seen Eli so spun up, and after what he and the kids had been through after his father and stepmother were murdered, that was saying something. He looked absolutely tortured.

"I never wanted you to know this," he said haltingly.

"Know what?"

"Growing up," he said, sounding resigned to having to talk about whatever it was, "I spent summers in California with my mother. I've told you before how she had some health issues, which made it so she didn't really supervise me. That drove my dad crazy, but the court required me to spend that time with her."

When he took a sip of his bourbon, Sam noticed his hand was shaking. Seeing him so upset made her want to protect him from whatever was causing him such pain. At some point since he and the twins had come into their lives, he'd become theirs, too.

"The summer I was seventeen, I became friends with the girl who lived next door to my mom. Her name was Candace. We went to the beach, the arcade, movies. All the usual stuff, except nothing about her was usual. She was... She *is* the most beautiful girl I've ever met, and I fell in love with her. At the time, her parents were going through a divorce that had gotten ugly, and I tried to be there for her since I understood what it was like to have parents fighting over you and everything else. We became each other's closest friend. I'd never had feelings like that before. It was overwhelming and amazing all at the same time. It was the first time in my life that I felt like I was exactly where I belonged, with who I was supposed to be with."

Sam glanced at Nick at the same time he looked at her.

They certainly understood the feelings Eli was describing.

"One thing led to another between us, and before long, we were having sex. I'm sorry if that's more info than you want or need, but that's how I ended up in trouble."

Sam held her breath, almost afraid of what he was going to say next.

"Her parents found out we were sleeping together and lost their minds. They... They called the police."

"Why?" Sam asked.

Eli's eyes filled as he looked down at the floor. "She was fifteen. I was seventeen. They charged me with statutory rape."

"Oh my God," Nick said.

"I loved her. I'd never have done anything to harm her, and her parents knew that."

"They also knew your dad was loaded, right?" Nick asked.

Eli grimaced as he nodded.

"Son of a bitch," Nick said.

"It was a complete nightmare. I was arrested, arraigned, charged with a felony. My dad hired the best lawyers money could buy, offered her parents whatever they wanted to drop the charges, but by then, it was out of their hands. The lawyers were able to get the charges reduced to a misdemeanor count, but I have a sealed juvenile record that we've been trying to have expunged since I turned eighteen and satisfied the terms of the original agreement. It's in the works, but it hasn't happened yet." After a long pause, he added, "The worst part is that I've never seen or spoken to Candace again since the night her parents found out we were having sex."

"I'm so sorry that happened to you, Eli," Sam said.

"It was the worst thing I'd ever been through until my dad and Cleo were murdered. I think about Candace all the time, and I just hope when she turns eighteen in January that she'll reach out to me."

"What happened to bring this up again?" Nick asked.

"Cleo's sister Monique knows about it. She emailed me to say how unfortunate it would be if that got out and how embarrassing it would be to my 'new' family, the president and first lady, to find out they have a rapist in their midst, not to mention what Princeton might have to say about it. She went on to say that we could avoid all that by settling the custody dispute out of court and doing the right thing for the twins, which of course means turning them over to her and her parents. She's the last person on earth I'd want raising them."

"I knew I fucking hated that woman the first time I met her," Sam said, feeling as if she could commit murder on behalf of the young man she'd come to love.

"Yeah, she's a prize," Eli said. "Cleo never got along with her, so I can't imagine she told her about it. But Cleo must've confided in her mother when it was happening, because they were close, and that's how Monique knows."

Nick withdrew his BlackBerry from his pocket and put through a call, putting the phone on speaker.

"Mr. President, to what do I owe the honor?"

"Stuff it, Andy," Nick said with a small smile. His friends loved to razz him every chance they got about his new title. "We've got a problem with the custody case."

"What's that?" Andy asked, all signs of amusement gone from his tone.

Nick gave him the condensed version of the story Eli had told them.

"She said this in an email?" Andy asked.

"She did," Eli confirmed.

"Will you forward that to me?"

"Sure." Eli pulled out his cell phone and sent the email to Andy, whose address he already had due to the ongoing case.

"Hang on a second," Andy said. "I'm reading it now." After a long moment in which Sam, Nick and Eli existed in painful silence, Andy said, "Wow, what a piece of work. She's threatening to blackmail a young man whose father and stepmother were recently murdered by revealing the details of a sealed juvenile record to the media. I think the judge will be interested in seeing this, and I'll be reaching out to the attorney representing their family to let her know her clients are resorting to some dirty tricks."

"Do you think that will help our case?" Eli asked.

"It won't hurt. Don't forget… We already have the advantage because your father and Cleo's wishes were clear. We have to go through the motions with the court, but I just did a quick check online and found that the California Supreme Court has ruled that the disclosure of the names of minors involved in crimes isn't considered an invasion of privacy."

"Great," Eli said. "So she could destroy my entire life and get away with it?"

"I'm going to file an injunction with the court to bar the release of that information in relation to the custody case."

"Will that work?" Nick asked.

"It should. The judge assigned to this case is a no-nonsense type who won't like that she did this. She may have helped us by putting her threats in writing. I'll send this to opposing counsel and the judge right now and ask for guidance on how to proceed. I know it's very stressful to have to wait, but you did the right thing telling us about this, Eli. It's better not to have any surprises in a situation like this. I'll be in touch as soon as I know more."

"Thanks, Andy," Nick said.

"You got it. Try to get some sleep. We'll take care of it."

"Thank you, Andy," Eli said. After Nick had ended the call, Eli said, "I would've told you sooner if I'd thought it was relevant to the custody case, but juvenile records are sealed, and my other lawyers told me there's no public record of them. It hadn't occurred to me that Cleo would've told anyone about it, but I know she and her mom talked every day."

"I don't blame you for not telling us about this before now," Nick said. "Juvenile records are sealed for a reason. The focus is on rehabilitation and not ruining the life of a young person who made a mistake."

"Candace wasn't a mistake," Eli said fiercely. "I didn't even know it was illegal for a seventeen-year-old to have sex with a fifteen-year-old. The age of consent in California is eighteen. I found that out the hard way."

"Is this why you don't see much of your mother these days?" Sam asked.

Eli nodded. "My dad was so mad that she let this happen, but it wasn't her fault. We were sneaky teenagers. She had no idea what we were doing."

"How did Candace's parents find out?" Sam asked.

"She got a UTI that led to an exam, and when the doctor asked if she was sexually active, she said she was. Her mom blew up right in the doctor's office and demanded the doctor call the police."

"I haven't been a mother very long, but I can't imagine ever doing that. A fifteen-year-old isn't a baby, and she was in a loving relationship."

"Candace's mother was the queen of the overreaction, from what she told me. She was super strict and wanted to know where she was every second of every day. I guess after her dad left her mom, she went a little crazy and wasn't as vigilant with Candace, which was such a relief to her. I'll never understand why she had to call the police."

"If I had to guess," Sam said, "it was probably more about sticking it to the dad for leaving and allowing this to happen than it was about you."

"And yet I'm the one whose life was nearly destroyed by it."

"We're not going to let your life be destroyed," Nick said fiercely. "We'll do whatever it takes, including play some hard ball of our own, to keep our family together and to protect you from people who'd harm you to get what they want."

Nick was never sexier to Sam than when he was in protector mode. The family they'd made for themselves with Scotty, the twins and Eli was the most important thing in Nick's life, and Sam had no doubt he'd do whatever it took to protect them from harm.

"Are you hungry?" Sam asked Eli.

"A little, but I'm not sure I could eat."

"Let's try. What do you feel like?"

"Pizza maybe?"

"Coming right up." Sam picked up the phone that connected them to butlers twenty-four hours a day and asked for a supreme pizza, knowing that was Eli's favorite, and a Coke.

"We'll be up shortly," the butler replied.

"Thank you so much."

"A pleasure, ma'am."

"If there's one thing to love about the White House, it's the room service," Sam said.

"There's only one thing to love about the White House?" Nick asked, amusement dancing in his gorgeous hazel eyes.

"Well, you live here, so there's that, too."

"Oh phew, that's a relief."

"I want what you guys have," Eli said wistfully. "What my dad and Cleo had. I had that with Candace. I miss her so much. I almost flunked out of school my senior year after all this happened. My dad helped me every night with my schoolwork so I wouldn't screw up my acceptance to Princeton. He was there for me every step of the way through the nightmare." His eyes filled, and he moved quickly to wipe away tears. "I never would've survived it without him. He was my best friend, and I miss him so much."

Sam went to sit next to Eli, putting her arms around him and holding him as he wept for his father. "I know what you mean. My dad was my best friend, too. There's no replacing them."

"Sorry," he said, attempting to rally. "I don't mean to dump my shit all over you guys. You've already done so much for us."

"Elijah, we love you and the twins," Nick said. "There's nothing you could want or need that'd be too much for us. I know it may seem crazy that we feel that way about you all after such a short amount of time, but it was instantaneous for me."

"Me, too," Sam said. "I took one look at those precious babies, and I was sunk. And then I found out they had a wonderful older brother, and that was the best kind of bonus."

"We love you guys, too, and I don't want to cause any trouble for you after everything you've done for us," Eli said. "I'd hate that."

"Don't worry about us," Nick said. "All that matters is that you guys and Scotty are safe and happy. The rest is just details we'll figure out as we go along."

"Thank you for letting me come here and talk this out with you. After I read that email, I almost had a heart attack."

"That email was egregious, and we'll make sure she regrets sending it," Nick said.

For the first time since he arrived, Elijah cracked a grin. "Don't eff with President Cappuano or his family."

"Damn straight, my friend," Nick said.

"I appreciate having you guys on my side."

"We'll always be on your side," Sam said, "and Andy will do his very best to make this go away."

"If it gets out, it'll be embarrassing to you."

"No, it won't," Nick said.

Eli gave him a skeptical look.

"Remember, I'm not running for anything, which makes me somewhat untouchable. Let them say what they will. I don't care. I only care about how it affects you, the kids and Sam. I don't care about being hurt politically, so please don't spend one minute worrying about that. I fully intend to do my very best for the American people over the next three years, but I refuse to be bullied by people like Cleo's sister."

Eli released a deep breath and seemed to relax ever so slightly.

"Do you feel better after talking about it?" Sam asked.

"Yeah, and I'm glad Andy's fired up about it."

"He's fired up because it's an awful thing to do to a young man who just lost his father and stepmother in the worst way imaginable," Nick said. "If anyone is going to come off looking bad in this situation, it's Monique and the rest of the family who thought it would be a good idea to use that information against you."

"In fact," Sam added, "I think we ought to find a way to let it slip that they tried to blackmail you."

"After the case is settled, of course," Nick said, giving her a stern but amused look.

"Of course," Sam said.

"You guys are funny," Eli said, perking up when a knock sounded on the door.

"That'll be your pizza," Sam said.

"I'll get it." Eli jumped up to greet the butler and thanked him profusely for the late night meal.

"You're most welcome," LeRoy Chastain said as he rolled in the cart that contained cutlery and china. "When you're done, just put the cart outside the door, and we'll take care of it for you."

"Thank you so much, LeRoy," Sam said.

"A pleasure, ma'am."

Eli walked him to the door, shook the older man's hand and closed the door behind him. "This place is the bomb."

"Don't say the word 'bomb' in the White House," Nick said with a teasing smile.

Eli laughed, and Sam felt herself relax at the sound of his laughter. She hated to see him upset like he'd been when he first arrived, and she hoped Candace would reach out to him as soon as she could.

It sounded as if the two of them belonged together, and Sam found herself rooting for them to find their way back to each other.

# CHAPTER NINE

A phone call woke Nick in the middle of the night, which meant it woke Sam, too. Nick sat up to take the call from one of his aides. He mumbled a few words of acknowledgment and put the phone down.

"What's up?" she asked when he settled back into bed. The nightlight they kept in the bedroom for middle-of-the-night crises of state made it so she could see the strain in his expression.

"I asked to be updated on any developments in Des Moines, and we have two more fatalities as well as confirmation that the father of the shooter has been arrested for failing to properly secure his weapons."

Sam reached for him, and he snuggled into her embrace as she ran her fingers through his hair. He'd probably never go back to sleep after being awakened. His insomnia was an ever-present challenge to his daily life, never more so than since he'd become vice president and then president.

"I can't stop thinking about all the poor families who'll never be the same after this," he said.

"I know. Me either. It's so awful."

"Part of me hates that we have to go there and make their grief ours when our own grief is so fresh."

He was referring to the loss of her father in October.

"The holidays were going to be hard enough on us without this, too," Sam said. "Saying that out loud makes me feel like an asshole."

"You're anything but that. It's only natural to want to avoid something that's going to hurt like this does, especially when we're already raw."

"That's it exactly. Thank you for understanding and for letting me say that out loud, even though I feel terrible even thinking that way. Of course we have to go there and show our support."

"Yes, we do, but we don't have to like it, and we need to be free to express those feelings to each other in the privacy of our own bedroom." He raised his head to kiss her cheek. "I could never do this without you by my side."

"Yes, you could."

"No, I couldn't. I'd never survive it if I didn't have you to come 'home' to every night. That's how I get through the days, thinking about you and this and us and the kids. You give me strength even when you're not with me."

"Likewise, my love. I'll find myself daydreaming about you when I'm supposed to be working."

"Is that right?" he asked, his hand smoothing down over her back to cup her ass and pull her in even closer to him.

"Uh-huh. It's like a fever I can't seem to shake."

He looked up at her with his heart in his eyes. "Please don't shake it."

She kissed him as sweetly as she possibly could. "I never will."

"Promise?"

Sam nodded as she kissed him again. "Hearing what Eli went through with Candace made me hurt for them both."

"Me, too. We know all too well what it's like to be separated from our true love."

"Yeah, I was thinking that very thing. I hope he hears from her."

"I know." He moved so he was on top of her, gazing down with love in his eyes.

"That was a very smooth move, Mr. President."

"You liked that, huh?"

"I like all your moves."

"How about this move?" he asked as he nudged at her with his hard cock.

Sam spread her legs and raised her hips to let him know what she thought of that particular move. "That's one of my favorites."

"What do you think of this one?" he asked as he filled her.

"That's another favorite," she said, gasping from the impact, the pleasure, the overwhelming desire that overtook her any time he touched her this way—or any way, for that matter.

His lips curved into a smile as he kissed her. "Of mine, too. Along with this." He picked up the pace, moving in her like he'd been born to love her and only her, which he had.

After loving him like this for two years, she was convinced no one else would've done for either of them but each other.

Her body responded to him the way it had for no one else—ever. What had been so elusive in past relationships was as easy as breathing with him, so easy that he had her on the verge of release in a matter of minutes.

"Not yet," he whispered against her lips. "Make me work for it."

"I can't. I'm easy where you're concerned."

Laughter made his body—and hers—shake. "Easy. That's the one word no one ever uses to describe you."

"Don't make me mad, or I'll take mine and deny you yours."

"You wouldn't do that to me."

"You want to bet?" She wouldn't, and he knew that, which made it fun to play with him.

Still smiling, he shook his head as he kissed her more intently this time, his tongue brushing up against hers and setting her on fire with the movement of his cock inside her. Because it was the middle of the night, she didn't try too hard to hold off the orgasm that had been building from the first second he touched her.

He groaned from the feel of her release and let himself go with her on the best kind of wild ride.

"You gave up easily," she whispered in his ear, making him grunt with laughter.

"Only because I want you to get some sleep."

"What about you? Will you be able to go back to sleep?"

"The odds are better after your middle-of-the-night treatment."

"It's been a while since we did that," she said, yawning.

"Because we're getting old, and going without sleep makes us cranky."

"You mean it makes me cranky, right? Since you go without sleep regularly."

"You said that, not me."

Sam laughed as she yawned again.

He withdrew from her and moved to his side, bringing her with him and holding her close. "Get some sleep. We've got some long days ahead of us."

"I know," she said, sighing. The trip to Iowa would be among the most difficult things either of them had ever done, and it was probably just the start of the difficult things that would be part of their new roles.

As long as they stuck together, she was confident they could get through whatever came their way.

Sam's first stop the next morning—after getting Scotty and the twins off to school—was the headquarters of the National Pipefitters Association in Alexandria, Virginia. "Had to be in freaking Alexandria, didn't it?" she asked Freddie, as they made their way through bumper-to-bumper traffic on the 14th Street Bridge. She'd picked him up outside the Metro Center station.

"Most of the associations in the DC area are headquartered in Alexandria and Arlington," he said between bites of the powdered doughnuts that made up fifty percent of his diet, or so it seemed to her.

"Thank you for that, Mr. Chamber of Commerce, and P.S., do you have stock in that doughnut company? Because if you don't, you should get some. You single-handedly keep them in business."

He popped another doughnut in his mouth and chased it with chocolate milk before burping loudly.

"You're revolting."

"I'm just a growing boy having his breakfast, and no, I don't have stock in the company."

"Don't get that powder crap all over my car."

"I'm not."

"You are!"

"You're in particularly rare form this morning," he said, "and that's saying something since you're almost always in rare form."

"I had a long day yesterday, getting called back to work the homicide, and then we had a situation with Elijah."

"What happened with him?"

Sam glanced at him. "You have to promise not to tell anyone, even Elin."

"I won't."

Since she trusted him with her life, she filled him in on what Elijah had told them the night before and how Cleo's sister was trying to use his history against him.

"That's totally lame. How can she do that to a kid who just lost his dad the way he did?"

"We said the same thing. We met them when they came to see the twins—after their parents' murderers had been caught and not one second before. They were awful people. Eli says Cleo was nothing like her sister and that she didn't get along with her."

"I can see why. What a crappy thing to do."

"What I want to know is why they want the kids so badly. Is it so they can raise them in a loving home or because they're attracted to the billions their father left them?"

"If I had to guess, I'd say the latter."

"Me, too." That gave Sam an idea that had her making a phone call to Andy. After she gave his receptionist her name, she was put right through with the now-predictable level of fawning that came with being the first lady. Sam rolled her eyes at Freddie, who was choking back a laugh.

"Hey, Sam. What's up?"

"I was telling Freddie about what Cleo's sister was up to and how I wonder whether they really want the kids or the billions. That led me to question their finances, and I was thinking I could maybe do a run on the family members to get some additional information on that, but I didn't want to do it without asking you first."

"Can you do it without alerting them that you're investigating them?"

"Yep."

"In that case, I say take a look and let me know what you find."

"Will do."

"Be careful, Sam. We have all the advantages thanks to Jameson and Cleo's very clear instructions on who they wanted to care for their minor children. We don't want to do anything to mess with that."

"I got you. Discretion is my middle name."

Freddie choked on his latest doughnut, sending a cloud of sugar into the air that had Sam scowling at him. "That was not my fault," he said.

"I'll be in touch, Andy." Sam slapped her phone closed and glared at Freddie. "Clean that up! Right now."

"I'm cleaning it." He ran a napkin over her dashboard, which only made the mess worse.

"When we get back to HQ, your first order of business is cleaning that up."

"Yes, ma'am. Can we talk about how discretion is your middle name?"

"What? It is. I can be discreet when I need to be."

"Sure, but it's not like you're *known* for it or anything."

"I knew for hours that Nick was going to be president, and I didn't tell *anyone* except Celia. You think it was easy to sit on that bombshell? I know lots of stuff that I never tell anyone."

"Like, super-secret stuff?"

"Wouldn't you like to know?"

"Yes, I would."

"Dream on and stuff another doughnut into your piehole. While you're at it, do a run on the financials of Monique and Robert Lawson and Leslie and Chad Dennis in California."

Freddie popped the last doughnut in his mouth and got busy working on his smart phone.

"And speaking of discretion, don't tell anyone I had you do that while we were on the clock."

"We're riding in the car, and I'm looking at my phone while we go. No rule against that."

"Thanks, Freddie."

"Sorry about the sugar dust."

"You're gonna clean it up."

"Yeah, yeah."

The traffic finally let up a bit as they crossed the 14th Street Bridge, but came to a dead stop on George Washington Parkway. "We shouldn't have done this first thing."

"I tried to tell you that."

"*When* did you try to tell me that?"

"When I got in the car and said traffic is going to be a bear at this hour."

"You didn't say that."

"Yes, I did, and besides, you already knew that. You've lived here all your life."

"Stop talking sense to me. It's irritating."

His low snort of laughter had her holding back a smile. Sparring with him made their dreadful jobs and long days together so much more fun than they would've been otherwise. In the back of her mind, she knew she was too close to him on a personal level and probably should switch up their team to make him someone else's partner, but she couldn't bring herself to do it.

"How do you think Gonzo's doing?" she asked, eager to change the subject of her own thoughts.

"So much better than he was."

"Yeah, but with the trial looming, do we need to be worried?" Sid Androzzi, also known as Giuseppe Besozzi, would be tried for the murder of Gonzo's former partner, Detective AJ Arnold. As the only witness to the shooting that had ended Arnold's life, Sergeant Tommy Gonzales was the U.S. Attorney's star witness.

"I think his recovery is solid, and he's stronger than he's been since it all happened."

"Hard to believe it'll be a year next month."

"I know. In some ways, it feels like five minutes, and in other ways, it's like we haven't seen Arnold in years." He glanced over at her. "Tommy asked Elin to help him organize the road race he wants to do in Arnold's memory. They're targeting the spring to hold the first one, hoping it'll be an annual event with the goal of raising money for after-school programs for middle and high school students."

"Yes, I heard about that. Sign me up to help."

"In your copious spare time?"

"I'll make time for that and lend my, you know, platform to help make it huge."

"You say 'platform' like it's a dirty word."

"If I had my druthers, I'd have no platform. But since I can't have my druthers *and* be married to Nick, the platform is what it is, and it's mine to use on whatever I want, such as a road race in honor of our beloved colleague."

"Your support will make a huge difference."

"Nick and I will run the race."

"Wait. What?"

"I said Nick and I will run the race. Do you need to get your hearing checked?"

"You're going to run a 5K?"

"Yes, I am."

"Um, okay," he said, clearly trying not to howl with laughter.

"How far is that, anyway?"

Freddie lost it laughing. "Three-point-one miles."

"No biggie."

"You'd better start training now, killer."

Sam made a mental note to get her ass on the treadmill ASAP. "I don't need to train for that. I can run three miles in my sleep."

"And when you come in last place, what will your platform have to say about that?"

"Shut up."

"What? It's an honest question."

"Are you going to run it?"

"Of course I am. Arnold was one of my best friends."

"So you'll be giving up your doughnut and junk food habit while you train?"

"Why would I need to do that?"

"So you don't drop dead?"

"Dude. I run three miles every day of my life and haven't dropped dead yet."

"Well, that's a freaking miracle considering your hellacious diet."

Sam pulled into the parking lot at the National Pipefitters Association on Mount Vernon Avenue shortly after nine thirty, having sacrificed forty minutes of her life she'd never get back to travel four miles. "Someone needs to do something about the traffic situation in this area."

"That's a novel idea. I'm sure no one has thought of it."

"You're being very sassy today, young Freddie," she said as she followed him from the car to the association's main door.

"Thank you, Captain Obvious."

"That's Lieutenant Obvious to you, Detective Clueless."

"Like you ever let me forget that." He rang the doorbell outside the association's main door.

"Hear that? A *regular, normal* doorbell that goes ding-dong and lets people know someone is at the door. You don't need gongs and symphonies and cymbals to get that job done."

"I hope your fount of wisdom never runs dry, Lieutenant. I benefit from it every day."

"Quit your sucking up and ring it again."

"Maybe louder would be better in this case." Sam looked up to see the building had a second and third floor. She made a fist and pounded on the door. "Police, open up!"

"Um, can I help you?" a female voice said from behind them.

As Sam spun around to find a young woman holding a tray with four coffees, it occurred to her that they could've been attacked from behind. But then she saw Vernon leaning against the black Secret Service SUV that had followed them to Alexandria and knew he wouldn't have let that happen.

"Oh my God. You're the first lady!"

"Do you work here?" Sam asked, gesturing to the door.

"Yes, I do. I went to get coffee."

"We need to speak to someone in charge."

"Ah, sure. Come in."

Sam stepped aside to allow the woman to use her key in the door.

"What's this about?"

"I'm afraid I can't say."

"You investigate murders, right?"

"I do."

She put the tray of coffees on a reception desk. "Has someone been murdered?"

"Could I please speak to your boss? I need the big boss."

"Yes, of course." The young woman picked up a phone and pressed a button. "Joyce, the, um, first lady is here to talk to you about a murder."

Sam wanted to commit murder herself as she glared at the woman, who seemed to wilt ever so slightly. "Tell her Lieutenant Holland from the Metro PD would like to speak to her right away."

"Did you hear that?" After a pause, the woman said, "Okay. I will." When she put down the phone, she gestured to a closed door across the hall. "You can wait for her in there. She'll be right down."

"Tell her to hurry up. We're busy."

"Yes, ma'am." She held up a pad of paper and a pen. "Could I get your autograph?"

Normally, she acquiesced to those sorts of requests on the job, but today she wasn't in the mood. "Sorry, I can't right now." She pretended to take a call on her cell phone as she walked into the conference room where Freddie was already seated. "What's up?"

"You talking to me or some imaginary person on the phone?"

"I'm on a very important call, so shut your yap."

"Sure, you are."

"Why do people have to do that whole first lady thing? Why can't I just be Lieutenant Holland on the job?"

"Is that a rhetorical question, or do you expect an answer?"

She slapped her phone closed with the satisfying smack she loved so much. "I want an answer! The whole world knows what I do for a living—and what my side hustle is. Why do we have to *talk* about it everywhere I go?"

"Again, is that rhetorical, or are you looking for an answer?"

"You're being a serious smartass today."

"No, I'm not," he said, laughing. "It just surprises me that you're still shocked when people mention your so-called 'side hustle.'"

"How long is that going to go on?"

"Still rhetorical?"

"Shut up and eat another doughnut."

"Is it lunchtime yet? I know some good places here in Del Ray we can hit."

"It's nine o'clock!"

"Never too early for first lunch."

"Where is this woman? I'm getting annoyed."

"You hit annoyed the second the receptionist said, 'first lady.'"

Sam went to ask the receptionist where the boss was and nearly collided with an older woman who was coming into the room. Somehow she managed to avoid crashing into her, avoid falling and stick the landing all in one smooth move.

"I'm Joyce Dougherty, the CEO."

"Lieutenant Holland. My partner, Detective Cruz. Could we speak in private, please?"

"Of course."

# CHAPTER TEN

They stepped back into the room, and Sam took great pleasure in shutting the door on the nosy receptionist.

"What is this about?" Joyce asked.

"Pam Tappen."

Joyce's expression immediately turned stormy. "That woman is dead to me. Do you have any idea what her incompetence has cost me? My board is outraged at the lack of professionalism she demonstrated by failing to appear at a conference she was paid in advance to manage."

"I'm sorry to tell you that she is actually dead."

Joyce's face lost all expression. "*What?*" she asked on a long breath.

"She's been murdered."

"Oh my God. Are you sure?"

"We're very sure. She was found bound and gagged in her minivan miles from her home. The medical examiner believes she was there for as long as two days before she died. We've placed the time of death around six p.m. on Sunday."

"Good Lord." Joyce dropped her head into her hands. "I just can't believe this."

"Where was your conference held?"

"Baltimore."

"And when was Pam due to arrive?"

"Friday evening to set up for registration and a welcome reception the next morning."

"What did you do when she didn't arrive?"

"We had to scramble to cover for all the things she was supposed to be handling. Our guests had to wear 'Hello, My Name Is' badges from CVS. It was an outrage. The board president told me he'd have my job for hiring someone so incompetent."

"This was the first time you'd worked with her?"

"Yes, and she came highly recommended by a number of other organizations that'd worked with her in the past."

"Did you notify anyone when she didn't show up?"

That question seemed to take Joyce by surprise. "Who would I notify? She worked alone."

"She didn't have an emergency contact on file with you?"

"No, we don't require that of contractors, but in light of this situation, we will in the future." Joyce leaned in, her expression earnest. "Please try to understand the position I was in when she didn't show up. I have a small staff of four that had to cover for months of work that Pam had done on our behalf that was now unavailable to us. Serving our membership is our most important mission. We did everything we could to provide them with a successful event with one hand tied behind our backs. I've never been through a more stressful situation in my entire life, and even though it all went as well as could be expected, I'm still worried about losing my job over this."

"Well, you can tell your board that your contractor was murdered," Sam said. "That should help."

Joyce recoiled from the sarcasm in Sam's tone. "I'm not in any way discounting the horror of what happened to her. I'm simply telling you the position I was in when she failed to show up to our event."

"I understand. In your dealings with Pam, did she ever indicate to you that anything in her life was amiss?"

"No, our relationship was strictly professional."

Sam realized she wasn't going to get anything more from this woman. "Thank you for your time."

"That's it?"

"That's it, unless you have information relevant to Pam's murder."

"I know nothing about that."

"Then we'll be on our way." Sam led the way past a group of

people gathered in the lobby, probably waiting for the chance to see the first lady on the job.

When they were back in her car and headed toward the District, Sam said, "That was a complete waste of time."

"Not entirely. We got to see the woman's shocked expression when she heard Pam had been murdered, which helps to eliminate her from our suspect list. We also know now that Joyce would've had no motive to harm someone she was relying so heavily upon."

"Yeah, that's all true, but it didn't give us any threads to pull, and you know how I love my threads."

"Yes, I do. So what's next?"

"I want to see the Tappens again. Find out where Officer Charles put them up."

"I CAN'T BELIEVE the department sprung for the JW Marriott, but when we travel, we're supposed to stay at the Motel 6."

Freddie laughed. "Right? Nothing but the best for everyone but us."

Sam pulled up to the front of the hotel on 14th Street and parked at the front door.

A uniformed man approached her and did a double take when he realized who she was.

"I need you to watch my car for a few minutes," she said.

"Yes, ma'am, Mrs. Cappuano."

Sam flashed her gold shield. "Lieutenant Holland."

"Got it."

"Will you take care of my friends' car, too?" she asked, gesturing to the Secret Service vehicle behind her.

"Yes, will do. Just leave the keys in both of them in case we have to move them."

"We're not leaving the keys," Vernon said. "Jimmy can stay with the car."

"I miss all the fun stuff," Jimmy said with a good-natured grin.

"Right there with you, brother," Freddie said, fist-bumping the younger of the two agents.

"If you two are done with your bromance, we've got work to do," Sam said.

"I'm with you, Lieutenant," Freddie said.

"As am I," Vernon added.

"I'll just be here minding the vehicles," Jimmy said.

Sam failed to hold back a laugh.

"Damned insubordinate kids," Vernon muttered.

"I feel you," Sam said, earning a glare from her partner.

As they made their way to the elevators, they turned every head in the lobby of the busy hotel—or she turned every head. Whatever. She pretended like she didn't notice people looking at her. On the seventh floor, they encountered a Patrol officer outside the elevators.

Even though he recognized her, they still went through the required steps to show identification.

"They're in 710 and 712," the officer said. "The friends are across the hall in 709."

"Thanks," Sam said.

She went to 710 and knocked on the door.

Bob Tappen answered, looking disheveled and exhausted. He stepped aside to let her and Freddie in.

Vernon waited in the hallway.

"Do you have any news about what happened to my wife?" Bob asked.

"Not yet. We're working the case as we always do, and we need more help from you and your family. As the people closest to Pam, you're our best hope of generating information that'll hopefully lead to answers."

"Whatever we can do."

"Would you ask your children and Pam's friend to join us?"

"Sure." Bob went to the door that adjoined his room with another and returned with his sons and daughter in tow. They didn't look much better than he did. "This is Molly."

Sam shook the hand of the pretty young woman. She had dark hair and blue eyes that were red and swollen from hours of tears. "I'm very sorry for your loss."

"Thank you."

Bob sent a text to Amy, who joined them a minute later.

"Is there news?" she asked. She was tall, with reddish-brown hair and green eyes that were also ravaged by grief.

"Nothing yet," Sam said, addressing the group. "We need your help to try to understand what happened to Pam." To Bob, she said, "Is it okay to speak freely about the murder in front of your children?"

He waved a weary hand. "They already know everything I know.

"The way she was murdered feels deeply personal, as if the person wanted her to suffer. I'm sorry to have to put this in such blunt terms, but she was left bound and gagged—and alive— inside her car in freezing weather. The person who did this to her wanted her to die a slow, agonizing death."

Molly's heartbroken sobs made Sam feel terrible to be adding to their despair, but if she was going to get them the answers they needed, she had to be truthful with them.

"Each of you has said you don't know of anyone who might've wanted to harm her that way."

"We don't," Bob said. "We've talked about it all night, and we can't think of anyone who disliked her, let alone hated her enough to do something like that to her."

"We're going to need a comprehensive list of people she came into contact with in all corners of her life. I know you gave us some names, but we need *everyone*."

"We figured you'd want that info, so we made you a list," Amy said, handing her a sheet of paper with names, addresses and phone numbers, separated by personal and business.

Sam liked this woman. They never got this kind of help. "This is excellent. Thank you."

"We want to do anything we can to help you find the person who took our beloved Pam from us," Amy said, her eyes fierce with love and heartbreak. "She and I had been close friends since college. We didn't see as much of each other as we'd like since we've been busy raising kids and working, but we stayed in close touch."

"And she never mentioned anything to you about having a conflict with someone?" Sam asked.

"No, never. She was so happy. Her business was doing better than she could've dreamed when she started it six years ago. The boys are excelling in school and sports. Molly made a smooth transition to college in Boston. Things between her and Bob were great, as always."

Bob hung his head as he battled with his emotions.

"They met in college," Amy continued. "They hit it off right away and have been together ever since. I was there at the beginning, and she still talked about him recently the way she did at the beginning."

"Excuse me." Bob stood and went into the adjoining room.

"This is so hard for all of us," Amy said, tears filling her eyes. "Pam was a wonderful wife, mother and friend. To think of how she suffered..." Amy shook her head and wiped away tears. "It's unbearable."

"We appreciate your help and this list of people to talk to."

"Whatever we can do to help," Amy said.

"I need you to keep thinking about anything she might've said, even months or years ago, about something that might've happened, a conflict with someone. It can be the smallest thing that'll blow the case wide open. We've seen that happen so many times."

"We'll let you know if we think of anything," Amy said.

The kids nodded in agreement.

"Thank you."

"When will they be able to get back into their home?" Amy asked.

"I'll let you know the minute our Crime Scene detectives are finished."

"Okay," Amy said. "We'll wait to hear."

Sam lowered her voice so only Amy would hear her. "In the meantime, you might want to help Bob decide what funeral home he'd like to use so he's ready when the ME releases her."

"I will."

As they rode the elevator to the lobby, Sam looked at the list of names Amy had given her. "Let's start with the friends. If anyone knew what was going on with her, it would be them."

"Even more than the family?" Freddie asked.

"Some women confide things in their friends that they wouldn't tell anyone else, even their husbands."

"You don't do that."

"I'm not like most women."

Freddie snorted out a laugh. "No, you aren't."

"I mean I talk to my sisters, and I have friends, but I don't tell them things that Nick doesn't know. Does Elin?"

"She has a lot of close friends, but I don't think she has secrets from me."

"I suppose it's not possible to ever fully know everything about someone. Even in the closest of relationships, people still hold parts of themselves back."

"I don't," Freddie said. "There's nothing about me that Elin doesn't know."

"Nothing at all?"

"Nope. I tell her everything. Except for things at work that I'm not allowed to tell anyone. What about you? Do you tell Nick everything?"

"Just about everything. I can't think of anything he doesn't know off the top of my head," Sam said. "The first two friends on the list are in Brentwood, so let's start there."

"I'm going to need food soon."

"It's only ten."

"The perfect time for first lunch."

"After we talk to the friends."

"Ugh, you're killing me."

"Nah, your diet is going to kill you long before I do."

While they worked their way through downtown traffic on the way to Brentwood, Sam took a call from Nick on the BlackBerry.

"Hey," she said, "what's up?"

"We're looking at Friday for the trip to Des Moines, but I wanted to make sure you can do it before I commit to the date."

"That's kind of soon after it happened, isn't it?"

"The thought is to get there before Christmas, and that's the only day I can do it. We've been assured by local authorities that they've consulted with the families, and we're welcome to come."

"Ah, okay. I'll need to clear it with Malone, since we're in the middle of a case. Can I let you know?"

"Sure, but as soon as you can. As you can imagine, the logistics are daunting."

"I'll call him right now."

"Thanks, babe."

"What's the latest from Des Moines?"

"Nothing new since last night. Just a bunch of families waking up to a whole new reality this morning. And some pretty significant pushback on my statement from yesterday about sensible gun control, but that's to be expected. It's a hot-button issue."

"Stay strong. What you said makes sense. You're not looking to take guns away from responsible owners. You're looking to get them out of the hands of people who shouldn't have them for whatever reason."

"Exactly."

"You might be in the best possible position to get something done on this issue, with no political fucks to give."

"That's what Terry said, too. I've got a meeting with Gretchen Henderson in ten minutes."

"Why are you seeing her again?"

"The party wants me to pick her for VP."

"I thought you'd decided on Senator Sanford, the Chanel No. 5 lady," Sam said.

Senator Jessica Sanford wore the same perfume his deadbeat mother had worn all her life, which had given Nick an intense aversion to it.

"They want Sanford to take Ruskin's place at State."

"Isn't it up to you?"

"Sanford wants the job at State. She told colleagues that was her dream."

"Ugh. I thought we didn't like Henderson."

"I didn't dislike her. I just liked Sanford more."

"I had a weird feeling about Henderson."

"I know," he said with a sigh, "and that's nagging at me. I've learned to trust that gut of yours, but you saw her for ten seconds."

"That's all it took."

"We've been through every other possible female candidate and eliminated them all for one reason or another. It's down to her, or I have to move on, and moving on would be to a man. I want a woman in this role. I want to be the first to have a female vice president."

"And I so admire you for that commitment. I'll shut my mouth and wish you luck with your new vice president."

"I never want you to shut your mouth for long, babe."

"Hahaha, don't be fresh with young Freddie listening."

Nick's laughter made her skin tingle with love and desire and so many emotions that only he could stir in her. "Have you heard from Roni?" Sam had asked her newly widowed friend to be her communications director and spokesperson at the White House, and while Roni had accepted the position, she'd since decided to take some time away to cope with her painful loss before she started in January.

"Not yet, and I'm starting to get a little worried. I'm going to have Darren get on it." Roni worked with Darren Tabor, the one reporter Sam could tolerate, at the *Washington Star*.

"He'll expect an exclusive in exchange."

"He can wish, and he can hope."

"Aw, he adores you. You need to cut him a break."

"The minute I do that, he'll become insubordinate like young Freddie has, and he'll be ruined."

"I can hear you," Freddie said.

"How's the case?" Nick asked.

"Frustrating. A well-liked mother of three is murdered in gruesome fashion, and no one around her can think of a single person who had a beef with her, let alone would do something like what was done to her."

"I'm sure you guys will figure it out."

"I hope so. Gotta run. We're interviewing one of her friends in a few."

"Good luck with it. See you when you get home."

"Love you."

"Love you, too, babe."

"How do you think he's holding up?" Freddie asked after Sam ended the call.

"Pretty well, all things considered. We're looking forward to escaping to Camp David after Christmas. I think he's feeling a little cooped up after a few weeks of not leaving there. At least when he was VP, he got to come home at night."

"Other presidents have referred to it as the gilded cage."

"That's an apt description. It's beautiful, and the staff is amazing, but being walled off from real life and surrounded by security makes for a confining existence even in the loveliest of buildings."

"I'd go mad," Freddie said bluntly.

"I would, too. I'm so thankful I can be out and about every day the way I always have been, even with Vernon and Jimmy trailing me. They're good about not being overly intrusive."

"That's working out better than I expected."

"Because they respect what I'm trying to do. I'm sure there're agents who wouldn't be so accommodating, or who'd be put out by the idea of the first lady pounding the pavement."

"Agents with that attitude wouldn't last on your detail. I'm sure Vernon and Jimmy were chosen because the higher-ups thought they'd be a good fit for you."

"Vernon's sarcasm is definitely a good fit for me."

"I never had a sarcastic bone in my body until I started spending all my time with you."

"And look at you now. I'm so proud of how you're coming along."

He looked over at her. "Are you? Really?"

She rolled her eyes. "Of course I am. You're my masterpiece."

"Means a lot to me that you're proud of me."

"Stop being schmoopy."

"I'm not being schmoopy."

"Yes, you are."

"No, I'm not. It does mean a lot to me that you're proud of me. That matters to me."

Sam parked a block away from the address they'd been given for Stella Gregorio and looked over at her young, handsome, earnest partner. "I'm very proud of the man and the detective you've grown up to be. I hope you know that."

"Thank you. And I'm proud of you and Nick and the way you've taken on these new roles with such class and dignity. It's amazing to me that my best friends are the president and first lady."

"We're honored to be your best friends and consider you one of ours, too. Now this officially ends the lovefest. Back to normal. Let's go see what Stella has to say about Pam."

"Yes, ma'am."

# CHAPTER ELEVEN

Freddie followed her up the walk to Stella's front door, which didn't have a doorbell.

Sam knocked on the door and peered into the side windows to see if anyone was home. "Here comes someone." She put her hand on her weapon, immediately on guard after having been recently shot at through a closed door.

The door opened to a man with a scowl on his face until he recognized Sam, and his expression became what she thought of as the "holy shit, it's the first lady" expression as he opened the storm door.

She showed him her gold shield. "Lieutenant Holland, Detective Cruz. We'd like to speak to Stella Gregorio."

"She's not doing well. Pam was one of her closest friends."

"I understand this is a very difficult time, but we're trying to figure out who murdered Pam. We need all the help we can get from the people who were closest to her."

"Come in. I'll get her." He stepped aside to let them in and gestured to a small sitting room off the foyer. "Have a seat."

While he went to retrieve his wife, Sam and Freddie sat together on a love seat.

Sam took a look at the framed photos of young adults that hung on the wall. "Another day, another love seat."

"Don't cross the middle line," Freddie said, pointing to it.

"Don't worry. I'm not buying what you're selling."

"My goods aren't available to you."

Before she could express her lack of interest in his goods, they heard footsteps coming toward them.

The man who'd greeted them had his arm around a woman who was nearly a foot shorter than him. "This is my wife, Stella." He helped her into a chair and hovered close by, as if waiting for her to fall out of the chair or something.

Stella had short, spiky gray hair and funky purple glasses. Her face was red and puffy from crying, her hands trembling in her lap.

"We're so sorry to disturb you at such a difficult time," Sam said.

"I can't imagine who could've done this to Pammy. She was..." Stella broke down into sobs. "She was the best friend I ever had."

"How did you meet her?"

"Her Molly was in kindergarten with my Jimmy. The two of them are the best of friends to this day, and so are we."

Damned that present tense that people used to refer to recently murdered loved ones. It made Sam sad for them every time.

"I can't believe she's gone. How can she be gone?"

"We're trying to determine what might've happened to her. Did she tell you about problems she was having with anyone in her life?"

Stella was shaking her head before Sam finished asking the question. "Things had been so good for her lately. Molly made a smooth transition to college, the boys are doing wonderfully in high school—both are great students and star athletes. She and Bob were always that couple you loved to hate—still so in love after more than twenty years together."

Sam hoped people would say the same thing about her and Nick when they'd been together twenty years.

"Her business was thriving after years of hard work building it from nothing," Stella added. "Her clients said the nicest things about her. The testimonials are on her website."

"How about her other friends? Was she having any issues with them?"

"Not at all. I've been awake all night trying to come up with something that might explain this, but there's nothing."

"Is it possible that something was happening that you didn't know about?"

"Highly unlikely. We told each other everything, even the difficult things."

"What were some of the difficult things she told you about her life?"

"Bob had a health scare three years ago with prostate cancer. He was treated and is doing well now, but there were a lot of challenges associated with that treatment, including impotency. We talked about that. They also went through a rough patch with Lucas when he was a sophomore and fell in with a group of kids that Bob and Pam didn't care for. They got through every challenge that came their way by pulling together."

"Tell me about these kids they didn't care for." It wasn't much, but it was more than she'd had coming in.

"I don't know much about the specifics. They were kids Lucas met through a job at one of the local restaurants, and they didn't care for the influence they had on him. He started to blow off school and miss practices. He's got the potential for a full ride to a Division 1 school through football. They weren't about to let him mess that up."

"How did they address the issue?"

"By making sure he was so busy with work, school and sports that he didn't have time to hang out with friends who were leading him astray. I thought they managed it in a very clever way—they got rid of the friends without making a huge scene."

Sam made mental note of that for the case, and for her own information should she ever need such a strategy with her own kids. She hoped she never would.

As fast as the possibility of troubled kids in Lucas's life had materialized, the lead had fizzled. If there was no big scene or fight, Lucas and his friends probably wouldn't have noticed what his parents were doing to separate them.

This case was pissing her off.

Sam gave Stella her business card. "Please call me if you think of anything else that might be relevant." As she always did, she added, "The smallest thing can blow a case like this wide open."

Stella took the card from her. "Pam would love that you're investigating her case. She admired you and your husband very much."

"That's nice to hear. We're sorry again about your friend."

"Thank you."

The husband saw them out.

When they were back in the frigid air, Sam glanced at Freddie. "That got us nowhere."

"I thought she was handing us something with the kid's friends."

"Me, too, but of course it can never be that easy. Let's try the next friend on the list."

Paula Baxter lived on Quincy Place, about five blocks north of Pam's home on M Street. Paula was sprinkling sand on her front stairs when Sam and Freddie approached her gate. When she realized who'd come to visit, she nearly fell down the steps. From outside the gate, Sam showed her gold badge while Freddie did the same.

"Lieutenant Holland, Detective Cruz with the MPD. Could we trouble you for a minute of your time?"

"Y-yes, of course. Please come in."

She went ahead of them into a warm, cozy home in which bright color was the focal point. Rooms were painted in primary colors, including yellow, red and blue. The place gave Sam an immediate headache.

"This is about Pam, right?" Paula asked.

"That's right."

Paula led them into an orange kitchen with a profusion of colorful fruit ceramics. "Would you like some coffee?"

"If it's no trouble," Sam said, earning a surprised look from her partner. She liked to think she could still surprise him once in a while.

"No trouble at all. I just made a fresh pot." She poured coffees for each of them and placed cream and sugar on the table.

"How did you hear about Pam?" Sam asked as she stirred cream into her coffee while Freddie dumped sugar into his.

"Our mutual friend Bev called me. Our boys play football together. They have since they were little. It's such a shock. Pam was the nicest person. Always willing to help out with rides for parents who couldn't get out of work. She'd say she was self-employed, and if she couldn't be there for her kids when they needed her, what was the point?"

"I want to ask you something that will sound judgmental when I don't mean it to be," Sam said.

"Okay..."

"When Pam worked conferences, she went off the grid with her family for days at a time."

Paula was nodding before Sam finished speaking. "I know, and she always made sure the rest of us were available for whatever the kids might need while she was away. She helped us the rest of the time, so we stepped up for her when she was working a show."

"I'll have to admit I feel better knowing it was part of a plan."

"The shows were super intense. Often, she was the one running the whole thing, along with staff from the various organizations she worked for, of course, but she was in charge. It was often as much as sixteen hours a day for up to five or six days in a row. Bob and the kids left her alone when she was on-site at a show. They knew they could contact her if there was an emergency, but they tried not to bother her if they didn't need to."

"This helps me to understand their routine a little better."

"She worked so hard for the companies she supported. She'd built that business from a very small company providing registration support to a full-service conference operation. We're all so proud of what she accomplished and heartbroken that she's been taken from her family and friends in such a senseless way."

"Do you know of anyone who might've wanted her dead?"

"Not at all. Everyone who knew her loved her."

Not everyone, Sam wanted to say but didn't. "Has she had any disagreements with clients, friends, other parents, coaches?"

"Not that I'm aware of. As far as I knew, she got along with everyone. People liked her. I never heard her say a bad word about anyone."

Sam wanted to scream with frustration. Pam's murder had been extremely personal. The person who killed her made sure she suffered before she died. Talking to the friends who'd loved her wasn't getting them anywhere. "We appreciate your help."

"I wish there was more I could do to find the person who did this to her."

Sam placed her business card on the table. "If you think of anything that might be relevant, please call me."

"I will."

"Is there anyone you think we should talk to who's not on this list?" She showed Paula the list of friends that the family had given her.

"Maybe Mark Ouellette, the boys' football coach. She was the president of the boosters and worked closely with him on a number of projects."

"Where can we find him?"

Paula reached for her phone, found his contact info and wrote it down on the pad that Sam provided. "He owns an insurance company."

"Add that info, too, if you would."

When Paula was finished, Sam retrieved the notebook. "Thank you very much for your time."

"I wish there was more I could do."

"This helped."

Paula walked them to the door. "I hope you find the person who did this."

"I hope so, too," Sam said. When they were outside, Sam zipped up her coat and pulled on gloves. "Thoughts?"

"This one reminds me of the Woodmansee case."

"How so?"

"Perfectly ordinary people turning up dead for no good reason."

"Yeah, that's true. How can she have had a beef with someone bad enough for that person to bind her, gag her and leave her to die a slow, torturous death in the cold, and no one in her life is aware of it?"

After they got into Sam's car, she started it to get the heat going.

"What's our next move?"

"Before we talk to Ouellette, I want to talk to Archie about what's on her phone and computer."

"Let's do it."

"I'VE BEEN through everything on her computer and phone for the last month, and I didn't see anything that would indicate a problem with anyone," Archie said thirty minutes later when Sam found him in his office at HQ.

"There has to be *something*," Sam said.

"If there is, it's not on her phone or computer."

Sam's frustration threatened to boil over, but that wouldn't help her find a murderer.

"Do you want me to go back further than a month?"

"Yeah, I guess so. There has to be something."

"Will do," Archie said, using his chin to point. "Did you see what's happening across the hall?"

"No, what?"

"Ramsey's packing up his stuff. Farnsworth fired him."

"*What?*"

"Crime Scene was able to tie him to the vandalism in your office. He's also being charged with malicious mischief."

"I need a moment to process this dream-come-true moment," Sam said, although she was aware that Ramsey's removal from the force didn't end the threat he posed to her.

"I thought you might be pleased to hear this news."

"How could he be so stupid as to think he wouldn't get caught?"

"Just like Stahl making phone calls to the media from the lieutenants' lounge."

"Exactly! If I was going to come after a fellow officer," Sam said, "I'd make sure no one could trace it back to me."

"Like if you were, say, to investigate someone like Ramsey and discover he was having an affair?"

"Just like that, but that wasn't me."

"Of course it wasn't," Archie said, his eyes dancing with amusement. "You're far too busy to involve yourself in such petty matters."

"That's right."

"Whoever investigated him did us all a big favor. We don't need his shit around here after everything with Stahl, Conklin and Hernandez."

"True."

"What're you hearing about your dad's case?"

"There's an evidentiary hearing after the holidays."

"You don't have to testify, do you?"

"No, I was kept at arm's length on that one. Avery Hill and the FBI are working with the U.S. Attorney."

"That's good. We can't afford any conflicts of interest on something that hot."

"Right."

"They're going down for it, Sam. Tell me you know that."

"I do, but it's weird how it matters so much less to me than it did when my dad was still alive. What difference does it make now that he's gone?"

"It makes *all* the difference," Archie said, all signs of amusement long gone. "What they did was monstrous, and they deserve to fry for it. And Conklin, sitting on what he knew for *four* years. It's total bullshit."

"Yeah, for sure."

"None of us can possibly know how hard this is for you, but trust me when I tell you that just about everyone on this force wants justice for your dad."

"That's good to know. Means a lot to me."

"We want justice for Steven Coyne, too."

"I do, too. For both of them."

Weeks later, Sam was still trying to get her head around the facts of the shooting that had left her dad a quadriplegic—and the connection to the drive-by shooting of his first partner twenty years earlier. All to protect a secret gambling ring run by City Councilman Roy Gallagher and his cohorts. And Paul Conklin, her dad's successor as deputy chief, had known all along who was behind the shooting and had sat on the information while pretending to be a close friend to her dad. It was beyond outrageous.

"Will you do me a favor?" Sam asked Archie.

"Anything you need."

"Check to see if the coast is clear of Ramsey before I head downstairs?"

"Yep."

While she waited for Archie to return to his office, she thought about how lucky she was to have friends like him and many others at work. The Stahls, Ramseys and Conklins had been the minority during her career, and she was relieved to be rid of Ramsey on the job.

"All clear," Archie said when he returned, "but I'll walk out with you just in case he resurfaces."

"Normally, I'd say no need for such things, but this time I'll just say thanks."

"You got it."

Archie walked her all the way downstairs to the pit, where she found her squad putting her office back to rights after the CSU investigation.

"Did you hear the news, Lieutenant?" Detective Jeannie McBride asked, smiling widely.

"I did."

"Rumor has it that the chief is going after his pension, along with that of Stahl, Conklin and Hernandez." They'd found out after the fact that Hernandez, the Patrol commander, had also known who was behind her father's shooting and had kept the information to himself.

"Good," Sam said. "None of them deserve to live fat off the city when they left the department in disgrace."

"No, they certainly do not," Jeannie said fiercely.

"Thank you all for doing this," Sam said to Jeannie, as well as Detectives Green and O'Brien.

"No problem," Green said. "We put your files back together as best we could, but you might want to flip through to make sure things are where you want them."

"I have no doubt they're better organized now than they were before. I sincerely appreciate this, you guys."

"You have enough to deal with," O'Brien said.

He'd recently joined the squad to replace Detective Will Tyrone, who'd left the department in the wake of his friend Detective Arnold's murder. O'Brien was fitting in nicely.

"What's the latest with the case?" Green asked.

"We're getting nowhere fast," Sam said. "Let's gather in the conference room in ten to go over what we have so far." She went into her office, which was cleaner than it had ever been, and tried to find the legendary mojo that was missing on this case.

"Knock, knock."

Sam looked up to find Dr. Trulo in her doorway. "Come in."

He came in and closed the door. "Heard about what happened with Ramsey tossing your office and getting himself fired."

"I got rid of him without having to lift a finger."

A smile teased at the corners of Trulo's mouth. "He remains a powerful enemy, however."

"Yes, I'm aware of that and will watch my back."

"I'm glad you have Secret Service to help keep an eye on your back."

"That doesn't suck in situations such as this."

"I came down to see if you need me to do anything for you before tonight."

Her mind went completely blank. What was tonight?

"Sam," Trulo said, sounding exasperated and amused. "The second grief group meeting is tonight."

"Oh, right." They'd agreed to get a second meeting on the schedule before the holidays so people could turn to each other for support if needed. "I knew that."

"Don't make it worse by lying to my face."

"I'm not lying. I remembered!"

"No, you didn't," he said, chuckling, "but that's okay. I've got you covered if you can't make it. I understand you have a lot on your plate these days, especially after the tragedy in Des Moines."

"It is a lot, Doc. Nick and I are really struggling with how best to support the families in Iowa."

"May I?" he asked, gesturing toward her visitor chair.

"Sure." Her team could wait five more minutes for her.

"The best thing you both can do is to go there and show you care about what happened to them, that you care about the underlying issues that cause these things to happen, that you're determined to do what you can to try to bring about change."

"It feels so inadequate."

"Having the president and first lady come to offer their condolences won't feel inadequate to the people affected."

"Are you sure?"

"I am."

"That's good to know. Thank you."

"I'm always here for you, Sam, whether it's department related or not. You have a friend in me."

"That's very comforting. I'll be there tonight."

"I requested a bigger room in light of the interest I've received since we were on the *Today* show."

"Oh wow. Has it been a lot?"

"More than three hundred departments have reached out to ask about our blueprint, and I've heard from quite a few people associated with past cases of ours who were interested in attending the next meeting. Thus the bigger room."

"Wow, that's amazing."

"It's all thanks to you and your brilliant idea."

"And thanks to your brilliant execution of my idea."

"We make a good team, you and me."

"Yes, we do. Speaking of that... You might be hearing from my husband."

Trulo's eyebrows lifted. "About?"

"Leading a task force looking to address the connection between mental health and gun violence."

"The president... wants me... to..."

Amused by his flustered reaction, Sam said, "Lead his mental health task force. If you're willing, that is."

"Of course I am. What an unbelievable honor that would be. I assume you suggested me for this?"

"Only when he thought I might make for a good chair."

Trulo laughed at that before he made a futile attempt to curb his amusement.

"It's okay to laugh. I thought it was funny, too."

"Would you be on this task force with me?"

"In sort of a figurehead kind of way, like I am with the grief group."

"Ah, I see how it is."

"You do all the work. I get all the glory."

They shared another laugh. "I'm happy to share the glory with you, my friend." He stood to leave. "Take good care of yourself while you're helping your husband care for others, especially in light of what you're already dealing with."

"I will," she said, touched by his concern for her after the recent loss of her beloved father. "Thank you again."

"See you later."

# CHAPTER TWELVE

After Dr. Trulo left, Sam gathered her hair into a twist that she secured with a clip, grabbed a half-empty bottle of water and her notebook before joining her team in the conference room.

"I saw you were with Dr. Trulo, so I took the liberty of updating everyone on what we have so far," Freddie said.

"Thank you. Unless anyone has a better idea, my plan is to see the sons' football coach next. I have no idea if he'll have anything to add, but we'll check that box."

"I've been thinking about it," Cameron said, "and I keep coming back to how she was killed. There're really only a few things that would spark the kind of emotions that would lead to that kind of murder—love, money, sex, power."

"Very good thinking," Sam said, impressed as always by the sharp young detective who'd joined them after Detective Arnold was murdered. "Let's take them one by one." They'd started a murder board for Pam, with photos of her in life and death, as well as a time line of what they knew so far. She went to the second dry-erase board and wrote the words *love, money, sex* and *power* across the top.

"What do we have under love?" she asked.

"Her family," Jeannie said. "Her friends. Her business. Her community."

Sam made notes of each one of those things. "What else?"

"I can't think of anything else we've learned about her that wouldn't be covered by one of those things," Freddie said.

"How about money?"

"We ran the financials for both her and Bob," Cam said. "We found nothing out of the ordinary. An upper-middle-class existence with the usual bills and expenses that come with having three children, one of them in college in Boston. There were no unusual deposits or withdrawals in the last six months."

"I checked her business accounts," Jeannie said. "The business made about three hundred thousand last year and was on track for a bigger year this year. According to the testimonials on her website, she was the best at what she did, and a wide variety of organizations relied on her to provide flawless events for their members and stakeholders."

"Next is sex. What stands out?"

"She was happily married," Freddie said. "Everyone we talked to mentioned how solid she and Bob were as a couple and all of them were as a family. Nothing like the vibe we picked up right away that something was rotten when we were investigating Ginny McLeod's murder."

"True," Sam said. "That family was in a class by itself." She pointed to the final column on the dry-erase board. "We're left with power."

"I haven't picked up a sense that either she or Bob were power hungry," Freddie said. "They seemed like the types to keep to themselves and their kids and the people closest to them."

"One thing to consider," Cameron said. "The sons are elite football players. Freddie said Lucas is on track for a scholarship with a D-1 college program. That's big time. We might want to do some digging into the dynamics of his football situation."

"That's a thread," Sam said.

"I'd suggest speaking to each of the kids individually," Jeannie said. "Sometimes teenagers pick up on tensions or arguments or things that they'd keep to themselves unless asked directly."

"That's a good idea, too," Sam said. "We'll do that after the football coach. In the meantime, the rest of you can stay on the computers, digging into each member of the family. As you know, no detail is too small. I want reports on the kids' social media as well."

"We're on it," Gonzo said. "We've got a few things to talk about from Stahl's files, too."

"Like what?"

"A missing teenager who was never investigated, to start with."

"Ugh," Sam said. "Tell me that's the worst of it."

"That's the worst of what we've found so far," Gonzo said.

"Is it safe to assume it was a Black teenager?" Sam asked.

"It is, a girl."

"Why did I know you were going to say that?"

"Because Stahl was a scumbag, and now we're finding out he was even more of one than we thought."

"He was a *racist* scumbag on top of all his other charms," Jeannie said fiercely. "With your permission, I'll dig into that unsolved case."

"Please do," Sam said. "Keep me posted."

"I will."

"All right, everyone, let's get to work."

SAM AND FREDDIE found Mark Ouellette at a nondescript office on Rhode Island Avenue with several employees working at desks in the outer office. Although he immediately recognized Sam, he didn't overreact, but he did seem nervous.

"You're here about Pam," he said. "We're all just shocked and heartbroken."

"How did you find out about her death?"

"My son, Aidan, heard it from some other kids on the team. He plays with Pam's sons, Lucas and Justin."

After he closed the office door, he gestured for them to sit in visitor chairs on the other side of his messy desk.

"Do you own this business?" she asked.

"I do. I have to make my own schedule to accommodate my second job as a football coach. What happened to Pam? No one has been able to find that out."

"She was found bound and gagged in her minivan in Southeast."

"Oh my God." He rubbed a trembling hand over his face. "And you're sure it's her?"

Sam gave him a perplexed look. "Of course we're sure." After a beat, she continued. "I have to be honest with you, Mr. Ouellette. Your reaction seems intense, considering we're talking about the mother of some of the kids you coach. You seem incredibly upset."

"I am incredibly upset. Pam was a wonderful person. She

helped so much with the management of the team. I'll be lost without her."

"And that's all it was between you and her?" Sam asked, working a hunch. "The management of the team?"

He gasped with outrage. "What're you asking?"

"You know what I'm asking. Were you involved with her beyond the team?"

"No, I wasn't. She's happily married, and so am I. I have a wife and four children. She has three kids and has been with Bob forever. Our families were connected through football for many years. I considered her a close friend, so yes, I'm very upset that she's been murdered."

While his words were convincing, the tingle that attacked Sam's backbone told her to look closer, to dig deeper. She'd learned to trust those tingles. "I'm going to say this once and only once, Mr. Ouellette. If you know something that might be relevant to this investigation, I urge you to come forward with it now. If we have to come back here, the next visit won't be friendly."

He swallowed hard enough that his Adam's apple bobbed in his throat. For a long moment, he said nothing as he stared blankly at the wall behind them. When he shifted his gaze back to her, he said, "I'd like to speak to an attorney."

While he made the phone call to the attorney, Sam texted Freddie. *Didn't see that coming.*

*I know, right?*

*My backbone was tingling.*

*Ew.*

*No, listen, that usually means I need to pay closer attention. It's like my intuition system or something.*

*Well, you and your tingling backbone were right. Something's up.*

*What do you think it will be?*

*I have no idea. Her marriage with Bob seemed solid.*

*At least HE thought so. Who knows what she was up to?*

"My attorney will be here in fifteen minutes."

Sam was thrilled to hear someone was on the way. Waiting for attorneys to arrive could take half a day or longer sometimes. "I'm surprised you were able to get someone that fast."

"He's my brother-in-law."

"Does he specialize in criminal law?"

Ouellette blanched at the word *criminal*. "No, he doesn't, but I don't need a criminal lawyer, because I haven't committed a crime."

Sam wanted to tell him he was a fool to trust something like this to a lawyer who didn't regularly work with the police, but she wasn't paid to hand out free legal advice. So she kept her mouth shut and read a text from Freddie.

*He's a fool to trust this to a hack.*

Sometimes it freaked her out the way he read her mind. *Was just thinking the same thing. But that's not our problem. He knows something. I want to know what that is. He wants a lawyer present, so we'll wait.*

*How long? I'm starving.*

Sam hoped the glare she sent his way sent the message that he needed to shut up about being hungry. He was always hungry. There was never a time when he couldn't eat a full meal, even if he'd just had one. Dreaming about the day his shit diet caught up to him gave her something to look forward to.

She received a phone call from Captain Malone and stepped outside to take it. "What's up?"

"That's what I'm calling to ask you. Where are we with the Tappen case?"

"We may have something, but I won't know for sure for a bit."

"What've you got?"

She explained about Ouellette and his request for an attorney.

"Interesting. If he's worried about having a lawyer there, it must be something."

"Your thought matches mine, which is why Cruz and I are waiting for the brother-in-law lawyer to get here."

"All right. Let me know what it turns out to be."

"Will do. I also gave McBride the green light to dig into one of Stahl's unsolved cases—the disappearance of a Black female teenager that was never investigated."

"Son of a bitch," Malone muttered. "What the hell was wrong with him?"

"It'd take all day to list the things that were wrong with him."

"That's for sure. You heard about Ramsey getting the ax?"

"I did. Assume he's going to appeal it through the union?"

"He already has and said he's going to spill a lot of dirt on the department and its so-called stars if we try to get rid of him."

"What dirt does he have?" Sam asked.

"We don't know, but we're not backing down. The chief has had enough of him."

"No one is happier about that than I am," Sam said.

"Just because he's no longer on the force doesn't mean you should let down your guard where he's concerned."

"I'm aware that he'll remain a powerful enemy, but I'm thankful he'll no longer be collecting a paycheck to be a waste of space."

"Agreed. After the last few months, the chief is not putting up with any bullshit. He hopes that in addition to getting rid of Ramsey, this'll send the message that bad cops have no place in this department."

"God, I hope so. I've had it up to my eyeballs with bad cops."

"Me, too."

"What are you hearing about the deputy-chief thing?" Sam asked, hoping the mayor had shifted her focus away from Sam, who'd declined the offer of a promotion she didn't want.

"Nothing new. She's still aiming for a woman."

"Have her look at Erica Lucas. She's an outstanding detective, as you well know."

"I do know that. I'll send the idea up the flagpole. On another note, are you planning to attend the hearing in your dad's case after the holidays?"

"I don't know yet. Do I need to be there?"

"Not in any official capacity. We kept your name out of the reports for obvious reasons."

"I don't want it to turn into a circus, and that seems to happen everywhere I go lately," Sam said.

"I understand. Let me know if anyone from the family plans to attend, and we'll take care of getting you all in and out."

"We'll figure that out after the holidays."

"In the meantime, can you brief the press on the Tappen case when you get back to the house?"

"Do I have to?" she asked, as she always did.

"I'm afraid so."

"Fine. I'll take care of it."

"Thank you, Lieutenant."

"You're welcome, Captain." She'd hated dealing with the media before Nick became vice president and then president. Now she hated it even more because they were forever trying to get her to tell them things about him even though she'd repeatedly made it clear that wasn't going to happen—ever. But that didn't stop them from asking irrelevant questions that she had no intention of answering every time she briefed them.

"Keep me posted on what you find out from the coach."

"Will do." Sam slapped her phone closed with a satisfying smack and went back inside. "When will your lawyer be here?"

Ouellette, who'd been slouching in his chair, sat up straighter. "Any minute now."

Sam sat in the chair facing his desk and trained her gaze on him.

He refused to look at her.

At least she knew for sure he had something big to tell her, or he wouldn't be so easily intimidated or asking for a lawyer.

Ten minutes later, the guy came rushing through the door, red-faced and huffing. "So sorry to keep you waiting, Mrs. Cappuano."

Sam rolled her eyes and showed him her gold shield. "Lieutenant Holland. My partner, Detective Cruz. Your name?"

"Joseph Holleran. Pleasure to meet you both. My wife won't believe I met the first lady."

"Enough with that," Sam said, scowling. "I'm here as a police officer, as you well know, and the one thing I hate is people who waste my time. I'm trying to figure out who killed Pam Tappen. Your client has information relevant to the case that I need, so let's get this moving."

"I'd like a moment to confer in private with my client," Holleran said.

Sam gestured for him to have at it. "Make it snappy." She and Freddie got up and left the room.

"I thought I'd have to hold you back for a second there," Freddie said, grinning. "When he added the part about his wife, I was ready."

"Why do people have to state the obvious? Why, why, *why*?"

"Um, probably because they've never had a first lady pounding the pavement as a cop before?"

"Why do *you* have to state the obvious? You're supposed to be on my side."

Laughing, he said, "I am on your side, but it's going to take a while for the novelty to wear off."

"Anytime now." She was giving them five more minutes before she went back in there to start kicking ass and taking names.

Three minutes later, the lawyer opened the door and invited them back inside. "My client is willing to speak to you about highly personal matters with the understanding that he's doing so voluntarily and out of a desire to find justice for Pam."

While Freddie cleared his throat to keep from laughing at the outrageous statement, Sam met the lawyer's gaze head on. "Let me clarify some things for you, Mr. Hapigan."

"It's, um, Holleran."

"Whatever your name is, this is a *homicide* investigation, which means I can arrest your client for failing to provide relevant information. He's not doing us a favor here. He's cooperating with a *homicide* investigation and thus saving himself from being arrested. Are we all clear now?"

"I didn't have anything to do with what happened to Pam!" Ouellette said.

"Shut up, Mark," Holleran said.

"I didn't! I cared about her. We were friends. I'd never harm her." His chin quivered and his eyes filled, and Sam again felt the tingle that came with a potential break in a baffling case.

"What is it you wish to tell us, Mr. Ouellette?" Sam asked, forcing herself to use a patient tone when she was tempted to rip his head off for dragging this out.

"I want you to know that Pam was a wonderful friend, mother, wife. She did so much for so many people and was always willing to lend a hand when needed."

"And?"

To her great dismay, he began to cry. For fuck's sake...

"I love my wife and my kids. My family is everything to me, and Pam's family was everything to her."

"But?"

"We, I... We had an affair."

Bingo. "When?"

"It started about a year ago."

"How long did it last?"

"It was ongoing."

"Who knew about it?"

"No one! We were very discreet."

"I want details. How it started, when it started, where the encounters took place."

"That's, um, kind of personal."

"Mr. Ouellette, I'll remind you again that Pam was *murdered*, which means nothing is personal."

He dropped his head into his hands. "I can't believe anyone would ever hurt her. She was the best person. Everyone loved her."

"I want the details, Mr. Ouellette. *Now.*"

Seeming to realize he had no choice, Ouellette released a deep sigh and began to talk. "She was the president of our boosters, and I relied on her for everything. We were in constant contact, and over time, we began to share confidences. At first, it was about our kids, who were teenagers and giving us the usual stress that goes along with that time in their lives. We commiserated, you know? One thing led to another, and we began to talk about our marriages and how as much as we loved our spouses, we both felt something was missing."

"And that something was sex?"

"No, it was more than that. Intimacy, connection and sex, too. We felt terrible for even talking about it outside our marriages, but we were both desperate for someone to talk to. She adored Bob. She truly did. She never had a bad word to say about him. He was an excellent father and provider and all the things anyone would want in a husband. But at some point, they'd lost the spark. I understood that better than just about anyone, because that's what's happened to me, too. My wife, Josie, is amazing. She's the best mother I've ever known and the sweetest person. I love her more than anything, but I'm not *in* love with her anymore. I haven't been for a very long time." He wiped away tears with his shirt sleeve. "I'm sure this sounds horrible to you, but Pam and I turned to each other for something that was missing in our marriages. We felt awful about betraying our spouses, but it was important to both of us to remain in our marriages and to keep our families together."

"I'll ask again. Who knew about the affair?"

"Neither of us told anyone. We made a pact at the beginning that it had to stay between us. Our lives would've been ruined if anyone found out."

Without taking her eyes off Ouellette, Sam said, "Detective

Cruz, would you please call up the images from the vehicle where Mrs. Tappen was found?"

"Yes, ma'am. Here you go." He handed her his iPhone.

"This is what was done to Pam, Mr. Ouellette."

After glancing at the image on the screen, he broke down once again. "Oh my God," he whispered.

"She was bound and gagged and left to die in the cold by someone who wanted her to suffer, so I'll ask you once again. Who did you tell about the affair?"

"No one. I swear on the lives of my children."

"Is there any chance your wife found out and didn't tell you?"

"I think I'd know if she did, and there's been no sign of that."

"Tell me where you met for sex."

He took a deep breath and released it slowly. "Hotel rooms mostly. Sometimes I met her when she was working a show."

"And that would require you to fly?"

"At times, yes."

"How did you pay for the hotel rooms and the flights?"

"I had a credit card just for that purpose, and the bills came here."

Sam was revolted by the notion of him having a special credit card to pay for an affair. "Where were you on Friday?"

"At an AAU football tournament in Delaware."

"When did you return?"

"Around midnight on Sunday. I was with my son the entire time and never left my house after I got home."

"Can you prove that?"

"I have an alarm system that I set when I returned home, and I didn't deactivate it until the next morning."

Sam glanced at Freddie, who'd know she wanted him to confirm that. "Did your wife go to the tournament?"

"No, she was home with our other children."

"You said you have four?"

"Yes. The oldest is my son, who was with me in Delaware. He's nineteen."

"And still in high school?"

Ouellette nodded. "He repeated eighth grade to give him an extra year to grow and mature as a player. He's one of the most highly recruited quarterbacks in this year's class. Everyone wants him."

"When was the last time you saw Pam?"

He thought about that for a second. "We had dinner last Tuesday."

"Where?"

"We drove over to a place in West Virginia."

"You drove all that way just for dinner?"

"We spent the night."

"Where did your spouses think you were?"

"Pam said she was meeting with a new client, and I was at an AAU meeting. Both are things we did frequently."

Sam couldn't believe the way these two had had an affair in almost plain sight.

"Did anyone suspect you and Pam were more than just friends?"

"Not that I'm aware of. We were very careful. We both had a lot to lose."

"Not even your son, who you spent so much time with, knew about it?"

"I never told him. If he found out, I was unaware."

"I'd like to speak to your wife."

He blanched and then looked at the lawyer, who seemed equally shocked. "Why?"

"I need to know if she knew you were having an affair with Pam."

"You're going to come right out and *ask* her that?"

"I am. And I'm going to ask Bob Tappen, too, because the two of them are the only people I've heard of yet that would've had motive to kill a woman everyone loved."

"You can't do that! You'll ruin my life!"

She held up another photo of Pam. "Her life has already been ruined, Mr. Ouellette, by someone who wanted her to *suffer*. Do you care at all about getting justice for her?"

"Of course I do, but you're asking me to implode my entire life to get justice for someone who's gone now."

"I'm sorry that it's come to this. We're not out to destroy anyone's life, but your wife and Mr. Tappen have motive because of the affair."

"Even if they didn't know about it?"

"You *think* they didn't know."

"I'm sure of it. My wife isn't the type to put up with something like this. If she knew, she would've killed me, not Pam."

"Did she know Pam?"

He nodded tentatively. "Our boys grew up together, played football from a young age on the same teams."

"Did she consider Pam a friend?"

"They were mom friends. They didn't run around together or anything like that."

"But they were friends."

"Yes, I guess you could say that they were."

"So if your wife knew, not only had she been betrayed by her husband, but also by a longtime friend."

"She would never do something like that to anyone," he said, gesturing toward the pictures of Pam on the phone. "She doesn't have that in her."

"Let me tell you something I've learned about people, Mr. Ouellette. When they've been betrayed by the people closest to them, they're capable of anything."

"Not my Josie. She'd never leave someone to die like that. She rescues birds with broken wings and takes them to the sanctuary. That's who she is."

"I'm sorry, but I'll need to speak to her, and I'll need to ask her if she knew about the affair."

Ouellette made a tortured-sounding moan.

"How could you do this to her, Mark?" Holleran asked. "That's my *sister*. You're on your own with this." When he would've stormed out, Freddie stopped him with a hand on his arm.

"We need you to keep the details of this investigation confidential until we've had the chance to speak to Mrs. Ouellette," he said. "Do you understand?"

"Yeah, I understand. I'm not allowed to tell my sister her husband is a dick. Got it." He pulled free of Freddie's grasp and walked out.

Sam put her notebook on the desk in front of Ouellette, who was now weeping quietly. "Write down the information about where we can find your wife. And please don't play any games or do anything to waste more of our time, or I will arrest you."

He took the notebook from her and started writing.

# CHAPTER THIRTEEN

"I hate this," Sam said to Freddie as they made their way through traffic toward the home of Mark and Josie Ouellette in the Woodley Park neighborhood.

"I do, too. She's at home minding her own business while her husband is at work and her kids are at school with no idea a bomb is about to go off in her well-ordered life."

"I have to be honest," Sam said. "I didn't have Pam pegged as the type to have an affair."

"Me either. If you'd asked me to bet my life..."

"I know. Same. It seems out of character from everything we've learned about her."

"I just wonder when she'd have the time between running her own business, taking care of a family, attending football games, helping with other people's kids. She seemed really busy."

"People make time for the things that're important to them."

"Yeah, I guess."

"Don't be disillusioned, young Freddie. Not all marriages end up this way."

"We run into an awful lot of them that are so far off the rails, you wonder how they ever got together in the first place."

"Doesn't mean that's going to happen to you."

"I know, but it makes me wonder *when* does it happen? At what point do you go from wanting to spend forever with someone to being so over them that you'd find someone else to sleep with?"

"If you're looking for an actual answer, I'd have to say it

happens gradually in most cases. In others, you realize almost right away that you made a huge mistake getting married in the first place. That's how it was for me with Peter. I knew I'd fucked up by marrying him almost from the start."

"Why did you marry him? I've always wanted to ask you that."

"You only knew him as the weirdo psychopath. You never knew the sweet, charming, romantic side of him. He really poured on the charm, and I was vulnerable after what happened with Nick—or what I thought had happened with Nick." It would burn her ass forever that Peter had withheld messages from Nick that she'd desperately wanted, because Peter had wanted her for himself. "He saw an opening, and he stepped right into it to give me what I needed." She glanced over at Freddie. "I know it may surprise you to hear that I wasn't always the ruthless woman I am today."

He snorted as he tried to contain laughter that spilled out nonetheless.

Sam held back her own need to laugh at the absurdity of her ever being married to Peter Gibson while Nick Cappuano existed in this world. "I made a big mistake marrying Peter for many reasons, but primarily because I was still in love with the man I'd shared one night with. That was on me. But I never would've cheated on Peter while we were married. Toward the end, I might've considered homicide, but not infidelity."

"Wouldn't have blamed you there. When he hassled you about spending time with your dad after he was shot... None of us could believe that."

"That was the end of the road for us. How could you know me for years and not know what my dad meant to me? To all of us? Between Peter at home, Stahl at work and my dad adjusting to being a quad while his shooter ran free, it's a wonder I didn't kill someone during that time."

"No one would've blamed you."

"Ah, but the paperwork wouldn't be worth it."

"True." He pointed to a row of four-story, luxury townhomes. "This is it." He took a closer look. "His business didn't look profitable enough to support something like this."

"Maybe football coaching is lucrative. What is AAU football, anyway?"

"It's for the really, really good kids, the ones with a chance at playing D-1 in college."

"I didn't want to ask in front of everyone back at the house, but what's D-1 mean?"

He gave her the side-eye. "Division 1. Top-level college."

"Ah, okay. So his kids and Pam's are very good football players."

"If they're playing AAU, then yes."

"What does AAU stand for?"

"I'm not sure. Let me go to the Google." He tapped around on his phone. "Amateur Athletic Union. It's a pretty big deal in the amateur-sports world. The site says more than seven hundred thousand athletes participate in more than thirty AAU sports around the country. According to the site, it was 'co-founded in 1888 by William Buckingham Curtis to establish standards and uniformity in amateur sports.' I remember it being a fairly elite thing when I was in school. You have to try out, and only the top kids in each sport end up at that level."

"I'm glad Scotty isn't into football. I'd be afraid of him getting hurt."

"But you let him play ice hockey?"

"That doesn't seem as bad as football."

"I hate to break it to you, Sam, but hockey is one of the most dangerous sports out there."

"Don't tell me that!"

"I shouldn't have to tell you that," he said as they got out of the car. "You've been to games. You know how rough it is."

"They aren't allowed to check in his league."

"But they will in high school."

"No one told me that!"

"I can't with you. I just *cannot*."

"How in the world am I supposed to know how high school hockey works when I've never had a kid play high school hockey?"

"While I'll acknowledge that's a good question, you had to know the checking started at some point."

"I figured they saved that for college."

"Nope."

"My husband and I will be having a conversation about that later."

"I feel like I should warn him."

"Don't you dare. I need the upper hand on this."

"That's a fight you can't win with your two hockey jocks."

Sam would rather spend the rest of the day arguing about

hockey with Freddie than tell Josie Ouellette that her husband had been having an affair with a woman who'd been murdered. "Ugh, this sucks so bad," Sam said as she looked up at the front door that was festively decorated for the holidays.

"Sure does. Let's get it over with."

They trudged up the stairs and rang the rather normal-sounding doorbell. That neither of them commented on its normalness was indicative of how stressful this sort of thing was for both of them.

A blonde woman wearing a red sweater and a shocked expression answered the door. "Holy. Shit. It's you! The first lady! At my door."

Sam held up her gold shield. "Are you Josie Ouellette?"

"I am."

"Lieutenant Holland, Detective Cruz. May we have a moment of your time, please?"

She stepped aside to let them in. "You work on murders, right? Oh, wait. We knew Pam Tappen. That's why you're here. We were so shocked to hear the news about her." Josie led them to a warm, cozy kitchen in the back of the home. "Can I get you anything? Coffee, tea, hot chocolate? It's so cold out there."

"We're fine, thank you," Sam said, taking the seat she was offered at a round wooden table with six chairs.

"I just feel sick about Pam. It's all I can think about. And poor Bob and the kids. They're such a great family. We've known them for years."

"How many years?"

"Oh, well… It has to be seven or eight since my Aidan started playing with their Lucas. They started at U8, which is the youngest group. They're both standout players and have won several championships together."

"How would you describe your relationship with Pam?"

"We were friends through our kids. When your children play at a highly competitive level, it takes over your life as well as theirs. We spent a lot of weekends away at tournaments, and the other families become like a football family of sorts. It wasn't uncommon for all of us to help each other out with rides and stuff, too. When she traveled for work, I brought Lucas and later Justin to practices, and she gave my kids rides home when I had to pick up my others. It takes a village to raise an elite athlete."

"Sounds like it. What was Pam's relationship like with your husband?"

Josie's brows furrowed with confusion. "With my husband? He's one of the team coaches and she was the head of the boosters, so she helped out with lots of things. We spent time together at tournaments and games, had dinners afterward, tailgated here and there. That kind of thing."

*Dear God,* Sam thought. *The woman truly has no idea.* In some ways, that was good news for Josie, as she didn't appear to be a suspect in Pam's murder. But in other ways...

"Why do you ask?"

"It's come to our attention that she and your husband were involved. Romantically involved."

For a heartbeat, Josie's face went completely blank as she shook her head. "That's not possible."

Sam remained quiet to give the other woman a moment to wrap her head around what Sam was telling her.

"How do you know that?"

"He told us."

She shook her head again with disbelief. "That's ludicrous. He's so busy, he barely has time to eat or sleep between running his business and coaching the team. When in the world would he have time for..." Josie stopped as if something had occurred to her that made her realize that what Sam was telling her might be true. She immediately began to weep.

Sam glanced at Freddie, who seemed as agonized over this as she was. "I'm very sorry to have to tell you this, Mrs. Ouellette, but we're trying to figure out who would've been angry enough with Pam to do what was done to her."

"It wasn't me," she said between sobs. "I didn't know she was sleeping with my husband."

Sam believed her. "Can you think of anyone else who might've had a beef with her?" She asked the necessary questions, even though she had to believe the affair played into what'd happened to Pam. It was the only thing out of the ordinary they'd discovered yet about the dead woman's life.

Josie shook her head as she wiped away tears. "Everyone likes her. Or they did. Or so I thought. Who knows what's true and what isn't?" She used a paper napkin to mop up her tears and blow her nose. "Does Bob know?"

"He's our next stop."

"This will devastate him. He adored her. That was obvious to everyone who knew them. Why would she do something like this to him? To her children? To my family?"

Sam wanted to remind her that it took two to tango, but she'd come to that conclusion on her own soon enough.

"How old are your children?" Sam asked her.

"Aidan is nineteen. Grace is eighteen, Michaela is fifteen, and my baby, Alexis, is eleven." She gave Sam a look full of despair. "What am I supposed to do now? My husband was having an affair with a woman who was murdered? And you're here because you thought I killed her?"

"We had to rule you out."

"I didn't kill her. I had no idea I had cause to want her dead. I've been heartbroken over what happened to her, and now I find out she'd been sleeping with my husband. For how long? Did he say?"

"A year."

"I think I'm going to be sick." She got up and rushed for the bathroom that was around the corner from the kitchen. The sounds of retching soon filled the air.

"Today, I truly hate this job," Sam said.

"Right there with you."

Sam's phone chimed with a text from her reporter friend Darren Tabor from the *Washington Star*. *Got a text from Roni. She's away until after the holidays. She said she'd check in with you and to please hold the job for her if you can.*

Sam texted him right back. *I'll hit her up and let her know the job is hers whenever she's available. Glad to hear she's ok.*

*Define ok, though, you know?*

*Yeah, for sure. I feel for her.*

*Me, too, but I think the job is giving her something to look forward to, so thanks for that.*

*Excited to have her on the team. If you're in the area and would like to come by the WH for a gathering on Christmas Eve, I'll leave your name at the gate.*

*Shut up. Don't mess with me that way.*

*I mean it! You're invited as a FRIEND. Off the record.*

*I need a minute to process this.*

Sam had to remind herself that it would be inappropriate to

laugh out loud amid Josie Ouellette's disaster. *Let me know if you're bringing a date. Got to clear her with the SS. And BTW it's formal.*

*You're serious.*

*Yes, Darren, but you're making me rethink the invite...*

*I accept! See you then. If not before. And if there's anything to tell me about the woman in the van, you know where to find me.*

*Go away.*

*We're FRIENDS now. You can't talk to me like that.*

*That's how I talk to my friends. Go. Away. I'm working.*

"Sheesh," Sam said, handing her phone to Freddie so he could read the exchange.

"Aw, you made his day, his week, his year, his life."

"I suspect I'll live to regret inviting him."

"No, you won't."

Josie returned a few minutes later, looking noticeably paler. "I'm sorry."

"Don't be."

"It's a terrible shock. I thought Mark and I..." She took a deep breath and let it out slowly. "I thought we had something special, only to find out I'm just another cliché wife who had no idea what her husband was really up to."

The door from the garage into the kitchen opened, and Mark stood in the doorway as if he wasn't sure he still lived there.

"Get out," Josie said, her eyes flashing with rage now.

"Please, Josie, let's talk about this."

"Did you sleep with Pam?"

"Let me explain."

"Get. Out. *Now.*"

Mark looked to Sam and Freddie, as if they were going to somehow help him out. They weren't. Thankfully, he turned and walked out before they had to get involved.

"What'll I do?" Josie asked, her eyes filling again. "I haven't worked since before Aidan was born. How will I support myself without his income?"

"Find a lawyer to help you through this," Sam said. "That's the best thing you can do."

"I didn't kill Pam," Josie said softly. "I'm not sad about her dying anymore, but I still feel for her kids. They don't deserve this, and neither do mine."

Sam put her business card on the table. "If you hear of anything that may be relevant to the case, please call me."

"You can't actually expect me to help you, can you?"

"I expect you to share any information relevant to a homicide investigation because you can be charged if you don't."

"This just gets better and better," Josie said with a bitter laugh.

"I'm sorry to have had to do this to you," Sam said. "Our job is to figure out who killed Pam."

"And it doesn't matter who gets run over in the process, right?"

"Are you saying you'd rather not know?"

She shrugged. "I liked my life the way it was thirty minutes ago."

Sam had no idea what to say to that. How could anyone not want to know their spouse was lying to them? "We'll, ah, see ourselves out." She couldn't get out of there fast enough.

"Ugh, that was horrible," Freddie said when they were outside. "I feel so bad for her."

"Why would she not want to know her husband was sleeping with someone else?"

"Because she needed to believe her life was exactly as she saw it. The happily married couple with the four accomplished children and a life anyone would envy. Now she's the scorned wife with no source of income and a husband who'll need to pay for two homes and probably can barely swing the one he already has."

"Wow, that's a lot of insight into marital meltdown from a newlywed."

"Am I wrong?"

"Probably not."

"What next?"

"I want to see Bob Tappen again."

"So we can spread the good news to him, too?"

"Yep."

"I really need some food before we continue on our path of destruction."

"Fine, but make it snappy."

"I'd rather make it greasy."

"I'm sure you know exactly where you want to go, so you can drive." She tossed him the keys and got into the passenger seat.

Freddie bounced in the driver's seat like a five-year-old who'd had too much sugar. "One of my favorite sandwich shops is up here."

Fifteen minutes later, Freddie got back in the car, bringing the mouthwatering aromas of grilled onions, peppers and steak. Because life wasn't fair, it was probably smothered in cheese, too.

"Here's your salad," he said, handing her a separate bag.

"Thanks."

They ate in silence—or rather, he powered through an extra-large sub while she picked at a tasteless salad. In the time it took her to eat half of hers, he'd also consumed two bags of chips and three chocolate chip cookies.

The salad would've been halfway appetizing if she hadn't had to watch his dumpster show while she was trying to eat it. She put the uneaten half back in the bag and rolled it closed. She sent a text to Captain Malone. *Will you please, please, PLEASE handle the media? We're on a roll out here, and I don't want to have to come back in. Just tell them we're working the case and expect to have more info soon. PLEASE??*

*Fine!*

*Thank you!*

*Yeah, yeah.*

"Phew. Malone is going to do the press briefing."

"That's good."

With one less thing to do, Sam relaxed a bit as Freddie pulled the car into traffic to head for the 14th Street hotel where the Tappens were staying. On the way, she called Lieutenant Haggerty from Crime Scene to ask where they were with the processing of the Tappens' home.

"Whatever happened to her didn't take place in the house," Haggerty said. "No signs of struggle or blood or anything that suggests a crime."

"Damn it. I was hoping you'd find a slam dunk."

"We rarely get that lucky."

"True. Thanks for trying. Send me anything you have when you can."

"You got it. We're cleaning up now. You can tell them they can come back around four."

"Will do." Sam slapped the phone closed with frustration. "I want to know what happened to her, and I want to know it right now."

"I hear you. How can it not be related to the affair?"

"It has to be. But how? That's the question. Josie didn't kill her. She didn't know about the affair. Bob gave off the blissful glow of happily married, so I'm gonna bet he didn't know about it either. So where does that leave us?"

"Someone knew."

"How do we find out who?"

"If I had the answer to that question, you'd be tempted to promote me."

Sam rolled her eyes. "After Bob, I want to circle back to the friend, Paula. If Pam told anyone about the affair, it would've been her."

"She said she couldn't think of anything that would've gotten Pam murdered."

"Perhaps she was trying to protect her reputation and her family's memories of her. As much as that would piss me off, I'd understand it. People are protective of the ones they love."

"I guess, but you were pretty clear about her keeping things from us during a homicide investigation."

"Maybe she was hoping we'd find that out somewhere else, and she wouldn't have to get into it."

"That's possible."

At the hotel, they ran into the same bellhop they'd seen earlier.

"Different day, same request," Sam said, handing him a five-dollar bill. "Watch my car, please." Then she remembered the Secret Service agents she tried not to think about while on the job and added another five-dollar bill. "And them, too." She used her thumb to gesture to the black SUV that had pulled in behind her.

"Yes, ma'am, Mrs. Cappuano."

Sam didn't take the time to correct him.

# CHAPTER FOURTEEN

They took the elevator to the Tappens' floor and went through the same routine with the officer on duty as they had before. By the time she knocked on Bob Tappen's door, she'd had more than enough of this day.

"Did you find the person who killed my wife?" he asked, looking hopeful and exhausted at the same time.

"Not yet. Could we please come in for a minute?"

"Oh, um, sure."

They followed him into the room. Lucas was stretched out on the second bed, scrolling through his phone. When he saw Sam and Freddie, he sat up.

"Crime Scene detectives are completing their work at your home. You'll be able to go home around four. I'll ask Patrol to arrange rides for you."

"Thank you."

Sam glanced at Lucas. "Could we speak to you in private please, Mr. Tappen?"

He nodded for Lucas to go next door, which he did, with a glance over his shoulder.

After the adjoining door closed behind him, Sam said, "Do you mind if we sit?" she asked, pointing to the bed Lucas had been on.

"No. Please, make yourselves comfortable." He sat across from them. "Have you got anything that might explain this? Because I'm telling you, I can't think of anything. I've gone over everything in my mind, every conversation, every day for weeks, trying to think of something that would've led to Pam being murdered. I can't think of a single thing."

Sam glanced at Freddie, giving him the floor without warning. She loved doing that to him and would certainly hear about it when they were back outside. But hey, her job was to train him, and that's what she was doing.

"Mr. Tappen," Freddie said haltingly, "we've encountered some information that may or may not be relevant to your wife's case."

"What information?"

"I'm sorry to have to tell you, sir, that we've discovered your wife was having an affair."

For a long, long moment, he stared at Freddie, his expression unchanged. And then he began to laugh. He laughed so hard that he couldn't breathe.

Freddie looked to Sam for guidance she didn't have. She shrugged.

"You find that funny, sir?" Freddie asked.

"Pam was *not* having an affair." Tappen wiped away tears of laughter. "That's preposterous."

"The other party has confirmed that she was, in fact, having an affair with him."

"What other party?"

"Mark Ouellette."

His expression went immediately thunderous. "There's *no way* she'd have an affair with that douchebag."

Freddie said nothing, letting his silence speak for him.

*Nicely done*, Sam thought. *Give him a minute to let it set in.*

"Pam didn't like him. None of us like him. He's a jackass."

Still, Freddie said nothing.

"There's no way she was sleeping with him," Tappen said, his tone losing some of its edge.

"Mr. Ouellette has confirmed a year-long relationship."

Tappen shook his head in what seemed to be complete disbelief. "Pam thought he was a windbag. She said it all the time. 'How can Josie stand to be married to him?' she would ask. 'All he talks about is himself, his quarterback-star son and how he's going all the way to the NFL, when we know the closest many of these kids will ever get to the NFL is attending a game on a future Sunday.' I wish I could tell you how many times she said those and other things. My boys don't like him either, and they can't stand his son."

"I'm not sure what reason Mr. Ouellette would have to lie about such a thing, as it made him a person of interest in a homicide investigation," Sam said. "Not to mention we had no choice but to interview his wife and present her with the same information we're giving you. Needless to say, his marriage is now in serious jeopardy."

"There's just *no way*," Tappen said again.

"We're forced to operate on the assumption that Mr. Ouellette was telling us the truth, as there would be no reason for him to detonate a nuclear bomb in his life if it wasn't true."

"People are going to hear about this and wonder what kind of life we had together. *I'm* going to have to wonder about that, because I thought I knew."

"We're sorry to have to bring you this news at what's an already difficult time for you."

"What am I supposed to tell my kids?"

"I'd suggest you go with the truth, and do it before it gets out as part of the case," Sam said.

"How can I tell them such a thing about their mother? They won't believe it, especially since I don't believe it."

"We need to ask you who Pam would've told about the affair."

"She wouldn't have told *anyone*. Something like this... It would've set off a nuclear bomb in *her* life if people found out. You have to understand... Our football family was tight. Everyone knows everyone, and this would've been a *huge* scandal. And I promise you, if anyone knew, it would've gotten out. People wouldn't have kept it quiet. It would be too salacious, too tempting." He took a deep breath and let it out in an even deeper sigh. "It wasn't bad enough that she was murdered. Now this."

"We're sorry to add to your grief," Freddie said.

He shrugged. "You're just doing your jobs. It's not your fault that my wife cheated on me with a complete asshole." After another long pause, he looked to Sam. "Did he say why she did it?"

"I, uh, he said they were both in long marriages, and some of the spark had gone out."

"That's a fucking lie," Tappen said, his eyes flashing with outrage. "The spark was very much alive in our marriage."

"I'm, ah, just telling you what he said."

"Maybe that was true for him, but not for her. I'll never believe she thought that."

"Can you think of anyone who might've learned about the affair and would be upset enough about it to do what was done to Pam?" Sam asked.

"Other than myself or Josie, no, and from what you tell me, she didn't know about it any more than I did."

"Would it be possible that one of your children knew?"

He stared at her in disbelief. "You think one of my children, who adored their mother, could've heard about an affair and murdered their mother in the most torturous way possible? They wouldn't have murdered her. They'd have been too heartbroken to even think up such a diabolical plan. If you don't believe me, do you want to be the ones to tell them what their mother was up to with Ouellette? You can see for yourself that none of them knew, because if they did, they would've raised holy hell about it with her and with me."

Sam absolutely did *not* want to be the one to tell Tappen's kids about the affair, but she *did* want to see their reactions to hearing about it. "If you'll bring them in, we'll ask them if they knew."

Freddie gave her a "holy shit, are you for real?" look, letting her know he wanted nothing to do with this either.

She couldn't blame him.

Tappen went to get his three children. When they were in the room, he said, "Go ahead. Tell them what you told me."

Sam once again looked to Freddie.

If looks could kill, she'd be so dead.

"It's come to our attention," he said, "that your mother was having a romantic relationship with Mark Ouellette."

Justin snorted through his nose. "No way. She couldn't stand him."

"She said all the time what a blowhard he is," Lucas said, glancing at his dad for confirmation.

"My mother wouldn't do that to my father," Molly said. "That's not who she was."

"Mr. Ouellette has confirmed the affair. He'd have no reason to make himself a potential person of interest in a homicide investigation if it wasn't true."

"You think he did it?" Lucas asked, sounding incredulous.

"He has an alibi for the time your mother most likely went missing," Sam said. "He was at a football tournament in Delaware."

"We were there, too," Lucas said, including his brother. "We saw him and Aidan there."

"We have to ask this, as difficult as it may be," Freddie said. "But did any of you have any inkling whatsoever that your mother was involved with Mr. Ouellette?"

"Hell no," Justin said. "That's so disgusting."

"I didn't," Lucas said.

A long beat of silence passed before Molly said, "I didn't know."

Sam zeroed in on her with the laser stare that made criminals wilt in the interrogation room. "If you know anything, now is the time to say so, Molly. If we find out that you withheld information pertinent to our investigation, that can cause you trouble."

"Did you know, Molly?" her father asked her, his expression conveying complete astonishment.

"I knew something was off," Molly said, blinking back tears. "She wasn't herself since I went away to college. Every time I talked to her, she was distracted, and there were times she didn't take calls from me, which wasn't like her."

"Did you know about Mark?" her father asked again, more sharply this time.

"I suspected something was going on with him. She mentioned his name a lot to me."

"Are you *kidding* me? And you didn't say anything?"

"What was I supposed to say, Dad? 'I think Mom might be banging Mr. Ouellette'?"

"To start with, yes. That might've kept her from being murdered."

Molly's face collapsed in the second before she broke down into heartbroken sobs.

Bob immediately realized what he'd done and went to comfort his daughter. "I'm so sorry, honey. Of course, none of this is your fault."

"I sh-should've said something."

"No, it wasn't your problem."

"I'm s-sorry, Dad."

Her father hugged her until she'd calmed down.

"Why would she do such a fucked-up thing, and with him of all people?" Justin asked, his expression making his feelings known. "She couldn't stand him. None of us can."

"Can you think of anyone else who may have known about the affair and been angry enough to do something like murder your mother?" Sam asked.

"Other than our dad and the coach's wife, who would care that much?" Molly asked.

"One of their kids?" Justin asked.

"Nah," Lucas said. "They're all decent kids, except for Aidan and his overblown ego. But that's not really his fault. All his life, he's been built up to be the next Peyton Manning or Tom Brady. It's gone to his head."

"Is he that good?" Freddie asked.

"Yeah, he really is," Lucas said. "If any of us is headed for pro football, he is."

"If you think of anything that might be relevant, even if it seems out there, will you please let us know?" Sam asked. "I believe you have my card."

"We will," Bob said for all of them.

"I'm sorry to have had to add to your grief with this information."

"You think you know someone, really know them," Bob said, shaking his head. "It's unbelievable."

What could she say to that? "I'll have Patrol get you home later this afternoon."

"Thank you."

Sam couldn't get out of that room fast enough.

Freddie was right behind her. "Freaking brutal," he said.

"Ugh, I know."

"And thanks for giving me the lead on that without any warning."

"I do what I can for the people," she said, earning a scowl from her partner.

At the end of the hallway, Sam stopped to speak to the Patrol officer who had been chatting with Vernon while he waited for her. "CSU has finished at the Tappen home, and they're cleared to return around four. Would you please see about transport for them?"

"Yes, ma'am. We'll take care of it."

"Thanks." She pushed the down arrow, and when the elevator arrived, she got on with Freddie and Vernon. "This case sucks."

"Don't they all?" Freddie asked.

"Yeah, but this one is suckier than some."

"What's the sticking point?" Vernon asked.

"A well-liked wife and mother found murdered in her minivan after having been bound and gagged and left to either suffocate or freeze to death over a period of days, meaning whoever did this wanted her to suffer. Her sons play in an elite football league, and we've determined she was having an affair with the father of one of the other players, who was also a coach. Neither of their spouses had any idea about the affair—and we believe them—so who else would hate her enough to do what was done to her? And how can it not be related to the affair, which was the only thing in her life that was out of whack?"

"That's the only thing you've found to be out of whack," Vernon said. "Doesn't mean there isn't more."

"That's true," Sam conceded. "It's just that, by all accounts, she was a wonderful wife, mother, friend, businesswoman. She doesn't seem like the type to have bodies buried all over town."

"Maybe the affair with Ouellette wasn't the first she's had," Freddie said.

"Ugh, that's also possible."

"What's the plan?" Freddie asked.

"I want to talk to Paula again, and then we'll call it a day." To Vernon, she said, "Thanks for the input."

"Anytime."

Sam was punched in the gut by a wave of longing for her dad. Normally, she'd be asking for his input at this point in a confounding case. Even two months later, it still came as a shock to realize he was gone forever.

Outside, she thanked the bellman and Jimmy, who'd stayed with their cars.

"Merry Christmas to you and your family, ma'am," the bellman said. "We hope you enjoy your holiday in the White House."

"Thank you. Happy holidays." There it was again, that punch to the gut that came with thinking about what it would be like to celebrate Christmas without her father. He'd absolutely loved Christmas and had been the best gift giver. She'd heard that the "first" of everything after a big loss was the worst, and that was probably true, but she already knew that nothing would ever be the same in her life without Skip Holland around to tell her how to live.

While she drove back to Paula's home, she put through a call to her new friend Roni. If this holiday was going to be torturous for her, she couldn't begin to imagine what it would be like for Roni after having lost her new husband when he was struck by a stray bullet on 12th Street in October.

The call went through to voice mail. "Hey, it's Sam. I just wanted to call to let you know I'm thinking of you. Darren told me you'd checked in with him, and I wanted to assure you the job is yours whenever you're ready. No rush, no deadline. Take care of yourself, Roni."

She ended the call by slapping her phone closed.

"It's nice of you to check on her."

"I really like her."

"Which makes her the rarest of unicorns, because you don't like anyone."

"I like more people than I used to. My other new friend is Gideon Lawson, the chief usher at the White House. He gets me, *and* he's sarcastic."

"Another unicorn. I'm looking forward to meeting him."

"He's cool. You'll like him."

"I can't believe we're spending Christmas Eve at the White House. It's so surreal."

"How do you think we feel? That's why we wanted all you guys there with us, to make it feel less surreal."

"I can't imagine how strange it must be to call the most iconic house in the world home."

"I need to stop by Ninth Street and get a box of family ornaments I packed to bring to the White House, but somehow they didn't make it into the move. I'm afraid that if I go there, I'm not going to want to leave."

"Do you hate living at the White House? You can tell me the truth."

"No, I don't hate it. It's like the most luxurious hotel on earth. Last night, we ordered pizza for Eli at one in the morning, and the butlers were right there twenty minutes later, rolling in a cart with a midnight snack fit for a king."

"I'd be in big trouble if I had that kind of service available to me."

"Maybe if you did, you'd finally gain the nine hundred pounds you deserve to weigh."

"You're being a nasty cow again."

"Better than a filthy pig."

"That's your opinion."

"Oink, oink."

"Mooooo. Anyway, about the White House…"

"I don't hate it, but it doesn't feel like home."

"It'll take a while."

"I'm sure it will. I keep telling myself that the only thing that matters is where Nick and the kids are. That's home. The building doesn't matter."

"In most cases, I'd say that's true, but when you live at the White House, the building matters."

"I guess. I don't want you to think I'm complaining, because I'm really not. It's a beautiful place to live, and I'm so proud of Nick for having this incredible opportunity, even if it scares the crap out of me, too."

"What scares you?"

"He literally has the weight of the world on his shoulders, for one thing. The other night, there was an incident with pirates attacking ships in the Gulf of Suez that required him to spend hours in the Situation Room in the middle of the night. I don't even know where the Gulf of Suez is or what goes on there."

"He's got great people helping him."

"Does he, though? A lot of those great people were Nelson's people. Are they loyal to Nick? Will they do right by him or focus on their own agendas? That's another thing I worry about, in addition to the increased risk to his safety simply because of the office he holds and how he came to be there. A lot of people are outraged that he was never elected, and now he's president."

"He's going to prove to them, one situation at a time, that they're lucky to have him."

Sam shrugged. "I guess."

"He said all the right things yesterday after the shooting. That'll matter to those who were directly affected and everyone who's looking for someone to make sense of it."

"Shooting babies in line to see Santa will never make sense."

"No, it won't." He looked over at her. "You want me to go with you to Ninth Street?"

"That's okay, but thanks for asking."

# CHAPTER FIFTEEN

They arrived in Paula's neighborhood a few minutes later and parked a block from her house as the afternoon light began to wane. The short days in December were downright depressing, Sam thought as they hoofed it through the cold toward Paula's house.

"I suppose you're going to make me ask Pam's best friend if she knew about the affair."

"Haven't decided yet."

"Let me know when you make up your mind."

"I'll tell you one thing, if she knew about it and didn't tell us the first time we were here, I'm going to be pissed." Sam knocked on Paula's front door. "You know how I hate people who waste our time."

"Yes, I do."

She knocked again. "Metro PD."

The inside door opened, and Paula seemed surprised to see them there. "You're back," she said as she opened the storm door.

"We're back," Sam said. "We have some follow-up questions."

"Come in."

Once again, they followed her back to the kitchen, where Paula turned down the heat under a pot on the gas range.

Sam wouldn't live in a house with gas. Her first year on the job, she'd responded to a house explosion that was later tied to a leak in the gas line. The house had been reduced to splinters, killing two people inside. Sam had never forgotten what she'd seen that day. She wondered if the White House had gas. If it did, it was probably inspected regularly. She'd have to ask Gideon about that so she'd have something else to worry about.

When they were seated at Paula's kitchen table, Sam glanced at Freddie, giving him the ball.

He gave her a withering look before turning his attention to Paula. "Did Pam ever give you any indication that she was unhappy in her marriage?"

"No, not at all. She and Bob were solid."

"Did she mention interest in other men?"

Paula recoiled. "Of course not. She was married."

"It's come to our attention that Pam was having an affair with Mark Ouellette, one of the coaches of her sons' football team."

"That's not true."

"We have reason to believe it is."

Paula was quiet for a long moment, and Sam was pleased that Freddie waited on her. That's what she would've done, too. "How did you find out?"

"Mark told us."

"Why would he do that?"

"Because we're trying to figure out who killed Pam, and we made it clear to him that withholding information in a homicide investigation is a crime."

"How do you know he's telling the truth?"

"His story was convincing, as was the fact that he'd have nothing to gain by telling us this and everything to lose." Sam waited a beat before adding, "You heard the part about withholding information pertinent to a homicide being a crime, right?"

"Yes." She ran a trembling hand through her hair. "I hope you understand... Pam was my friend. My best friend. When you were here the first time, my only thought was to protect her family. She's gone, you know? But her husband and kids... They have to live with the fallout of what happened."

"Tell us what happened," Sam said.

"She... She loved Bob very much. I never heard her say a bad word about him, even when the rest of us were husband-bashing. She said he was a wonderful father and husband and a hard worker."

"But?"

Paula released a deep sigh. "In the past few years, he'd stopped wanting a physical relationship with her. Everything else between them was as it had always been, but that part of their lives had come to an end."

"Had she talked to him about it?"

"She had, and he'd seen several doctors who couldn't find any physical reason for his sudden lack of interest in sex. He'd recovered from the prostate cancer he'd been treated for and was back to full health, so it wasn't that. They'd been to counseling, which had also failed to solve the problem. It was a very difficult situation for her. She was forty-seven years old and not ready for that part of her life to be over."

"So she had an affair?"

"Several of them, actually. Mark was the most recent and the longest lasting."

Sam's spine began to tingle with the realization that they were on to something. Finally. "I'll need a list of the men she was involved with."

Paula stared at her, seeming shocked. "I... I'm not sure I know them all."

"How many were there?"

"Four."

"Starting when?"

"About three years ago. The first two were one-night stands while she was away at conferences. The third was a friend of ours who lost his wife to cancer several years ago."

"His name?"

"You really have to involve him in this? He's been through so much already."

"I really do have to involve him. His name?"

"Tyler Markham."

"Where would we find him?"

Paula dropped her face into her hands. "He's an obstetrician at GW."

His name rang a bell with Sam, but she couldn't immediately place him. "Is there anything else?" Sam asked. "Is there anything else you know that we should know, and let me warn you that failing to disclose information a second time will result in charges."

"There's nothing else. You won't tell Bob that this came from me, will you?"

"I doubt I'll have to. Who else would know this?"

"No one," Paula said tearfully. "There's no one else who knows."

"I FREAKING hate when people waste our time," Sam said as they left Paula's and returned to the car.

"I can sort of understand why she didn't go there the first time, though," Freddie said. "In her mind, her friend is dead, and protecting her memory is the friend's top priority."

"Whereas finding her killer is *our* top priority."

"Different perspectives, different priorities."

"I suppose," Sam said. "But honestly, why do we have to tell people that withholding information in a homicide is a crime before they'll tell us what we need to know?"

"My very wise partner would tell you this is an everyday thing to us, but it's all new to them."

"Stop making so much sense. It's irritating."

Freddie barked out a laugh. "I'll add that to the things I'm not allowed to do."

"That list has to be getting very long."

"It's twenty-six pages."

Sam shot him a look. "You don't really have a list, do you?"

"I'll never tell."

She tossed him her keys. "Drive me to GW. I have some calls to make."

"Yes, ma'am."

When she was belted into the passenger seat, she put through a call to Dr. Anderson, her friend at GW. His voice mail picked up, so she left a message. "Hey, it's Sam Holland wondering how to find one of your colleagues in the maze you call a hospital. Call me if you get this message in the next twenty minutes or so."

She ended that call and put through another to Captain Malone.

He answered on the second ring. "Hey, how's it going?"

"We might have a small break." She explained what they'd learned from Pam's best friend. "We're on our way to talk to one of the other guys and operating under the assumption that the two one-night stands aren't worth pursuing. Right now, anyway."

"And you've ruled out the wife of the current guy and Pam's husband?"

"Both were legitimately shocked to learn of their affair. Josie Oucllette had no idea, and Bob Tappen said Pam couldn't stand Mark, or so she said. He and his children were stunned to hear that she'd been having an affair with him, 'of all people,' as they put it."

"This is very strange. The person who did this wanted her to suffer, so who else would have motive besides the spouses?"

"Their children would, if they found out about the affair and were revolted by it, but a crime like this takes a certain level of sophistication. Luring her from her home without leaving a digital trail, tying her up in a way that would keep her from being able to help herself, abandoning her in a freezing car and waiting to hear she was dead. A full-on sociopath did this."

"I'd take a low-level look at the kids and see if anything stands out."

"Will do. Tomorrow. After we see the third guy, a doctor at GW, we're going to call it a day. We'll get back to it in the morning."

"Don't you have your grief group meeting tonight?"

"Shit, fuck, damn, hell."

Captain Malone cracked up laughing. "I won't tell Dr. Trulo that you forgot."

"I didn't forget. Exactly."

"Sure, you didn't. See you when you get back to the house."

"What are you SFDHing about?" Freddie asked.

"I may or may not have forgotten that grief group is tonight."

"Ah, right. I should've reminded you."

"I shouldn't need a reminder."

"But alas..."

"Stop enjoying this so much. That's also irritating."

"Adding it to my growing list."

"You keeping a list of things that irritate me is also irritating."

"Duly noted."

"Am I allowed to skip the grief group that I founded?"

"I don't think so."

"Why did I know you were going to say that? Ugh. I have so much to do and no time to do any of it."

"What else do you have to do?"

"I haven't bought a thing for anyone, and Christmas is next week."

"You have people who can help you with that."

"Nothing says how much you love someone than farming out your Christmas shopping to other people."

"Everyone would understand, Sam. We're all well aware of the changes to your life recently."

"Still, I don't want a stranger shopping for my kids and Nick."

"Then ask Celia and your sisters to do it."

"They have enough of their own people to shop for."

"Ask for help, Sam. That's the only way you're going to be able to survive having three full-time jobs."

"I hate when you're right. Add that to your stupid list."

"That's number one on the list."

Sam didn't want to laugh, but couldn't help it. "I also hate to encourage you, but that was a good one."

"Thank you. I learned from the master."

"Clearly, I've taught you too well. So what do I get the man who has everything because he has me for Christmas?"

"Not sure where to even start to unpack that question."

"Seriously, Freddie. What do I get him?"

"How about working with the Secret Service to arrange a family ski trip while the kids are on vacation? There's nothing he'd rather have than more time with you and the kids."

"We're supposed to go to Camp David after Christmas."

"Ah, right. Do something for June when they're all out of school. That way, he'll have it to look forward to."

"That's a good idea, and I'll probably do that, but I need something to give him that's for right now."

"I'll give that some thought and get back to you."

"Think fast. We've got a week."

"Will do."

Sam's phone rang with a call from Dr. Anderson. "Hey."

"Who you looking for?"

"Tyler Markham, an OB." Again, Sam tried to recall how she knew that name.

"You'd probably find him at his office on K Street at this time of day, unless he's delivering."

"I'll try the office first. Thanks for the info."

"Haven't seen you in a while. You must be due for some sort of catastrophe soon."

"Shut your mouth."

His laughter rang through the phone. "We offer two-for-one specials on your frequent-flier punch card during the holidays."

"Good to know. Since I won't be seeing you, have a nice Christmas."

"You do the same."

"Thanks for the help."

"Anytime."

Sam slapped her phone closed. "Let me see your phone."

"Why?"

"So I can look up the doctor's office address."

"You could do that on the iPad," he said, gesturing to the screen that was mounted to her dash.

"I'd rather do it on your phone."

"Why? Because you never bothered to learn how to use the iPad?"

"Why do I need to know how to use it when you do?"

"For times like this when I'm driving."

"Give me your phone, or you're fired."

Rolling his eyes, he dug the phone out of his back pocket and handed it over to her. "P.S., you can't fire me for not letting you use my personal phone."

"You wanna bet?"

"No, I don't. You'd lose."

"What's your code?"

"I'm not required to provide that information."

"Freddie!"

Laughing, he said, "Six, two, zero, three."

Sam punched in the numbers. "Now what do I do?"

"Oh my freaking God."

"Are you swearing *and* using the Lord's name in vain?"

"You drive me to it."

"My work with you is nearly finished."

"Click on the blue icon with the red-and-white dial. That will get you to a thing called the World Wide Web. From there, you can conduct your search for the doctor's office address."

"Now was that so hard?"

"It's excruciating to realize you have no idea how to use a smart phone."

"Again, why do I need to know that when I have you?"

"For times when I can't be at your beck and call, such as when I'm driving."

"He's at 920 K Street. Check me out. I successfully found something on a smart phone all by myself."

"You hardly did that by yourself."

"Who punched all the buttons?"

"You did," he said with a long-suffering sigh.

"I rest my case."

"Speaking of cases, why aren't they waiting until after Christmas to start Androzzi's trial?"

"A good question. I guess the judge wanted to get as much in as he could before the holidays because he's got another big trial right after this one."

"I'm not sure I'm ready to relive Arnold's murder."

"I know. Me either. The first time was more than enough."

"Imagine his poor parents, sister, girlfriend. And Gonzo... Ugh, we just got him back."

"We'll all be there to support him and get him through it," Sam said, but she was worried, too. Gonzo had done several months in rehab to combat the pain pill addiction he'd developed in the throes of grief and was doing so much better. The thought of all that hard work and progress being undone by the trial was unbearable. They couldn't let that happen.

Parking at GW was always a competitive sport, but they got lucky with a space on the street a few blocks from the doctor's office.

"Remind me to come here late in the day more often," Sam said.

"I'll see if I can help to time your injuries accordingly."

"You're very saucy today, young Freddie."

"Just keeping it real, Lieutenant."

He'd never know how much that meant to her, especially since her entire life had imploded on Thanksgiving with the phone call from the White House that had changed everything. Keeping it real with him was essential to her sanity in the new normal.

As they hoofed it to the medical office building, Sam took a call from Andy. "What's up, Counselor?"

"Just wanted you to know your guy Thorn has been served with a big fat lawsuit."

"Excellent. Thanks for letting me know. You made it hurt, right?"

"Big-time."

"Thank you so much, Andy."

"Pleasure to help you and your husband."

"Anything new with the custody case?"

"Waiting to hear if we can get a hearing next week before the holidays. I'm holding out hope that the involvement of the president and first lady will help to move things along."

"If it helps to get this taken care of, I'm all for being married to the president."

Andy laughed. "I'll keep you posted."

"Thanks again."

Sam slapped her phone closed and updated Freddie as they stepped inside the office building.

"I'm really glad you're sticking it to that guy Thorn. He totally deserves it."

"He certainly does."

# CHAPTER SIXTEEN

They found the doctor's name in the directory and took the elevator to the fifth floor. "What're the odds he's actually here and available?"

"If I had to guess, I'd say the odds are low."

"I don't like that answer."

"Figured you wouldn't. I suppose we're working this weekend."

"Probably. If you can, that is." She often had to remind herself that the people under her command had lives in addition to their jobs. Not to mention she was eager to spend time with Scotty and the twins. Weekends had become precious commodities since the kids came into her life, but murder stopped for nothing.

She'd ordered ornament-decorating kits for each of the kids as well as her nieces and nephews from an online vendor and was hoping they'd arrive in time for some craftiness this weekend. Yes, it was out of character for her, but she'd made it a goal to try to spend more one-on-one time doing things outside her comfort zone with the kids. Holiday crafts certainly counted as outside her comfort zone.

"I can work Saturday morning, if need be," Freddie said. "Elin is working, and then we have a birthday party for one of her nieces in the afternoon."

"If we have to work, I'll make sure you're free by then."

"Thanks, boss."

"But let's make it our goal to sew this fucker up quick so we can be done before the holidays."

"I'm on board for that."

They stepped into Dr. Markham's office, which was all but deserted late on that Tuesday afternoon. The shocked receptionist slid open the window. "May I help you?"

Sam and Freddie showed their badges. "Lieutenant Holland, Detective Cruz to see Dr. Markham."

"Is he expecting you?"

"No, he's most definitely not expecting us."

"Could you please hold on for one minute?"

"I can, but that's about all the time I have."

"I'll be right with you." The woman closed the window and then disappeared into the corridor off the office.

"I appreciate her," Sam said.

"Why's that?"

"She obviously recognized me, but didn't make a red-hot fool of herself, and when I asked for Markham, she asked if he was expecting me. Not 'do you have an appointment?' when she knows damned well I don't. And then she went right off to get him. I give her an A-plus in *receptionisting*."

"That's not a word."

"I can make it a word. I'm the first lady, you know."

He rolled his eyes. "So you're playing that card when it's convenient for you?"

"When else should I play it?"

Before he could respond to that, the receptionist came through a door to the inner sanctum. "Right this way, please."

"A-plus-*plus*," Sam said to Freddie.

They followed the receptionist past dark exam rooms to an office at the end of a long hallway. The second Sam caught her first glimpse of Dr. Tyler Markham, she realized why his name was familiar. She'd once come to him for fertility treatment while married to Peter. If he recognized her as anything other than the first lady, he didn't let on. The sight of his face instantly transported her back to one of the most difficult times in her life, and she had to fight through the swell of emotion that came with those memories so she could stay focused on the job she was here to do.

Sam went through the ritual of introducing them and showing their badges.

He stood behind his desk, handsome in a strong, competent

sort of way that reminded her a bit of Nick, although Markham's hair was dark blond, and his eyes were blue. "What can I do for you, Detectives?"

"We're investigating the murder of Pam Tappen. During the course of our investigation, we've come to learn that you once had a relationship with her."

Judging by his shocked expression, he hadn't expected that. "Pam is *dead*?"

"Yes," Sam said. "She was found yesterday bound and gagged and left to freeze to death in her minivan, which was located miles from her home."

"Oh my God," he said, sitting. "That's horrible."

"Yes, it is."

"What does it have to do with me? I haven't seen her in years."

"How many years?"

He thought about that for a minute. "Three. I spent some time with her shortly after I lost my wife to breast cancer. We were introduced by a mutual friend at a dinner party and had a lovely conversation over dinner. She reached out to me the following week, asked if I wanted to meet for coffee."

"And you knew she was married?"

"I did," he said, grimacing, "and it's so not my style to get involved with a married woman. But things were a bit of a mess in my life at that time. I'd been left to finish raising three teenagers on my own, and Pam... She was so warm and understanding, and I just... I needed that."

"How and why did it end?"

"It ended when I couldn't handle the guilt of being with a married woman. After a couple of months of seeing her, I started to snap out of the initial fog of grief and didn't like what I saw when I looked in the mirror. I worried about her husband and kids and about people finding out and thinking poorly of me—and having that reflect on my children. I couldn't do it anymore."

"How did Pam respond when you broke it off with her?"

"She was sad about it. We both were. We'd found something we both needed in the other, and it was hard to let it go, but it was the right thing to do." He took a deep breath before he added, "I'm not proud of being involved with a married woman, but I had genuine feelings for her, and she helped me through the most difficult time in my life. However, it ended a long time ago."

Sam appreciated his candor and forthcomingness. Those were two things that could be hard to come by in her line of work. "We're trying to understand why someone like Pam, who had a husband and three children she was obviously devoted to, would seek out men outside her marriage. And I ask that with zero judgment. It just seems out of character for the person we'd come to know before we received this information about her extracurricular activities."

Markham seemed to sag somewhat as he contemplated the proper response to her question. "It *was* out of character for her. She struggled horribly with it. She loves Bob and didn't want to divorce him or break up their family. But things between them had changed, and she was in a tough spot."

"I know you said you hadn't been in touch with her in years, but when you were, did she mention anything or anyone that was causing her particular stress?"

"Her son Lucas's football was always a source of strain. It was nonstop tournaments, weekends going here, there and everywhere. As much as she loved Lucas and wanted to support him, she hated those tournaments and the endless commitments. Her younger son was also a gifted athlete, so her years as a football mom were feeling overwhelming to her."

"This has been very helpful." Sam stood and placed her business card on his desk. "If you think of anything else that might be relevant, even the smallest thing, please give me a call."

"I will." He glanced at her. "Do you remember meeting me before?"

"I do."

Nodding, he said, "It's nice to see you again."

"You, too. Thank you again for your time."

"I wish there was more I could do. Pam was a lovely person. I'm very sad to hear that she's been killed."

"We'll see ourselves out," Sam said.

In the elevator, Freddie looked over at her. "How do you know him?"

"I went to him for fertility treatment years ago when I was married to Peter. His name rang a bell, but I didn't put it together until I saw him."

"Yikes, that must've been an unpleasant blast from the past for you."

"It was, but that was a long time ago now. It's not as raw as it used to be before Scotty, Eli and the twins came into my life." They walked to her car in frigid late-afternoon darkness. "Do you want me to take you to HQ or the Metro?"

"The Metro works. Are you sure you don't want me to go with you to Ninth?"

"I'm sure. It's no big deal. Just a quick errand."

"Okay, but I'm happy to go with you if you want me to."

Sam appreciated that he was offering, knowing how eager he always was to get home to his wife at the end of every long day. "I got it, but points to you for offering."

"I'll add them to my running tally of points earned on the job. I'm still waiting to hear how I can redeem them."

"We'll get back to you on that." She pulled up to the curb outside the Farragut North Metro station. "Thanks for everything today."

"You got it."

"Hey, Freddie?"

"Yeah?"

"I just want you to know how much I appreciate that we can still be us in the middle of the insanity swirling around me these days. It means so much to me to keep things normal with you."

"We'll always be us, regardless of how famous and important you become to everyone else."

"Thank you."

"If you need to talk after grief group, you know where to find me."

"You're the best."

"I know! I tell you that every day!"

"Get out."

"She gives and she takes away, all in the same minute." He got out of the car and gave her a jaunty wave before he took off in a jog toward the train that would take him home to Woodley Park.

Sam loved him unreasonably. It occurred to her once again that she probably ought to not partner with him, because she'd protect him over herself in any situation. But she simply couldn't imagine doing this horrible job without him riding shotgun and making her laugh all day. As she drove toward Capitol Hill, she told herself it was no big deal to be running home to Ninth Street for a few minutes. Because it wasn't a big deal.

But as she pulled onto the street and drove past where the Secret Service checkpoint had been before they moved to the White House, she was struck by how deserted and forlorn the street seemed without all the activity that had surrounded them when Nick was vice president. The neighbors were probably singing hallelujah that they'd moved out and taken their three-ring circus with them.

As Sam pulled up outside the double townhouse she and Nick had called home, the sight of the ramp leading to their front door that Nick had built for her dad tugged at her heart. Outside, as she stood on the sidewalk, she glanced toward the ramp outside her father's now-dark home and reflected on the massive changes that had occurred in her life since her father died in October. Everything was different now, and she couldn't help but yearn for what had been just a short time ago.

She went up the ramp to her front door and realized it'd been more than a year since she'd had to use her key to get in. On many a night, she'd returned home to chaos inside this house, kids chasing each other around, screaming with delight as Nick stood watch over them. Tonight, she was greeted by silence and an odd echo as she walked through the first floor on her way upstairs to the third-floor storage room where the Christmas decorations were stored.

Passing Scotty's abandoned room as well as the bedroom the twins had shared, she reflected on how a house was just a building without the people who made it a home. In just a few short weeks, this place no longer felt like home, because the people who made it one lived elsewhere now. She found the ornaments right where she'd thought they'd be and brought the box downstairs. In the kitchen, she eyed the table where they'd had so many meals and conversations and mornings with the kids.

Sam saw Shelby bustling around the kitchen with her son, Noah, strapped to her chest and yearned for the simplicity of only a few weeks ago. She poured a glass of ice water from the fridge and sat at the table, which already bore a faint layer of dust on its surface. She used her fingertip to draw a heart in the dust.

This was where she belonged, on Ninth Street in the heart of the Capitol Hill neighborhood where she'd grown up in a modest, middle-class family. As much as she respected the historical significance of the White House, living in the midst of opulence and being ma'am'd nonstop by butlers and other household staff would never feel normal to her.

She had no idea how long she sat in the kitchen, wallowing in the familiar before she had to return to the new normal. The ringer on the BlackBerry startled her out of her thoughts. "Hey."

"Hey, yourself," Nick said. "Where are you?"

"At Ninth Street, actually."

"What're you doing there?"

"I came to get some of our ornaments for the tree in the residence."

"Ah, I see. You sound a little weird. Are you okay?"

"It's strange to be here. It's like all the life has been sucked out of the place or something."

"Do I need to come get you?"

Knowing it would take a huge effort by the Secret Service to bring him the short distance across town, she said, "Nah, no need. I'm leaving in a few."

"I'd come get you if you needed me to."

"I know you would."

"Do I need to be worried that you might choose to stay there?"

"Not even kinda."

"Part of me wouldn't blame you if you did."

"I won't, Nick. I want to be wherever you and the kids are. This place is just a building without you guys here to make it a home."

"We need you here to make this place a home."

"I've got the grief group tonight. I'm going for the first part at least. I'll be home after."

"We'll be here."

"How was your day?"

"Not terrible, but not over yet. Gretchen Henderson is coming in shortly."

"Hmmm."

"I know, babe. I'm going to have a very frank conversation with her and make sure I'm comfortable."

"Good luck. I know it's a tough decision."

"Every minute around here is a tough decision. Do I send troops in to defend the Gulf of Suez from pirates, risking a confrontation with any number of countries that would love nothing more than to wipe us off the planet? Or do I hold off and hope the Egyptians and others can confront the pirates on their own?"

"Jeez, that makes my day seem simple by comparison. What're you going to do?"

"We're giving it another twenty-four hours before we decide anything. The thought of sending U.S. troops into harm's way gives me incredible anxiety, even if I'm well aware that it's part of the job."

"I'd be worried if that *didn't* give you anxiety. I have no doubt that whatever you decide to do will be the best possible decision you could make with the information you have available at the time."

"Thanks for the vote of confidence. This is the stuff that makes me wonder why anyone would want this job. On another note, the communications team would like for you to make a statement about the Des Moines shooting on the FLOTUS accounts. Lilia is going to reach out to you with some suggestions."

"Sure, I can do that."

"The thought is for you to address it from a mother's perspective."

"I can't even imagine what those families must be going through."

"The media is publishing stories about each of the victims, and it's just heartbreaking."

"As sad as I am to have lost my dad, I can't begin to conceive of it being one of the kids."

"Let's not go there. Our kids are very well protected, which is the one major benefit of this job."

"Well, the butlers don't suck."

"No," he said, laughing, "they certainly don't. I'm going to have to add a second daily workout to my schedule to keep from gaining twenty pounds a year while we live here."

"I need to add a first workout to my daily schedule."

"No, you don't. I love you just the way you are."

"You have to say that."

"That isn't true, and you know it. Now, go finish your stuff and get your sexy ass home to me ASAP. I have a surprise for you."

"What surprise?"

"You'll have to wait and see."

"Ugh, why did you have to tell me about it when I have to wait hours to see it?"

"Because I knew you'd flip out about it, and that makes me laugh."

"You'll pay for this later."

"I can't wait. Love you."

"For some strange reason, I love you, too."

Nick ended the call laughing, leaving her with a big goofy grin on her face. That was his superpower—making her laugh and smile when the rest of her life was often chaotic and full of the darkness that came with working the homicide beat. His love sustained her through good times and bad, and all it took was one ten-minute conversation with him to brighten her mood.

She stood to wash and dry the glass she'd used and put it back on the shelf with the rest of the dishes that would be waiting for them to return to their home when their time at the White House came to an end. Part of her couldn't wait for that day, but another part of her was determined to enjoy this adventure of a lifetime to the best of her ability while it lasted.

There was literally not another man alive for whom she would've taken on the role of first lady. For Nick, she'd proven once again that there was nothing she wouldn't do for him—and was certain that worked both ways.

Leaving the house, she felt energized to return to HQ for the grief group meeting and to leave as soon as she could make a clean escape so she could get home to her family. At her request, Dr. Trulo had scheduled this meeting for six rather than seven so she could get home that much earlier. Her plan was to attend the first part of the meeting and leave during the break. She felt strongly about being present for the group she'd founded, but didn't feel obligated to attend every second of every meeting.

She hoped the attendees would understand.

# CHAPTER SEVENTEEN

Her regular cell phone rang with a call from Lilia, her chief of staff at the White House. "Hi there," Sam said. "I heard you were going to call."

"Hope I'm not disturbing your work."

"Not at all. I'm driving, so your timing is perfect."

"Excellent. So we're thinking a post from the first lady expressing her condolences to the families in Des Moines might be in order."

"I'm in favor of that. What do you have in mind?"

"How does this sound? 'The president and I wish to express our heartfelt condolences to the families and loved ones of the people lost in Des Moines to this senseless tragedy. As a mother, my heart breaks for the loss of innocent children enjoying an annual tradition. As a law enforcement officer, I agonize over the toll gun violence is taking on our society and vow to work closely with the president to bring about sensible changes that will make all of us safer.' What do you think?"

"That's perfect. Couldn't have said it better myself."

"Great, we'll get it posted to your social channels and then monitor them for commentary."

"Thanks, Lilia. You always make me look good."

"That's my job."

"I left a message for Roni today and told her we'll hold the job for as long as she needs us to. I know that puts an extra burden on you—"

"I don't mind at all. You should have the person you want in that role, as she'll often be speaking for you."

"Thank you for understanding. We'll see you and Harry on Christmas Eve?"

"We wouldn't miss it for anything. Who gets the Lincoln Bedroom?"

"We have a plan for deciding, which will provide much laughter."

"I can't wait."

"See you then, if not before."

"Sounds good."

Sam so appreciated the wonderful, competent professional known as Lilia for running her offices as second and first lady with such wisdom and attention to detail. With a full-time job outside the White House, Sam didn't make it easy for her staff, but they managed each situation with aplomb that astounded her.

When she walked into the Homicide pit twenty minutes later, she was surprised to find Gonzo still there. "Hey, what're you doing here long after your tour ended?"

"I'm going to the meeting."

"Oh. Okay."

"Is it?"

"Of course it is. We'd love to have you there again."

"Thanks. I figured it couldn't hurt anything with the trial coming up."

Sam leaned against O'Brien's desk, facing Gonzo, who turned toward her. When he made sergeant, he'd chosen to remain in the pit rather than take one of the offices. "How're you holding up with the trial looming?"

"As well as can be expected, I guess. I've been meeting with Hope and Faith to make sure my testimony is rock solid." The Assistant U.S. Attorneys would prosecute Arnold's accused killer. Grimacing, Gonzo added, "Nothing like being the only witness to the murder of your partner."

"It's a very tough thing to have to do, Gonzo. I hope you'll reach out if there's anything we can do to support you."

"I will. Thanks. It's just something I have to power through to get justice for him."

"As long as it's not at your expense. You've been doing so great."

"I'm a lot stronger than I was a few months ago and determined not to let this be a setback."

"I can't tell you how glad I am to hear that."

"It's a daily effort not to let the darkness win, but I'm fighting that battle for myself as well as Christina and Alex and you guys. I've got too many people counting on me."

"I'm really proud of you. I try to put myself in your shoes, and I just can't do it, even for a second."

"I pray that none of you ever have to know what it's like. We're going to get justice for AJ, and we're going to do everything we can to keep his memory alive, starting with the road race in the spring to raise money for after-school programs."

"Let me know what I can do to help with that."

"I will." He glanced at his watch. "We'd better get upstairs before Dr. Trulo sends out an APB for you."

"I'm sure he regrets taking on this project with me. I can barely remember my own name these days, let alone when the grief group is meeting."

"You're holding up okay, though, right?"

Sam appreciated him asking. Over the last year, they'd learned the hard way to keep a closer eye on each other during difficult times. "I am, but thanks for checking."

"It's a lot on top of a lot after losing your dad. Don't let it overwhelm you the way I did."

"I'm working on trying to stay focused on the immediate moment and not let my mind get too far down the road. Kids, husband, work, friends, first lady duties, grief group... One thing at a time."

"I still can't believe you're the first lady and Nick is the president," Gonzo said with a chuckle.

"How the hell do you think we feel?"

"It's got to be insane."

"In every possible way. I'm thankful I get to still come here every day where things make sense to me—most of the time, anyway."

"Anything new with the Tappen case?"

"We've discovered she had long-term affairs with two men and one-night stands with two others after the spark went out of her marriage."

"Huh, that's interesting."

"From what I knew of her before I knew she had affairs, I would've bet my life that she was the type to suffer through marriage difficulties, but not to stray. My dad once said that no one knows what goes on inside a marriage except the two people who are in it, and that's the truth. Bob would tell you they were solid. Pam apparently didn't agree, but stayed in it for her kids and to keep the family together."

"Life is so fucking complicated."

"It really is."

"Do you like either of the long-term guys for her murder?"

"Nope."

"What about their spouses?"

"One of them was a widower when they got together. The more recent guy's wife was shocked speechless to hear he was having an affair with her."

"So you still don't have a person of interest?"

"Nope."

"Keep digging. You'll get there. In the meantime, Jeannie has been working on the Carisma Deasly case and finding that Stahl never did even the barest minimum when she was reported missing."

"What I want to know is where the commanders were when he was ignoring the report of a missing teenager." Sam realized that question might encompass her own father if the timing lined up, but it was still a question that would need an answer.

"I think it was at a time when they were severely shorthanded around here. Detectives were working alone, which made it easier to get away with shit."

"That would explain it, I guess. What time is it?"

Gonzo checked his watch. "Five to six."

"We'd better get upstairs before Dr. Trulo thinks I forgot, which I didn't."

"Did he have to remind you?"

"That's not the point."

Gonzo lost it laughing as he followed her up the stairs. "Crazy about Ramsey, huh?"

"Yeah, I can't believe I no longer have to worry about running into him up here."

"I know, but you need to worry about running into him elsewhere."

She flashed him a cheeky grin. "That's where Secret Service protection comes in handy." They stepped into a room packed with people. "Holy crap, Batman."

"No kidding. Looks like your group's a hit, Lieutenant."

Sam saw a swarm of faces she recognized from past cases, people who'd come last time and some new ones, including Charles and Diana Weber, parents of Tara Weber, who'd been murdered recently.

"It's nice to see you again," Sam said as she accepted hugs from them.

"You as well, Lieutenant."

"How's the baby?" she asked of Tara's son, who was a newborn when she was killed.

"He's doing wonderfully," Diana said. "My sister insisted on watching him so we could come tonight. She thought it would be helpful to us."

"I hope it is. There's a community here of people who've been through the same thing you have, and it helps to be with people who understand."

"We appreciate everything you did to get justice for Tara," Charles said. "We still can't believe her friends were involved. It'll take the rest of our lives to understand how two people she loved so much could've betrayed her the way they did."

"I'm so sorry again for your loss."

"Thank you," Diana said, softly. "We'll get through this. Somehow."

"Your grandson will be a great source of joy to you."

"Oh, he already is."

Sam caught the eye of her and Nick's close friend Derek Kavanaugh. "Excuse me while I say hello to some other friends."

"Of course," Diana said. "Thank you again for making this resource available to us."

"Thank you for coming." Sam went to hug Derek. He had dirty blond hair, brown eyes and a wiry but muscular build. "Good to see you here."

"I would've told you I didn't need it, but the holidays bring it all back." He shrugged. "The last couple of weeks have been rough."

Sam hugged him again. "I wish there was more we could do for you."

"Everyone does all they can, and I wouldn't have survived losing Vic without you guys and the rest of my friends."

"We'll always be here for you and Maeve."

"That helps. We're looking forward to Christmas Eve at the White House. Maeve wants to know if Santa will find her there."

"He absolutely will. Tell her we sent him a very long letter with a list of all the good boys and girls who'll be in the residence on Christmas morning so he knows where to find them."

"I will," he said, chuckling. "She'll be happy to hear that."

"You've heard from Gideon, right?" Sam asked him.

"I have. He's the best."

"He really is." The chief usher at the White House was working with each of the parents who'd been invited to ensure that Santa's visit was covered for each child.

"We really appreciate you inviting my parents, too. They would've been disappointed to miss seeing Maeve open her presents on Christmas morning."

"Of course they're invited. We wouldn't have wanted them to miss that."

"If everyone could please take a seat," Dr. Trulo said from the front of the crowded room.

Sam noticed several Patrol officers carrying in additional chairs to accommodate the overflow crowd. "We're going to need a bigger boat," she said to Derek.

"Excellent *Jaws* reference," he said, grinning.

"I know my shark movies."

"Lieutenant?" Dr. Trulo said, gesturing for her to join him.

"Duty calls," she said.

"Knock 'em dead," Derek said. "Oh, wait. Bad pun in this crowd."

Sam laughed, squeezed his arm and headed for Dr. Trulo.

"Me or you?" the doctor asked.

"You. All you."

"Why did I know you'd say that?" To the group, Dr. Trulo said, "Thank you so much for joining us tonight for this second meeting of our new grief group for victims of violent crime. Lieutenant Holland and I are honored to have each of you here to share in this special community of people who understand the unique grief that comes with losing a loved one to violence. I'd like to begin with a moment of silence for the families suffering this week in Des Moines."

Sam bowed her head and contended with the lump that suddenly lodged in her throat. Anytime she thought about what had happened there, she felt unbearably sad. She hoped she'd be able to hold it together when they met with the families.

"Thank you for that," Dr. Trulo said. "I see some familiar faces from our last meeting and lots of new people. We're so glad to have you here. Who'd like to begin?"

Danita Jackson raised her hand. Her fifteen-year-old son, Jamal, had been gunned down on a city street during a series of random shootings that were later tied to a disgruntled city employee. "I just want to say thank you from the bottom of my heart for this amazing group. Since our first meeting, I've become close friends with so many people I met here, and it truly helps to share this terrible burden with people who understand what I'm going through. That's all I wanted to say. Just thank you."

"Thanks, Danita," Sam said. "We appreciate hearing that."

Gonzo raised his hand, and Dr. Trulo signaled for him to take the floor.

"I'm Detective Sergeant Tommy Gonzales. My friends call me Gonzo, and all of you should feel free to call me that. As I told you guys the last time, I lost my partner to murder almost a year ago, and I've had a really, *really* rough year since that night last January when he was killed right in front of me. I've struggled with so many things, but I'm finally getting back on track. I recently married my love, Christina, who's been such a rock through all this, and I'm back to work after a few months away to get my head together.

"My biggest challenge now is the trial for the man who killed my partner that starts next week. As the only eyewitness to the senseless killing of an amazing young man, I'm fully aware of what I need to do in order to get justice for my partner. But the thought of reopening that painful wound is a bit overwhelming, to say the least. Well, that's all I wanted to say, other than thanks again to Sam and Dr. Trulo for starting this group. It's going to help a lot of people."

Sam led a round of applause for her colleague and friend that left him flushed with embarrassment. "I know I speak for everyone in the department when I say how much we admire everything you've done and are doing to honor Detective Arnold's legacy."

"Thank you," Gonzo said softly.

"I want to ask my friend Derek Kavanaugh if he'd mind saying a few words as someone who's eighteen months out from the terrible loss of his wife. Sorry to put you on the spot, Derek," Sam said, smiling at him. "But I think your perspective might be helpful to those of us dealing with more recent losses."

"Sure," Derek said. "Although, sometimes it still feels like it happened a week ago, and other times, it feels like years. My wife, Victoria, was murdered in our home, and for a time, our one-year-old daughter was missing. You've all heard the story about how presidential candidate Arnie Patterson planted Victoria with one of President Nelson's aides in a years-long plot to gain intel on Patterson's biggest rival. When Victoria refused to cooperate, they eliminated her. That's the short part of the story. The longer part is about me coming to terms with some pretty screwed-up facts about our relationship that were later put to rest with a letter from Vic that let me know that the things that mattered between us were as real as it got.

"She protected me at the expense of her life. That's something I'll live with every day, but Maeve and I are doing better. The grief that was like cut glass at the beginning has dulled around the edges some as we get further out from that awful time. I hate that Maeve won't remember Victoria. She was a wonderful mother, and I try to keep her present in our lives as much as I can. I guess I would tell those of you who are just starting this journey to allow yourself to feel all the things so you can move through it, rather than trying to avoid it. Not that avoiding it is really an option. I'm happy to talk to anyone who needs a friend in this process, if you think it would help to talk to someone who's been at it awhile."

"Thank you so much, Derek," Sam said. "Nick and I have so admired your devotion to Maeve over this last year and a half, and we're so proud of you."

"Thank you. That means a lot. My family and friends have been key to my survival of this unimaginable loss."

When they took a short break a while later, Sam noticed Derek talking to Trey Marchand, who'd lost his six-year-old daughter, Vanessa, in a drive-by shooting.

"You really struck a chord with this idea, Lieutenant," Dr. Trulo said, sounding like a proud father. Naturally, that thought gave Sam a pang of longing for her own father.

"It's nice to see some good coming from the madness," she said, glancing at him. "If it's okay with you, I'm going to duck out now so I can get home to see the kids before bedtime."

"Of course. I'll check in with you tomorrow to update you on the rest of the meeting."

"Thanks for doing all the work here," she added. "I think it's making a difference."

"It is for sure. Before you go... The first holidays after a major loss can be very difficult. You know where to find me if you need anything."

"I'll keep that in mind. You're the best." Once upon a time, Sam would've resisted any kind of shrinking, but that was before Dr. Trulo saved her sanity and her career after former lieutenant Stahl attacked her. Now she knew that everyone needed help at various times in their lives. The secret was being self-aware enough to know when to ask for it.

While the attendees were occupied with each other and the snacks Dr. Trulo must've arranged, Sam made her escape and was headed home ten minutes later, with Vernon and Jimmy following her in a black SUV. She was halfway to Ninth Street when she realized she was going the wrong way. After making a U-turn at the next intersection, she made her way to Pennsylvania Avenue while wondering when thinking of the White House as "home" would feel normal.

Almost three weeks later, she wasn't there yet.

EAGER TO GET upstairs to see the kids, Nick was stuck in the Oval Office waiting for Gretchen Henderson to arrive for their meeting. She'd been in New York City when she received Terry's call asking her to come in and had caught the first flight she could get back to DC. Thus, Nick was stuck waiting.

Not that he didn't have plenty to do. Information flowed toward him like rapids in a river, flooding every corner of his conscience with details that needed to be managed with differing levels of urgency—briefings, meetings, phone calls. It was nonstop for as much as twelve hours a day. In addition, the media was on him twenty-four seven, picking apart every word he said, everything he did and every action of his administration with a ruthlessness that defied description.

He was trying hard to love it, but by this time of the day, he was ready for some family time. He'd had a long conversation with his senior adviser and close friend Senator Graham O'Connor earlier. Talking to him always helped Nick find perspective on the most difficult issues. It was all Graham's "fault" that Nick was in this office in the first place. Nick smiled when he thought about how excited Graham was that he was president.

Graham's son Terry came in carrying the ever-present briefing book that Nick took "home" with him each evening to prepare for the next day. "I heard from a contact at State that the inspector general is opening an inquiry into what went down in Iran. Interestingly, the director of the Diplomatic Security Service is demanding a congressional hearing because his agents have a very different story than the one Ruskin is peddling. I also heard on the deep down low that Justice is taking a look at the situation, too."

"I'd be very happy to see Ruskin held accountable." Since Nick had fired former secretary of State Martin Ruskin after the bizarre incident in Iran, Ruskin had been ruthless in his public criticism of the country's youngest president, who lacked, as Ruskin put it, the "gravitas" to do the job he hadn't been "elected by anyone" to do. Not to mention, Ruskin was fond of saying, he didn't even want the job.

The guy was a windbag, but the cable news shows were eating up his criticism of the new president, who'd had just about enough of the guy.

Terry brought Gretchen into the office shortly after six thirty. "Mr. President, Gretchen Henderson to see you." Tall with dark hair done in spiral curls that framed a strikingly beautiful face, Gretchen came toward him with a smile and an extended hand.

Nick stood to greet her with a handshake. "Thank you, Terry. Good to see you again, Gretchen."

"You, too, Mr. President. Sorry to keep you waiting."

"No problem. I didn't give you much notice."

Per their earlier conversation, Terry left the room but kept the office door open to avoid any hint of impropriety. Nick hated having to think that way, but he didn't know her and still wasn't sure he trusted her. "Have a seat." Nick gestured to the sofa next to the chair he settled into. "Please help yourself to the refreshments."

She leaned forward to pour herself a cup of the coffee one of the butlers had brought in earlier. "Thank you."

"The cookies are to die for," Nick said. "I've had to limit myself to one a day."

"I remember how good they were the last time I was here." She smiled and chose one of the sugar cookies, placing it on a napkin. "I'm sure you could get away with two."

"I'm afraid to risk getting addicted. The White House staff takes very good care of us."

"It has to be such a huge adjustment for you and your family."

"That's for sure, but we're settling in and figuring out how to find our way around. This place is so much bigger than it appears from the outside."

"I liked what you said after the shooting," she said between bites of the sugar cookie. "It was the right tone and the right time to raise the topic—again—of some sort of reasonable gun control."

"That was unscripted and came directly from the father in me who can't imagine what those families must be feeling today."

"It's unfathomable."

"Indeed. I'm sure you're wondering why I asked you to come in again on short notice."

"The question did cross my mind," she said with a small smile that made her brown eyes sparkle.

"I'm still in need of a vice president, and I was hoping you might still be interested."

"I'd be honored, but I thought you'd settled on Senator Sanford."

"I'll admit she was my first choice, but she's more interested in the opening at State."

"Ah, I see, although I'm surprised she'd pass up the opportunity to be the first female vice president."

"I believe she feels she could be more effective as secretary of State, and that's probably true. Having served as vice president, I can attest to the lack of a clear role and how challenging that can be. However, as I mentioned in our first meeting, I'd like my vice president to be a true partner in governing. After just a few weeks in office, it's clear to me that I need serious help to manage everything that comes my way on any given day. I'm not looking for a vice president to relegate to the cheap seats. I want someone willing to get their hands dirty with real work."

"That appeals to me very much, Mr. President. I've become accustomed to keeping a frantically busy schedule between my work and my children. I'm afraid I'd be terribly bored without a real role to play in your administration."

"That's good to know. Again, I have to ask if you and your children are prepared to move to the VP residence on the grounds of the Naval Observatory and to accommodate the intrusiveness of Secret Service protection."

"After you had me in the first time, I had a long talk with my kids about what would change if I were chosen for this position. While they had some concerns about privacy and safety, they agreed it would be worth the sacrifice for me to have this historic opportunity."

"In that case, I'm pleased to formally offer you the position, pending the approval of Congress, of course."

"I accept with profound gratitude for your faith in me. I promise you'll never regret asking me."

Nick stood to indicate the meeting was over. "I appreciate you coming in and look forward to working with you." After they shook hands again, he added, "Terry will be in touch in the morning about making it official later in the day tomorrow with a press event in the East Room to announce you as our nominee. You're welcome to bring anyone you wish to invite. Terry can help with that. We'll put your nomination before Congress after the holiday recess."

"My parents will be thrilled beyond measure."

He walked her to the door. "I look forward to meeting them and your children."

"I'll see you tomorrow."

"See you then."

As he watched her leave, he hoped he'd made a good decision. It'd been important to him to elevate a woman into the vice presidency for the first time and to open the door in the near future to the possibility of a female president.

He was back at the Resolute desk, gathering what he needed to take upstairs with him to review after dinner with the family, when his BlackBerry buzzed with a text from Andy. *Good news. We got a judge to issue a gag order on all parties involved in the custody case, and it was extended to include all members of Cleo's immediate family. Tell Eli his secrets are safe. I've also requested an emergency hearing to dispose of this matter before the holidays. Waiting to hear. Fingers crossed.*

*Thank you SO MUCH, Andy. Eli will be so relieved, and we are, too. Keep us posted.*

*You got it.*

Nick forwarded Andy's text to Sam and Eli. *Good news!*

*Thank God,* Eli responded.

*What he said,* Sam added.

Terry appeared at the door to the Oval Office. "We've got a report of shots fired in the Gulf of Suez, Mr. President. You're needed in the Situation Room."

Nick sighed as he realized he might not get to see the kids before bed. So much for the advantages of working from home, but he felt a whole lot lighter after getting Andy's text.

# CHAPTER EIGHTEEN

Cameron debated whether he should go back to Gigi's again that night or take a night off so he wouldn't appear to come on too strong. He debated the pros and cons while enjoying a hot shower after work. All he'd thought about all day was what a relief it had been to tell her how he felt about her and to finally get the chance to kiss her.

Who was he kidding? He was going back there again tonight and probably every night from now on—if she'd have him.

After his shower, he dressed in a dark blue Henley and faded jeans and put a leash on his pug, Jeffrey, before heading out to pick up dinner at an Italian place she'd raved about when he brought her food from there last week. He'd decided it was time to introduce Gigi to Jeffrey because if the two of them didn't get along, there'd be no hope for them as a couple. As he approached his car in the lot, something looked weird, which had him immediately reaching for the weapon he never left home without. When he got closer, he saw that all four of the tires on his Dodge Charger were flat.

"Motherfucker," he muttered, holstering the weapon on his hip and reaching for his cell to call in the report to Dispatch. "This is Detective Green, badge number 9822. My personal vehicle has been vandalized." He gave his Adams Morgan address and was told Patrol officers were on their way. While he waited, he sent a text to Sam to let her know what'd happened.

She called him. "What the hell?"

"No idea," Cameron said. "I stopped at home after work to shower and was here for about thirty minutes. When I came out, every tire was flat."

"What do you have for security cameras in the area?"

"I'll run over to the management office to check."

"Okay, let me know, and get Archie's team looking at our cameras in the area, too."

"Will do."

"Was it only your car?"

"I took a quick look and didn't see any others."

"So this is something personal. Any idea who might have a beef?"

The realization hit him like a fist to the gut. She wouldn't. Would she? "Jaycee."

"Your girlfriend?"

"Ex-girlfriend. I took your advice and made some changes to my life, beginning with ending my relationship with her. She didn't take it well."

"How do you mean?"

"She was pissed. Said I led her to believe we'd be getting married when that's absolutely not true. I never talked to her about marriage. I swear to God, Sam. That never happened."

"I believe you, but I think you need to entertain the possibility that she's acting out."

"I just can't believe she'd do something like this."

"I never imagined my ex-husband would try to kill me. Watch your back, Cameron. If she's capable of vandalizing your car, who knows what else she might do?"

"Gigi."

"What?"

"I've been spending time with her..." His heart beat so fast, he feared he might hyperventilate. "If she's been following me..."

"Hang on. I'm sending Patrol to her place."

Cameron could hear Sam on the radio ordering Patrol officers to respond to Gigi's apartment immediately. The urgency he heard in her voice spiked his anxiety as he fired off a text to Gigi. *Someone flattened all my tires. Thinking it could be my ex. Sam is sending Patrol to your place just in case. If anyone comes to the door besides me, don't let them in. Please respond to let me know you got this. And sorry about this...*

She wrote back right away, thank goodness. *OMG, Cam... I'm fine. I won't let anyone in.*

*I'll be there as soon as I can.*

This was the last freaking thing she needed after having been recently assaulted by her ex. The next hour was spent dealing with Patrol officers, filing a report and answering questions. "I think I might know who did it, but until we have proof, I don't want to throw her name into this," he told the shift supervisor, who asked him the same questions the Patrol officer had asked. "The building is pulling security footage for me, and as soon as I can take a look, I'll let you know if I see anyone I recognize."

"Let us know what you find out."

"I will." He was dying to get to Gigi's, but he waited twenty more minutes for the security people to review the video.

"I think we have something, Detective Green," the security director said, inviting Cameron into the office to take a look.

As the other man played the video, Cameron watched without blinking, holding his breath until he saw a white Nissan Altima stop next to his car. When the driver got out, he gasped, recognizing the woman he'd been dating for the last year by her height and body shape. And then she looked up at his townhouse, showing her face to the camera before systematically puncturing all four of his tires.

"You know her?" the security guy asked.

"Yeah. She's my ex."

"Ended badly, huh?"

"No, it just ended, and thank God it did if this is who she really is. Can you put that on a thumb drive for me?"

"You got it."

With the drive in hand, Cam went outside and put through another call to Sam. "Sorry to bother you again, Lieutenant, but I've got video proof it was Jaycee."

"What do you want to do?"

He thought about that for a minute, debating whether he wanted to press charges. Glancing toward the parking lot, he saw that the Patrol commander was still on-site. "I think I want to press charges."

"I think you should, or she's apt to keep this up."

"That's my fear."

"Do you want me to take care of it?"

"That's okay. The Patrol commander is still here. I just wanted you to know what was going on."

"I appreciate the info. Are you okay?"

"I'm confused, honestly. If you'd asked me to bet my life, I would've said she wasn't capable of something like this."

"It's better to find out this way than after you say, 'I do.'"

"No kidding."

"You're a nice guy, Cam, so it goes against everything you believe in to send the police for her, but she committed a crime and needs to be held accountable."

"I agree."

"Go tell the Patrol commander to pick her up, and call me if you need anything."

"I will. Thanks for the support, LT."

"Anytime."

As Cameron walked back to where the Patrol commander was waiting, he hated having to do this.

"Any luck with the video?"

"Yep. It was my ex, Jaycee Patrick."

"Are we picking her up?"

Cam appreciated the professional consideration offered to him by his colleague. If Cam didn't want to pursue it, that would be that. But the lieutenant was right. If he let her get away with this, what would be next? "Yes, please." He recited her address in the Kingman Park neighborhood, feeling like shit as he did it.

"We'll take care of it."

"Will you let me know when you've got her?" Cameron asked, handing him a card that had his cell number on it.

"Will do."

"Thank you, Sergeant."

Cameron used an app on his phone to summon an Uber to take him and Jeffrey to Gigi's. Tomorrow, he'd figure out what to do about getting new tires. What a pain in the ass at an already busy time of year. Now that the shock was beginning to recede, he was seriously pissed. How could he have dated a woman—slept with a woman—who'd do such a thing? How did he not see that she had that level of vindictiveness in her?

As the Uber transported him to Gigi's, it occurred to him that he ought to stay away from her until Jaycee was in custody. The thought of endangering Gigi in any way, especially after what she'd been through with her own ex, made him sick. But he couldn't bring himself to stay away from her. He wouldn't leave until he got word that Jaycee was in custody.

When he arrived at her building, Cameron stopped to speak to the officers in the Patrol car in the parking lot, showing his badge. "I'm Detective Green, and I asked for assistance here."

"Everything's quiet," one of the officers said.

"Thanks for coming. I'll take it from here."

"Sounds good."

Cameron knocked on Gigi's door a few minutes later. "It's me." A series of locks disengaged before the door opened. He was so damn happy to see her.

She grabbed his hand and pulled him inside before closing and locking the door again.

Jeffrey had trotted in with him and was taking a good look around at the new place.

"Are you all right?" she asked, surprising Cam with a tight hug.

He put his arms around her and released the tension that'd gripped him since he first noticed his tires were flat. "I'm fine. Just pissed. The security film showed it was my ex who did it."

"Wow. I'm sorry, Cam."

"I should be apologizing to you. After everything that's happened, the last thing you need is to be afraid that my crazy ex is coming after you."

She gave him a fierce look. "I'm not afraid."

Smiling, he leaned in for what he intended to be a quick kiss. But she had other ideas. When her arms linked around his neck and her lips parted, the touch of her tongue on his lower lip ignited a fire in him. *Go easy with her*, he told himself. *She's still recovering.*

"Gigi," he said, sounding as breathless as he felt. "Wait."

"I don't want to wait. I want to kiss you. Right now."

What was he supposed to do when she said that but give her what she wanted? One kiss became two and then three, and before he knew it, he was stretched out on top of her on the sofa.

Annoyed at being ignored, Jeffrey let out a bark that made him laugh. "Gigi, this is my son, Jeffrey. Jeffrey, meet Gigi."

"Aww, he's the cutest boy ever."

Jeffrey sat next to the sofa, staring at them, panting dog breath all over them.

"Stand down, buddy. All is well."

The dog let out a deep sigh and curled up on the floor.

Cameron returned his focus to Gigi. "Um, we should, you know..."

"Keep kissing," she said. "We should definitely keep it up."

"Oh, it's up," he joked, pushing his arousal against her core.

"It feels so good to kiss you, Cam. I've wanted to for the longest time."

"Me, too." After a few minutes, Cameron broke the kiss, sat back and extended a hand to help her up.

Gigi made a cute little pout as she took hold of his hand. "More kissing, please."

He looked down at their linked fingers.

"What are you thinking about?"

"I hate that I'm sending cops to arrest her."

"I know, but you have to. She can't be allowed to get away with this."

"That's what Sam said, too. But still... I spent a year with her, and I knew she could be intense at times, but I never saw anything to indicate she was capable of vandalism."

"At least that's all she did. I had a few rough moments when I thought about how she could've been waiting for you out there with a gun."

"Yeah, I guess I'm lucky it was only my tires."

"You're very lucky."

"I don't understand why I'm not allowed to say this relationship isn't working for me anymore without having to worry about having her come for me or my stuff or other people I care about."

"People are crazy."

"You're not."

"I've got a tiny bit of crazy in me. I bet you do, too."

"Maybe a little, but I'd never flatten your tires or burst your spleen if you told me you didn't want to be with me anymore."

"Well, since I no longer have a spleen, that's good to know."

Smiling, he reached up to caress her face. "I'd never hurt any part of you, no matter what you said you wanted—or didn't want."

"Same. I don't have puncturing tires in me, in case you were wondering."

"I wasn't, but that's good to know."

"Can we get back to kissing now?"

Smiling wider now, he said, "If we must."

"We must. We absolutely must."

WHEN SAM GOT HOME to the residence, she had to go looking for the kids, who were in the third-floor conservatory playing a game of Jenga with Eli.

"You're still here," Sam said to him as she hugged Aubrey and Alden and messed with Scotty's hair. "I thought you had to go back to Princeton."

"Tomorrow. The one class I had today was canceled, so I decided to stay. Celia got invited out to dinner with her sisters, so I told her I'd hold down the fort here."

"We're glad to have you, and I bet these guys are, too."

"I'm so happy Lijah is here," Aubrey said. "He gets to come for a whole month next week."

"That's going to be so much fun," Sam said, smoothing her fingers over the little girl's damp hair. "Thanks for overseeing baths."

"My pleasure," Eli said. "I wish I could do it more often."

"You'll have a whole month together very soon."

"I can't wait."

"No sign of Dad yet?"

"We heard he got called to the Situation Room around seven," Scotty said.

"Ugh," Sam said. "What now?" She'd already grown to hate the Situation Room and everything that went on there.

"Mom, wait until you see how high Eli can get the Jenga," Scotty said.

Sam hung with them for an hour, heard everything that'd happened that day, was impressed by Eli's Jenga skills and delighted by the squeals of laughter from the twins when the tower collapsed with a huge crash. She and Eli wrangled the Littles into bed around nine.

"Three more school nights, and then you're on vacation," she told them as she tucked them in after one quick story from their big brother.

"Will you be here in the morning, Lijah?" Alden asked.

"I certainly will. I'll see you before school, and then I'll be back this weekend." He gave them both noisy kisses that made them giggle before leaving them to sleep. "They're so damned cute."

"They certainly are."

He ran a hand over the back of his neck, his expression tense. "I hate having this custody thing hanging over us with Christmas coming."

"Hopefully, the judge will agree to hear the case this week. If there's any benefit to living here, it's that when the president asks for something, people tend to listen."

"I sure hope so. I've got some work to do for class tomorrow."

Sam gave him a quick hug. "I'll see you in the morning. Keep reminding yourself what Andy said about having the advantage in this situation because your dad and Cleo were very specific about what they wanted for the kids."

"I'll try. Thanks for everything, Sam."

"We love you guys. We'll do whatever we can for you."

"We love you, too. Your support means everything to me."

"Try to get some rest."

"You, too."

She left him at the door to his room and went to knock on Scotty's door.

"Enter."

Sam stepped into a room that looked remarkably similar to his room on Ninth Street. He had the Caps game on the TV as he did homework. "You put up your posters."

"Yeah, Eli helped me do it earlier."

"Looks like home."

"Starting to feel like it, too."

She went in to sit on the edge of his bed. "I'm glad to hear that. How'd school go today?"

"Another day in paradise."

"That's one of my lines, and it's trademarked."

He rolled his eyes. "Whatever you say." After a pause, he said, "Can I ask you something?"

"Anything."

"This custody thing with the twins…"

"I don't want you to worry about that."

"I'm worried. It's the weirdest thing. They've only been with us for a couple of months, and it's already like they've been here forever."

"I know. We feel the same way."

"We can't lose them," Scotty said, his chin quivering.

Sam moved closer to hug him. "We're not going to lose them. Andy says our case is really strong because their parents were very clear about who they wanted to be their guardian. Eli gets to decide where they live and make all the important decisions for them."

"But now that Dad is president, the judge might think they're in danger or something."

His concern made her sad and mad at the people causing it. "They have the best security in the world looking out for them."

"I love our family," Scotty said softly. "It's the family I've always wanted."

"Same, buddy. Dad and I will fight to keep everything just the way it is. I don't want you to worry."

"I can't help it. I love them—and Eli. For the first time in my life, I have siblings. I don't want to lose them."

"You won't."

He hadn't let her hug him that tightly since he became a teenager who disdained maternal affection. But he clung to her just as tightly.

"It's going to be okay," she said. "I promise." As she said those words, she prayed it was a promise she could keep.

"Will you tell me what's happening?"

"Of course. Try to think about the good things—Christmas is coming, we're all going to be on vacation for a week together at Camp David, which I hear is very fun, and no algebra for, like, two whole weeks."

"That's better than Christmas," he said with the dry humor that was more like his usual disposition.

"Tracy, Angela, Celia, Shelby and all the kids are coming, too. You'll have so much fun."

"I am looking forward to all that, but do I really have to wear a tux on Christmas Eve?"

She gave him a playful bop on the head. "Take that up with your dad. He's the one who thought it would be fun to make Christmas Eve formal."

"Ugh. He becomes president, and suddenly he gets all fancy."

Sam laughed. "I know, right?" In truth, she thought the formal party with their friends and family would be a lot of fun, but she couldn't tell Scotty that. She was especially excited about the designer gown her friend Marcus was creating for her to wear. "I want you to talk to us about how you're feeling about the custody situation."

"I will."

"But I also want you to not worry. Andy is all over it, and he's the best."

"I know."

"You want to know something else?"

"Sure."

"I loved you a whole lot before the twins came to live with us, but I love you a hundred million times more after seeing you as a big brother."

"I love being a big brother—and a little brother, too. It's the best."

"We won't let anything mess that up."

"Thanks for that and everything else, too."

"Love you to the moon and back."

Again, he rolled his eyes. "People say that to babies."

"I didn't get to say it to you when you were a baby, so you gotta let me make up for lost time."

"If you say so."

"I say so, and what I say goes."

"I'm glad I'm only your son and don't work for you. Poor Freddie."

"Haha, very funny. He knows how lucky he is to work with me."

"Sure he does."

She kissed his forehead and got up to leave. "Don't stay up too late."

"I'm staying up *all night* on vacation."

"I used to do the same thing when I was your age. Drove my dad crazy."

"I sure do miss him."

"Me, too. Can't you picture him rolling around the halls of the residence, being into everything?"

"He'd love it—and he'd be ordering all the food on the menu from the butlers."

"Especially the endless ice cream."

"That's my favorite, too."

"We're going to need to make frequent use of the gym with the way they feed us here."

"I'll go if you go."

"It's a date. Add it to our vacation to-do list. See you in the morning, buddy."

"Night, Mom."

*Mom.*

God, she never got tired of hearing him call her that.

# CHAPTER NINETEEN

After hearing Scotty's concerns about the custody case, she wanted to hunt down Cleo's family and let them know what their frivolous custody case was doing to innocent kids. She sent a text to Freddie. *Did you ever get a chance to run the financials for the Lawsons and Dennises?*

*Doing it now,* he replied a few minutes later when she was in the bathroom attached to their bedroom getting changed into leggings and a T-shirt.

*Let me know.*

*Who else would I tell?*

*Stop being fresh. In other news, Green's psycho ex slashed all four of his tires.*

Her phone rang with a call from him.

"Seriously?"

"Yep—and he identified her on the security film from his place."

"Jeez. That's screwed up."

"This is where I tell you something you can't tell anyone else."

"I'm here for that."

"He's seeing Gigi."

"*Our* Gigi? And how do you know that, and I didn't?"

"Yes, our Gigi, and people confide in me because I'm known as a tremendous source of wisdom."

"I just threw up in my mouth. Gotta say I didn't see that pairing happening."

"He showed up at the hospital after she got hurt, and I knew right away something was up. In fact, I think I knew it before he did."

"What do you mean?"

"When I asked him about it, he seemed surprised that someone had noticed. He was deeply conflicted because he'd been with Jaycee for a year. It was almost like he needed someone to give him permission to have feelings for Gigi."

"Wow, and now Jaycee is coming for him. What about Gigi?"

"We sent Patrol to her place as soon as he realized it might've been Jaycee who did his tires."

"Imagine being that insane that you'd do something like that to someone you claim to love."

"I know. It's like trying to blow up your ex and the guy you kept her from for six years."

He huffed out a laugh. "Just like. Hey, so pay dirt on the Lawsons. They filed for bankruptcy last year, and the Dennises' business is in trouble. They had a customer sue them last year, and the case is looking to go against them, which will wipe them out."

"No way. So none of them are interested in the kids. They want their money. Those motherfuckers."

"What're you going to do with this info?"

"I'll pass it on to Andy and have him request they submit their financials to prove they have the means to care for the kids. Thanks for doing that for me."

"Happy to do anything I can to help."

"Even somewhat unethical things?"

"Even that."

"Have a good night."

"You, too."

Sam fired off a text to Andy. *Those MF'ing Lawsons filed for bankruptcy last year, and the Dennises are being sued by a customer, and it's not looking good for them, so they're on a fundraising mission with this custody suit.*

Andy responded right away. *How do you know?*

*I can't say... What can we do with it?*

*I'll request financials as part of the discovery.*

*I was hoping you'd say that. This is good info to have, right?*

*It doesn't hurt...*

*On top of them blackmailing Eli...*

*Yeah, they're really showing their asses.*

*Everyone is so upset. This is unbearable.*

*I've requested an emergency hearing to try to get this resolved before Christmas. I'm fairly confident that the judge will throw it out when he sees the airtight custody plan Cleo and Jamison drafted.*

*What if he doesn't?*

*Then we go to war.*

The thought of that made Sam's stomach ache fiercely. *Thank you for all you're doing.*

*I'd tell you not to worry, but I know that's pointless. I'll let you know about the emergency hearing.*

*Thanks, Andy.*

He responded with a thumbs-up emoji.

Sam slapped her phone closed with more than the usual velocity.

"Uh-oh," Nick said from the doorway. "What's wrong?"

The sound of his voice, the sight of his handsome, tired face... That was all it took to calm and settle her. How did he do that just by coming into the room? "Scotty and Eli are stressing big-time about the custody case."

His deep sigh said it all. "I hate that for them, for all of us."

"I do, too. Freddie and I did a little digging. Get this—the Lawsons filed for bankruptcy last year, and the parents' business is in trouble."

"You don't say, and now their fabulously wealthy niece and nephew are looking pretty good to them."

"Something like that. Since we can't come right out and tell them we know this, Andy is going to request their financials as part of the discovery. He's also hoping the judge will throw out the case when he sees the plans Cleo and Jameson made for the kids, hopefully as soon as next week if he can get that emergency hearing."

Nick dropped his heavy bag of work inside the door, pulled off his tie, unbuttoned the top two buttons on his shirt and came over to kiss her. "That'd be good. It'd be nice to not have this hanging over us for Christmas."

Sam finished unbuttoning his shirt and ran her hands over his chest and abdomen, feeling his muscles ripple through his T-shirt as she breathed in the unmistakable scent of home. "I know. You're late tonight. Everything okay?"

"Nope."

"You want to talk about it?"

"Absolutely not. I'm starving. Did you eat yet?"

"No, I only got home an hour ago and was hoping I'd get to eat with you."

"You had grief group tonight. How'd that go?"

"Really well. Gonzo came and Derek, too."

"He told me he was going to try to make this one. He wanted to support what you're doing."

"It was great to have him there. People appreciated hearing from someone who's been at it awhile."

"I'm glad he was able to do that. Let's order some dinner, and then I want to show you my surprise."

"I can't wait to see whatever it is."

They called down to the butlers' office to inquire about dinner.

"The chef has prepared salmon and risotto with asparagus in anticipation of your call," LeRoy said. "We can bring it up whenever you're ready."

Sam's mouth watered as he listed the menu. "That sounds perfect."

"I'll be up shortly."

"Thank you so much."

"Pleasure, ma'am."

She put down the housephone and turned to look at Nick, who'd stripped down to boxers. "The next time I complain about being first lady, remind me of the salmon and risotto that was waiting for us when I made that call."

Smiling, he said, "I'll be sure to do that. The butlers are the best part of living here."

Sam went to him and ran her hands over her favorite muscles. "They're even better than the pool and the bowling alley."

He bent his head to kiss her neck. "A million times better."

Her hands slid down over his back to cup his tight ass.

"Don't start something we can't finish before dinner arrives."

She rubbed herself against his instant erection. "Will it keep until after dessert?"

With his arms tight around her, he said, "It'll keep forever if you're around."

"This and the time with the kids is the best part of my day."

"Same. I hate that I didn't get to see them before bed."

"Scotty is still awake if you want to see him. We had a good talk about what's happening with the custody case. I hate how it's stressing him out."

Nick pulled back from her and gave her another quick kiss. "I'll go see him before dinner comes." He went into the walk-in closet and came back wearing sweats and his favorite ratty Harvard T-shirt.

Even dressed down, he was the sexiest man she'd ever laid eyes on.

"Be right back."

"I'll be here."

"Counting on that."

When he returned to their suite fifteen minutes later, dinner had arrived, and Sam had lit the candles LeRoy had put on the table. She appreciated his attention to detail.

"This is nice," Nick said when he sat across from her.

Sam poured white wine for them. "How's our boy?"

"He's okay. He said it helped to talk to you about it and to know Andy is doing everything he can to make it go away."

"I hate that he's suffering over it. That Eli is, too."

"Yeah, and knowing it's probably all about money just enrages me."

"Same."

The dinner was as delicious as it had sounded, and the wine helped take the edge off the day.

"I'm ready for my surprise now."

"I can't believe you lasted this long without making me show you."

"Only because I was hungry. Now that I've eaten, I'm fresh out of patience."

"Go put on something sexy."

"What?" she said, gesturing to her T-shirt. "This isn't sexy enough?"

"Everything about you is sexy, but you're going to want to dress up for this."

"Challenge accepted." She got up from the table and went into the closet to change into a getup she'd bought for their upcoming vacation. These days, she had everything sent to her sister Tracy's house so some poor White House staffer wouldn't have to open the package full of lacy bits for the first lady.

As she battled her way into the complicated contraption, she giggled at the thought of that happening. What the hell had she been thinking ordering something with so many straps and snaps? By the time she had it on, she'd broken into a sweat. She put on the vanilla and lavender lotion Nick loved and donned the black silk robe he'd given her for her birthday in October.

When she stepped back into their bedroom, she found that the candles had been extinguished, and he was nowhere to be found. Her gaze was attracted to something on the floor.

A rose petal.

Oh, game on, she thought, smiling as she grabbed her phone, dropped it in the pocket of her robe and followed the trail he'd left her to the stairs to the third floor. She went past the conservatory to a closed door down the hall from Celia's apartment.

While everything around them was changing, some things remained exactly the same, Sam thought as she followed the rose petals to the door where the trail ended. Her heart raced with excitement and anticipation as she opened the door and was immediately hit with the coconut scent of the candles from their loft at home.

Smiling, she took in the sight of her gorgeous husband stretched out on the double lounge he'd bought to remind them of their honeymoon in Bora Bora. As she closed the door behind her, she said, "I'm looking for the president. The bat line is ringing downstairs."

"Liar." He grinned as he gestured to the phone on a table next to the lounge. "They can find me no matter where I am."

"Well, that's a drag."

"You have no idea." He held out his hand to her. "As much as everything has changed, some things never will."

Sam put her phone on the table before she took his hand. "Funny, I was just thinking the same thing as I followed the path you left for me."

"Having an in-house florist comes in handy at times like this."

"You must've made their day when you asked for rose petals."

He snuggled her into his warm embrace. "They were pleased to receive a direct request from the Oval."

Sam kissed his bare chest and up his neck on the way to his lips. "I love that you found a way to bring our loft here."

"We need this too badly not to find a place for it in our new life."

"Yes, we do."

"Every day here seems crazier than the last. Nonstop meetings, obligations, photos, interviews, decisions... Every decision is a big decision. The little ones don't make it to me. Only the big ones, and all of them have so many consequences." As he spoke, he ran his hand up and down her arm and over her back. "You know what gets me through all that?"

"What?" she asked, even though she knew because the answer was the same for her.

"You, this, us, our family. It's the payoff that makes everything else worth the struggle."

"Yes, it does. I can't wait to have a whole week with you and the kids and my sisters, nieces and nephews. And Shelby, Avery and Noah, too."

"You know I'll have to work part of the time, right?"

"I do, but you'll still have downtime."

"I'm looking forward to it, too. The last few months have been unreal. Between losing your dad, the twins and Eli coming into our lives and my job change—"

Sam sputtered with laughter. "Your job change. You say that like it was a minor promotion when it was *the* promotion."

"It's been a lot, especially since we had to leave our home just when the Littles were getting comfortable there. Despite all that, you and me, we're the glue that holds it all together, and as long as we still have this," he said, sliding a leg between hers, "then I can handle the rest of it."

"Same goes for me, babe," Sam said, moved by his sweet words. "If anyone knew how much I think about you when I'm not with you, they'd make fun of me mercilessly."

"I have the same problem. In fact, I heard that *Saturday Night Live* is ready to debut the actors who'll play us while I'm in office, and the first sketch is apparently going to focus on our obvious *affection* for each other."

"Oh jeez. I can only imagine what they'll do with that. When can we look forward to seeing it?"

"Not sure. It was supposed to air this week, but they're delaying it out of respect for the victims in Des Moines."

Sam released a deep sigh at the reminder of that tragedy.

"Enough of everything that isn't this." He kissed her as he tugged at the knot in her robe belt. Tucking a hand inside, he stopped short at the feel of skin and satin. "What've we got here?"

"This old thing? I bought it for vacation."

Nick pulled back. "I need a full demonstration, and then I need to know how you bought it and whether it's going to cause an international incident."

Laughing, Sam rose to her knees and shrugged off the robe, giving him a full view of the "thing" that barely hid anything. Black satin strips covered her nipples and crisscrossed over her abdomen, coming together with a single snap between her legs.

"Holy Moses," Nick said with a low whistle as he lifted himself to one elbow for a closer look. "That's the sexiest freaking thing I've ever seen, and I've seen a lot of sexy things since I found you the second time."

"Thought you might like it."

"I *love* it. Bring it over here so I can see it better."

Sam moved across the mattress on her knees until she was right next to him. "Is this close enough?"

He shook his head and reached for her, bringing her down on top of his aroused body. "Even this isn't close enough. I can never get you close enough."

"I can get closer," she said, reaching down to unsnap the garment, if you could call it that.

"I'm down for that."

"I'm down for it, too." She raised herself up and slid down on his cock, taking him to the hilt in one smooth move that had them both groaning.

"How close is this room to Celia's again?" Sam asked. "Wondering for next time."

"Three doors down."

"That ought to be far enough away to keep me from being inhibited."

He cupped her breasts and smoothed his thumbs over the satin that barely covered her nipples. "We don't want you inhibited. We want you *loud* and *un*inhibited."

"We aren't on top of Eli's room are we?"

"Nope. I made sure of that. We're safe."

"Safer than we were at home with the Secret Service at the bottom of the stairs."

"That's true." He placed his hands on her hips. "Now that you have me where you want me, what're you going to do with me?"

"Haven't decided yet," she said with the slightest of movements that drew a sharp gasp from him. "Maybe some of this." She picked up the pace and then slowed right down. "Or this." Rising, she nearly lifted herself off him before she came back down. "Any preferences?"

"I like it all. Lady's choice."

"Hmmm... Let me think..." She could tell she surprised him when she lifted up and off him, turning to give him her back. "Here's something new."

"We like new things."

She'd read about "reverse cowgirl," but she hadn't done it. As she took him in from the new angle, she wasn't sure she liked it until his cock touched something deep inside that nearly made her howl. She leaned forward, her hands on his thighs as she moved carefully until she found a rhythm.

And then his hands were on her ass, squeezing and shaping and making her crazy as she took them on a wild ride that had her thigh muscles screaming from the exertion. She'd feel that tomorrow.

"The view is extraordinary," he said, making her laugh and then groan when he pressed his thumb against her back door.

The pressure alone was enough to trip an orgasm that touched every part of her and had him surging into her with his own release.

"Come to me, my little cowgirl." He helped her up and off him and then situated her next to him to catch her breath. "That was awesome."

"Glad you liked it. I do my best work with you."

His rumble of laughter made her smile. "My wife is full of surprises." He traced a line over the strap that crossed on her back. "Now tell me how you bought this and whether my press secretary is going to get asked about it tomorrow."

"I had it sent to Tracy, and she brought it to me still in the package."

"Ah, good call. We don't need the rest of the world knowing our first lady is a sultry vixen."

"I've never been a sultry vixen with anyone but you."

"I hate that there was ever anyone other than me."

"I do, too. And I don't know the half of what came before me."

He pinched her rear. "None of them mattered, as you well know."

"Still, you know about Peter and Archie... I know very little about yours."

"Does it matter so much?"

"Not really, but it's this weird blank space for me. I'm not a fool. I know there were others before me."

"There were a few, but none who mattered to me the way you do."

Sam had no idea why she was picking at this when she had no reason to worry about who he might've cared about in the past. "It's fine. I just wonder sometimes, that's all."

"You don't need to wonder about anything or anyone." He turned on his side to face her and tucked a strand of hair behind her ear. "Sometimes I feel like the first part of my life officially ended and the rest of it began two years ago this week when I found John dead and you came strolling into his apartment to work the case. Everything before that is like a black-and-white blur. Everything after that is in vivid color."

"You ought to go into politics. You've got a way with words."

Smiling, he said, "Only when I'm talking about the love of my life, who brought the color and the fun and the love and the family I yearned for. She's the secret to everything."

"Who is she, and how do I have her killed?"

His laughter rocked his entire body. "You're the only one, and you know it. Now stop being silly and kiss me."

She was about to do just that when her phone rang, making her moan. "That'd better not be Dispatch."

Nick reached over her to grab the phone off the table and handed it to her. "I'm afraid it is."

# CHAPTER TWENTY

S am took the phone from him. "Mother-effer. I've already got one ridiculous case that refuses to be solved with vacation looming." She opened the phone to accept the call. "Holland."

"Lieutenant, we have a report of a homicide in Spring Valley." The dispatcher gave her an address that sent a tingle down her spine. It was a coincidence that she'd been there the day before. She hoped that was all it was... a big fat coincidence. "I'll be there shortly. Please contact Detective Carlucci and Sergeant Gonzales as well."

"Yes, ma'am."

Sam ended the call and then made another to the number she'd been given to request a Secret Service detail after hours. "I have to leave for work," she said to the agent on duty.

"We'll have a detail meet you outside momentarily, ma'am."

"Tell them they have ten minutes."

"Yes, ma'am."

"Thank you."

"You have no idea how much I appreciate you making that call, babe," Nick said after she'd closed the phone with a satisfying slap.

"I'm trying to make it part of my routine."

"Thank you."

She shrugged. "If it gives you peace of mind, it's a small price to pay. I have to admit I barely notice them during the day."

"I'm glad it's working out okay."

"So, um, the murder happened at the Thorn home."

Nick's eyes went wide. "As in the guy who released the images from the party?"

"One and the same."

"Oh shit."

"If it's him, it'll be a thing, since we just slapped a lawsuit on him."

"If it's a thing, we'll handle it. Keep me posted?"

"I will." Sam leaned in to kiss him. "Thank you for this."

"Thank you, my sexy cowgirl."

"Yeehaw!"

"And the outfit, too. Keep those coming."

Sam got up to put on her robe. "I'll see if I can top this one."

"Yes, please."

"Don't forget to clean up your rose petals, Mr. President, or you'll set off a scandal among the housekeeping staff."

"I'll take care of it. Be safe out there, Samantha. I love you madly."

She was about to leave the room, but returned to him for one more kiss. "Love you just as madly, and I'm always careful. I have so much to live for." After another kiss, she said, "Get some sleep."

"I'll try."

The last thing she wanted to do was leave him, but she tried to respond to every homicide, even if that meant leaving her husband to sleep alone while she hit the streets and went without sleep. The job stopped for nothing—even the president.


As Sam stood over the bludgeoned body of Bryson Thorn, she knew she had to take a step back from this one, which was why she'd requested Gonzo be called to the scene.

"What've we got?" he asked when he arrived ahead of Carlucci, who'd been asked to assist SVU with a sexual assault.

"Bryson Thorn, age forty-one. Found out here in the yard by his wife when she returned home from dinner with friends. That's her over there." Sam nodded to the hysterical woman being comforted by Patrol officers on the pool deck. "Full disclosure— Nick and I just sued him for violating the terms of the NDA he signed by releasing photos of Nick at the twins' birthday party."

"Oh shit."

"I'm going to need you to take the lead on this."

"Yeah, sure. I can do that. What do we know?"

"Nothing yet. His wife came home and couldn't find him, so she came outside to see if he was in the pool and saw him over here."

"A place like this must have cameras."

"That was going to be my next question."

"Before you go, will you hold the flashlight so I can take photos?"

"Sure."

After he was done taking photos of the body from every angle, Gonzo said, "I'll take it from here."

"Thanks," Sam said, frustrated to have to take a back seat on this one, but the last thing they needed was conflict-of-interest claims. She returned to her car and called Nick on the BlackBerry.

"Didn't I just see you?"

"You did, and you're going to be seeing me again very soon. Our vic is Bryson Thorn, so I've asked Gonzo to take the lead. I'm giving you a heads-up so you can prepare for when word gets out that the guy we're suing has been murdered."

"I'll let Christina know."

"Sorry to add to your already overflowing plate."

"Not your fault. You didn't kill him. Did you?"

"Stop! Don't say that on a line the NSA is probably tracking."

"They're not tracking it."

"I bet they are."

Laughing, he said, "See you when you get home. This night is looking up."

"Not for Thorn it isn't."

"I'm sorry that happened to him, but I'm not sorry we sued him."

"Same. See you in a few."

"I'll be here."

Sam ended the call and then used her flip phone to call Captain Malone.

"Hey." He sounded like he'd been sleeping. "What's up?"

"So remember how I told you Nick and I are suing the guy who violated the NDA and released the photos of him at the twins' party?"

"What about it?"

"He's been murdered by bludgeon."

"Oh shit."

"I've put Gonzo on lead."

"Good call."

"I wanted to let you know it's apt to be a bit of a thing that he turned up dead shortly after Nick and I sued him."

"You'll need to keep your distance from this one."

"That's why I put Gonzo in charge. I've got my hands full with Pam Tappen, which is going nowhere fast."

"Let's start from scratch on that one in the morning. On another note, this afternoon, the chief asked me to talk to you about reopening Stahl's cases."

"What about it?"

"He's not in favor."

Sam was shocked to hear that. "Why?"

"Because we've had all the bad publicity we can handle in the last couple of months. Letting it be known that we have a bunch of badly handled cold cases under review isn't the coverage we need."

Sam was truly stunned. "Jeannie is working on a missing-person case in which nothing was done to try to find a teenage girl. Are you saying we need to stop what we're doing there?"

"That's what I'm saying."

"You can't be serious."

"I am, and so is he. The last freaking thing we need is coverage of all the shit we've screwed up over the years."

"What about the missing child's family? What do we owe them?"

"We can't save them all, Sam."

"We can at least fucking *try!*"

"This is coming from the top. If you have a beef, you're going to have to take it up with him—and I'd recommend you tread lightly on this. He's very adamant that he doesn't want it. The FBI report is looming in January, and it's apt to be damning. We don't need to invite in more. Not now."

Sam's heart sank at the thought of having to abandon the review of the cold cases that'd been overlooked by Stahl.

"I know this isn't what you want to hear, but he's right, Sam. With the FBI report coming, Stahl being convicted, charges pending against Conklin and Hernandez, Ramsey being fired, and you solving the Worthington case in a single afternoon, the media has been merciless in its criticism of the department, the chief and everyone who works for him. Our deputy chief was arrested for withholding information on the shootings of two fellow officers. That's a stain that's going to stick to us for years. Morale is already low. We don't need to do anything to make it worse."

Sam sighed as she listened to him. Although she understood where he and the chief were coming from, she couldn't bear to know there were cases that hadn't gotten even the most rudimentary of effort from Stahl. She started the car and drove away from Thorn's house, leaving the details of that case to Gonzo to supervise.

"Tell me you get it," Malone said.

"I do, but I don't like it."

"We don't either. We hate that corners were cut and cases were given little or no effort. That's not who we are as cops or human beings, but unfortunately, not everyone we work with feels the way we do. Having you on the job while you're first lady gives us a chance to change the narrative around the department. Your appearance on the *Today* show was very well received, and the grief group is getting national attention. That's the publicity we need now, as well as the bump of sympathy we'll receive for the trial of Arnold's killer, not another cold case solved in two days because we finally decided to care about it."

"But solving cold cases is *good* PR for the department. It shows the community we never stop looking for answers."

"In this case, it shows the community that we had officers in command positions who didn't do the bare minimum for victims. That's the story we can't afford right now. We're not saying never on this. We're just saying not right now when Stahl has just been convicted of attempted murder and we've got Conklin and Hernandez facing charges in your dad's case. With Calvin Worthington, people are focusing on the outrage of it taking only an afternoon to solve a case that should've been solved fifteen years ago."

Sam had so much more she wanted to say, but she recognized a brick wall when she was banging her head against it. "I hear you. I hate it, but I get it. You can let the chief know that we'll stand down on the cold-case review."

"Thank you. He'll appreciate your understanding."

"I'd also like to go on record as objecting to us working the sympathy card during the trial."

"We're not going to work it, but we *will* benefit from it. It's just the nature of these things. You know that."

"Sometimes this world is just too fucked up for me to stand. *How* could Stahl have let a teenage girl go missing and done nothing to try to find her? How did he live with himself?"

"I don't know, and I'm glad I don't know what it's like to be that kind of person. He's going to have the rest of his life to sit in prison and think about all the many ways he could've been a better person."

"He won't think about that. He'll think about how I ruined his life just by being born."

"You're probably right about that. He lacks the ability to be introspective."

That made Sam laugh. "Indeed he does."

"One other piece of news, and then I'll let you go. Ramsey has been charged with vandalism and B&E."

Breaking and entering was a felony. "Wow. Forrester isn't fooling around."

"The chief asked the USA to throw the book at Ramsey. He wants to be sure something sticks so we aren't forced to take him back when he gets off on some random technicality."

"That'd be good."

"We all agree that you need to be careful, Sam. He, too, is going to blame you for everything that's gone wrong in his life."

"I know," Sam said with a sigh. "It sure gets tiring taking the blame for men who can't keep their own shit together."

"I'm sure it does, but the threat is real nonetheless. On another note, how does Gonzales seem to be doing ahead of the trial?"

"As well as can be expected. He says he's ready and looking forward to getting it over with. Justice for Arnold is his only concern. He assures me his recovery is solid, and he's not going to allow a backwards spiral. I'm keeping an eye on him, and having him in charge of the Thorn investigation will be good for him."

"Agreed. Please let me know if you feel he needs anything at all. If we've learned anything in the last year, it's that we need to do more to support our people when they suffer trauma on the job."

"Yes, we do." She hated how much Gonzo had suffered after his partner's senseless murder and how he'd kept the worst of it hidden from the people closest to him. "I'm going to head home and get some sleep while I can. I'll see you in the morning."

"See you then."

Twenty minutes later, she crawled into bed with Nick, who put an arm around her and drew her in close to him. She released a deep breath and tried to calm her racing mind so she could get some rest, but all she could think about was Bryson Thorn's murder and what kind of shit storm might erupt in their lives as a result.

GONZO'S first order of business was to speak with Thorn's distraught wife. "Did you get her name?" he asked the Patrol officer who'd been first on the scene.

"It's Tiffany. She said she came home from dinner with friends to find Bryson dead in the yard."

"Did you ask about security cameras?"

"She said the security system was off because Bryson was home."

"Of course it was. Please do a canvass of the property. See if you can find me a murder weapon."

"Yes, sir."

Gonzo walked over to speak to the woman who was being comforted by a female Patrol officer. Thorn's wife reminded Gonzo of a Barbie doll, right down to the blonde hair that fell in perfect waves around her shoulders. "Mrs. Thorn, I'm Detective Sergeant Gonzales with the Metro PD. I'm very sorry for your loss."

"Wh-who could've done this to him?" she asked between sobs, looking up at him with red, swollen eyes. "Everyone loved Bryson."

*Not everyone*, Gonzo thought. "When was the last time you spoke to him?"

"Before I left for dinner with my girlfriends. He said he was going to make dinner for our son, and they were planning to watch a movie before bed."

"And your son? Where is he?"

"Asleep in his bed."

"What time does he usually go to bed?"

"Around eight thirty on school nights."

"And you got home at what time?"

"At ten twenty. I noticed the time on my dash when I pulled into the driveway."

That information gave Gonzo a timeline to work with. Thorn had been killed sometime between eight thirty and ten twenty. "Can you think of anyone who was at odds with him?"

"Other than your boss and her husband?" Tiffany asked with a hard edge to her voice. "They were suing him for a million dollars for violating the NDA at the party."

Gonzo didn't blame Sam and Nick one bit for enforcing the NDA and for trying to make it hurt after the trouble Thorn's photos had caused for Nick in the first days of his presidency. "Anyone else?"

"You're going to investigate them, right?"

"No, I'm not."

She didn't care for that response. "Powerful people always get a pass with things like this."

"My boss and her husband are under twenty-four-hour-a-day protection from the Secret Service, which would make committing murder rather difficult."

"That doesn't mean they couldn't hire it done," she said forcefully, as if she honestly believed Sam and Nick would hire someone to kill her husband.

"I believe the lawsuit spoke for itself. They were far more interested in causing him financial pain than physical pain."

"Believe what you want. You'll never convince me they didn't have something to do with this, and I'll bet the media will be interested in that angle, too."

"Is that your plan? To take your case to the media with zero proof of their involvement in the hope that the president and first lady will be convicted in the court of public opinion?"

She squirmed a bit under his intense stare. "How could it not be related to the lawsuit?"

"I can think of a million ways this could be unrelated to the lawsuit. We'll do a full investigation, and at the conclusion of that, we'll hopefully find the person who did this to your husband. In the meantime, I'd suggest you refrain from spouting bullshit to the press that might affect our ability to get justice for your husband. That's what you want, right? Justice for him?"

"Of course that's what I want," she snapped.

"Then let us do our jobs, and keep your baseless theories to yourself."

"Can you be objective when your prime suspects are your friends?"

"They're not the prime suspects."

"I guess that answers my question," she said bitterly.

"I'd suggest you refrain from venting about them unless you want another lawsuit to deal with."

"They might have me killed, too."

Gonzo realized he wasn't going to get any more useful info from her and decided to cut his losses. "Write down your full name and phone number in case I have follow-up questions. Also write down the names and numbers of the women you were with tonight."

She took the notebook from him, wrote the information for herself, used her phone to get the numbers for her friends and then thrust the notebook back at him.

"If you know anything about what happened to your husband, Mrs. Thorn, I suggest you tell me now."

"I told you! I was at dinner with my friends. I don't know anything." She began to cry again, her body shaking from the effort expended to project intense grief.

He no sooner had that thought than he realized she was faking it. How he knew that and why he knew it, he couldn't say. But he was one hundred percent sure she was putting on a show for him.

As he started to walk away, the medical examiner's van pulled into the driveway. Gonzo went over to speak with Dr. Byron Tomlinson, the deputy ME.

"What've we got?"

"One vic in the backyard, possibly bludgeoned."

"Lead the way."

Gonzo took him to the body, glancing again at his face and head, which had borne the brunt of the attack. The grass around him was soaked with blood.

"Yikes." Byron crouched for a closer look, using a flashlight to scan the body from top to bottom. "You took photos?"

"Yes," Gonzo said. "Do you agree that it seems as if the attack happened out here?"

"I think that's a safe assumption."

Byron signaled for his colleagues to bring the body bag and gurney for transport.

The Patrol officer Gonzo had asked to look for the murder weapon returned empty-handed. "There's a lot of landscaping on this property," he said. "I looked as best I could, but it was hard to see even with the flashlight."

"I'll have Crime Scene take a closer look in the daylight. In the meantime, I want Patrol officers here to preserve the crime scene and provide security. I'm going to ask Mrs. Thorn to relocate with her son."

"Yes, sir."

Gonzo returned to Tiffany, whose tears had miraculously dried up. "I'm going to need you and your son to move to a hotel tonight."

"*Why?*" The single word was full of privilege and outrage that someone like him would tell someone like her what to do.

This woman was pissing him off. "Because someone killed your husband, and if they come back for you and your son, I'd assume you'd rather not be here."

They engaged in a visual standoff that he won when she blinked.

"Fine."

"Patrolman Watts will help you get settled in a hotel."

"That won't be necessary. I can go to my sister's. She lives locally."

"He'll accompany you to make sure you arrive safely."

"I'll need a minute to pack for myself and my son and to get him up."

"We'll wait."

As she stormed off, Patrolman Watts said, "She's a pleasant sort."

"I'll be taking a hard look at her." Gonzo wished he had more to go on than a hunch that she was involved so he could transport her to HQ. Since she had an alibi, he needed evidence he didn't have yet before he could do that. He'd confirm her alibi the first chance he got. "Are you okay to wait for her and make sure she gets to her sister's?"

"Yes, sir."

"Let me know if you see or hear anything I should know about."

"Will do."

As he walked toward his car, he put through a call to Sam.

"Mmm, what?"

"Sorry to wake you, but Tiffany Thorn is making noise about accusing you and Nick of arranging her husband's murder. I think I talked her out of going to the press with that, but I'm not entirely sure, so I figured I'd give you a heads-up."

"'Kay."

"Sam? Did you hear me?"

"Yeah."

"What did I say?"

"Thorn's wife thinks we did it and is going to the press."

"Yes. You should probably tell Nick's people to be on alert."

"I will. In the morning. Thanks for calling."

The line went dead.

"Welp, I did what I could," he said as he started his car and headed for HQ to do some digging on Mrs. Tiffany Thorn—and her husband.

# CHAPTER TWENTY-ONE

C ameron hadn't intended to sleep at Gigi's place, but somehow, he'd ended up wrapped around her with a blanket over them as they slept together on her sofa. The feel of her pressed against him caused a predictable reaction that he hoped she wouldn't notice. She was still recovering from her injuries and didn't need him and his hard cock disturbing her.

He needed to get moving so he could go home and change before he had to be at work.

She roused when he started to move.

"Sorry to disturb you, but I have to go to work."

She turned onto her back and smiled up at him. "We fell asleep."

All he wanted to do was spend the entire day kissing her. "I see that."

She reached up to run a finger over his jaw, her touch like a bolt of lightning through his entire body. "I wish you didn't have to go."

"So do I." As she bit her lip and gazed up at him, Cameron was tempted to call in sick for the first time in his professional career. But with the Tappen case at a standstill and Sam trying to get away for a couple of badly needed weeks off for the holidays, he couldn't do that. "I'll take a few days off after Christmas. We can go somewhere to rest and relax."

Her dark eyes glittered with excitement. "That'd be great."

"Where should we go?"

"Out to the mountains where we can snuggle in front of a fireplace while it snows outside."

"I'll see what I can do to make that happen."

"Is this real, Cam? Are we really together now?"

"It's as real as it gets, and we're absolutely together."

"I still can't believe that you wanted me this way and never said anything."

"We were both with other people. The time wasn't right."

"And it's right now?"

He smoothed the dark hair back from her face. "Nothing has ever felt more right to me than being with you, but I don't want to rush you into something you might not be ready for."

She thought about that for a second before she replied. "I've been with Ezra my entire adult life, and all that time, I was trying to make it work with him because I thought I had to do that. I thought that constant struggle to make our relationship work the way it was supposed to was normal, but I know now that nothing about it was normal. It was over between us long before the night he hurt me. I think everyone in my life knew that but me—and him. My mom and sister are so glad it's over between us—and they were before he took my mom and nephews hostage."

"I'm so sorry you went through all that, sweetheart."

"I'm not."

He tipped his head. "No?"

"Nope. If I hadn't gone through what I did with him, I might not realize that this, with you, is something very special."

Even though he didn't have time, Cameron put his arms around her and held her close. "It's very special, which is why I want to be careful with you. Things are crazy for you, and the last thing I want to do is make anything worse."

She pulled back so she could look into his eyes. "Don't you see, Cameron? You're what's making everything better."

He needed to leave her, but how could he do anything other than kiss her after she said that to him? For the longest time, he'd suspected it could be this way between them, but with Gigi in a long-term relationship, he'd allowed himself to get involved with Jaycee.

He could see now that'd been a huge mistake—for more reasons than just the fact that she was obviously unstable if she'd do what she did the night before. But it had also been unfair to both of them when his heart was yearning for someone else.

Gigi broke the kiss and smiled up at him. "You need to go to work."

Cameron glanced at the time on his watch and winced. "Would you mind if I borrowed your car and your shower? I don't have time to go home and change." He'd be going to work in jeans and a Henley for the first time ever, which would set tongues to wagging, but he couldn't be bothered to care what anyone else thought. Not when he was finally with the woman he'd wanted from the first time he ever laid eyes on her.

"Yes, you can borrow my car and my shower, and if you want to leave Jeffrey here, I'll ask my sister to bring me some food for him."

"Jeez, you've got me forgetting all about my poor son."

"I'll take good care of him today." She ran a hand over his chest. "Mr. Pressed and Polished is going to start a scandal showing up in the pit wearing a Henley and jeans."

"It'll be worth it for fifteen more minutes with you."


WHEN SAM WOKE UP, she thought for a second that she'd dreamed the call from Gonzo. But when she checked her phone and found that he'd called at eleven forty-five, she knew she hadn't dreamed it. Nick was already up and gone, so she called him on the BlackBerry.

The call rang multiple times. He was probably in the morning security briefing, his most dreaded meeting of the day, the one he called "the little shop of horrors."

When his voice mail answered, she got to hear the message he'd recorded for her for the first time.

"Hi, babe. I can't take your call right now, but there's nothing I'd rather be doing than talking to you, so leave me a message, and I'll call you back as soon as I can."

*Swoon.*

"Hey, it's me. Love the voicemail message. So I told you Bryson Thorn was murdered last night. Gonzo called to tell me his wife, Tiffany, was accusing us of arranging it and asking how could it not be related to the lawsuit. Apparently, she's talking about taking her claims to the media. He said he tried to talk her out of it, but who knows what she'll do? Let me know that you got this message."

Sam ended the call and decided to text the same information to Christina, just in case Nick didn't get the message.

When she'd done what she could to tip them off, she got up, showered and got dressed for work before she went to rouse Scotty and the twins. With just a few more days of school until Christmas vacation, they moved slowly and were grumpier than usual as they ate the pancakes she made for them in the family kitchen.

During their upcoming vacation, she was determined to cook as many meals for their family as she could so her kids would know she was capable of making more than pancakes.

Elijah's presence helped to elevate the mood, but they were all sad to hug him goodbye for a few days as he headed back to school for final exams.

Scotty left with his detail, and the twins were fifteen minutes behind him with theirs. She left shortly after they did and arrived at HQ minutes before her tour was to begin at eight.

She was greeted by Captain Malone, who appeared in her office doorway five minutes after she arrived. "Morning."

"We have Green's ex in lockup making a huge stink about being unjustly accused."

"Did you tell her we have her on video damaging Green's vehicle?"

"She says it wasn't her."

Sighing, Sam gathered her hair into a ponytail that she twisted and secured with a clip. "I'll go have a talk with her, and then I'm getting everyone into the conference room to start at the top with the Tappen case."

"Thank you for dealing with Green's ex, and let me know when you're meeting. I'll join you."

"That'd be good. Any word from Gonzo about the Thorn case?"

"He's been here all night working the case. He can report on it at the meeting, and then we'll divide and conquer."

"I need some threads to pull on Tappen. I just keep coming back to the affair she was having with the father of one of her son's teammates. How can that not be related to her murder?"

"We'll talk it through and find you some threads."

Sam stood to follow him out of the office. When he took a left to go to his office, she took a right toward the stairs that led to the jail in the basement. She heard Jaycee before she saw her.

"I'll sue your asses off for unlawful incarceration," she shrieked at the top of her considerable lungs.

"One of yours, Lieutenant?" the sergeant at the desk asked her.

"The ex of one of mine."

"He dodged a bullet. She hasn't shut up since they brought her in last night."

"I'll see what I can do."

"We'd appreciate that."

Sam approached Jaycee's cell right as she started a fresh diatribe about cops using their authority to persecute innocent people. "Shut up," Sam said, amazed to think she'd found the woman in the cell attractive on previous meetings while she'd been dating Cameron.

Stunned by Sam's sudden appearance, Jaycee slammed her mouth shut, but it stayed that way for only a second. "How dare you tell me to shut up?" She was a curvy blonde with blue eyes, a looker who was no doubt accustomed to getting her own way in life and love. It would've been a shock to her system to be dumped by Cameron, Sam decided.

"How dare you vandalize Detective Green's property?"

"I didn't do that!"

"We have you on video, Jaycee, so you can quit all your bullshit about persecution and cops having an unfair advantage."

"The video isn't admissible. It's entrapment if I don't know there were cameras."

Sam rolled her eyes to high heaven. "Obviously, you've been watching too much *Law & Order*. The video footage *is* admissible, and it's *not* entrapment. You committed the crime, and you'll be charged accordingly."

"Cameron committed a crime when he made me believe we were going to get married and then dumped me for some brown-skinned bitch—"

Sam was glad there were bars keeping her from slapping her across her nasty face. "Are you seriously going there?"

"Does she or does she not have brown skin?"

"The Dark Ages called. They're looking for their hateful village idiot."

Her frosty blue eyes flashed with outrage. "He made promises to me."

"No, he didn't, and that's probably because he knew that under your shiny veneer is a hateful, vindictive, racist *bitch* who doesn't deserve him."

"How dare you? You don't know me at all."

"In these delightful five minutes with you, I know everything I'll ever need to know, and I'm deeply thankful that my friend and colleague has removed you from his life. Here's how this is going to go—when you're arraigned later this morning, you'll plead guilty to malicious mischief and take your punishment, including making restitution for the damage you did to Cameron's vehicle. After that, he'll be filing for a restraining order that will keep you more than a thousand feet from him and Detective Dominguez. You'll follow the letter of that restraining order, or we'll be happy to invite you back for another stay in our city jail. Is there any part of that you don't understand?"

Jaycee crossed her arms and stuck out her chin. "I want my lawyer."

"Sure, we can call one for you, but you should know that until he or she arrives, you'll be staying right here. We won't be able to arraign you until your lawyer gets here. That can sometimes take a day or two, and your lawyer is likely to give you the same advice I did when he or she sees the video footage of you committing a crime. It's up to you."

Her posture lost some of its rigidity when it sank in that her choices were somewhat limited.

"Am I calling a lawyer for you, or shall we move forward with the arraignment and get you released on personal recognizance with an order to stay far away from Detectives Green and Dominguez?"

She shifted her weight from one foot to the other.

Sam was a tiny bit ashamed at the pleasure she was taking in the other woman's discomfort.

"It's not fair."

Sighing, Sam said, "What isn't?"

"He led me on, made me believe we were going to be married."

"He never once mentioned the word 'marriage' with you."

"How do you know that?"

"He told me he never said anything of the sort because he never wanted it."

She recoiled from that information. "What else did he tell you about me?"

"That he felt bad that he didn't feel for you what you felt for him, but he couldn't force that to happen if it just wasn't there."

"It was there! He's a liar!"

"No, he isn't. He's one of the most honest, ethical people I've ever met in my life. I have no doubt at all that he was always honest and upfront with you. If you read more into it than what was there, that's on you, not him."

"I love him."

"So much that you flattened his tires?"

"I didn't want him going to her! How can he want her and not me?"

"Uh, is that a rhetorical question?"

"What does that mean?"

"Never mind. I've given you enough of my valuable time. Am I calling a lawyer or putting forth your arraignment?"

Jaycee released an indignant huff. "I'll take the arraignment."

"And you'll stay away from my detectives?"

She gave a tiny nod, but it was enough of an acknowledgment to satisfy Sam. "Let me be very clear—if we meet again, I won't be anywhere near as friendly as I've been today. If you get the big idea to bother, harass or threaten Detective Green or Detective Dominguez, I'll make your life a living hell. You got me?"

Tears filled her big blue eyes as she nodded.

"Excellent."

Sam turned to walk away and nearly collided with Cameron Green. She wasn't sure which was more shocking—that he was wearing jeans or that he hadn't shaved. Sam directed him back toward the stairs and followed him up. "Were you listening to that?"

"I was. Thank you, Lieutenant."

"No problem."

When they were upstairs, he turned to face her. "I'm very sorry to have brought this nonsense into your house."

"You didn't. She did. It's not your fault."

"What she said about Gigi..." His normally amiable expression hardened. "I had no idea she was like that."

"You're lucky to be rid of her."

"I feel sick after hearing the stuff she said."

"Try to put it behind you and focus on the future. You were upstanding in your dealings with her. You know the truth, and that's all that matters. What she read into it isn't your responsibility."

He released a deep breath. "Yeah, I know. It's just hard to fathom that I spent a year with her and had no idea who she really is until now."

"At least you found out before you shackled yourself to her for a lifetime."

Shuddering, he said, "No kidding."

"How's Gigi?"

His entire disposition changed at the mention of her. "She's great."

"I take it things are progressing there?"

"Yeah, you could say that."

"I'm happy for you both."

"It won't get in the way of the work, LT. I swear to you."

"You're both professionals. I'm not at all concerned about that."

"Okay, good."

"We're meeting in the conference room in ten to go over the Tappen case. Can you let everyone know?"

"I'll take care of it. And thank you again, Lieutenant, for your support and for handling the mess downstairs."

"I've got your back, Detective. Always."

"Likewise."

Satisfied that she'd handled things with Jaycee as well as she could, she returned to the pit to get to work.

# CHAPTER TWENTY-TWO

"It's now been more than twenty-four since Pam Tappen was found bound and gagged in her minivan, which was three full days after she left her M Street home to attend a conference in Baltimore." Sam gestured to the photos that were taken of Pam in the van that were now on the murder board. "Our review of her phone and computer show nothing out of the ordinary on the day she presumably went missing, which we're assuming was last Friday. Dr. McNamara has put her time of death around six p.m. on Sunday."

Sam paused to let that information sit with her detectives to imagine what two days bound and gagged in a freezing minivan would've been like for their victim.

"Pam's company provided conference support for a wide variety of clients. We've learned it wasn't uncommon for Pam to be out of touch with her husband and children when she was working at a show. We spoke to the company she was due to support in Baltimore and learned she was a no-show. Their efforts to reach her beginning on Friday were unsuccessful. The CEO of the company was furious with Pam until she learned she'd been murdered."

"What's your theory on how the murderer contacted or waylaid her?" Green asked.

"I think she might've been approached either outside of her home or somewhere along the road on the way out of her neighborhood."

"Archie has checked all our cameras in a one-mile radius surrounding her home, and nothing popped," Freddie said.

"We need to expand our radius beyond a mile." Sam felt a buzz for the first time since this baffling case began. "Imagine she's driving along her expected route on the way to the highway north to Baltimore. She sees someone she knows, who flags her down. Naturally, she pulls over. I think that's how it happened, except I can't figure out who among the people she knew wanted her dead. We've uncovered an affair she was having with the father of one of her sons' AAU football teammates. Both spouses were legitimately shocked to hear of the affair. Bob Tappen said that as far as he knew, Pam didn't even like Mark Ouellette. Bob was stunned to hear that not only was she having an affair, but that she was having it with him of all people. Josie Ouellette was equally shocked."

"What about the kids?" Gonzo asked. "What did they know, and when did they know it?"

"The Tappen kids were unaware," Freddie said. "We witnessed their reactions at hearing the news, and they were revolted."

"What about the Ouellette kids?" Malone asked.

"We haven't spoken with them yet," Sam said. "But you're right. Maybe one of them found out and decided to eliminate the threat to their family. I just have a hard time picturing a teenager doing what was done to Pam. There was an almost diabolical element to it. The killer not only wanted her to die. They wanted her to suffer first."

"It's a stretch to picture a kid doing that, but it's not impossible," Malone said. "I'd take a close look at all the kids. I remember being in high school, and one of my classmates found out her dad was having an affair with another kid's mother, and she was so angry. So, so angry that her dad would do that to *her*. She took it *very* personally."

"That's interesting," Sam said.

"I agree with the captain," Jeannie McBride said. "Kids are so caught up in what their friends think of them that something like this would be hugely embarrassing, especially if everyone at school found out about it. Or even one person found out about it and said something to one of them."

"I hear what you all are saying, but I keep coming back to the torturous way in which Pam died," Sam said.

"What if it was one of the kids, and he or she didn't intend for Pam to die?" Freddie said.

"What was their goal, then?" Sam asked.

"To make her suffer a little, but not to kill her."

"Hmm, I don't know. This felt almost professional to me."

"Have we examined that possibility?" Malone asked. "That it was a professional hit?"

"Again, it goes to motive," Sam said. "The only people we know of who had motive to want her dead would've been the spouses of the people doing the cheating—and not for nothing, they're probably the only ones who could've afforded a professional hit. Neither of them even knew about it."

"What about the guy?" Jeannie asked. "Ouellette? What if Pam had become a liability to him, and he needed to get her out of his life?"

"I suppose that's possible, although he wept when we told him how she'd been murdered."

"Doesn't mean he didn't hire it done," Freddie said.

"True. Cam, will you look into his financials and see what you can find on his four children? Let me know what we find in the kids' social media."

"Will do," Jeannie said as Cameron nodded.

"This helped," Sam said. "It gave me some threads to pull. Now, where are we with the Thorn murder, Gonzo?"

"I think his wife was involved," Gonzo said emphatically.

"How so?"

Gonzo distributed printouts containing the financials for Tiffany and Bryson Thorn. "Note the twenty-five-thousand-dollar withdrawal from their joint account yesterday. I spoke to the branch closest to their house, and the manager confirmed Mrs. Thorn was there yesterday."

"Very interesting indeed," Sam said. "Of course, it doesn't mean that she used the money to have her husband killed."

"No, but I went through her social media and found a post about how excited they were to attend a party at the home of the vice president. I read through the comments other parents made about being 'wicked jealous,' and then 'holy shit, he's the president now, is the party moving to the WH?' Tiffany said no with a sad face, adding, 'But next year, we'll be there!' Imagine how pissed she must've been to learn her husband was the one who released the photos and ruined her chance of ever being invited to the White House."

Sam glanced at Malone, who nodded. "That's enough to pick her up and bring her in. Good work, Sergeant."

"She was a real piece of work last night." Gonzo stood and signaled for Cam to come with him. "Wouldn't break my heart to make a case against her."

"I'll help look into the Ouellette kids as soon as we're back," Cam said as he went with Gonzo, his partner, to pick up Tiffany Thorn.

"Thank you. Jeannie, can I see you for a minute after we're done here?"

"Sure. I'll be in the pit."

When the others had left the room, Sam glanced at Freddie and Captain Malone. "I never really considered it could be one of the kids."

"You make a good argument about the crime being diabolical," Malone said. "Hard to think of a teenager having that kind of a murder in them."

"I look at Scotty and even Eli, and I try to picture someone their age doing what was done to Pam, and I can't for the life of me picture a young person doing such a thing."

"Evil resides in people of all ages," the captain said in a world-weary tone that came from thirty years of seeing the worst of humanity.

"Yes, I suppose it does," Sam said. "I should've looked in this direction sooner."

"Could still be another dead end," Freddie said. "Who knows?"

"Let's go talk to Bob Tappen and the Ouellettes again," Sam said. "We'll start there while the others do some digging online."

"I'm with you, LT," Freddie said.

"Keep me posted," Malone added.

"Will do."

Before she left HQ, she asked Detective Jeannie McBride to join her in her office. "Shut the door, will you?"

"Everything all right?" Jeannie asked.

"Yes and no. So the chief is asking us to take a step back from the review of Stahl's files."

Jeannie looked as shocked as Sam had felt the night before. "Why?"

"Because we can't handle any more bad PR, especially with the FBI report due after the first of the year. We don't expect that to be flattering. And I guess the fact that I solved the fifteen-year-old Worthington cold case in an afternoon isn't exactly being greeted with praise. People are outraged—and rightly so—that it took us so long to solve what should've been an open-and-shut case."

"I think I'm on to something in finding Carisma Deasly."

Sam hesitated, but only for a second. "What've you got?"

"A friend of the mother's, Daniella Brown, went missing around the same time as Carisma did. Daniella had been in and out of trouble and rehab for a number of years, while the mom, LaToya Deasly, had put herself through paralegal school and had bought a townhouse for herself and her children. She's always believed that Daniella took Carisma, but couldn't find either of them or prove her ex-friend was involved."

Sam released the clip holding her hair and ran her fingers through the tangled length as she tried to figure out what to do.

"I can't stop now, LT. I just can't. We might be able to find them. I've tracked down a guy Daniella was dating at that time, and he's willing to talk to me about what he knows. I'm supposed to meet him tonight."

"This was a direct order from the chief to stand down."

"I'll do it on my own time. Carisma's family has waited eleven years for answers. They think it's possible that Daniella has held her hostage all this time, that Carisma would escape from her if she could. How do I go on with my life knowing she might be out there somewhere waiting for someone to care enough to bother to rescue her?"

Sam's head felt like it might explode at any second. "Go ahead with it, but report only to me. Don't tell anyone else what you're doing, but take Matt with you when you meet with the boyfriend. Tell him it's about the Tappen case." She was going straight to hell for defying a direct order from the chief and for encouraging Jeannie to lie to her partner. "We're out on a huge limb here. We can't let this blow up into a BFD that makes the department look like shit—again."

"I understand. I'll do everything I can to keep that from happening."

"Since both our jobs may depend on it, see that you do."

.  .  .

"WE HAVE A PROBLEM," Christina said when she entered the Oval Office with Trevor Donnelly.

Terry was in the process of briefing Nick about the latest in the situation in the Gulf of Suez, which had deescalated in recent hours. That was a huge relief. Nick had been sick over the thought of sending in troops, especially right before Christmas. Terry stopped speaking in midsentence to turn to face his press secretary and communications director. "What's the problem?"

"You and the first lady are suing a man named Bryson Thorn?"

"We were until he was murdered overnight," Nick said.

"His distraught wife is on TV spouting off about how the president and first lady sued her husband, and then he ended up dead the next day." Christina held up her phone. "Sam called both of us to try to warn us this was possible."

Nick picked up the BlackBerry on his desk and put through a call to Sam.

She answered on the third ring. "Sorry, I couldn't get this stupid thing out of my pocket. Did you get my message about Tiffany Thorn?"

"Nope, but I just heard from Christina that she's on TV and making not-so-subtle accusations against us."

"The wife is about to get her ass arrested for arranging her husband's death," Sam said. "She's probably trying to sow some reasonable doubt before the evidence points right back to her."

"Why do you think she killed him?"

"We think it was because he ruined her chances of being invited to the White House for the twins' birthday next year."

"Are you serious?"

"Afraid so."

"Wow."

"People are so fucked up."

"We already knew that," Nick said.

"Yes, we did, but this is further proof. How's your day going?"

"So far so good. Things seem to be calming down in the Gulf of Suez, which is the big news. We've got a big meeting on cybersecurity at noon. And then a bunch of tech CEOs are coming in to talk about forming a public-private partnership to deal with the issue of hacking and ransomware attacks."

"It's very sexy when you use words like public-private and ransomware."

His lovely wife never failed to amuse him. "I'll have to remember that later."

"You do that. Have a good meeting."

"Thank you. Can you be here for the Henderson announcement? It's at six thirty, so maybe aim for six?"

After another long pause, she said, "I'll be there."

"Take care of my gorgeous wife out there. She's the sun and the stars and the moon and my whole world."

"Swoon."

"You're set to go with me on Friday, right?"

"Yes, all set."

"Thank you, Samantha."

"You're welcome, Nicholas. Gotta run. See you later."

"Love you."

"Love you, too."


SAM ENDED that call and juggled the phones to put through a call on her flip to Captain Malone.

"Can you try to keep the car on the road while you're doing that?" Freddie asked.

"I've got this. Don't worry."

"Right."

Malone picked up the call. "Didn't I just see you?"

"You did, but I forgot to tell you I'm going to Iowa with Nick on Friday, just in case we don't have this all sewed up by then."

"No problem. Do what you have to do. You've got a good team to cover for you when you need to be out."

"Thanks for the support, Cap."

"We all agree that having the first lady working for the department while in office is going to be awesome PR. We're fully prepared to support you in every way we can."

His words made Sam feel oddly emotional. "That means so much to me. Thank you."

"Your dad would be so incredibly proud of you both."

That brought tears to her eyes. "I hope so. Scotty and I were talking about how he'd be all over the White House in his wheelchair, asking questions and bothering everyone."

Malone laughed. "I can see that so clearly. I sure do miss him. I can't imagine how hard this is for you, especially with Christmas coming."

"Thanksgiving was the tough one. He loved that day more than anything."

"I can still picture him gnawing on the turkey neck while everyone else was dry heaving."

Sam cracked up. "There was literally nothing he wouldn't eat. By the way, I've got a thing at La Casa Blanca at six tonight."

"Ah, yes, the announcement of our nation's first female vice presidential nominee. Exciting stuff."

"What do you know about her?"

"Just what I read in the paper this morning. She's been instrumental in get-out-the-vote efforts for the party over the last few years and has fired up young voters. People are excited to have a young, dynamic team in the White House, not to mention the young, dynamic first couple."

"Not to mention."

"Why do you ask?"

"I got a weird vibe from her the one time I met her, but I was in her company for about ten seconds."

"That's usually all it takes for that gut of yours to get a reading."

"I hope I'm wrong about her."

"I hope so, too. Let me know what Tappen has to say."

"Will do."

"You got a weird vibe on Gretchen Henderson?" Freddie asked after she hung up.

"Yeah, but like Nick said, I met her for ten seconds. I need to give her a chance."

"Your vibes are usually spot-on."

"That's what I'm afraid of."

She would give the woman a chance because it'd been a huge deal for Nick to nominate the nation's first female vice president. As someone who thought such things were long overdue, Sam wanted to be supportive of him—and Gretchen. She wanted to be supportive of women everywhere who'd celebrate the elevation of a woman to the second-most powerful office in the world. And she hoped Gretchen proved her—and her gut—wrong.

They arrived at the Tappen home at eleven thirty. Judging from the cars in the driveway, the family was home, which was a relief.

She didn't have time to waste during her final workweek before vacation.

Snow was beginning to fall as she and Freddie went to the front door and rang the bell.

Lucas Tappen answered the door. "Oh. Hey. Did you figure out who killed my mom?"

"Not yet," Sam said. "We're still working on it, though. Is your dad home?"

"Yeah, he is. Come in. I'll get him."

"Thank you."

They waited in the foyer while Lucas went to the back of the house to get his father.

Holding a dishtowel, Bob Tappen came out from the kitchen.

Sam noticed that the man looked terrible, like he hadn't slept in days. Her heart went out to him. In the span of a few days, not only had he lost his beloved wife, but he'd also learned she'd been unfaithful. "We're so sorry to bother you again."

"It's no problem."

With Lucas lurking behind him, Sam said, "Could we speak to you in private?"

"Sure. Come on into the office." He handed the towel to Lucas. "Finish up the dishes, will you, son?"

Lucas eyed Sam and Freddie before he said, "Sure."

Bob showed them into the office and closed the French doors. "This was Pam's office," he said, glancing around at the disarray left behind by the Crime Scene detectives. "What can I do for you?"

"We have a slightly delicate question, and we're sorry we have to ask this," Sam said hesitantly, still not convinced this was a reasonable line of investigation. "But is it possible that any of your children or the Ouellette children might've found out about the affair and been angry enough to do what was done to Pam?"

At first, Bob seemed too shocked to answer. "Not my children. They *adored* their mother."

"Molly knew about the affair. Is there a possibility that she—"

"Absolutely not! You're implying that one of my children is a psychopath, because that's what you'd have to be to do something like that."

"What do you know about the Ouellette children?"

"I only know Aidan. I've met the younger siblings in passing, but I don't know them at all."

"Have you ever heard anything about any of them that would raise a concern?"

"Not that I can recall."

"Thank you for your help."

"You aren't seriously looking at my kids for this, are you?"

"We're looking at everyone until we find the person who killed your wife."

"My kids didn't do it. The boys were in Delaware with me, and Molly was in Boston."

"Thank you for reconfirming your whereabouts."

"Please don't upset their lives any more than they've already been," he said with a pleading edge to his voice. "There's no way any of them could've done this. Pam was everything to them."

"Thank you again for your time," Sam said. "We'll be in touch."

He saw them out and was still standing in the doorway when they drove away.

"What're you thinking?" Freddie asked.

"That he's a father who naturally wants to protect his children and can't possibly imagine any of them being capable of something like this."

"No parent wants to believe they raised a murderer. Are we going to Josie Ouellette next?"

Sam thought about that for a second. "No, I want to see Paula again." If anyone knew the scoop, it would be Pam's best friend. "Give her a call and find out where she is."

# CHAPTER TWENTY-THREE

Freddie made the call and learned Paula was at work at a doctor's office on Connecticut Avenue Northwest. He put the directions into his phone.

They arrived twenty minutes later after navigating around frustrating traffic delays caused by construction. "I'll never understand why they can't do all the road shit in the middle of the night."

"Agreed. It makes no sense to do any of it during the day around here."

"And it irritates me."

"I'll add that to the list."

"I'm going to have Nick call the mayor and ask her why they have to do road construction during the day."

"Are you really?"

"I'll suggest to him that he might want to ask about that."

"I'm sure he'll get right on it since he has nothing better to do."

Sam shot him a look and caught him trying to hold back a laugh, which led her gaze to the sign for the doctor's office. "Oh my God. Paula works for a proctologist? No way. My ass would have to be falling off before I brought it to a proctologist."

He couldn't hold that laugh in. "I'll make a note to bring you here only if your ass is actually falling off."

"Not one second before."

Inside the doctor's office, Sam noticed that none of the patients in the waiting room gawked at her, which was a welcome relief from the usual routine. If she were a patient here, she wouldn't want to make eye contact with anyone either. Not that there was anything wrong with proctology. Of course there wasn't.

Paula waved for them to come on back and led them to a conference room.

"We're sorry to bother you at work," Sam said.

"It's okay. Whatever I can do to help you find who did this to Pam."

"Did she talk to you at all about Mark's children?"

The question seemed to surprise Paula. "Aidan is a teammate of her sons. He's a big deal. Everyone expects him to go all the way with football."

Since Aidan has an airtight alibi for the time of murder, Sam moved on. "What about his sisters?" Sam consulted her notes. "Grace, Michaela and Alexis. Did she ever speak of them?"

Paula thought about that for a full minute. "She said the older one, Grace, was troubled."

"Did she say how so?"

"Just that Mark and his wife had a lot of issues with her. She was very willful, didn't listen to them, constantly broke their rules. That kind of stuff."

Sam's backbone tingled with the sensation that told her they might be on to something. "Has she ever been violent that you know of?"

"I honestly don't know that."

"Is there anything else you can tell me about things Pam might've told you about Mark or his family?"

"I really can't think of anything, but if I do, I'll call you."

"Thank you for your help. We really appreciate it."

"I really hope you find the person who did this."

"So do we."

When they were back outside, Sam said, "Call McBride and tell them to focus on Grace Ouellette first. Get me everything they can find on her first and then her brother, Aidan, and her sisters Michaela and Alexis."

While Freddie conveyed her orders to Jeannie, Sam drove to Mark Ouellette's insurance office.

"They're on it," Freddie said. "What's our next move?"

"I want to talk to Mark Ouellette again. If one of his kids was pissed off about his affair, he might know about it. I want to see his face when I ask him about that."

"Good call. Let's do it."

WHEN GONZO and Cameron arrived at the home where Tiffany Thorn and her son were staying, he showed his badge to the officer standing outside the front door.

"She just came back a short time ago, Sergeant," the patrolman said as he handed their badges back to them after a thorough examination. "A real *nice* lady."

The young man's voice dripped with sarcasm.

"I had the unfortunate opportunity to spend time with her last night," Gonzo said.

Grinning at his comment, the officer said, "Her mother came to stay with the boy while she was on TV going off about your boss and her husband."

"Thank you for the info, Officer McDaniels," Gonzo said.

"Happy to help."

"We're here to pick her up for a formal interview at HQ. Will you back us up? I don't expect her to go easily."

"You got it, Sarge."

Cameron stood next to Gonzo as he rang the doorbell. When Tiffany Thorn answered it, he noted that her hair and makeup were flawless, as if maybe a professional had prepared her for her TV appearances.

"Did you find Bryson's killer?"

"We think so."

Her eyes went wide. "Oh good. That's such a relief. So we can go home, then?"

"Not quite yet. I'm going to need you to come downtown to MPD headquarters with me."

"Why?"

"I have some follow-up questions I need to ask you."

"Why can't you do that here?"

"Because this will be a formal interview of a person of interest in the murder of Bryson Thorn."

It took a second for his meaning to register with her, and then her eyes flashed with unmistakable rage. "I hope for your sake you aren't saying I had something to do with it."

"I'm saying you need to come with me for a formal interview to discuss the evidence we've uncovered thus far. If you come with me without making a scene, I won't cuff you until we're in the car."

"I'm not going anywhere with you."

He grasped her arm and had her cuffed before she could begin to gauge his intentions. "Then I guess we have to do this the hard way. Tiffany Thorn, you're under arrest for suspicion of murder by hire in the death of your husband, Bryson Thorn." Gonzo recited the rest of the Miranda warning as she fought him like a caged tiger trying to break loose. After Gonzo made sure Tiffany's shocked mother was there to care for the young boy, it took him, Cameron and McDaniels to get her out of the house and down the sidewalk to Gonzo's car.

Tiffany screamed the whole way about police harassment, that she'd have their badges, their careers, their boss's career and every dime they'd ever made in their entire lives.

"*I want a fucking lawyer!* Look at how they're treating someone who lost her husband yesterday!" People on the street stopped what they were doing to watch in stunned amazement at the way she was carrying on. She screamed that the only reason they were doing this was because she'd accused their boss, the first lady, and her husband, the president, of murdering her husband.

Gonzo slammed the door in her face, cutting off her diatribe. "That was fun."

"Most fun I've had all week," McDaniels said. "Good luck with the ride to HQ."

"We'll ignore her," Green said. "We're good at that."

"Keep an eye on the mother and son," Gonzo said to McDaniels, "just in case we're wrong about the wife. But I don't think we are."

"Will do, Sarge. And if I might say, we're all behind you with the trial coming."

Gonzo shook the younger man's hand. "Thanks. Means a lot." He got into the car and closed the window to the back seat to mute the bullshit coming from Tiffany. "Some days are definitely more fun than others on this job," he said as he pulled into traffic to head for HQ.

"No kidding," Cameron said.

"Can't help but notice you're not your usual pressed-and-polished, put-the-rest-of-us-to-shame self today."

Cameron grunted out a laugh. "Had a rough night. My ex slashed my tires."

Gonzo looked over at him. "Seriously? Did we pick her up?"

"Yeah, she's in the can awaiting arraignment. Sam gave her a talking-to this morning that should alleviate any further trouble from her."

"What brought this on?"

"I guess she's been following me and found out I'm sort of seeing someone else."

"Who?"

"Um, Gigi."

"*Our* Gigi?"

"Yeah."

"Holy crap. Didn't see that coming."

"I didn't either until her ex tuned her up, and I wanted to commit murder for the first time in my life. The LT was the one who sort of brought it into focus for me."

"Huh, well... That's great, Cam. I'm happy for you guys."

"We're happy for us, too, except for the two exes who aren't going quietly."

"It's hard to be patient when you've found someone special and the whole world seems to be conspiring against you. Christina and I had been together for like ten minutes when I found out about Alex." At the time, finding out he had a son he'd known nothing about had been the biggest shock of his life. Alex had since become one of his greatest blessings.

"That must've been wild."

"It was, but Christina... She never wavered. Stuck by me through the whole thing. That's when I knew she was the real deal, you know?"

"Yeah, for sure. That's a lot to ask of a new girlfriend. It's cool that she stepped up that way."

This was, Gonzo realized, the first time he'd spoken with his new partner as a friend and not just a colleague. They were long overdue for that, and he probably ought to say so. "Hey, so, I'm sorry it's been such a rough transition into being my partner. I hope you know it's nothing personal."

"Of course I do. I can't begin to know what you've been through since losing Arnold."

"Worst day of my life, hands down."

"By all accounts, he was a good guy and a great cop."

"He was," Gonzo said, smiling, able now to remember his partner with fond affection rather than only raw grief. "He was funny and goofy and often a huge pain in my ass, but I loved the guy. Losing him the way I did was a fucking nightmare."

"It would be for anyone, Gonzo."

"Ah, well, I'm just hoping we can get justice for him at the trial. Not sure what I'll do if that guy walks."

"There's no way he's going to walk. No way in hell."

Gonzo appreciated having Cam's support. "From your lips to God's ears."

Back at HQ, they walked the still-shrieking Tiffany through processing, including the strip search that nearly took her straight over the edge. The female officer who performed the search returned her to Gonzo and Cam in an orange jumpsuit.

"She's all yours."

"Oh joy," Gonzo said, taking Tiffany by the arm to walk her to interrogation.

"You're looking at the biggest lawsuit this department has ever seen," she said, seething.

"Okay."

"I want a lawyer!"

"Okay."

He ducked into one of the interrogation rooms and pointed to the landline on the table. "Do you have the number for your attorney? I'll dial it for you." That was the least he could do for her, since she was cuffed.

She sputtered as she tried to come up with a name. "I don't know him. Bryson handles that stuff."

"Shall I request a public defender, then?"

"Absolutely not," she said, cringing.

"I need a name so I can put through the call for you."

"I don't have it!"

"Then I'll call the public defender's office. They're usually pretty backed up, so it might be a day or two before they can get someone over here. In the meantime, let's go."

"Where?"

As he took hold of her arm, Gonzo ignored the question and walked her to the stairs to the city jail in the basement.

Anticipating a struggle, Cameron took her other arm.

"Where are you taking me?" she asked, fighting them.

"To lockup to wait for your lawyer to get here."

"You're not putting me in a cell! I haven't done anything!"

"Okay."

The sergeant working the desk at the jail looked up when he heard them coming. Seeing that Gonzo and Cam were struggling to get her down the stairs, he went to open a cell for them. They deposited her inside and quickly shut the door.

"This is harassment! You've got nothing on me! I'm going to have all your jobs!"

"Okay."

"You're doing this on purpose," she said, her eyes narrowing with vindictiveness.

"What am I doing on purpose?" Gonzo asked.

"Making this as hard on me as you possibly can."

"Ah, no, Mrs. Thorn, you're doing that all on your own. If you come up with the name of an attorney you'd like to call, the sergeant at the desk can help you. Otherwise, we'll wait for the PD's office to send someone over."

"You're going to regret this!" she screamed at them as they walked away and headed up the stairs. "I'm going to have your ass!"

"No, you're not, sweetie," Gonzo muttered under his breath. "I'm going to have yours."

AFTER HE AND Gonzo had deposited the shrew in the can, Cameron took a second to text Gigi to make sure she was okay.

*All good*, she responded. *Just bored and lonely except for Jeffrey, who is very good company.* She sent heart eyes and kiss faces that made him instantly hard—at work—as he remembered the sweet pleasure of sleeping with her in his arms the night before.

*I'll be there as soon as I can. Let me know what you want for dinner. See you soon. Xoxo*

Cam was so eager to see her he wanted to leave work early. He'd never felt that way about any woman. He thought about what the LT had told him about meeting Nick years earlier and having her malicious ex-husband conspire to keep them apart. She'd known the first time she met him that he was it for her, and no one else would ever do. Cameron was beginning to realize the same thing had happened to him the first time he met Gigi Dominguez. He just hadn't known it then. Hindsight was indeed twenty-twenty, and as he picked over the various clues that'd been there all along, he felt a bit stupid for missing what'd been right in front of his face.

Or maybe he hadn't missed it. Maybe he'd had no choice but to push it to the far back burner while both of them were involved with other people. Now, nothing stood in the way of them being together, and he couldn't recall a time when he'd been less interested in work than he was today.

"Get it together, man. You've got a job to do." He logged onto Facebook and searched for Grace Ouellette of Washington, DC, and picked through the search results until he found the girl he was looking for by noting that her parents and siblings, Aidan, Michaela and Alexis, were among her friends.

As he scrolled through Grace's posts, he detected a fascination with the occult in the books and movies she recommended. In most of her photos, her eyes were lined with black makeup that gave her an ethereal appearance when paired with her pale skin. A post from three weeks ago caught his attention. *Trust no one*, she'd written. *Absolutely no one.* He took a screenshot of the post and printed it along with the comments that included things like, "Yo, girl, who F'd you over?" and "What's that about?" and "Uh-oh, what now?"

To the first question, Grace had replied, "You won't believe who."

Since that was the only comment Grace had responded to, Cameron made a note of the girl's name: Cory Bachman. After he located an address for the girl, he reached for his phone and called the LT.

"Hey, what's up?"

"You might've heard from Gonzo that we have Tiffany Thorn in custody, and what a peach she is."

"I've heard she's something else."

"You have no idea. In other news, I did some digging into Grace Ouellette's Facebook account and found something from three weeks ago where she posted, 'Trust no one. Absolutely no one.' A bunch of friends responded, but she only replied to one who asked who effed her over. She said, 'You won't believe who.'"

The friend's name is Cory Bachman, and I've located an address for her a few miles from the Ouellettes' home."

"Great work, Cam. You gave me a thread."

"I'm going to keep digging with Jeannie and Matt on Grace and the rest of the Ouellette and Tappen kids to see if anything else pops."

"Let me know."

"Will do."

# CHAPTER TWENTY-FOUR

S am ended the call with Cameron and updated Freddie on what they'd learned.

"Interesting that Grace referenced being unable to trust anyone," Freddie said. "I wonder if she meant her father."

"That's my guess. Let's see what Mark says about what his kids knew and when they knew it." She glanced at the clock to find it was inching closer to two, which gave her four hours before she had to be at the White House for the announcement of Nick's VP nominee.

"What're people saying about Nick's choice of Henderson for VP?" she asked hesitantly. Part of her didn't want to know what people were saying.

"Women are celebrating the huge milestone of the nation's first female vice president."

"I'm very proud of Nick for sticking to that plan, even when it became far more difficult than he expected to find someone who wanted the job."

"The right is appalled by the choice of someone who's never held elective office, even though she's worked in politics her entire adult life. I read a quote from the minority leader about how we'll have the most inexperienced president and vice president in history, neither of them elected by anyone, leading our country."

Sam swallowed hard, regretting that she'd asked. "Leave it to Stenhouse to piss on our parade."

"Others are celebrating the youthful vitality of the top leadership, indicating that we're long overdue for the next generation of leaders to take command."

"You're remarkably well informed, young Freddie."

"One of my two best friends is the new president. I'm devouring every word that's written about him and his wife."

"Gulp. What're they saying about his wife?"

"You really want to know?"

"No. Never mind."

"It's not bad," he said, laughing. "Women are also celebrating the first first lady to hold down a job outside the White House. Editorials have been mostly favorable about the example you're setting for women and working moms."

"I don't want to be a role model for working moms. I don't spend nearly enough time with my children. That's something I want to change in the new year. I'm not sure how I'm going to do it, but I'm determined to spend more time with them. Scotty is already fourteen. *Fourteen!* He's only going to live at home for four more years. I refuse to be absent for most of that time."

"I think it's great that you want to spend more time with them, and I'll do anything I can to help make that possible for you."

"Thanks. I appreciate that. And I'll return the favor when you have kids."

"You've got a deal."

"The time just goes by so bloody fast. Nick and I are together two years this week, which means John O'Connor's murder was already two years ago."

"And I met Elin two years ago this week."

"Oh my God, that's right! That was quite a week, but how is it already two years ago?"

"Look at everything that's happened in those two years."

"The head absolutely spins when I do that. How did I go from dating a chief of staff out of a job because his boss was murdered to living at the White House with the president?"

Freddie laughed. "Imagine the books and movies that'll be made about your story someday."

"As long as they get someone sexy to play me, like Scarlett Johansson."

"She'd be perfect. Who'll play me?"

"You won't be in it," Sam said, holding back the laugh that was trying to bust loose.

He gave her an offended look. "I'm one of the *stars* of your story."

"If you say so."

"Maybe I'll just write a tell-all instead of starring in your movie."

"Don't you dare."

"Get me into the movie, then."

"That's blackmail!"

Tutting, he said, "Sam, 'blackmail' is such a dirty word."

"That's my line, and it's trademarked!"

"You'd better be thinking of your partner and how much he knows when Hollywood comes calling."

"You used to be such a nice boy. What happened to you?"

"*You* happened," he said, as he always did when she posed that question.

She pulled into the parking lot of Mark Ouellette's insurance agency and turned to Freddie. "If you see anything written about either of us that you think we need to know, tell me, okay?"

"You've got a whole team of people to do that for you."

"But I've only got one you, and you know better than anyone what I need to know—and what I don't."

"I got you covered. Don't worry."

"Thanks." Sam paused before getting out of the car. "For this." She gestured between them to indicate the nonstop banter and nonsense that made up their days. "I think you might be the only thing keeping me sane through all this."

"I'm here for you *always*," he said fiercely.

Moved by his loyalty and support, she said, "That makes all the difference. Let's go talk to Mark."

When they walked into the office, Mark seemed startled to see them again. "Did something happen?"

"We need more information." Sam glanced toward his personal office. "May we speak in private?"

He noticed his employees looking at him and them with naked curiosity. "Sure."

They followed him into his office.

Freddie closed the door and sat next to Sam while Mark went around to sit behind his desk.

"What's this about?"

"Talk to us about your children, Mr. Ouellette," Sam said.

The question shocked him. "M-my children? What about them?"

"Did any of them know about the affair with Pam Tappen?"

"I, uh, I think Aidan and Grace knew."

"You *think*?" Sam's backbone buzzed with the feeling she got when they were on to something. "You're not sure?"

"They, ah, they knew."

"You told us before that no one knew."

"I didn't want to bring them into this."

As a mother, Sam understood that. As a cop, it pissed her off that he'd wasted her time. "How did they find out?"

"Grace followed me one of the times I met Pam and confronted us."

Yep, this was a major thread. "Confronted you how?"

"She came up to us in the parking lot of a restaurant and started screaming at us that we were liars and cheaters and that she hoped we got what was coming to us."

"Is that all she said?"

He hesitated.

"Mr. Ouellette, I'd advise you to tell us the full story right now. If we later find out you once again withheld information, you could be charged."

Mark broke down into sobs. "She's my *daughter*. My little girl. She couldn't have done this."

"What else did she say?"

It took five whole minutes for him to pull himself together, which only added to Sam's growing irritation. "She said she'd end us both if we didn't stop our revolting relationship."

Sam had to hide her reaction to that bombshell. "How long ago did that happen?"

He thought for a second. "Six weeks or so."

"Is that how Aidan found out about the affair? Grace told him?"

"Yes. I begged her not to tell anyone. I told her we were going to end it."

"And did you?"

Mark's face flushed with color. "Not entirely, but we saw less of each other after that."

"What were your interactions with Grace like after that night?" Freddie asked.

"She hasn't spoken to me since."

Sam nodded to Freddie to continue that line of questioning.

"Has the rest of your family noticed she's not speaking to you?"

"It's not unlike Grace to go silent, so no, they don't think anything of it. But I've noticed."

"Mr. Ouellette, is it possible that your daughter wanted your mistress out of your life badly enough to kill her?"

His mouth flopped open as his eyes bugged. "*Absolutely not.* Grace would never do something like that. You'd have to be a monster to do what was done to Pam. My Grace couldn't do that. There's no way."

The waver in his voice on those final three words told Sam he wasn't entirely sure his Grace would be incapable of such a thing. To Freddie, she said, "Have Malone pull a warrant and get Crime Scene to the house. I want her computer, her phone and a full search of her room."

"Yes, ma'am," Freddie said, stepping out of the office to see to her orders while Mark looked on in horror.

"Where can we find her?" Sam asked.

"You're not seriously looking at her."

"I'm asking where we can find her."

"She goes to Burke," he said with a deep sigh. "She's a senior."

"Are your other children there, too?"

He nodded and ran a trembling hand through his hair. "Aidan is also a senior. We held him back a year for football."

Sam stood and turned for the door.

"So that's it? You're going to go there and bother her at school?"

She looked back over her shoulder. "That's exactly what we're going to do, and if you tip her off that we're coming, we'll be back to arrest you. Any other questions?"

His dark scowl spoke for him.

They walked past Ouellette's shocked staff and stepped out into frigid air that was a welcome relief from the stuffy office.

"How happy am I that Grace Ouellette is eighteen, and I don't need her parents' permission or involvement in any of this?"

"We're both very happy about that. Grace, on the other hand, is not going to be so happy."

Sam snorted out a laugh at his witty comeback. "What do we know about the school?"

"It's a really swank place. Some friends of mine from church went there." He tapped around on his phone. "Like 44K a year per kid."

Sam blew out a low whistle. "Is there that much money in insurance?"

"I wouldn't have thought so, but he's paying nearly two hundred grand a year to send four kids to school. And he's still got to put them through college."

"Where do the Tappen kids go?"

A minute later, he said, "Coolidge."

"Interesting. Ouellettes are private, and Tappens are public. Ask Cam and Matt to do a deep dive on the Ouellettes and their finances."

"Texted and Cam said okay."

"Call Archie and ask where we are with the expanded search of the film from the area where Pam lives and where the minivan was found," Sam said, buzzing from the adrenaline that came with a possible break in a complex, baffling case.

While Freddie put through the call, Sam drove toward the campus of Edmund Burke School on Connecticut Avenue.

"He says nothing yet, but they're working two miles out from both locations."

"Tell him thanks and let us know."

When Freddie ended the call with Archie, Sam said, "Call Burke to let them know we're coming to speak with Grace Ouellette, and we'd appreciate their cooperation."

While he made the call, Sam looked for a parking spot in the vicinity of the school. She ended up double-parking and leaving her hazard lights on while they made their way toward the leafy brick-fronted school with the huge BURKE sign out front. Because they'd called ahead, a school staffer met them at the main door and escorted them to a conference room in the office.

Sam appreciated that sort of cooperation and wished it happened more often on the job. "I like this place," she said after the staffer had left them to wait for Grace to join them.

"I knew you were going to say that."

"Cooperation is such a rare and special gift."

"That it is."

The same staffer escorted Grace Ouellette into the room five minutes later.

At first glance, Sam noticed the girl was stunning. She wore all black, her hair was dyed jet black, and her eyes were rimmed with heavy black makeup. A backpack hung from her shoulder.

"Who are you?" she asked, her gaze darting between them as she propped her hands on slender hips.

Sam had found the one unicorn in America who didn't know who she was. She showed her badge while Freddie did the same. "Lieutenant Holland, Detective Cruz from the Metro PD. We'd like to speak to you about the murder of Pam Tappen."

To her credit, her expression offered no reaction to the mention of Pam's name. "Who?"

"The woman your father was having an affair with."

"My dad isn't having an affair."

"We already know you confronted your father and Pam about the affair in the parking lot of a restaurant."

She stared blankly at them.

Sam gestured for Freddie to check her backpack and waited while he produced a slim silver laptop and an iPhone, both of which would be entered into evidence.

"I'd like to speak to a lawyer," Grace said.

"We can arrange that for you downtown." Sam took a pause to allow that information to register with Grace, who seemed to flinch at the realization she was being arrested. "If you come quietly, we can escort you out of here without cuffs, but we'll need to cuff you for the ride."

Her subtle nod was the only acknowledgment she gave.

The three of them walked out of the conference room together and toward the main doors as the woman who'd met them came after them.

"You can't just take her!"

"Yes, we can," Sam said. "We're trying not to make a scene of it. Maybe you could do the same?"

The woman stopped in her tracks as she cast a frantic look at Grace, probably fearing parental retaliation for allowing the police to take her from the school. That wasn't Sam's problem. Outside, they walked a block from the school before they cuffed Grace and led her to Sam's car, helping her into the back seat for the ride to HQ.

Their passenger never made a sound on the fifteen-minute ride.

Sam drove around to the morgue entrance to avoid the press camped outside the main door. If they were wrong about Grace, she had no desire to ruin the young woman's life, but she didn't think they were wrong.

Acting on a hunch, she brought Grace with her when she stepped into the cold, antiseptic-smelling morgue, where Dr. Lindsey McNamara was downing a wrap for lunch while she worked on the computer.

"Hey, LT, Detective. What's up?" Lindsey asked, eyeing Grace.

"We'd like to see Pam Tappen, please."

"What?" Grace said, recoiling. "I don't want to see her!"

"Too bad."

Every instinct she had told her this young woman had played a role in Pam's death. She nodded to Lindsey as she tightened her grip on Grace's arm so she couldn't escape.

"You can't make me look at dead people!"

"Yes, I can."

"I want a lawyer!"

"I'll get you one."

"You have to get me one the minute I ask."

"No, I have to get you one before I can interview you."

From inside the actual morgue, Lindsey signaled to Sam to come in.

"Let's go," Sam said.

It took both her and Freddie to walk Grace into the morgue, where Pam was laid out under the bright lights.

Lindsey had revealed only her face.

"Show her the rest."

As Grace continued to fight them, Lindsey pulled the sheet down to reveal the dark abrasions on Pamela's wrists and ankles that indicated a violent struggle to get free of her bindings.

"Take a good look," Sam said. "Can you imagine that someone kidnapped her, tied her up, gagged her and left her to either freeze to death or asphyxiate in her car over the course of several days? You'd have to be a complete monster to do what was done to her."

Grace's entire body vibrated with tremors in the second before she vomited onto the floor.

"Sorry for the mess, Doc," Sam said.

"No worries." Lindsey wiped Grace's face and mouth with a tissue. "It happens."

"Freddie, will you please take Grace to processing?"

"Yes, ma'am," he said, taking her by the arm to lead her out.

"That was intense," Lindsey said when they were alone.

"I'm ninety-nine percent sure she's our killer."

"Oh Lord," Lindsey said, her green eyes warm with compassion. "She's so young."

"I know, but she found out her father was having an affair with the victim, confronted them in a parking lot and threatened to 'end' them both if they didn't stop the affair. He said the affair continued after that."

"Wow."

"We just heard that part of the story today after we decided to dig into the kids. I was slow to look in this direction because I couldn't imagine someone her age doing what was done to Pam. That was my bad."

"That wouldn't have been my first thought either. Let me know what you find out. In the meantime, the tox screen came back on Pam, and she had no drugs or alcohol in her system."

"Thanks for the update. I'll keep you posted."

"Are you going to Des Moines?"

Sam nodded. "Friday."

"God, Sam."

"I know, but there's no way I'd let him go alone if I could avoid that."

"No, of course he can't go alone."

"I'm afraid I'll cry the whole time."

"If you do, you do. They'll appreciate your compassion and that you're human."

"I hope so."

Lindsey stood to hug her. "And when you get back, your friends and family will be here to help you and hug you and put you back together."

"I'm going to need that."

"We're here, Sam. Through it all. We're here."

"That's a source of tremendous comfort to me and to Nick."

Lindsey flashed a grin that made her eyes sparkle. "We're all looking forward to the sleepover on Christmas Eve. That's going to be epic."

"I can't wait. It's going to be so fun to dress up and be together after these insane last few months."

"Tell me the truth. Who gets the Lincoln Bedroom?"

"You'll see," Sam said with a coy smile as she left her friend to get back to work.

# CHAPTER TWENTY-FIVE

S am returned to the pit, where Gonzo watched as Patrol officers escorted Tiffany Thorn into interrogation.

"Can't help but notice that a night in jail and the orange jumpsuit seem to have taken some of the starch out of her spine," Gonzo said.

"Happens to the best of them," Sam replied.

"And the worst. Charity Miller is in the observation room," he said of the Assistant U.S. Attorney who'd prosecute the case against Tiffany. "I'm just waiting for Archie to bring me his report on text messages from her phone that he says I'm going to enjoy very much."

"Here it is," Archie said as he came into the pit with a printout he handed to Gonzo. "I've highlighted the good parts where she talks to her Salvadoran gardener, Holman Aguilar, in very bad Spanish as she tries to convince him that her husband beat her and her son and needed to be dealt with. You'll also note she was banging the gardener on the side and promised to give him some rather salacious favors if he did this 'one small thing' for her."

Gonzo scanned the messages that added to the growing murder-for-hire case against Tiffany Thorn. "Wow, she promised him anal if he took care of her husband. 'That's something even he has never gotten,' she told the gardener."

"It gets better," Archie said. "Wait until you get to the part where she promises to marry him and help him get his green card if he'll only get her husband out of the way."

"Wow, she sure did make it easy for us," Gonzo said. "Thanks, Archie. This is awesome."

"My pleasure. I took the liberty of providing a list of pings for his phone that put him at the Thorns' at nine ten last night. I figured you'd want his whereabouts today, and here's that report. The first ping is his home address in Northeast. The others are other homes in the Thorns' neighborhood."

"Great work, Archie," Sam said. "Thank you."

"You got it. We're still working on the expanded search for Pam Tappen's route from her home last Friday," he said as he headed for the stairs to his IT kingdom upstairs. "I'll let you know if we find anything."

"McBride." Gonzo held up the page with the pings from Aguilar's phone. "Can you and O'Brien pick up Holman Aguilar on suspicion of murder for hire?"

Jeannie took the page from him. "Sure thing. Let's go, Matt."

"Thanks." Gonzo glanced at Sam. "You want to join me in there? After all, she accused you and Nick of murdering her husband when she knew all along who'd done it."

"Nah, take Cam. I'll watch from observation. You guys have got this locked and loaded."

"She did all the heavy lifting for us."

"Hey, Gonzo?" Sam said when he'd started to walk away.

"Yeah?"

"It's so, *so* nice to have you back. We missed you more than you'll ever know."

"Thanks. It's nice to feel more like my old self." He rubbed at a spot on his chest. "Albeit with a great big hole right here that I'm learning to live with."

A lump filled her throat whenever she thought of Detective Arnold and his violent death. "What do you want to do for the one-year anniversary?"

"I thought maybe we could all go out somewhere—not O'Leary's," Gonzo said, frowning. That place was dead to them after they'd learned the owner had been involved in the shooting of Sam's dad. "We need a new place."

"We could do it at my place so Nick can come," she said with a sheepish grin. "The service is second to none."

"That sounds perfect," Gonzo said. "He would've been so stoked to see you guys living there."

"Invite his parents, sisters and girlfriend, too, will you?"

"I'll take care of it. Thanks, Sam."

"You got it. Now go nail that bitch Tiffany Thorn to the wall."


GONZO WALKED into the interrogation room with Cam, ready to do battle with Tiffany and her scumbag lawyer. Not all defense attorneys sank to the level of scumbags, but this one had that word stamped all over his cheap suit, greasy hair and sleazy smile. He didn't recognize the guy from the PD's office.

"Who are you?"

He slid a business card across the table that Gonzo ignored. "Von Cressley."

Cameron turned on the recorder and made note of everyone present in the room.

Gonzo forced her to look at him by staring her down. "Mrs. Thorn, you were brought in as a person of interest in your husband's murder—"

"I didn't do it! I told you! I was out with my friends when he was killed. Have you even asked them? They'll tell you I was with them. There was *no way* I could've done it."

Gonzo placed the financial records on the table that showed a twenty-five-thousand-dollar cash withdrawal from a joint account shared by Tiffany and Bryson Thorn the day before the man was killed.

"We have video footage putting Mrs. Thorn at the branch office and receiving the withdrawal in cash."

Her expression registered shock for a moment before it switched back to outrage.

"Can you please tell us what you used that money for?" Gonzo asked.

Tiffany's gaze darted toward the lawyer, who brought the document in for a closer look.

"You can answer that question," the lawyer said.

Tiffany obviously didn't want to, which gave Gonzo tremendous satisfaction.

"I, uh, used it on a down payment on a new car."

"In cash?" he asked, hoping his expression conveyed skepticism.

"That's what they requested."

"At what dealership?"

"I don't recall the name."

"What brand?"

"Lexus."

"What city or town?"

"Rockville."

Without blinking as he stared at her, Gonzo said, "Detective Green, will you please check with the Lexus dealership in Rockville and find out if they accepted a twenty-five-thousand-dollar down payment from Mrs. Thorn the day before yesterday or yesterday? We'll wait." He figured he'd let her hang herself even further before he showed his hand on the rest of what they knew.

Cameron stood and headed for the door. "Will do."

Gonzo also stood. "We'll be back when we confirm your story."

"Wait!"

He turned, raising a brow in inquiry.

"You have to let me out of here. I have to take care of my son. He just lost his father. I need to be with him."

"I'm afraid that's not going to happen until we're able to prove you had nothing to do with your husband's murder."

"I didn't!"

"Great. Once we can prove that, you'll be free to go. In the meantime, hang tight."

Gonzo took great pleasure in leaving the room, certain they had their killer—or at least the person who'd arranged the killing.

"Do you want to bet there's no Lexus?" Sam asked when she emerged from the observation room with Charity Miller.

"I'll take that bet and raise you a Mercedes-Benz," Charity said.

"Is it wrong for us to be so giddy about nailing a murdering scumbag?" Gonzo asked.

"We have to get our jollies where we can on this job," Sam said, "although I feel a little bit responsible for Bryson Thorn's death. If we hadn't made a federal case out of him releasing those photos, he'd still be alive."

"You're not the one who killed him, Lieutenant," Gonzo said. "This is on her—and her gardener."

Green joined them two minutes later. "Shocker that the dealership has no record of anyone by the name of Thorn putting a cash down payment on a Lexus this week."

"Somehow I knew you were going to say that." Gonzo felt

almost gleeful to have further proof that Tiffany Thorn was a lying sack of shit. "Let's go back in and see what other bullshit she's got for us."

When they burst back into the room, Tiffany startled, which gave Gonzo additional pleasure. He was having way too much fun with this one.

"The Lexis dealership confirms they have no record of you or your twenty-five grand this week."

"That's outrageous! I'll never do business with them again!"

"You can sit there and lie to us all day, and we'll take the time to debunk every single lie before we get to the truth of how you hired your gardener to murder your husband because you were infuriated that he'd ruined your chance to ever be invited to the White House."

Her expression went completely blank with shock.

Bull's-eye.

"I... That... That's not what happened."

"Isn't it? When did you find out that your husband was the one who leaked the photos of the president at the birthday party? Was it when cops came to see him, or was it when the president and first lady slapped a lawsuit on him?"

Tiffany crossed her arms and gave him a bullish look, but he noticed her entire body was trembling, as if she'd been plugged into a wall socket. "I don't know what you're talking about."

"Sure, you don't. It must've made you really mad that your husband was the one to violate the NDA. Were the other mommies pissed at you for maybe ruining their chances of being invited to the White House for the twins' party next year?"

Her mouth flopped open, but nothing came out.

Sometimes this horrible job was awfully fun. Gonzo shuffled through the pages of text messages that Archie had provided. "Your gardener, Holman, must've been excited when you offered him anal if he killed your husband. What was he more excited about? That, the money or the green-card marriage you promised him?"

Tiffany's eyes bugged. "That's revolting. I've never done that."

"I know. You said as much to Holman, promising him a prize that not even your husband had gotten. So which was he more excited about? The twenty-five large or the anal?"

"You're vile."

"At least I'm not a murderer."

"I never laid a hand on my husband," she said, her voice much less venomous than it had been before it became obvious to her that she was totally screwed, glued and tattooed, as the lieutenant would say.

"No, but you hired Holman to take care of him for you. He's on his way in. I'm sure he'll be happy to tell us how it all went down to keep from spending the rest of his life in prison."

"My client would like a deal," the useless lawyer said.

Gonzo leaned in, waited until he was certain he had their attention and said, "No deal."

"OH MY GOD," Sam said when she met him in the hallway. "That was fucking awesome." She gave Gonzo and Green high fives.

"I'll talk to Tom about filing murder and murder-for-hire charges against her," Charity said, referring to the U.S. Attorney, Tom Forrester.

"What about the gardener who did the actual deed?"

"He's looking at murder one as well," Charity said.

"What if we can get him to testify against her?" Gonzo asked. "She was the ringleader. He's an undocumented immigrant with a lot to lose if anyone finds out he's banging one of the customers on the side, and he believed the husband was knocking her and the kid around. She pressured the living hell out of him to do this for her, and we've got proof of that."

"I'll see what I can do for him, but at the very least, he's looking at murder two—if he's willing to testify against her."

With Tiffany Thorn on her way to life in prison, Sam went to find Freddie, who hadn't returned yet from Central Booking. He wasn't there, so she went to check downstairs and ran into him coming up, looking harried.

"I've got to admit I was skeptical that Grace Ouellette could've killed Pam Tappen until I spent a little time with her, and now I'm almost positive she has murder in her."

"What makes you say that?"

"There's just this hard edge to her, and get this. I told her we needed access to her phone, and she gave it to me along with the code. I think that despite her tough exterior, she's scared shitless and doesn't realize she shouldn't give us access to her phone without making us get a warrant first."

"Let's not do anything with it until we have the warrant. I don't want to make any mistakes that will let a killer off the hook."

"My next move was to get the warrant and have her sign the release giving us permission to review it. In the meantime, I put her in an interrogation room—with the phone—hoping she might send some texts that help our case."

"Good idea. Let's leave her for a bit and then see who Grace has been in touch with."

It took an hour to get the warrant that gave them permission to open Grace's phone to check her emails, texts and internet search history. In the meantime, Jeannie and Matt returned with a sobbing Holman Aguilar, who was willing to tell them anything they wanted to know about the plot hatched by Tiffany.

And yes, he was willing to testify against her to save his own ass from a lifetime in prison.

With Gonzo sewing up the parts and pieces of that case, Sam and Freddie turned their attention to Grace Ouellette's phone.

"Look here," Freddie said after scrolling through everything from around the date of Pam's abduction. "She texted Lucas Tappen on Friday to ask if he might put her in touch with his mom because she was interested in an internship. Lucas responded that his mom was heading out of town later that day to do a show in Baltimore, but he could ask her to get in touch when she got home."

"So she knew Pam would be leaving that day and which way she'd be going to get to Baltimore." Sam jumped up from the conference room table where they'd been camped out. "I need to see Archie about that footage."

"One step ahead of you." Archie came in holding a thumb drive. "We hit pay dirt two miles from Pam's house where she picked up a young woman by the side of the road."

As he put the thumb drive into the conference room computer and called up the footage, Sam's entire body buzzed the way it did when they were about to close a case.

"Wait for it," Archie said as the camera picked up Pam's minivan coming toward it. The next frame showed a young woman dressed all in black by the side of the road. She waved to Pam, who pulled the car over. Grace leaned into the open passenger window and then got in the car.

"Why would Pam pick her up if Grace had threatened to 'end' her for having an affair with her father?" Freddie asked.

"For the same reason I didn't think to look sooner at any of the kids." Sam felt sick for Pam. "She didn't believe Grace was capable of following through on her threat. She saw her lover's child by the side of the road and pulled over to check on her the way any mother would do for a friend's kid. I bet Grace pulled a weapon on her, and Pam did what she was told, hoping it would save her life."

The others were silent as they absorbed the impact of Pam helping Grace and how it had cost her her life.

"The threat she made to her father and Pam, the video putting her with Pam right before she was killed and the text with Lucas are enough to charge her," Freddie said. "Do we even need to talk to her?"

"We're going to be hard-pressed to get the dad to testify against his own kid, so we need more," Sam said.

"While she was in interrogation earlier," Freddie said, "she texted Lucas again to say she'd been arrested."

"Did he reply?"

"Nope."

The Crime Scene Unit commander, Lieutenant Haggerty, approached them, carrying a plastic evidence bag. "Honda keys found in Grace Ouellette's bedroom. We checked it in the ignition of the car, and it's a match."

"And with that, we have enough to charge her," Sam said. "Great work, Lieutenant. Thank you."

"No problem."

A scream from the lobby had them all rushing in that direction to find Josie Ouellette locked in a battle with two Patrol officers who were trying to stop her from progressing any farther into the building.

"*Where is my daughter?*" she screamed at the top of her lungs as she flailed against the tight hold the officers had on her.

Sam approached her. "Mrs. Ouellette, if you'll please calm down, I'll be happy to talk to you."

"What have you done with my child?" she asked in a low, sinister-sounding tone that completely changed her countenance.

"Your 'child' is actually an adult, and we've detained her on suspicion of murder in the Pam Tappen case."

"You fucking *cunt*!" Josie's eyes flashed with rage as she lifted a leg to kick Sam.

The Patrol officers pulled her back before she could follow through. One of them had cuffs on her in a matter of seconds.

"My daughter didn't kill that whore!"

"How do you know that?" Sam asked.

"I know that because *I'm* the one who killed her. Grace didn't do it."

Huh. Sam hadn't seen that coming. She also didn't believe her, but she would prove that in the interrogation room. To the Patrol officers, she said, "Take her to Central Booking and let me know when she's in a room."

As Sam began to walk away, Josie screamed after her. "I just confessed. Now let my daughter go."

Sam turned back to face her. "I'm afraid it doesn't work that way."

"What does that mean?"

"You can confess all you want. But until we prove you did it and Grace didn't, your confession is just words." She continued on her way back to the pit as Josie screamed at her to let Grace go.

"What do you think?" Freddie asked.

"She's lying to protect her kid," Sam said.

"That was my thought, too."

"But we'll let her tell us her tall tale and see what we get from it."

"What was that about?" Captain Malone asked when he joined them in the pit.

"Grace Ouellette's mother claiming she's the one who killed Pam, not Grace," Sam said.

"And she tried to kick the LT and called her a see-you-next-Tuesday," Freddie added.

Sam gave him a disdainful look. "You can say the word."

"I choose not to," Freddie replied indignantly.

She rolled her eyes. "We're bringing her in through Central Booking and seeing what she has to say, but we like Grace Ouellette for the murder of Pam Tappen."

"Carry on, then."

To Freddie, Sam said, "See where we are with comparing

Grace's prints to the ones Lindsey found on the duct tape during the autopsy."

"On it."

"We already have enough to charge the daughter," Sam said. "The prints will just confirm what we already know."

"As soon as you have it nailed down, let's update the media on the Tappen and Thorn cases," Malone said.

"I'd like Gonzo to take care of the brief on Thorn. That was all him, and he did a great job of wrapping that one up quickly, which also takes the heat off me and Nick."

"Fine by me. They're clamoring for info on all fronts."

"We'll take care of that."

Malone checked his watch. "Looks like you're going to make your self-imposed deadline of getting both cases wrapped before you leave on vacation."

"So it seems," Sam said, her stomach aching when she thought of the trip to Des Moines. "I'll be working my other two jobs for the next two weeks."

"Enjoy the holidays with your family. It's been a rough few months. You deserve the break and the time away."

"Thanks, Cap. I will."

"You can tell me, though. I'm getting the Lincoln Bedroom on Christmas Eve, right?"

"You'll have to wait and see," Sam said with the same mysterious smile she'd given the others.

# CHAPTER TWENTY-SIX

They'd invited all their closest people to spend Christmas Eve at the White House, and every bed in the house would be occupied that night. Which reminded Sam that she needed to check in with Gideon to make sure everything was ready, and with Shelby, who was overseeing many of the details. Shelby was settling into her new official role as the White House social secretary, while remaining a daily presence in the lives of Scotty, Alden and Aubrey, all of whom adored her.

Since she was waiting for the report on Grace's fingerprints, Sam went into her office and put through a call to Gideon to take care of some first lady business.

"Good afternoon, Mrs. Cappuano."

"Hi there, Gideon. And you can call me Sam when it's just us."

"Yes, ma'am."

"Not ma'am. Sam."

"Okay, Sam," he said, laughing. "How's it going?"

"Well, we're wrapping up two homicide investigations in time for me to accompany the president to Des Moines. Other than that... all is well."

"I know how hard that will be, but it'll mean so much to the families that you care enough to come."

"It's such a sad and tragic thing."

"It's horrible. Those poor families."

"Because the show must go on even in difficult times, I called to check in with you about Christmas Eve to make sure we're all set."

"Everything is coming together. We've got RSVPs from everyone you invited. The Gonzaleses aren't spending the night because his parents will be in town for Christmas, so they'll come for the party and go home after. The rest of your guests have accepted with pleasure—and quite a bit of excitement."

"I'll tell Gonzo to bring his parents to the party."

"I'll make a note of that and notify the Secret Service."

Sam couldn't wait to wake up on Christmas morning with their kids, her nieces, nephews, Nick's half brothers and their friends' kids. They were hoping to do it every year they were in the White House.

"When you return from Des Moines, we'll do a final review of the menus for dinner and Christmas brunch, if that meets with your approval."

"That'd be wonderful. Thank you again for all your hard work to make this happen for us, Gideon."

"It's a pleasure. The staff is enjoying having a young family back in the White House."

"That's nice to hear. Do let me know if any of them—or the dog —are getting on your last nerve."

"They're all doing great and making a very nice transition, it seems."

"I can't wait for time off to spend together and to check out Camp David."

"You'll find that to be a grand adventure, for sure. I'll check in with you over the weekend, if that suits you?"

"It does. Thanks again."

"You're more than welcome."

"Before I let you go, I wanted to ask whether the White House uses natural gas."

"Yes, ma'am."

"Huh."

"Is that a problem?"

"It's just that I'm not a fan after having worked a house explosion due to a natural gas leak early in my career."

"I understand, but I can assure you our gas line is inspected monthly and is kept in pristine condition."

"That's comforting. Thanks for letting me know that."

"Of course. You know where to find me if there's anything else I can do for you."

"Thanks, Gideon."

Sam ended that call and put through another to her designer friend Marcus, who'd come to their attention when Nick was a U.S. senator from Virginia.

"As I live and breathe," he said when he picked up the call, "is this the first lady of the United States of America?"

Sam huffed out a laugh at his outrageousness. "So I'm told."

"I was planning to call you today about a quick fitting before next Thursday."

"I meant to call you to thank you for sending the clothes for President Nelson's funeral. You made me look very first ladyish."

"I'm glad you were pleased."

"How are we coming with red, formal and sexy for Christmas Eve?"

"I've got you covered, my love."

"And you remember I've gained a couple of pounds since my father died, right?"

"Not to worry. Will Marcus get some free publicity out of this?"

"We can release a photo and credit the hip designer who made Mrs. C look so good."

"In that case, I'll have something to you by Tuesday. We'll do a quick fitting just to be sure it fits perfectly?"

"That works."

"Um, shall I meet you at the White House, then?"

Sam smiled at how he could barely contain his excitement as he said those words. "Since that's where I live these days, I guess so."

"Oh my God, my mother and grandmother are going to *die*!"

"Why don't you bring them with you?" If there was one great thing about living in the people's house, it was the ability to share it with her people.

"Stop it."

"Why not?"

"Are you serious?"

"Very serious. Text me legal names, dates of birth and addresses for all of you, and I'll leave word with the Secret Service to let you in."

"Sam... I mean, Mrs. Cappuano—"

"Please call me Sam, Marcus."

"You'll never know what this means to me—or to them. That I'm dressing the *first lady of the United States*. You honor me beyond all measure."

"I love your clothes, and I hope we can work closely together to keep me looking good over the next few years."

"Whatever you need, whenever you need it."

"Since you offered, what've you got in black that I might wear to Des Moines?"

"I'll courier over a few options right away."

"I'll let them know to expect the package from you."

"Should I include shoes?"

"Do you know me at all, Marcus?"

His laughter came ringing through the phone. "I'll fix you right up."

"Thank you, my friend."

"No, thank you. I hope you know that you'll be making my career with this."

He sounded like he was on the verge of tears. "I'm very happy to have the chance to work with you. I'll see you—and your mom and grandmother—very soon."

"I'm going to call them right now. They're going to *lose their minds!*"

Sam hung up with him, delighted by his excitement. She had to admit there were some positives to being the first lady. Inviting people to the White House was definitely one of them.

Freddie came to the door. "Dr. McNamara was able to determine that Grace's prints are a match for the ones she found on Pam during the autopsy."

"Is Grace's attorney here yet?"

"She arrived a few minutes ago and is waiting in the lobby."

"Excellent. I don't want to jinx us, but how nice would it be to wrap up two cases in the same day?"

"It would be very nice, and I can't believe you said that out loud."

"I know, right? I'm walking on the wild side lately. You can let her attorney in to see her. And let's finish with her phone in the meantime." It surely seemed as if the stars were aligning in her favor today, Sam thought, as she went into the conference room to finish going through Grace's messages from the days prior to Pam's disappearance and afterward. One of them, from the day after, stopped her in her tracks.

Lucas Tappen texted, *Did you do it?*

*It's taken care of. Now it's your turn.*

*I don't know if I can.*

*You agreed this needed to happen. Now do your part, or I will if you're not man enough.*

*I said I'd do it, and I will.*

*He's at his office every morning by seven. His staff doesn't arrive until eight. There's your opportunity. He also stays late after they leave at four. I'll be waiting.*

"Holy shit," Sam whispered, grabbing the receiver of the phone on the table and putting through a call to Patrol. "This is Lieutenant Holland. I need people on Mark Ouellette immediately." She gave his office and home addresses. "I believe his life is in imminent danger."

"Yes, ma'am," the Patrol sergeant said. "We'll dispatch officers to both places right away."

"Thank you."

When Freddie returned from taking Grace's attorney in to meet with her, Sam said, "Grace was in cahoots with Lucas Tappen. She'd take out Pam if he did her dad."

"Come on."

"It's all right here." Sam showed the texts to Freddie, who scanned them quickly.

"Lucas knew she was going to kill Pam, and he's planning to take Mark out."

"These are high school kids plotting murder."

"They're high school kids who caught their parents having an affair and decided to take matters into their own hands, except only one of them followed through with it."

"Are we picking him up?"

"He knew his mother was going to be murdered and did nothing to stop it. You bet your ass we're picking him up. Let's go."

They were almost to the Tappens' home when Sam took a call from an unknown number on speaker. "Holland."

"This is Patrol Sergeant Kramer. When my officers arrived at Mr. Ouellette's office, we found the subject deceased from multiple gunshot wounds."

"Oh *fuck*," Sam muttered as she slammed her hand against the wheel and pressed the accelerator to the floor, planning to go by the Tappens' home to look for Lucas before proceeding to Mark's office. "We'll be there shortly."

To Freddie, she said, "Get Gonzo, Cameron, Jeannie and Matt over to Mark Ouellette's office to process the scene and put out an APB for Lucas Tappen. List him as armed and dangerous."

"On it."

They were two blocks from the Tappens' house when Freddie said, "Sam, look."

As they went flying by a parked car, she caught a glimpse of a young man bent over the steering wheel and slammed on the brakes to make a U-turn.

While Freddie called Gonzo and updated him on the situation with Mark Ouellette, Sam pulled up behind the parked car, got out and withdrew her weapon as she approached the vehicle. Knowing he was armed, she stood back when she knocked on the window. The young man inside startled and looked up at her, his face red and his eyes ravaged. His shock at seeing her registered in the second before he aimed a weapon at her.

She kept her weapon trained on him, praying she wouldn't have to use it. "Put it down and get out of the car!"

Freddie appeared on the other side of the car with his gun drawn.

She took a step forward, hoping to make eye contact with him. "Put it down, Lucas, and get out of the car!"

He took a shot through the window that caught her in the arm. The shock and impact knocked her off her feet. Son of a bitch, if he shot her again while she was down, that could be game over. But damned if she could make her limbs work to get herself out of harm's way.

Freddie was upon them before Lucas could fire again. "Put it down and get out of the car with your hands up. Now!"

While Sam moved out of the line of fire, Freddie waited for Lucas to emerge from the car. The second he got out, Freddie cuffed him.

"Are you hit?" Freddie cried as Vernon and Jimmy joined them, guns drawn.

"Glancing blow." When she tried to get up, the world spun around her, so she sat.

Freddie called for backup and a bus and then put pressure on the wound that had her howling in pain.

"Son of a bitch," she hissed through clenched teeth. "Cut that out!"

"No, you're bleeding like crazy."

He pushed even harder on the wound, and she passed out.

AN HOUR before he was due to formally announce his new vice presidential nominee, Nick conducted a press scrum in the Oval Office. They surrounded his desk with lights, boom microphones, cameras and a relentless onslaught of questions covering everything from the shooting in Des Moines and his call for common sense gun control to former secretary Ruskin's accusations of incompetence, the situation in the Gulf of Suez, Nick's youthful inexperience, his choice of a vice president, his wife's career, the custody case that Cleo's parents had made public before the gag order was issued and so on.

By the time Terry and Trevor finally cleared the room, Nick was tapped out.

"Can you remind me again why people want this job so badly?" he asked Terry when they were alone.

"They want the power of it, but if they knew what it was really like, they'd probably run for their lives."

"No kidding. I need a drink after that."

"We can arrange for one."

"Nah, I'd better wait until the next press event is over. Once I start, I might never stop."

"Can't say I blame you, but you're doing great so far. Your approval rating is holding right around fifty percent, which is damned good in this polarized climate."

The thought that half the people polled didn't approve of him was daunting, though. "Lots of room for improvement."

"We're seeing many comments on the POTUS social media accounts about how it's high time for some young blood and new ideas in the White House. For every person that doesn't approve of you being the youngest president in history, ten more think you're just what we need."

"I guess that's something," Nick said, certain his upcoming thirty-eighth birthday wasn't going to do him any favors, as it would remind people once again just how young he was, although he could feel the job aging him at a rapid clip. He wondered if his hair would turn gray or white while he was in office like it had for so many previous presidents. Cheery thoughts.

"It's a good place to start," Terry said of his approval rating. "Dr. Flynn is here and was wondering if he could have a minute."

"Of course. Ask him to come in."

"I'll be back to get you for the ceremony."

Nick checked his watch, saw it was edging closer to six and wondered if Sam would get there in time. Or if she'd even remembered she was supposed to come. He wouldn't be surprised if she'd forgotten, so he sent her a quick text to remind her the press event to announce Gretchen was at six thirty.

Harry came into the office as Nick's lead Secret Service agent, John Brantley Jr., appeared in the door, signaling that he needed a minute.

"Just one second, Harry," Nick said as he went to confer with Brant.

"Vernon has let us know that Lieutenant Holland sustained a wound to her arm in a shooting," Brant said. "She's being taken to GW Trauma, but the wound is not considered life threatening."

Nick heard the words coming from Brant, and he understood what the agent was saying, but hearing that she'd had another near miss was like a shot to Nick's heart. *The wound is not considered life threatening...* But a few inches to the left or right, and it'd be a whole other story.

"Mr. President?"

Nick focused on Brant.

"Is there anything we can do for you, sir?"

"No, thank you. If you hear any more, please let me know."

"Yes, sir."

Nick turned to walk back into the Oval Office on legs that felt oddly rubbery, the way they did anytime he was reminded of how dangerous her work could be.

"Everything all right?" Harry asked.

"Apparently not." He told his friend what'd happened to Sam. "I'd go there, but I've got to be here for Gretchen Henderson's nomination announcement." Every part of him wanted to go to Sam, and he hated that he couldn't. "Let me check in with Freddie and see how she is."

"Do whatever you need to."

Nick used the secure BlackBerry they'd given him for personal use to make the call to Freddie. Thankfully, Freddie answered the call from an unavailable number.

"Detective Cruz."

"It's Nick. How is she?"

"She's okay. We just got to GW, and Dr. Anderson is with her now."

Nick felt better knowing her doctor friend was caring for her. "Will you text me when you hear an update?"

"I will, and I'll make sure she gets home when they let her out of here."

"Thanks, Freddie."

"No problem."

Nick ended the call and passed the info along to Harry. "She got lucky. Again. I have nightmares wondering when her luck will run out."

"She's okay, Nick." He appreciated that Harry dropped all the formality at a moment like this. "I know it's got to be so hard to hear that she's hurt, but she's okay."

"This time." Nick made an effort to shake off the sick feeling that always came with hearing she'd been hurt on the job. "Anyway, what's up with you?"

"It's nothing that won't keep."

"I'm fine, Harry. Really. What's on your mind?"

"I was going to ask if I might borrow a corner of your White House for some personal business on Christmas Eve."

"Do tell."

"I'm going to propose to Lilia, and I thought it might be fun to do it here."

"That's fantastic news, and my house is your house. Whatever you want to do is fine with me."

"Thank you. I appreciate that."

Nick extended a hand to his close friend. "Congratulations, pal. She's amazing and perfect for you."

"She really is. I waited a long time for her, and she's made that long wait so worth it."

"When it's right, it's right."

"Exactly. You'll be my best man, right?"

"I'd be honored."

"My mom will flip her lid about me having the president as my best man," Harry said, grinning.

"She's known me for years," Nick replied. "Nothing to flip her lid about."

"You really don't see it, do you?"

"See what?"

"How exciting it is for the rest of us to see you here," Harry said, gesturing to the iconic office. "My mom has known you for years as my friend, but not as her president. That's a whole other level."

"It's just still so weird, you know?"

"I do, and the way it happened makes it harder to wrap your head around it, but you're doing great. People are excited about your presidency."

"Not everyone."

"Pish," Harry said, "as my grandmother would say. Focus on the positive and ignore the detractors. They're going to be there no matter what you do. Don't give them any mental energy."

"That's easier said than done, but I'm trying to follow that plan. I can only do what I can do and hope for the best, right?"

"Exactly. You're giving the job your best effort, and that's all anyone can ask, even if it's not enough for some people."

Terry returned a few minutes later to tell Nick it was time to go to the East Room for the announcement about Gretchen Henderson.

"Since it looks like my date is going to stand me up," Nick said to Harry, "will you join me?"

"I'd love to."

# CHAPTER TWENTY-SEVEN

S am was confused about where she was and what had happened until a searing pain in her left arm brought it all back. Lucas Tappen had shot her after he'd murdered Mark Ouellette to keep up his end of the bargain with Grace Ouellette. Teenagers committing murder over an affair between their parents. Just when she thought she'd seen everything...

"Be still," Dr. Anderson said as he did something to her arm, which was strangely numb other than a tugging sensation.

"How bad is it?"

"A pretty nasty flesh wound, but you're going to survive. We're cleaning and suturing."

Sam glanced at the clock on the wall and saw that it was ten after six.

Six... She was supposed to be somewhere at six... Oh shit, fuck, damn, hell, the vice president thing. "I have to go." She tried to sit up, but was put right back in her place by a nurse.

"Please don't move. The doctor is suturing your arm."

"Hurry up, Doc. I have to go to the announcement of the new VP. I promised Nick I'd be there."

"You're not going anywhere for a while, Sam. You lost a lot of blood. We need to keep an eye on you for the next couple of hours."

"Oh, come on! It's a flesh wound."

"That resulted in significant blood loss. You need to take it easy and let us monitor your vitals until we're sure it's safe to release you."

Resigned to doing as she was told, Sam asked for Freddie.

"He's in the waiting room."

"Can you get him? I need to talk to him. It's urgent."

"If you promise not to move, I'll send someone to get him," Anderson said.

"I won't move."

He nodded to one of the nurses, and she left to get Freddie.

"Do you have a first name?" Sam asked the doctor.

He huffed out a laugh. "I do."

"What is it?"

"Rob."

"Huh. I didn't picture you as a Rob. I thought more like Melvin or Myron. Or maybe Warren."

"Gee, thanks," he said, chuckling. "If you don't watch out, I might slip and poke you with my needle in a spot that's not numbed up."

"Don't do that. I hate needles."

"I know. So quit making fun of your favorite doctor."

"Who said you're my favorite doctor?"

"I have to be the one you see most often."

"You think you're so funny."

"I am funny, and don't worry, I already punched your frequent-flier card and gave you an extra punch for the holidays."

She was surrounded by comedic wannabes. "Is this going to hurt later?"

"Like a bitch, which is why you're going to take the painkillers I'm going to prescribe and take it easy for a few days."

"I'm on vacation after tomorrow."

"*Including* tomorrow."

"Is she behaving?" Freddie asked when he came into the room.

"As well as she ever does," Anderson replied.

The two of them shared a laugh at her expense.

"If you two are done, Freddie, I need the BlackBerry. Can you find it for me?"

"Sure." He located her blood-soaked coat, tossed over a chair, and retrieved the BlackBerry from her pocket. "Here you go."

"Thanks." Since her left arm was completely immobilized, she said, "I need you to call Nick for me. The number is star six nine."

Both men and the nurse cracked up laughing.

"That's his warped sense of humor," Sam said. "Please don't tell anyone about that, or it'll be all over the news."

"Our lips are sealed," Anderson said.

Freddie dialed the number and handed her the phone.

Sam wasn't surprised when the call went through to voice mail. "I'm so sorry about missing the thing with Henderson," she said. "I got myself into a bit of a jam at work, which I'm sure you've already heard about from my babysitters. I'm totally fine, and I'll be home as soon as I can. I hope it went well, and I'm really, really sorry I missed it." She handed the phone back to Freddie. "Can you push the button to end the call?"

"All set."

"That right there is why I'll never leave my flip. You close it, and you're done."

"Shall we list all the things you *can't* do on a flip phone?" Freddie asked.

"No, we shall not. What's happening with Lucas, and what're you hearing from Gonzo at the Ouellette office?"

"Lucas is at HQ being processed on multiple charges. Gonzo is at the scene at Mark's office and waiting for the ME. The rest of the staff had already left for the day, so there were no witnesses, but Gonzo says there're security cameras. He's working on getting a warrant."

"Okay, good," she said, relieved. "That's good."

"See?" Anderson said without looking up from what he was doing to her arm. "They *can* function without you."

"But we'd rather not," Freddie said with a smile for her.


SAM SPENT three hours steaming in a hospital bed before Anderson signed the discharge papers with orders for her to rest and relax for the next few days so she wouldn't risk reopening the wound.

"Take me to HQ," Sam ordered Freddie when they were in her car with him at the wheel.

"The only place I'm taking you is home."

"I gave you a direct order!"

"Which I'm defying. You heard what the doc said. If you

reopen that wound, you're going to be right back in the hospital again. You're going home."

"I'm going to write you up for this."

"Knock yourself out. Oh wait, you already did that today."

"You think you're so funny, but I'm not kidding. I want to check in at work before I go home."

He drove toward Pennsylvania Avenue. "I'll check in at work and report back to you."

"I mean it when I say you're going to take a rap for this."

"Okay."

"At what point did you stop being afraid of me as your boss?"

"Um, like, the first day?"

"That is not true! You were afraid of me for a long time after that."

"Nope."

"Yes!"

"Not even kinda."

While she fumed at his insubordination, he drove up to the White House security gate.

"I've got the first lady," he said, showing his badge and ID as required by the Secret Service.

The agent working the gate bent to make sure Sam was actually in the car before waving them through.

Freddie drove up to the entrance and put the car in park before getting out to come around to help her.

"I don't need help. My arm is injured, not my legs."

"You got *shot*, Sam. Do what any sane person would do after getting shot and take a minute to recover."

"I guess I'm not sane, then, because I don't want to sit around and recover when I could be *at work* recovering."

"Have a nice evening," he said as he walked back to her car.

"I'm going to report that car stolen."

Laughing, he said, "You do that."

"I want half-hour updates on what's happening."

"You got it."

The insubordinate ass drove off in her car with a toot and a jaunty wave. She'd make him pay for this, she thought as she went inside, was greeted by the doorman and headed up to the residence, determined to enjoy the evening with her family if she wasn't allowed to be at work. And since when did a detective decide what a lieutenant was allowed to do?

Her cranky mood disappeared when she arrived in the residence to find Aubrey and Alden having a race in the hallway that was being timed by Scotty and Skippy the dog, who was running between Scotty and the twins like the wild child she was. Only Scotty could see Sam, so she held up a finger to tell him to wait a minute before outing her presence to the twins. In the meantime, she removed her coat and hung it just so over her shoulder so the kids wouldn't see the blood.

"Alden wins this one," Scotty declared. "Best two out of three."

"What does that mean?" Aubrey asked.

"You won one, and Alden won one. So now we do it one more time to see who wins. Best two out of three."

The little girl's wrinkled nose indicated that she still wasn't sure she understood the term, but she was ready to race again.

"On your mark," Scotty said. "Get set. Go!"

The twins ran their hearts out, with Aubrey beating Alden by an inch.

Sam stepped into view, and they both ran back to hug her as Skippy came for her like a heat-seeking missile. "Go easy. I hurt my arm." She bent to give the dog a pat on the head and a scratch behind her soft, silky ears.

"How did you hurt your arm?" Aubrey asked.

"I bumped it," she said, not wanting them to know she'd been shot.

"Does it hurt?" Alden asked.

"Not yet, but it's going to later when the medicine they gave me wears off. Did you guys already eat?"

"Not yet," Celia said when she joined them. "We were waiting to see if you guys got home in time to eat with them."

"Is Nick here?"

"He got home ten minutes ago and is grabbing a quick shower. The chef prepared barbecue for dinner."

"Oh, that sounds good."

Shelby came down the stairs from the third floor nursery, carrying Noah. "Hi there," she said as the twins ran to greet her and Noah with hugs. "Did everyone have a wonderful day?"

"Everyone but Mom," Scotty said as he accepted a one-armed hug from Shelby. "She hurt her arm."

"Are you okay?" Shelby asked.

"I'm fine. Can you stay for dinner?"

"We'd love to. Avery has a meeting tonight, so we're on our own."

"It's barbecue," Scotty said.

"Yum. We're here for that."

"Let me just get changed," Sam said. "We'll find you in a minute." She gave Scotty a kiss on the forehead before proceeding through their living room, where the white lights on their personal Christmas tree twinkled, into the bedroom where Nick was just coming out of the shower with a towel around his hips. "I'm so sorry I missed the Henderson thing."

"How's your arm?"

"It's fine right now. I hear it'll hurt like a bitch when the numbness wears off."

Nick winced at the sight of her blood-soaked blouse. "Another close call."

"He got off a lucky shot."

Nick kissed her cheek and then her lips. "Too close for comfort."

"I'm fine. I swear. Did it go okay with Henderson?"

"All good."

"Did you apologize to her for me?"

"I told her you were detained at work but sent your regards. She said she looks forward to getting to know you."

"Thanks for covering for me. I really wanted to be there."

"I know you did. It's no big deal."

"This is going to happen sometimes. You're going to need me for some first lady thing, and the cop thing is going to get in the way."

"I'm well aware of that, and I don't want you to worry about it. You'll do what you can, and I'll understand when you can't make something."

"As long as you know I'd always rather be wherever you and the kids are than anywhere else."

"That's what matters, babe." He gently wrapped his arms around her and held on for a long moment, seeming to need the reassurance that she was really all right. "Let's not worry about the shit we can't control."

"I hear there's barbecue for dinner," she said.

"I'm starving."

"Me, too. Let me grab a shower, and I'll find you guys in the dining room."

"You need help?"

"Nah, I've got it."

Nick released her, seeming reluctant to let her go. "Did you get the guy?"

"We got them all. Two homicide cases locked and loaded today. All in all, a very good day that's better now that I'm home. Oh, and I'm supposed to be on R&R tomorrow, so bonus Thursday off, although I'll have to call in to work and do some paperwork and stuff."

"So we'll both be working from home. Maybe we can sneak some alone time into the schedule."

"I'm here for that," she said, borrowing Shelby's term.

"Me, too." He kissed her again. "Take your shower."

"I'll be quick."

Dinner was in full swing by the time Sam joined her family in the dining room. The smell of the barbecue made her mouth water as she took in the chatter of kids and adults. "How is it?"

"*So good,*" Scotty said around a mouthful.

"The best," Nick added.

Both the twins and Noah had smears of sauce on their faces that only added to their over-the-top cuteness.

As Sam took a seat next to Celia and across from Shelby, she experienced a feeling of profound happiness that caught her by surprise. She wouldn't have expected to feel this kind of happiness with the first Christmas without Skip looming. But with her family gathered around the dinner table like it was any other night in any house in America, Sam was happy.

Nick had been right when he said it didn't matter where they lived. As long as they were together, they were home. Even if home was the most famous house in the world.

# CHAPTER TWENTY-EIGHT

The next morning after she saw the kids off to school, Sam called in to work for the shift-change meeting at eight o'clock. "Update me, people."

"How's your arm?" Freddie asked.

"It's fine." The numbness had worn off in the middle of the night, and it hurt like seven angry bitches, but she wasn't admitting that to anyone. "Talk to me."

"Bob Tappen made almost as big of a scene as Josie Ouellette did after he heard Lucas had been arrested," Gonzo said. "We showed him the video of Lucas entering Mark's office and shooting him. The poor guy completely lost it when he saw that. We had to call the paramedics to tend to him."

"I feel for him," Sam said. "His family has been nearly destroyed in the span of a week."

"We've presented the cases against Grace and Lucas to Charity, and she's proceeding with charges against both of them. Lucas will be charged as an adult."

Sam felt sick at the waste of two promising young lives. "Did they honestly think they wouldn't get caught?"

"I suspect that's exactly what they thought," Green said. "It never occurred to either of them that anyone would think they did this."

"Hell, I didn't think they had done this," Sam said. "I wish it had occurred to me sooner so we could've saved Mark."

"We got there as fast as we could after we realized he was a target," Freddie said. "And not for nothing, he flat-out lied to us at the beginning when we asked him if anyone else knew about the affair. Grace had already confronted them about it and made her threats. If he'd told us that she and Aidan knew, we could've talked to them and maybe figured this out sooner."

"That's true," Sam said. "Did someone brief the media?"

"Gonzo did it, and he did a great job," Jeannie said.

"Aw, shucks," Gonzo said.

"Did they ask about the lawsuit against Thorn?" Sam asked.

"They did," Gonzo said, "and I was able to deflect the attention away from that and right onto Tiffany, where it belongs."

"Thanks for that. Well, since Gonzo and the rest of you have everything well in hand, I'm officially on vacation from job number one. Try not to eff anything up while I'm gone."

"We'll try not to," Gonzo said, chuckling.

"I'll see you all on Christmas Eve?"

"We can't wait," Jeannie said. "Good luck tomorrow in Des Moines. We'll be thinking of you both."

"Thanks. Good work on both cases, everyone. I was hoping to have the chance to say this in person, but I want to thank you all for the great work this year. We've had a rough year losing our beloved Detective Arnold, and I'm proud of the way we've come together to continue the work, despite our heartbreak. Cameron and Matt, we appreciate the contributions you've made since you joined our squad. Cam, it wasn't easy for you to come in and replace someone who was irreplaceable to the rest of us, but you've done an admirable job of making it work."

"Thank you, Lieutenant. It's an honor to work with you guys."

"We lost my dad, and we solved his case and a bunch of others. Detective Tyrone decided to leave us. Freddie, Jeannie and Gonzo got married. A few things changed in my personal life..."

The others laughed at her understatement.

"Through it all, we kept our eye on the ball, and we got the job done. I'll always be proud of us for surviving this year. Homicide is a tough, often thankless job, and I'm glad I get to do it with all of you."

"Likewise, LT," Jeannie said. "If I may add, we're so proud of the way you handled the outcome of your dad's case and how you didn't let it break you or ruin your love of the job. None of us would've blamed you if it had. And we're also proud to have the country's first lady leading us and to be able to say our wonderful new first couple are our friends."

The round of applause Jeannie started embarrassed Sam. "Thanks, Jeannie. You guys make me look good every day. I'm looking forward to celebrating with you all on Christmas Eve. I'll see you then, if not before."

"We'll be there," Freddie said for all of them.

AFTER A DELICIOUS LUNCH of tomato soup and a salad that was delivered by Roland, one of the butlers, Sam was on her laptop, reviewing the reports on the arrests of Grace and Lucas, when Nick walked into the bedroom. Upon kicking the door closed, he removed his suit coat, dropped it on the floor, pulled off his tie, unbuttoned his shirt and T-shirt, tossing them into the pile on the floor, revealing the sculpted chest and abs that made her mouth water.

"Is there any charge for this presidential striptease?" Sam asked without looking up from what she was doing, although she watched everything *he* was doing with keen interest.

"It's free to you," he said as he unbuckled his belt and dropped his pants.

"Do others have to pay?"

"I only perform this act for you." With his hands on his naked hips, he whistled a stripper tune as he bumped and grinded that had her cracking up laughing and closing her laptop as he approached the bed with all his considerable assets on full display. "My wife is working from home today, so I had to take full advantage of living above the store."

"If the media could see you now..."

"Thank God they can't. Now, I'd like to remind you that my birthday is coming up, so if you want to get a jump on birthday-level services, I'm *up* for that." To emphasize his point, he did an added little jig that made his hard cock slap against his stomach.

"I had no idea you had a stripper living in there."

"I like to think I can still surprise you."

Sam held out the hand of her good arm for him. "You definitely surprised me with the Magic Mike routine."

He took her hand and brought it to his lips. "Thought you might like that."

"How long do we have?"

"Ninety beautiful minutes."

"Did you lock the door?"

"As Scotty would say, *duh*. How does your arm feel?"

"Not bad as long as I stay on top of the pain meds."

"May I help you out of your clothes?"

"Yes, please." Sam sat up so he could gently remove the oversized T-shirt of his that she'd worn to bed the night before. Before he'd left to go downstairs to the office, he'd changed the dressing on her wound and treated it with the antibiotic ointment she'd been prescribed.

"You sure you're feeling up to some naked fun?" he asked as he traced his index finger over her collarbone.

"As long as it's not too athletic."

"Slow and sultry it is." He moved her laptop to the bedside table, eased her back and leaned over her, propped up on muscular arms. "I'm so glad you're still here with me."

"Where else would I be?"

Nick planted a kiss on her chest. "A few inches to the left and..."

"Shhh. Don't go there. I'm fine."

He propped his forehead on her chest for a long moment while she ran her fingers through his hair. "You can't let anything happen to my Samantha. I'd die without her."

"She's going to be around to drive you crazy for many more decades."

"I'm counting on that." As he kissed a path from her chest to her neck and then her lips, her entire body felt electrified.

She wrapped her good arm around him and held on tight as he kissed her with sweet tenderness.

He kept up the tender theme as he moved down to her breasts and belly, kissing every part of her with soft lips that skimmed over her sensitized skin. Usually, he dragged out the torture during the slow and sultry program, but he took mercy on her today and slid into her slowly and carefully so he wouldn't jostle her sore arm.

"Tell me if anything hurts."

"Nothing hurts, but I do have this particular ache. Why don't you see if you can find it?"

Laughing, he said, "I'll see what I can do, but you don't mind if

I take my time, do you? After all, I have..." He stopped moving to check his watch. "Seventy-eight minutes left."

"I don't mind if you take your time." She was thrilled to be on vacation from work, to have this stolen time with him in the middle of the day, to share this life and this love with him. If he wanted to take his time, she was going to let him, because for once, she had all the time in the world to give him.

NICK HELD her close to him as their bodies cooled and calmed after slow and sultry resulted in epic orgasms for both of them. He couldn't recall being this relaxed since he took the oath of office. His days were frantic and busy and stressful with decisions that impacted the lives of so many people coming at him one after another, but he had put all that aside to enjoy this stolen interlude with his beloved in the middle of a workday.

He needed the connection after she'd been injured yet again on the job. She rolled with each disaster, but every one of them shaved years off his life as he pondered what *could've* happened.

"I've got a secret," he said after a long period of contented silence.

"Do tell."

"How bad do you want to know?"

"*Bad.*"

His Samantha was impatient, impertinent, nosy, mouthy and perfectly imperfect. He wouldn't have her any other way. "Harry asked if we'd mind if he proposes to Lilia at some point on Christmas Eve."

"Oh my God! That's huge! I can't believe you waited this long to tell me!"

"You conked out early last night."

"You should've woken me up for this."

"Not when you needed the rest."

"We need to get her people here and surprise her with them after the engagement. I'll coordinate it with Harry."

"That's a good idea."

"Everyone wants the Lincoln Bedroom."

"I know. How are we going to decide who gets it?"

"I've got a plan."

"I can't wait to hear all about it.

. . .

THE NEXT MORNING, they departed from the White House on *Marine One*, which transported them to Joint Base Andrews, where *Air Force One* waited on the tarmac for their arrival. Nick had requested minimal press coverage of their trip to Des Moines and had only five reporters and one cameraman making the trip, along with Terry, Derek and Harry, who, as Nick's personal physician, went anywhere he did.

Also along for the ride was Gretchen Henderson, who was taking her first trip as the vice presidential nominee.

She was already on board when Sam and Nick arrived, and Nick once again introduced the two women.

"It's lovely to see you again," Gretchen said to Sam, who shook her hand.

Sam was determined to give her a chance, even if she had the same inexplicably negative reaction to her that she'd had the first time they met. Why? She couldn't say, but she'd be keeping an eye on the woman going forward. "Likewise. Congratulations on your nomination. I'm sorry I was unable to be there the other night."

"No problem at all. I understand you were detained at work."

Was *detained* another word for *shot*? "Yes, I was."

"I so admire what you're doing as a first lady with a job outside of the White House. It sets such a lovely example for women and girls everywhere."

"Thank you, but I'm not trying to be any kind of example. I'm just doing what I do."

"It means a lot to women."

Before Sam could reply, they were asked to take their seats for takeoff, after which they were provided with a delicious hot breakfast consisting of eggs, bacon, potatoes and Danishes as well as coffee. Nick was in his onboard office for his morning security briefing. When that was completed, Gretchen was invited to join him and his team for a policy meeting.

Sam tried not to seethe as the stunning woman got up to join Sam's sexy husband and his aides in a closed-door meeting. "You're being a fool," she muttered to herself.

"Did you say something?" Lilia asked from across the aisle, where she was seated with Andrea, Sam's current communications director.

"Nope." Sam couldn't very well admit to being enraged by the idea of her gorgeous husband working hand in hand with a woman who looked like Gretchen Henderson. Not that she had a single reason to be jealous. She knew she didn't. It wasn't that. It was that Gretchen put her on edge for reasons she couldn't explain, and that made her uncomfortable. "Thanks for coming today, ladies."

"We wanted to be here to support you both," Lilia said.

"This will be your last trip, Andrea," Sam said, trying to make conversation to keep her mind from wandering to places it had no business going. It wasn't like they were alone in there or anything, and even if they were, that wouldn't matter. If there was one thing in her life Sam was completely sure of it was that her husband would never want anyone but her. Her angst where Gretchen was concerned wasn't romantic in nature. That she even had angst about a woman she'd spent all of an hour with was maddening, but her gut had guided her well throughout her life, and she'd learned to trust it.

She realized Andrea had been telling her about her upcoming wedding and the plan to move to Boston with her new husband, who had taken a job at a think tank associated with MIT.

"It sounds like an exciting new adventure," Sam said. "Congratulations to both of you."

"Thank you so much. We're looking forward to it, but I'm afraid that no future adventure will surpass the adventure of working at the White House."

"We've received a request for you to keynote a conference on learning challenges next summer," Lilia said to Sam. "Is that something that might interest you?"

"Potentially." Although speaking to large groups would never come naturally to her, after dealing with dyslexia her entire life, Sam wanted to use her platform to shed light on that and other issues of concern to her. "Send me the details."

"Already in your FLOTUS email."

"Which I need to check at some point."

"I keep an eye on it," Lilia said. "Don't worry."

"Thank goodness for you."

An hour later, Nick emerged from the office, having shed his suit coat and rolled up his sleeves. He gestured for Sam to join him.

"Excuse me, ladies." As she got up to walk toward him, the plane hit a bump that made her stumble.

He was right there to take her elbow and guide her into their personal cabin.

"Have I mentioned that I hate flying, even on *Air Force One*?" she asked him after he'd closed the door.

"I seem to recall hearing that once or twice before." He took her hand and led her to an easy chair, where he sat, bringing her down on his lap. "Are you feeling okay?"

"My arm still hurts, but not like it did yesterday. My stomach aches thinking about where we're going and why."

"I know. Mine, too, but I have a bit of good news."

"What's that?"

"A judge has agreed to hear an emergency request for relief in the custody matter on Monday."

"What does that mean? An emergency request for relief?"

"Andy has asked them to dismiss the case in light of the airtight custody clause in Cleo and Jameson's will. Their estate attorney is willing to testify that they never considered anyone but Elijah to be the twins' legal guardian, and as such, he has the right to set up any arrangement for them that he sees fit, provided they're in a safe and stable home."

"Our home is stable, but the argument could be made that it's not safe."

"It's safer than any home that doesn't have round-the-clock Secret Service protection. Andy really believes it's going to be fine."

"I won't breathe easily until it goes away entirely."

"Me either," he said with a sigh that revealed his true feelings on the matter.

"Are we going to be able to get their financial situation into it somehow? You know this is all about the billions that come with those two angels."

"Andy's working that angle."

Sam rested her head on his shoulder. "How will we ever get through the weekend with this hanging over our heads?"

"We'll focus on the kids and getting ready for Christmas, and it'll be Monday before we know it."

"I hope so."

"We have to believe that the wishes of their parents will take primary precedence," Nick said.

Before Sam could reply to that, the pilot announced their initial approach into Des Moines, and just that quickly, her stomach began to ache even harder. She wished she hadn't eaten so much for breakfast. "Stay close to me down there, will you, please?"

"You got it, babe."

# CHAPTER TWENTY-NINE

S am had spent her entire adult life working with victims of violent crime, but nothing could've prepared her to meet with the grieving families of those killed in Des Moines. The children who died had ranged in age from six months to ten years, and the adults were twenty to eighty. They'd included parents, grandparents and volunteers who'd left their homes that morning to help bring the magic of Christmas to local schoolchildren and their younger siblings.

In an elementary school gymnasium, they hugged devastated parents and siblings, listened to them talk about the children they'd lost and offered all the compassion and empathy they possibly could, knowing it would never be enough to soothe shattered hearts.

"Thank you so much for coming," a tearful mother named Cath said. She'd lost her six-year-old daughter and four-year-old son. "The kids were so excited for Christmas. What are we supposed to do now?" She looked at Sam for answers she simply didn't have.

"What were their names?" Sam asked, dabbing at tears that refused to quit. She'd stopped trying to contain them when it quickly became clear that nothing could stop them.

"Julia and Mason," Cath said. "Julia was in first grade and Mason in preschool. He was so excited to come to Sissy's school to meet Santa."

"Do you have pictures?" she asked, even though she'd seen pictures of all the victims.

Cath produced photos of her blond, blue-eyed children.

Sam studied them, wondering how their mother would possibly survive losing them. How did anyone survive such a thing? "They're beautiful."

"It makes me feel better to know they're together wherever they are now. They were inseparable when they were here."

Sam held the woman's hand. "I'm so, so sorry for your loss. I wish there was something else I could say."

"There isn't anything anyone can say. I just wish we lived in a country where things like this didn't happen."

"I wish that, too."

"I hope people won't forget about what happened here. I hope something will change."

The other family members echoed that comment over and over, and by the time they were back on the plane, heading home after three excruciating hours on the ground, Nick was on fire with determination to try to do *something, anything* to make it stop. "After the holidays, we're going to give this issue some time and attention," he said. "We're going to try to do something. I don't want to ever again have to do what we did today."

While Sam wholeheartedly supported his desire to fix an issue that had vexed previous administrations and Congresses, she understood better than most how difficult that challenge would be. But if anyone was up for it, Nick was, especially if he stuck to his determination not to run in the next election. Having nothing to lose might make him the perfect president to find a way to bring about real change on the emotionally charged issue.

During the flight, he asked her to go with him to speak briefly to the small group of media traveling with them.

Sam's inclination was to avoid the media, but she went with him because she sensed he needed the extra support after the grueling day.

The reporters in the back of the plane sat up straighter when they walked into their part of the cabin.

"I wanted to just say that Sam and I were deeply moved by the families we met today. Their grief is overwhelming, and our hearts are broken for them. Part of my job as president is to be the comforter-in-chief, and that's a role I willingly embrace, but at times like this, when it's something that shouldn't have happened, I'm also angry. I'm angry as a father, as a man, as a human being and as the president. I can't believe there isn't a way to find a path to common sense gun legislation that zeroes in on the people who simply shouldn't be in possession of a weapon that can do what was done in Des Moines. We face an uphill battle, but it's one I'm willing to undertake if it means Sam and I never again have to do what we did today. After the holidays, my administration will be addressing this issue on every possible front. While I'm well aware we may not succeed, doing nothing simply isn't an option. That's all I wanted to say."

They threw questions at him, and Nick answered every one with patience and thoughtfulness and the empathy that made her love him so fiercely. He spoke from his heart, and she had to believe that sincerity would connect with the American people when they saw the footage and read his comments.

*Marine One* landed on the White House lawn at just after five o'clock, which got them home in time to eat dinner with their own children, for whom they were ever more thankful after the dreadful day they'd spent with grieving families.

"Was it awful?" Scotty asked after they'd had dinner as a family, watched a movie with the twins and gotten them off to bed with four stories.

Skippy was curled up in Scotty's lap as he petted her.

"Yeah, it was," Nick said. "I'm glad we decided it would be better for you to sit this one out."

"I wouldn't know what to say to people after something like that," Scotty said.

"All you can do is listen and let them know you care," Sam said. "That's what we tried to do."

"I'm sure it meant a lot to them that you went there," Scotty said.

"We hope so," Nick said.

"I saw what you said on the plane," Scotty said. "You're trending on Twitter. People are tired of this crap. They want something done about it."

"Not everyone would agree," Nick said, "but I'm determined to put together the best possible group to home in on mental health considerations, criminal background checks and other sensible things that can be done. I want responsible gun owners to be able to carry on with no interference. They aren't the ones we're concerned about."

"I think as long as you keep saying that, you may actually get somewhere," Scotty said.

They spent the weekend with the kids and Elijah, who returned home from Princeton for a monthlong break from college. On Saturday morning, they had Sam's nieces and nephews as well as Shelby and Noah to the White House to decorate ornaments and make Christmas cookies. Having a pastry chef on staff came in handy when Florence taught the kids how to apply fondant and decorations that made their cookies into works of art.

Sunday afternoon, they entertained the families of the White House staff and then played multiple competitive games in the bowling alley with the kids before settling in to watch *Elf* together in the theater.

By Monday morning, Sam felt rested and ready to do battle to keep the Littles with them where they belonged.

Celia stayed with the kids while Sam, Nick and Elijah went to court. A custody battle that involved the president and first lady of the United States was bound to draw some attention, but they weren't prepared for the massive media presence outside the courthouse.

Apparently, the Secret Service had expected it. They got the three of them inside and delivered to the appropriate courtroom with a minimal amount of fuss.

"Sometimes, having Secret Service protection doesn't suck," Sam said to Nick when they were inside the courtroom, where Andy and two of his associates greeted them with handshakes.

"No matter what happens, just stay calm and remember the law is on our side," Andy said before Sam, Nick and Elijah took a seat in the front row behind their attorneys.

The courtroom was soon called to order with the judge hearing from the attorneys on both sides, each making a case for why the Armstrong twins would be better off with their clients.

"The Cappuano family has provided a loving home for the children since the night of their parents' murder. Their older brother, Elijah, who was appointed by his father and stepmother to be the twins' guardian in the event of their deaths, is in daily contact with the twins and their custodial guardians. In addition, due to their proximity to President and Mrs. Cappuano, the twins are afforded world-class security through the Secret Service. I'd go so far as to say that the twins are among the safest children in the world—and they're among the most loved.

"As a longtime friend of both President and Mrs. Cappuano, I can assure the court these are two people who've never been happier than since their son, Scotty, the twins and Elijah have come into their lives. It's important to note that prior to the apprehension of their parents' killer, Mrs. Cappuano, in her capacity as the lieutenant of the MPD Homicide division, had contact with Mrs. Dennis as well as her daughter, Monique Lawson.

"During the course of their conversations, neither the twins' grandmother nor their aunt asked about them or how they were coping after losing their parents in a violent home invasion that Alden Armstrong witnessed in part. They didn't ask where they were or who was caring for them. They only expressed interest in the twins after their parents' killers had been arrested. We've furnished the court with financial records that indicate that Mr. and Mrs. Dennis are deeply in debt and on the verge of losing their business due to a lawsuit that isn't expected to go their way. In addition, Monique Lawson and her husband declared bankruptcy last year. We find the timing of this petition interesting, since it's no secret that the Armstrong twins and their brother came into an immense fortune upon the deaths of their parents. We ask the court to honor the provisions of the Armstrongs' will and to keep the twins where their brother wants them to be. His father and stepmother trusted him to do what was best for the children, and that's exactly what he has done by asking the Cappuanos to care for them while he's away at college. Thank you for your consideration of our request for an immediate dismissal of this matter."

The opposing attorney stood and cleared her throat. "My clients wholeheartedly object to Mr. Simone's implication that this case is about money. This case is about two young children who need their *family* more than ever after the tragic loss of their parents. This case is about two children who don't need to be thrust into the relentless glare of the public eye at this tender time in their lives. My clients were concerned enough when President and Mrs. Cappuano were the vice president and second lady. But recent events have significantly altered the equation. The thought of their grandchildren living in the White House, surrounded by Secret Service, isn't at all what these loving grandparents want for Alden and Aubrey. We can't believe it's what their parents would've wanted either. We ask the judge to award emergency custody to my clients so the twins may recover from their heartbreaking loss in the privacy and safety of their grandparents' home."

*Ugh*, Sam thought. *I hate how concerned they are* now. *Where was all that concern after their parents were* murdered?

After the attorney took her seat, the judge sifted through several papers on his desk, leaving them to twist in the wind, waiting to hear what he would say.

Nick took hold of Sam's hand, and she reached for Elijah's.

His tight grip indicated his current stress level.

"I've reviewed the supporting documentation submitted by both sides, including the financial reports for both the Dennises and Lawsons that indicate significant financial concerns that do make me question the timing of this petition. Mr. President, Mrs. Cappuano, Mr. Armstrong, let me be clear. Under any other circumstances, my ruling today would be clear cut in favor of Mr. Armstrong continuing as the twins' guardian, which is what his father and stepmother clearly wanted. I'm also aware of the threatening email Mrs. Lawson sent to Mr. Armstrong, and I want to express my outrage at such tactics. That alone would be enough to deny your petition under normal circumstances."

Sam's heart sank, and her palms began to sweat at his use of the words *normal circumstances*. He wasn't going to give custody to those wretched people, was he? He couldn't. She began to feel as if she might vomit at the thought of such a thing.

"However, with the Cappuano family's move to the White House to take into consideration, I want more information. I've assigned a social worker to do a visit with the twins tomorrow, as I understand the urgent desire to get this settled before the holidays, which is my intent. Because she's already familiar with the children, Ms. Dolores Finklestein from Child and Family Services will be at the White House at ten o'clock tomorrow morning to conduct her visit. Once I receive her report, I'll issue my decision."

He banged the gavel to signal their business before him was completed.

Sam's heart lifted somewhat at hearing Ms. Finklestein had

been assigned to the case, as the woman had worked with them when the twins first came to live with them.

"I can't believe this," Eli whispered, sounding as if he was on the verge of tears.

"I think it's going to be okay," Nick said. "We know Ms. Finklestein, and she's already agreed once that the twins are well cared for with us."

"Still... How are we supposed to breathe until this is over?"

That's when Sam realized she had somewhere else to be the next morning. "Gonzo is testifying tomorrow morning. I have to be there."

"Uh, I hate to say it, babe, but I don't think we can risk you not being there to assure Picklestein"—as Nick had called her—"that the twins are in good hands with us. I'm texting Terry to clear my schedule for the morning."

Sam knew he was right, but she had to be there to support Gonzo when he testified against the man who'd killed his partner. Maybe she could start with Picklestein and leave her with Nick and Elijah to finish up.

When they were back in the car to return to the White House, she texted Gonzo to tell him about what'd happened in court.

*Do what you need to for the kids. I'll be okay.*

*I'll get there the second I can and will be sending you all the love and support in the whole world.*

*Thanks. I appreciate it. I feel ready to do what needs to be done for Arnold. Christina will be there. Arnold's parents and sisters, too, along with the rest of the squad, Farnsworth and Malone. Please don't worry about me. Do whatever it takes to keep those babies where they belong.*

*Will do. Hugs to you.*

Sam would do what needed to be done for her family at home, and then she'd join her work family to support Gonzo.

Ms. FINKLESTEIN WAS nothing if not prompt. She came into the White House at the stroke of ten a.m., appearing to have zero fucks to give—or so it seemed to Sam—for the house, the history, the Christmas decorations, the president, the first lady or anything other than Alden and Aubrey, who remembered her from their previous meeting. Sam feared her presence would trigger painful memories for them, but they seemed to roll with her without any sign of trauma, which was a relief.

The woman asked first to see their bedrooms and allowed the twins to tow her along the red-carpeted hallway to their rooms. While Sam, Nick and Eli hovered outside the door, she asked them about their school, their routine, what they thought of their new home and how they were liking living with Sam, Nick and Scotty.

"How's it going?" Scotty whispered when he and Skippy joined them. He'd put the puppy on a leash in deference to their visitor.

"So far so good."

"My stomach hurts," he said.

"Mine, too," Sam said, putting an arm around her son and kissing the top of his head.

"I like the pool the best," Alden said. "It's really fun to be able to swim, even though it's cold out."

"That must be fun."

"It is! I can dog-paddle, and Nick is teaching me to kick my feet. He swims with us every night after dinner. It's so much fun."

"What about you, Aubrey? What do you like best?"

"The theater. We can watch any movie we want and eat popcorn."

"How's school been going?" she asked.

"We're on bacation!" Aubrey announced. "We're going to..." She looked up at Sam in the doorway. "Where's that place again?"

Sam smiled at how adorable she was. "Camp David."

"We get to ride on a heliclopter," Alden said.

"That's very exciting. Does it ever bother you to have the agents with you when you go to school?"

Aubrey shook her head. "They always have a treat for us after school. They're our friends."

Sam hadn't heard that about the treats, and it made her appreciate the Secret Service agents even more.

"And you like living with Nick and Sam and Scotty?"

Alden nodded as Aubrey smiled. "We have lots of fun with them," she said, her smile dimming somewhat before she said, "But we miss Mommy and Daddy so much."

Sam's heart went out to the sweet little girl who was concerned about being disloyal to her late parents by expressing her happiness at living with her and Nick.

They took Ms. Finklestein to the third-floor conservatory that doubled as a family and play room and showed her the movie theater, the bowling alley, the pool and the playset on the South Lawn that Nick had gotten for them. As they moved through the White House, various members of the staff stopped to say hello to the first family.

"When can we bake more cookies?" Aubrey asked Florence.

"Whenever you want, Miss Aubrey. You come see me, and we'll bake up a storm."

"Can I?" Aubrey asked Sam.

"Sure, we can do that later."

"I'll look forward to it," Florence said. "Miss Aubrey is one of my very best assistants."

Aubrey beamed with pleasure at hearing that.

When they returned to the sitting room in the residence, Reginald came in with a tray of refreshments. They introduced him to Ms. Finklestein.

"Pleasure to meet you, ma'am. Mr. Alden, I included those chocolate snowmen you liked yesterday."

"Thank you so much," Alden said, smiling at the older man.

His smile had been slow to return after he'd witnessed some of the horror perpetrated on his parents, which was why they celebrated every one of them.

"Scotty," Ms. Finklestein said, "would you mind taking the twins to play for a bit while I talk to your parents and Elijah?"

"Sure," he said, casting a wary glance at Sam and Nick before he led the twins and Skippy out of the room.

"He's good with them," Ms. Finklestein said.

"He adores them," Sam said bluntly. "He considers himself their older brother and Elijah to be his older brother. They're the family Nick and I always hoped for but never dared to dream would happen for us. We may not be the most conventional parents, but I assure you we love those kids with every fiber of our beings. Our connection to them was instantaneous, and it's only grown in the months that they've lived with us."

"I can see they're happy and as well-adjusted as we could hope, considering their terrible loss. The judge's primary concern is the change in your circumstances since they first came to live with you."

"If I may address that," Elijah said haltingly. "Sam and Nick... They're the same people they were when they lived on Ninth

Street. None of the things that matter in this situation have changed. They spend time every day with the twins, and when they can't be with them, Mrs. Holland and Mrs. Hill are here with them, providing stability and care. They're part of a family here, and that family has been critical to my brother and sister's recovery from the loss of our parents. They didn't have a big extended family around them when my parents were alive. We'd had to leave all that when our dad was threatened by his ex-business partner. Here, they not only have Scotty, but they have aunts, uncles, cousins and close friends who are like family to them. Their recovery will take years, but I believe with all my heart that keeping them a part of *this* family will ensure they do eventually recover." He blinked back tears. "I understand that the arrangement I have with Sam and Nick might seem unconventional to outsiders, but it works for us—and most importantly, it works for Alden and Aubrey. I'm not sure if they'd survive another massive upheaval after what they've already endured." He cleared his throat. "That's all I wanted to say."

"If I could add," Nick said, taking hold of Sam's hand, "we love all three of these kids very much, and the six of us have become a family in the last couple of months. There's nothing Sam and I wouldn't do for any of them, including Eli."

"I've heard what you've said, and I'll make note of it in my report," Ms. Finklestein said, standing to leave. "I appreciate your time this morning, and I wish you all a merry Christmas."

Sam wanted to tell her that the only chance they had of a merry Christmas was if she recommended the court keep the twins with them. But she held her tongue, walked her out with Nick and thanked her for coming.

When the sturdy older woman was out of sight, Sam rested her head on Nick's chest. "I can't handle this."

"Me either."

"She absolutely has to be on our side. I don't know what I'd ever do if we lost custody of them."

"I can't bear to think about it."

"I hate to say that I have to go. If I leave now, I might catch Gonzo's testimony."

"Go ahead and go. I've got the rest of the morning free to spend with the kids, and Celia will relieve me at noon until you get back."

Sam went up on tiptoes to kiss him. "It's going to be okay."

"It has to be," he said, hugging her.

"Love you. Love our sweet family."

"Love you, too."

"I'll be back the second I can."

"Tell Tommy I wish I could be there, too."

"I will."

As she went to meet Vernon and Jimmy, who were driving her to court, she thought about how it would devastate them all to lose the twins. But it would break Nick and Scotty, both of whom finally had the family they'd never had before.

That absolutely couldn't happen.

# CHAPTER THIRTY

"Please state your name for the court," Assistant U.S Attorney Faith Miller said after Gonzo had sworn to tell the truth.

Since entering the courtroom, he'd managed to avoid looking toward the defense table. "Detective Sergeant Thomas Gonzales."

"And you've been with the Metropolitan Police Department for how long?"

"Thirteen years as of this coming February."

"And a Homicide detective for how long?"

"Five years."

"What is your position within the Homicide squad?"

"I'm second-in-command to Lieutenant Holland."

"Thank you, Sergeant. Would you please take the court through the investigation that led to you and your partner, Detective AJ Arnold, attempting to apprehend the defendant, Sid Androzzi?"

In the calm, cool tone he'd practiced with Faith as well as his wife, Christina, over the last few weeks, Gonzo went through the Androzzi investigation from the beginning, starting with a rash of stabbings, several of them fatal, that had eventually led to a man known as Giuseppe Besozzi, who was believed to be Italian. Later, they'd learned that Besozzi was actually Sid Androzzi, who was on the FBI's Ten Most Wanted list for his role in a multicity human trafficking ring. The trial had been combined to include Arnold's murder and the stabbings. Androzzi also faced federal human trafficking charges. Gonzo's testimony was part of a trial that was expected to take up to a month to try.

"Can you describe the events leading up to your encounter with Mr. Androzzi?" Faith asked, with a warm, compassionate look that only he could see.

This would be the hard part.

Before he began speaking, he saw Sam sneak into the room and take a seat in the back.

Fortified by her support as well as the rest of his squad, including Detective Dominguez, who'd surprised him by coming, Gonzo took a deep breath and began to tell the story of the worst night of his life. "Detective Arnold and I had been staked outside of Mr. Androzzi's local residence for several hours. It was long after our regular tour had ended. We were cold, hungry, tired and impatient. At least I was. Arnold was complaining about the cold and being hungry and asking how much longer we were going to wait for Androzzi to come home. I told him we were waiting as long as it took, and if he'd shut up about the inconvenience, I'd let him take the lead with Androzzi."

Gonzo paused and offered a small smile. "He was so excited to take the lead for the first time. Arnold... He was a great young guy, full of enthusiasm for the job and for life. He was becoming an exceptional detective, but he was still young, you know? I used to say he was like a puppy, but the best kind of puppy. Lovable and smart, but with some growing up left to do. Arnold asked me to go through the steps with him so he'd be ready. We did it a few times, going over each aspect of what would need to happen once Androzzi arrived on the scene. Arnold was ready. I'd known that for quite some time, but I hadn't given him the chance yet."

Gonzo's voice broke, and he gave himself a second to get his emotions under control. *This is for Arnold*, he told himself. *You have to get through this for him.*

Arnold's weeping parents, sisters and girlfriend didn't help, but after a minute, he got himself together enough to proceed. "When we finally saw Androzzi, we got out of the car and walked toward him. Arnold showed his badge and began to identify himself. Before he could finish the sentence, Androzzi had fired the shot to the face that killed Arnold. I got off a couple of rounds, but I didn't hit him. In the second it took me to process what'd happened, Arnold was dead, and Androzzi was gone."

Gonzo pulled a tissue from the box on the witness stand and wiped the tears from his eyes. "The thing I remember most was the gurgling sound that came from Arnold's throat. I'd never heard anything like that before, and I hope I never do again."

"What happened then?"

"The Patrol officers who'd been providing coverage for us went after Androzzi. I stayed with Arnold until EMTs arrived and pronounced Arnold dead, and then I went with him to the morgue."

"Is the man who shot your partner in this courtroom today?" Faith asked.

Gonzo finally allowed himself to look at the defendant, who stared back at him with soulless black eyes. "That's him."

"Let the record show that the witness has identified the defendant, Sid Androzzi," Faith said. To Gonzo, she said, "Thank you, Sergeant. Nothing further."

The defense attorney stood to cross-examine Gonzo. "You said the whole thing happened quickly."

"Yes," Gonzo said, his body filled with tension as he anticipated what the defense attorney might ask him.

"How quickly?"

"Thirty seconds, start to finish."

"And in that half a minute, during which your partner was fatally shot, you got a good enough look at my client to identify him without a shadow of a doubt?"

"Yes, I did. I'd know him anywhere."

"What happened after your partner was murdered?"

"We, uh, continued to work the case against Androzzi, who was eventually apprehended. We supported Arnold's parents, sisters and colleagues through the tragic loss of an outstanding young man."

"What happened to you personally?"

Gonzo knew he shouldn't be surprised that someone had fed the information to the defense, but he was, nonetheless. They probably had Ramsey to thank for that. "I went through a very difficult struggle with grief and guilt that included a dependency on pain medication that I've since overcome with the help of therapy and rehab."

Clearly, the attorney hadn't expected him to be so forthright, but Gonzo had learned to own his truth so it wouldn't have destructive power over him anymore.

"During your dependency on pain medication, did you ever do anything illegal to procure the pills?"

Faith jumped to her feet. "Objection! Sergeant Gonzales is not on trial here."

"Sustained," the judge said with a glare for the defense attorney.

Obviously annoyed to have that line of questioning shut down, the defense attorney said, "Nothing further."

"You're dismissed, Sergeant Gonzales, with the court's thanks and sympathy for your loss."

"Thank you, Your Honor."

"We'll take a ten-minute recess."

Gonzo left the witness stand and went straight to Christina, who wrapped her arms around him and held him as tightly as she could. "You did great, Tommy. You were so strong up there."

"Not really."

"No one would ever know that."

Holding his wife's hand, Gonzo left the courtroom and waited outside for his squad and Arnold's family. Everyone hugged him and told him he did great, including Arnold's parents.

"He'd be so proud of you, Tommy," Mrs. Arnold said.

Gonzo found that hard to hear, in light of the fact that he still blamed himself for walking Arnold into a slaughter. But he'd learned the hard way that he couldn't change the facts of that night, as much as he might wish otherwise.

"You were rock solid," Sam said when everyone else had had their moment with him. "I'm so proud of you."

"Thanks. That means a lot. I just hope it was enough." The thought of Androzzi somehow walking free was too much for Gonzo to bear.

"Added to everything else they have on him, it'll be enough. He's going away for the rest of his life."

"I sure as hell hope so."

"You've done everything you can," Sam said. "Now you have to let it go so you can enjoy Christmas with your family."

"Is it fair for me to enjoy Christmas with my family when Arnold can never again do that with his?"

"What would he say to that?"

"He'd tell me to quit saying stupid shit and go home with my wife and son to enjoy my life."

"Then maybe you ought to take his advice, huh?"

Gonzo offered his longtime friend and boss a small smile and nodded. "I'd give just about anything to have him back."

"We all would."

Since there was nothing any of them could do to make that happen, Gonzo put his arm around Christina and led her to their car to go home to their son. For whatever reason, the universe had seen fit to take his partner and leave him to carry on without him. Gonzo was determined to live for both of them while ensuring that no one ever forgot the name of the earnest young officer who'd given his life in service to the District.

WITH ONE DAY TO finish shopping for everyone, Sam hit the local stores on Wednesday with Vernon and Jimmy along for the ride. She let them drive her so she wouldn't have to worry about parking and so she could pop in to surprise startled store owners, many of whom she'd known for years, having grown up in the District.

Thankfully, people mostly left her alone to do what needed to be done, and by that afternoon, she felt somewhat ready. She'd struggled over what to get for Nick and had decided to surprise him with an "experience" rather than a gift. In January, they'd spend a weekend at a spa in Virginia with private accommodations that would keep them separate from the rest of the guests so they could enjoy the time away without intrusion. Their package included facials, a couples massage and a wine tasting, among other things. Now if only the rest of the world would cooperate to allow him to take an entire weekend off...

With the help of online shopping, she'd gotten what she needed for the kids and Elijah as well as her sisters, nieces, nephews, Celia, Shelby, Noah, Freddie, Gonzo's son... The list felt endless, but she was done. She stayed up late on Wednesday wrapping and drinking wine with Celia.

"How're you holding up?" Sam asked her stepmother as she refilled their glasses for the second—or was it the third?—time.

"I'm surprisingly okay," Celia said. "Thank you again for asking me to be here with you all. I think that's made such a difference for me."

"You're helping me more than I could ever help you."

"We're helping each other equally, and I love being part of this exciting time in your lives."

"We love having you."

"If only we'd hear something from the judge," Celia said.

The wait was wearing on all of them. "I know. It's ridiculous."

Sam was on the way to drunk by the time she crawled into bed with Nick shortly after two a.m., thrilled to have her gifts ready to go.

Not surprisingly, he was still awake and wrapped an arm around her to tuck her in close to him.

"You'll be glad to hear that this won't be the year without a Santa Claus."

"Mom for the win," he said.

"I had to get four more stockings for this Christmas, including one for Skippy."

"What a year, huh? We got three more kids and a dog out of it."

"In some ways, the best and worst year of my life."

"I know, babe."

"I can't wait for tomorrow night."

"It'll be fun. Everyone is so excited."

"And you've got it locked down so it's entirely private, right?" she asked.

They were concerned about sending the wrong message after the tragedy in Des Moines.

"We did everything we could, and we'll be confiscating cell phones until everyone is in their rooms. Even though we can totally trust everyone who's coming, people get excited about being at the White House and forget they're not supposed to post anything."

Sam yawned. "Yeah, that's a good call." The next thing she knew, sunlight was streaming into the room, and through the monitor on the bedside table, she could hear Elijah talking to the twins as he got them up and dressed for a Christmas visit with their former nanny. They'd invited Milagros, who remained faithfully devoted to the children, to the White House for lunch with the kids.

She checked her phone for messages and found nothing from

Andy, the one person she most wanted to hear from. The only thing she and Nick wanted for Christmas was confirmation that the twins would remain in their custody. Yawning, she put through a call to Gonzo to check in at work.

"Morning," he said. "Merry Christmas."

"Same to you. How're you doing?"

"I'm better now that it's over and done with."

"I remember that feeling from after I testified against Stahl. It's such a huge relief to know you never again have to lay eyes on the son of a bitch."

"For sure. That was the worst part. Having to actually look at him."

"You were great up there. You did everything you could for Arnold and his family. We're all so proud of you."

"I still feel like I don't deserve that, but I'm doing better at accepting that it was his time to go, not mine."

"I'm glad to hear you say that. How's everything going there?"

"All good. We've got the reports finished for the Thorn and Tappen investigations, and everyone has been arraigned. Josie Ouellette is still raising hell and threatening lawsuits, but there's nothing she can do. We've got the evidence we need that this was all Grace's idea and that she pressured Lucas relentlessly to hold up his end of the bargain they made. Grace threatened to come for him and the rest of his family if he didn't do his part."

"If only he'd come to us rather than kill Mark," Sam said with a sigh.

"We've all been saying that," Gonzo said. "Why not just come clean to us rather than make it worse by killing Mark?"

"I'll never believe a couple of high school kids were behind this."

"Charity is asking for a psych eval for Grace. She seems almost devoid of emotion and doesn't seem to understand the magnitude of the charges she's facing. Jeannie thinks that's an act, that she knows exactly what she did and would do it again if she had it to do over."

"I tend to side with Jeannie on that, but the psych eval will be telling. Thanks for taking this one over the finish line."

"No problem. I'll see you tonight."

"Can't wait."

Sam ended the call, pleased to hear that everything at work

was covered in her absence. Before she'd had a family of her own, she would've wanted to be smack in the middle of it all, but now she had other things she wanted to do, such as spending the rest of the day with her kids. That was her idea of a perfect day now.

Much later, she was putting the finishing touches on the outfit Marcus had put together for their Christmas Eve party when Nick came into the bedroom and stopped short at the sight of her standing before a full-length mirror, marveling at the miracle brought about by the White House glam squad, as she called the in-house hair, nail and makeup team. Having them at her disposal was another major perk of being the first lady—as well as sharing them with her mother, stepmother, sisters, nieces and Aubrey, who'd loved the mani-pedi she'd received earlier.

"Holy bombshell." Nick made a spinning gesture with his finger. "Let me see the rest."

She made a slow, sultry turn so he could see the back, which featured more skin than red silk.

"My first lady is one hot mama." He came up behind her, put his arms around her and placed a kiss on the base of her neck that made her shiver in anticipation of being alone with him later.

"You know what the very best part of a night like this is?" she asked, gazing at him in the mirror.

"Time with our closest friends and family?"

"That's going to be great, but the very best part is at the end of the night when I get to go to bed with you."

"I'm already counting the hours."

"Me, too. Everything all right in the free world?"

"For the moment."

"And no word from the judge?"

"Not yet," he said, sounding as dejected as she'd felt all day hoping for news.

"Since we can't do anything about that, what do you say we have some fun?"

"Let's do it."

# CHAPTER THIRTY-ONE

He was simply devastating in a tuxedo. Sam knew it was uncouth to gawk at her own husband, but she couldn't resist the temptation to let her gaze follow him as he made the rounds, greeting friends and family. The White House photographer was hot on his trail and got an adorable photo of him with his dad, stepmother and two half brothers, who were also decked out in tuxedos.

They'd debated whether to make the party formal, and Sam was glad now that they had. The kids were crazy excited about their fancy outfits, and everyone looked stunning.

Tracy and Angela came up to Sam and linked their arms with hers.

"Most fabulous Christmas Eve party ever," Tracy said. She'd worn a black gown with one shoulder bare and her hair up in an elaborate style.

"The kids are so cute." Angela, whose abdomen was round with the pregnancy of her third child, pointed to her son, Jack, who was following Scotty around the way he always did, and her daughter, Ella, in a fancy green velvet dress, in the arms of her dad, Spencer.

Tracy's kids, Brooke, Abby and Ethan, were taking a tour of all the decorations with Celia and her sisters, who were possibly the most excited members of the group tonight. Sam had taken all the kids to see the famous White House gingerbread house that the twins were obsessed with. They wanted to know when they'd be allowed to eat it.

"Jack was so excited about sleeping at the White House that I was afraid he'd wet himself on the way over here," Angela added.

Sam laughed. "Jack is way past the point where that would happen."

"The White House might be the exception."

"Are the kids okay with Santa coming here?" Sam asked.

"We had a lot of questions from Jack," Angela said, "but I think he understands that Santa will find him and Ella wherever they are."

"Gideon was terrific about coordinating all the gifts so everything is ready for an epic Christmas morning," Tracy said as she accepted another glass of champagne from the waitstaff that circulated through the East Room. They'd be dining shortly in the State Dining Room and then back to the East Room for dancing.

"He's the best," Sam said of the chief usher, who'd been so integral to pulling off this evening.

Shelby, Avery and Noah approached them.

Sam took Noah from Shelby and gave him a tight squeeze. "How's my big boy doing?"

"Santa," he said.

"That's his only word these days," Shelby said, glowing with excitement.

"Only you could pull off the sexiest pink maternity gown in history, Tinker Bell," Sam said, in genuine awe of how Shelby managed to rock pink for every occasion.

"I do what I can for the people," Shelby said with a saucy wink.

"Hey, that's trademarked," Sam said, laughing.

Everyone they loved was there—Freddie and Elin; Freddie's parents; Gonzo, Christina and Alex as well as Gonzo's parents; Joe and Marnie Farnsworth; Jake Malone and his wife; Lindsey and Terry; Harry and Lilia; Graham and Laine O'Connor; Scotty's former guardian, Mrs. Littlefield; Derek, his parents and daughter, Maeve; Andy and his wife, Elsa; Darren Tabor and his girlfriend; Jeannie and Michael; Archie, Cameron, Gigi, Dani and Matt.

Sam and Nick had invited the Reverend Canon William Swain, the childhood friend of Skip's who'd presided over his funeral, to say a blessing before dinner.

"Let us please join hands and bow our heads to ask for God's mercy," Swain said when the group was gathered around a large square table that took up most of the gorgeous State Dining Room.

Sam reached for Nick on her left and Scotty on her right, closed her eyes and bowed her head.

"In this season of Christmas, let us give thanks for this meal, the devoted White House staff who prepared it for us and the company of the loved ones gathered around this table as well as those who couldn't be here tonight. Let us pray for our new president, first lady and first family. May they find comfort in each other as they lead the country and the world through these turbulent times. Let us pray for the families of those lost in Des Moines last week and ask the Lord to provide them with peace and comfort in their time of grief. Let us pray for those we've lost this year, especially our beloved Skip Holland and AJ Arnold. And let us pray for all who suffer from poverty, loneliness, illness and despair this holiday season and ask the Lord to care for them in their time of need. May God bless and keep this family and protect you all in the coming year so that we may gather again next Christmas Eve to once again give thanks for His many blessings. Amen."

"Amen," Sam said as she continued to fight the wave of sorrow for her dad that had been tugging at her all day. More than anything, she wished he could be with them at the White House for their first Christmas. He'd have enjoyed it more than anyone.

"He's here," Nick whispered. "I feel him all around us."

Sam could barely breathe at the way he read her mind. "Thank you for that. I hope he's here."

"He is. I'm sure of it. I've been hearing his voice so much in the weeks since I took the oath. He's very much a part of me, too."

Sam contended with the huge lump that landed in her throat and blinked back tears. "That's so nice to hear."

They'd requested a traditional turkey dinner in Skip's honor, since it was his favorite, and the White House staff had gone all out with every possible side dish.

Sam helped Aubrey cut up her turkey while Eli helped Alden. Elijah had been quiet all day as the stress of waiting to hear from the judge had him as tense as Sam had ever seen him.

As dessert was being served, Nick stood and picked up the wireless microphone the staff had set at his place, per his request. "Sam and I want to thank you all for being with us to celebrate our first Christmas at the White House. We still can't believe that sentence is real, but here we are in the historic State Dining Room with the amazing White House staff taking such beautiful care of us, and we're deeply thankful to them for taking time away from their own families on Christmas Eve to be with us." He led a round of applause for the staff.

"I can't say enough about how incredible the staff is or how grateful we are to them for helping us to make this transition as smoothly as possible. We're also incredibly thankful to all of you for the love and support you've provided us at home and at work as we processed this tremendous change in our lives. A very special thanks to our wonderful Shelby and Celia for all their help with making sure that Scotty, Alden and Aubrey are incredibly well loved. We couldn't do this without you two, and we're so blessed to have you both in our lives." The entire group cheered for Shelby and Celia, whose faces turned bright red.

Nick smiled as he looked over at the kids. "A very special thanks to Scotty, Elijah, Alden and Aubrey for coming on this journey with us. You guys make every day fun and special. You're the family I always dreamed of having, and I love you all so much. And to my beautiful first lady, Samantha... You certainly didn't sign up for the White House, but you've been there for me every step of the way over this last surreal month, and I'll never have the words to tell you how much I love and appreciate you." He raised his glass of champagne. "To the first lady!"

The others cheered for her until Sam was completely mortified. "Thank you," she said to Nick and the others.

With a delighted smile, Nick said, "This is for you, babe."

Jon Bon Jovi came strolling into the room like he lived there, and Sam let out a very un-first-lady-like squeal of excitement that only intensified when another man sat at a piano she hadn't even noticed earlier. When the opening notes of "Hallelujah" played, tears filled her eyes when she recalled how much her dad had loved that song.

Sam took hold of Nick's hand. "Best Christmas present ever."

"It was a little hard to shop this year."

She laughed through her tears at the understatement of the century.

"This is for our new president and first lady, with all my best wishes," Jon said.

As he sang the beautiful song, Sam's heart was filled with so many emotions—love, gratitude and joy for the people closest to her and sorrow for the ones who were gone.

Jon performed an entire set of many of his biggest hits and then asked Sam and Nick to join him.

"This song might bring back some memories from one of our earlier meetings." He performed their wedding song, "Thank You for Loving Me."

Nick wrapped his arms around Sam, and for a few minutes, there was only him, only them as they danced to the song that meant so much to them.

"Thank you so much," Sam said, blowing a kiss to Jon when the song ended.

Next, Jon asked Dr. Harry Flynn to join him.

Knowing what was coming, Sam was on pins and needles as Harry walked up to take the microphone from Jon. He looked ridiculously handsome in his tuxedo, and his big smile put his adorable dimples on full display.

"I gotta say that I never expected to be in the White House taking the microphone from Jon Bon Jovi and looking on as two of my best friends have made us so very proud as our new president and first lady."

Harry led a warm round of applause that embarrassed Sam and Nick.

"Since we were going to be together tonight, I asked my buddy Nick if I could borrow his house for a minute to take care of some very important business. Lilia, would you mind joining me up here?"

Lilia looked around with a confused expression as she made her way to Harry. Her shock was further compounded when her parents, grandparents and siblings, as well as Harry's parents and brother, came in to join the party.

"What is happening?" Lilia asked.

"Come here, and I'll tell you," Harry said.

"This is so freaking exciting," Sam whispered to Nick.

Nick put his arm around her as they watched Harry hold out a hand to Lilia.

"Lilia, my sweet love, you've changed my entire life since we met by chance in Sam's office at the police department, and I'll be forever thankful to her for bringing you to me. For so long, I'd been searching for something, and I had no idea what it was until I had you and realized I'd been looking for you."

He dropped to one knee as Lilia contended with a flood of tears. "Will you please marry me and make everything even more perfect than it's been since the day I met you?"

"*Yes.*" Lilia covered her heart as tears fell from her eyes. "God, yes."

Harry rose to his feet to kiss and hug her before sliding a ring on her finger while everyone else exploded in applause.

Sam wiped away her own tears as she clapped and whistled as loudly as she could for two of her favorite people. She'd wanted this for Harry for as long as she'd known him, and Lilia was simply the best. She'd done some good work with those two, if she said so herself. "That was *perfect.*"

"Couldn't agree more," Nick said.

They went to congratulate the happy couple with hugs and more champagne.

"Did you know about this?" Lilia asked Sam, who'd never seen her friend look happier.

"I might've heard a rumbling or two. I'm so happy for you guys. He's the best of the best, and so are you."

"Thank you for introducing us. He's the best thing to ever happen to me."

Sam glanced at Nick, who had one of his five-year-old brothers on his shoulders as he talked to his dad, Leo, and stepmother, Stacy. "There's nothing better than seeing two great people who deserve all good things finding each other in this crazy world."

"Couldn't agree more," Lilia said. "Best night of my life."

Then Sam got to hug Jon Bon Jovi, which made her year and her Christmas. "Thank you so much for taking time away from your own family to be here."

"It's a tremendous honor to perform for you guys," he said. "We wish you all the best during your stay in the White House."

Nick shook his hand and thanked him for coming.

"When the president calls and asks for a favor that'll earn him a year's worth of points with the first lady, I couldn't say no to that."

Sam and Nick laughed and walked him out to fly home to New Jersey to join his own family for the holidays.

As they returned to the East Room, where the party had moved for dancing, Jeannie asked for a moment with Sam.

"I'll be right in," she told Nick.

"I won't keep her too long," Jeannie said.

"Take your time, ladies," Nick said as he walked away.

"You two look beautiful tonight," Jeannie said.

"So do you. You're positively glowing in that gown." Jeannie's dress was a midnight blue with the faintest hint of sparkle.

"The glow is because of one of the things I wanted to tell you." She paused before she said, "I'm pregnant."

Sam hugged her friend and colleague. "That's wonderful, Jeannie. Congratulations! I'm so happy for you and Michael."

"Thank you. I was almost afraid to tell you…"

"Please don't feel that way. I have what I need with Nick and the kids. My life is very complete. Things don't always happen the way you plan, but they work out the way they're meant to."

"Yes, I guess that's true. The other thing I wanted to tell you is I think I've located Daniella Brown, the woman believed to have abducted Carisma Deasly."

Sam glanced into the East Room, where the chief was laughing at something the captain was saying. "Where?"

"She's living in the Richmond area. I'm almost one hundred percent sure it's her, but I won't know for certain until I go there and dig a little deeper. I know this isn't the time, but I'd be happy to walk you through the evidence."

"Let's talk the day after Christmas about how best to handle this. As much as I hate to make Carisma's family wait one more day, we need to be very careful how we proceed in light of the clear orders we were given."

"Understood."

"We'll find a way to make this right. I just need to figure out how."

"You know where to find me when you're ready."

"I don't have to tell you how important it is that we keep this quiet until we have a plan."

"I haven't told anyone else, and I don't plan to."

"Thanks for the great work, Detective."

"I wish I could say it was a pleasure, but it's an outrage."

"It sure is. We'll do everything we can to fix this. Somehow."

Sam walked with Jeannie to the East Room, where a local band had everyone up and dancing. Over the next few hours, they danced, drank too much champagne, exchanged gifts with friends and laughed—a lot. Sam noticed Cameron dancing with Gigi and thought about how great the two of them looked together. She hoped that whatever was starting between them would bring them both nothing but happiness.

At nine p.m., Sam stepped up to the microphone. "I hope everyone is having a good time!"

The cheers of their guests confirmed that their party was a huge hit.

"There's been tremendous competition for the honor of sleeping in the Lincoln Bedroom tonight. Nick and I have given this some significant thought and have decided on a contest. A *dance* contest." The announcement was met with equal parts groans and cheers. "Everyone on the dance floor will be considered a contestant. If either Nick or I tap you on the shoulder, you're eliminated. Are you ready to dance?"

She gave the band leader the signal. They'd prepped the band in advance, asking them to play some old-time swing music for the contest, and when they launched into "In the Mood," the younger members of the party had no idea what to do, so they stepped aside, yielding the floor to the older folks.

Within minutes, it became clear that Joe and Marnie Farnsworth had been preparing for this moment their entire married lives and were quickly and unanimously declared the winners by Sam, Nick and everyone else in the room.

"Holy crap, Uncle Joe," Sam said. "That was awesome."

"Your old uncle still has a little gas in the tank," he said, breathing hard from the exertion.

"Congratulations, guys," Nick said. "I'm super impressed."

They'd no sooner crowned the winners with stovepipe hats reminiscent of President Lincoln than Andy came over to them, smiling and holding his phone.

Sam could barely breathe as she, Nick and Elijah waited to hear what he would say. "The judge has denied the Lawsons' petition for custody. The twins will be staying right where they belong."

Upon hearing the news, Elijah broke down.

Sam hugged him tightly as relief flooded her entire body.

"This is what he said," Andy added. "'The twins' parents were very clear about what they wanted for their minor children. They put their faith in their son, Elijah, and I must do the same. While

Elijah has chosen an unconventional arrangement for his brother and sister, it's one that seems to be working for everyone involved, and the children are obviously well loved and cared for in their new home. This court can find no reason to disrupt the current custody arrangement. The petition is denied.'"

As Sam wiped away tears, Nick hugged Elijah and said, "I guess that makes us officially a family."

"We were a family long before this," Eli said. "Thank you so much, Andy, Nick, Sam... Thank you for going to bat for us."

"We've got your backs," Sam said, hugging him again. "Always."

Scotty came over with Alden and Aubrey each holding one of his hands. "What's going on?" he asked, his brows furrowing with concern when he saw tears on the faces of Eli, Sam and Nick.

"Good news from the judge," Sam told him, picking up Aubrey as Nick reached for Alden.

"Oh, thank God," Scotty said, his shoulders sagging with relief.

"You said it, buddy," Nick said.

"First family," the White House photographer said, "everyone say, 'Happy holidays.'"

The six of them stood together, arms around each other, wearing smiles of relief and innocent joy, as the photographer captured the moment for history, having no idea whatsoever that they had just officially became a family forever.

# CHAPTER THIRTY-TWO

A short time later, they moved the party up to the third-floor conservatory, where Nick gathered the kids around him to read "'Twas the Night Before Christmas." The photographer took numerous pictures of the president with Alden and Aubrey on his lap, his brothers, nieces, nephews and friends' kids on the floor, in front of a ten-foot Christmas tree.

As Sam watched and listened, her heart was so full of love for him and the kids they'd made their own. They'd never dared to dream of the family they now had.

Elijah came to stand next to her. "I'm so fucking relieved," he whispered.

"Right there with you, pal." She slipped an arm around him and rested her head on his shoulder as he put his arm around her. They hadn't known him or the twins a year ago, and now they were firmly woven into the fabric of their lives, as if they'd always been there.

After the story, Terry appeared with a printout that he handed to Nick.

"You know what this is?" Nick asked the wide-eyed kids.

They shook their heads.

"It's a map from NORAD that shows Santa is on his way."

The kids scooted closer so they could see.

"He's coming across the ocean right now," Nick said, pointing to the picture of the sleigh on the map, "which means all good boys and girls need to be tucked into bed before he gets here."

"Are you sure he knows where to find us?" Angela's son, Jack, asked.

"I'm positive. I sent a letter from the president to the North Pole with a full list of all the good boys and girls who'd be sleeping at the White House tonight. Now it's time for everyone to go to bed and get to sleep so Santa can come."

Reginald appeared with cookies and milk that the children put on plates for Santa and special White House reindeer food Sam and the kids had made that was left for Santa's team.

Parents claimed their children and took them off to the rooms they'd been assigned earlier as Gideon and several of the butlers stood by to offer help and directions to bedrooms.

"This was the most fantastic night ever," Freddie declared as he and Elin said good night to Sam with hugs.

"It was absolutely magical," Elin declared.

"I'm so glad you enjoyed it," Sam said.

"Thanks so much for including my parents," Freddie said. "They're going to dine out on this for years."

"Of course we included them. Family is family."

Freddie hugged Sam. "Love ya."

"Love you, too," she said as she hugged him tighter than she usually did. "Merry Christmas." Then she hugged Elin. "No sex in the White House, you two."

"What*ever*," Freddie said, laughing as he took his wife's hand to head to one of the third-floor bedrooms.

Sam went downstairs to check on Elijah and the twins, who were tucked into the bed they shared.

Sam leaned over to kiss them both good night. "Sweet dreams, my loves."

Aubrey looked up at her with tears shimmering in her expressive eyes. "I wish Mommy and Daddy were here."

"I know, sweetheart. But I think they're somewhere nearby keeping a close eye on you and Alden and Elijah. They know you're so loved by all of us."

Seemingly satisfied to hear that, the little girl popped her thumb in her mouth and snuggled up to her twin, who put an arm around her.

Alden was wise beyond his years and took care of his sister with a tenderness that never failed to move Sam to tears.

"We'll see you in the morning," Nick said when he came in to kiss them good night.

"What time do you think they'll be up?" Sam asked Elijah when the three of them were in the hallway.

"They were up at five last year."

"Oh my Lord," Sam said. "We'd better get some sleep while we can."

Elijah hugged them both. "I know I keep saying thank you, but... I just... You guys are the best, and I'm so, so grateful to have you in our lives."

"Right back at you, buddy," Nick said. "We can't remember what life was like without the three of you."

"Merry Christmas," Eli said.

"Sleep well," Sam said.

"I'll sleep very well knowing that damned custody case is over."

After Eli walked away, Nick said, "So will I."

"No kidding."

"Gideon and the staff have all the Santa stuff set out in the conservatory," Nick said. "They made the cutest signs so each child will know which gifts belong to them."

"They're the best. Tomorrow is going to be crazy."

"I can't wait to see all the excitement," Nick said. "Let's check on Scotty and then hit the sack. I hear we're in for an early wakeup."

Scotty was in bed with Skippy, who was curled up next to him. Parts and pieces of his tuxedo were scattered about the room. "I know she's not supposed to be in my bed, but you try telling her that. The woman has a mind of her own."

"She's good training for your future wife," Nick said, earning him an elbow to the gut from his wife.

"Oof," Nick said, grinning at Sam.

"I'm so happy the judge saw things our way," Scotty said. "I kept worrying about how we'd ever give them up."

"Now we don't have to," Nick said.

"Are you guys as relieved as I am?"

"We sure are," Sam said. "Even though we knew we had the advantage because of their parents appointing Elijah, you just never know what a judge is going to decide." She leaned over to kiss Scotty's forehead as she scratched Skippy's silky head. "Get some sleep, pal. Elijah told us to expect a five a.m. wakeup."

"Oh jeez. That's too early."

"Welcome to big brotherhood," Sam said.

"Best job I ever had. Merry Christmas."

"Same to you, buddy," Nick said as they headed for the door.

Gideon was still in the hallway, checking a clipboard and speaking into a walkie-talkie.

"How's it going?" Sam asked him.

"All good. Everyone is settled, and we're just making sure there're no last-minute requests before I send everyone home."

"We can't thank you enough for such a wonderful evening," Sam said.

"We all enjoyed it. Everyone appreciated you inviting the staff families in for the reception last weekend. They loved meeting you both and the kids. And, of course, Skippy, the internet superstar."

"She's the most famous one in the family," Nick said, offering his hand to Gideon. "Thank you for all you do. We're blown away every day by the incredible staff."

Gideon shook his hand. "We aim to please, sir. We'll see you in the morning."

With their guests settled in for the night, Sam followed Nick into their bedroom and closed the door, leaning against it with a deep sigh. "That was one hell of a Christmas Eve," she said.

"I'd say it was the best ever, but I sure did miss having your dad with us."

"Me, too, but it's okay to say it was the best ever. He'd certainly agree with that."

"It's nice to be able to have everyone here with us, even if I feel a little guilty about putting so much on the staff at Christmas."

"Gideon said they were happy to do it. They know about the twins and what they've been through. Everyone wants to see them have a magical Christmas."

Nick came to her and ran his hands down her bare arms, careful to avoid the bandage on her left arm, before linking their fingers. "Most beautiful wife I've ever had," he said, kissing her neck.

Sam laughed. "I'd better be the only wife you ever have, mister."

"Only one I've ever wanted, and you know it. How do I get you out of this getup?"

"There's a button right here," she said, pointing to the back of her neck.

When he released the button, the top half of the dress collapsed, leaving her nearly bare from the waist up.

"What've we got going on here?" Nick asked, eyeing the tape Marcus had convinced her to wear in lieu of a bra.

"Blame Marcus. He said, 'Tape up the girls so you won't have to wear a bra.'"

"How do I *un*tape the girls?" Nick asked, his brows furrowing adorably.

"Carefully," Sam said.

Working together, they tugged gently on the tape that had held her breasts in place inside the slinky red gown.

"Ah, there they are," Nick said when the last of the tape had been removed. "My best girls." He cupped them and ran his thumbs over her nipples. "You looked so beautiful tonight, but then again, you always do."

"Same to you. I love how you look in that tux. Hotter than the sun."

"Whatever," he said, as he always did when she commented on his hotness.

Sam laughed as she worked on removing the studs that held his shirt together. "Can you just take this over your head?" she asked, impatient as always.

"Yep." He lifted the shirt and the T-shirt under it up and over his head, revealing her favorite man chest of all time.

She slipped her arms around him and pressed her breasts against him.

"Mmm, now that is what I needed," Nick said, sighing with pleasure. "Best part of the day, hands down."

"Watching you read to the kids was pretty great, too."

"I've never been more relieved in my life than when we got that news from Andy," Nick said.

"I know."

"Having you and the kids... This life, this family, it's everything to me."

"It makes me so happy that you finally have that. The thought of anything messing with it was almost more than I could bear."

"It was brutal. Now, we can relax and fully enjoy the holiday."

"How should we start?" she asked, flashing a coy grin.

"You can start by showing me how to get this gown the rest of the way off you."

She tugged on a snap at her waist that dropped the dress to the floor.

"That was seriously hot, babe." With his sexy hazel eyes full of desire, he took her hand and helped her step out of the gown. Knowing how she was about designer gowns, he bent to pick it up and draped it over a chair before leading her into the bedroom.

"I hate to be a mood killer, but I need to brush my teeth," Sam said.

"Me, too."

Sam used the facilities, brushed her teeth and took preventative Advil to contend with the always-hideous hangover that followed too much champagne. Before joining him in the bedroom, she got him Advil and two melatonin pills to ensure he'd get some sleep. She refilled the water glass and brought it with her to dole out the meds to Nick, who sat on the edge of the bed waiting for her.

"This makes me feel eighty," he said, grinning as he chased the pills with a swig of water.

"You'll feel eighty in the morning after all that champagne if you don't take them."

"Very true." He put the glass on the table, placed his hands on her hips and brought her in close enough to kiss her abdomen. "Remember two years ago today?"

"Ah, yes, the day you convinced me to go all in with a future senator. How could I forget? And in case I forget to tell you, you're a big fat lying liar face. 'One year and out,' my ass."

His low chuckle made her smile. "I love your ass." He gave it a squeeze to make his point. "And in case I forget to tell you, talking you into taking this ride with me was the best thing I ever did, even if it hasn't unfolded quite the way we expected." As he spoke, he brought her onto his lap.

"That's the understatement of the century. Maybe even the millennium." Sam surprised him when she moved just so and sank down on his hard cock.

"*Whoa.* Smooth move, babe."

"You liked that, huh?"

"I love all your moves."

"Then you'll really love this one," she said as she pivoted her hips and drew a deep groan from him.

"Oh yeah, that's a winner."

Sam laughed at his dazzled expression. "I've got quite a few others where that came from."

"Let's see what you've got."

Just as Sam was about to bring out her big guns, the bat phone on the bedside table rang.

Nick groaned. "No, I'm busy!"

Because he couldn't ignore a call on that line, Sam reached for the receiver and handed it to him.

"Yes?"

Sam rolled her hips and stifled a laugh when his eyes rolled back in his head.

Though she wasn't supposed to listen when he got calls on that phone, she couldn't help but hear what the person on the other end was saying.

"Mr. President, a bomb has been found outside the gates to the White House."

∿

Have you been wondering about Roni Connolly's story in *Someone Like You*, book 1 in my all-new Wild Widows Series? Turn the page for a sneak peek of this exciting new series, which features appearances in book 1 from Sam and Nick!

∿

DON'T BE mad at me for leaving you with **a bomb at the gate!** Of course we have to have something to look forward to, right?! *State of the Union*, book three in the First Family Series, is coming in 2022, with much more excitement for Sam and Nick after that. I'm loving writing their new life in the White House, and I hope you're enjoying it, too. A big thank you to all the readers who gave *State of Affairs* such a huge welcome earlier this year and to all who've read *State of Grace*, too. You make this "job" so much fun!

Join the *State of Grace* reader group *www.facebook.com/groups/stateofgracereaders/* to dish about the details of this book and the Fatal/First Family group *https://www.facebook.com/groups/FatalSeries* to be the first to hear about the preorder for the next book, *State of the Union*. Don't forget to also join my newsletter list at *https://marieforce.com* to keep up with all my book news.

Special thanks to the team that supports me every day—Julie Cupp, Lisa Cafferty, Jean Mello, Andrea Buschell, Nikki Haley and Ashley Lopez. A big thank you Kristina Brinton for the gorgeous cover of State of Grace, my editors Joyce Lamb and Linda Ingmanson and my primary beta readers Anne Woodall, Kara Conrad and Tracey Suppo. A shout out to my home team of Dan, Emily and Jake, who are so supportive of my author career.

Retired Capt. Russ Hayes, of the Newport, RI, Police Department, has read every installment of Sam and Nick's story ahead of publication to check my police work, and I so, so appreciate his input into this series!

Thank you to my last line of defense beta readers, who check the final, final version for last-minute issues: Gwen, Irene, Maricar, Marti, Juliane, Jennifer, Jenny, Viki, Marianne, Sarah Jennifer, Karina and Gina.

And last but certainly not least... To the readers who show up for every new book with so much excitement and enthusiasm, this one is for you with my best wishes for a wonderful holiday season and a happy, healthy new year.

Much love,
Marie

# SOMEONE LIKE YOU

## THE WILD WIDOWS, BOOK 1

**"Tell me, what is it you plan to do with your one wild and precious life?" —Mary Oliver**

### Chapter 1

Five and a half months ago today, I married Patrick Connolly, the love of my life. During the spring semester of my junior year at the University of Virginia, where he was attending grad school, Patrick stopped by my dorm room with my roommate Sarah's boyfriend and never left. We were a couple from the moment we met. Sarah told me later she'd never witnessed such an immediate connection between two people. After Patrick was shot and killed on October 10, just over two months ago, she told me she's still never known any couple more "meant to be" than we are.

Or I guess I should say than we *were* because we're over now. He's gone at thirty-one, and I'm left to face the rest of my life without him. I'm a widow at twenty-nine, and it's my fault Patrick was killed. I wasn't the one who fired the stray bullet that hit him in the chest and killed him instantly. But I was too lazy to go to the grocery store the night before, which meant we had nothing for him to take for lunch. He'd left his office on 12th Street to go grab a sandwich and was on his way back when an argument across the street escalated into the shooting that left my husband dead.

Of course, Patrick could've gone to the store, too, but that was something I did for both of us, along with the laundry and the dry cleaning pickups. As an up-and-coming Drug Enforcement Agency IT agent, Patrick worked a lot more hours than I do as an obituary writer for the *Washington Star*. I can bring work home with me, but due to the sensitive nature of his cases, he couldn't do that. So I took care of the things I could for both of us, including the grocery shopping. For the rest of my life, I'll have to wonder if I'd gone to the store that night, would Patrick still be alive.

I've only shared my guilt about that once—at a grief group for victims of violent crime that my new friend Sam Holland invited me to attend. She's the lead Homicide detective for the Metro DC police department—and the nation's new first lady. For some reason, she's decided we need to be friends, which is funny because I've had a huge lady crush on her for the longest time. She's a badass cop who happens to be married to our new president, but she doesn't let that stop her from chasing murderers. The day Patrick was killed, she was the one who had to tell me the horrific news.

I'll never forget that day or how I went from being happily married to my one true love to being widowed in the span of ten unbearable seconds. I can't even think about that day, or I'll put myself right back at day one of a lifetime without Patrick. At first, I was surrounded around the clock by people who care, especially my parents, sisters, brother, extended family and close friends. They saw me through the dreadful first week and the beautiful funeral at the National Cathedral. They took care of the massive influx of food, flowers, gifts and sympathy.

One by one, they'd had no choice but to return to their lives, leaving me alone to pick up the pieces of my shattered existence. My mom held out the longest. She was with me for three weeks, and even slept with me many a night, holding me as I cried myself to sleep. Once, she found me on the floor of the bathroom at two in the morning. I have no idea how I got there or how long I'd been there when she found me shivering violently.

I shook for hours in bed afterward, unable to get warm.

Sometimes I wonder if I'll ever be warm again.

Our bed, which had once borne the scent of Patrick on the pillows next to mine, now smells like my mother. I'm left to love alone in the Capitol Hill apartment we chose together and furnished with loving care over a year of weekends spent at flea markets and antique sales. We'd wanted something different, funky and special, not just another living room or bedroom plucked from the floor of a furniture showroom. We wanted our place to reflect us—a little artsy (me), a little nerdy (him), with an emphasis on music (both of us) and cooking (both of us, but mostly me). We'd also wanted to be able to entertain our friends and family in a warm, comfortable space. Our apartment is gorgeous. Everyone says so. But now, like everywhere else that meant something to us, it's just a place where Patrick will never be again.

For something to do, I've been taking long walks through the neighborhood, getting lost on side streets for hours. Anything to keep me away from the apartment where I see my late husband everywhere I look, and not just in the framed wedding photos in the living room and on the bedside table. I see him on the sofa watching football, hockey and baseball. I see him lounging on the bed, completely naked and erect, a smile on his handsome face as he reaches for me and drags me into bed with him, making me laugh and sigh and then scream from the way he made me feel every time he made love to me.

I miss his hugs, his kisses and the way he had to be touching me if he was anywhere near me. Whether on the sofa, in bed or in the car, he was always touching me. I crave his touch, his scent, his smile, the way he lit up with delight any time I walked into a room. I fear no one will ever again look at me like that or love me the way Patrick did.

Our life together was perfection, from Ella Fitzgerald Sundays to Moody Blues Mondays to Santana Taco Tuesdays to Bocelli Italian on Wednesdays. Every week, seven different themes chosen by my music afficionado husband from the fifteen hundred records he'd been collecting since he was fourteen, when his late grandfather introduced him to the magic of vinyl.

The first minutes of every new day are the worst, when I wake up, reach for him and have to remember all over again that he's gone forever. He was the most important person in my life. How can he be *gone*? It makes no sense. He was thirty-one years old, with his whole life ahead of him, a dream career, a new wife and more friends than most people make in a lifetime.

One random second of being in the exact wrong place at the wrong time, and it's all over. That's what I think about as I walk for miles through the District, finding myself in places I've never been before even after living here for more than five years. I came to DC right out of college and lived in Patrick's nasty apartment in Shaw for a couple of years before we moved to our dream place on Capitol Hill after Patrick received a huge promotion—and a raise.

Fortunately, he also had awesome life insurance through work, which means I won't have to move. Not right away, anyway. Eventually, I'll probably want to live somewhere else, where the memories of the life I had with him aren't present in every corner of the home we shared.

In addition to the emotional trauma, no one tells you how much *work* death is. The endless forms to be completed, not to mention the number of times you need to produce a death certificate to close an account or change something simple. Every piece of mail comes with someone who needs to be told the news —a credit card company, an alumni association, an insurance agent. It's endless and exhausting and results in a slew of fresh wounds every time someone expresses shock at the news of Patrick's sudden death.

And then there's the criminal element, which is marching forward with hearings that must be attended by the loved ones of the murder victim. That includes the special joy of dealing with the anguished family members of the shooter, who made a tragic mistake and ruined two lives in the span of seconds. I feel for his heartbroken mother, sister and girlfriend. I really do, but he took Patrick from me, so my empathy for them only goes so far.

It's all so screwed up, and every day I'm left to wonder how my perfect, beautiful life has evolved into this never-ending nightmare. Thank God for my parents, sisters, brother and a few of my closest friends, who've been so relentlessly there for me. I say *a few* of my closest friends, because some have all but disappeared off the face of the earth since Patrick died.

Sarah, the college roommate who was part of us from the beginning, told a mutual friend who *has* been there for me that she just can't bear it. How sad for her that she can't bear the loss of *my* husband. The minute I heard that, a close friend of ten years was dead to me. If she can't put her own needs aside to tend to mine in my darkest hour, then I guess we were never friends to begin with. I'm tempted to cut her face out of the wedding party photos.

On top of this already huge mountain of crap, I feel like

absolute shit most of the time. I can't eat without wanting to puke. I can't sleep for more than an hour or two at a time. My head hurts, my eyes are probably infected from all the tears and even my boobs are aching as if they're mourning the loss of Patrick, too. I've lost fifteen pounds I really didn't have to lose, as I'm one of those women you love to hate—the one who struggles to keep weight on while everyone else is trying to lose it.

It's okay to hate me for that. I'm used to it. But losing fifteen pounds is not a good thing for me, and it has my family freaking out and insisting I see a doctor immediately. I have that to look forward to tomorrow.

In the meantime, I walk. It's barely seven in the morning, and I've already been out for an hour when I circle back to Capitol Hill to head home. I'm walking along Seventh Street near Eastern Market when I see a man on the other side of the street, moving in the same direction I am so I can't see his face. He's built like Patrick, with the same lanky build and fast-paced stride that used to annoy the hell out of me when I tried to keep up with him. We fell into the habit of holding hands anytime we walked somewhere together so I wouldn't get left behind.

I pick up my pace, curious to see where the man is going. I'm not sure why I feel compelled to follow him, but hey, it's something to do. I went back to work two weeks after Patrick died and decided I just wasn't ready to be there writing about death, so *The Star* management insisted I take paid bereavement leave for a few more weeks. That's super generous of them, but it leaves me with way too much time with nothing much to do. Following a man who looks like my husband from the back seems like a good use of fifteen or twenty minutes.

When he ducks into one of my favorite coffee shops, I follow him, standing behind him in line. He's wearing gray pants and a black wool coat that I stare at while we wait in line to order. He also smells good. Really good. What the hell am I doing here? I don't even drink coffee. I hate the taste and smell of it, and Patrick tended to his morning addiction after he left the house most days so I wouldn't have to smell it.

I glance at the menu and see they have hot chocolate and decide to order that and a cinnamon bun because I need the calories, and the pastry looks good to me. I can't recall the last time food of any kind tempted me. My mom bought me those Ensure drinks they give to old people in nursing homes because she's so alarmed by the weight I've lost since Patrick died.

I lean in a little closer so I can listen to the man in front of me order a tall skinny latte and an everything bagel with cream cheese to go.

That's all it takes to send me reeling. Patrick *loved* everything bagels loaded with cream cheese. I used to complain about the garlic breath they gave him after he ate them.

I turn and leave the shop before I can embarrass myself by bursting into tears in a crowd of strangers who just want their coffee before work. They don't need me or my overwhelming grief in the midst of their morning routine. Tears spill down my cheeks as I hustle toward home, feeling sick again. I'm almost there when the need to puke has me leaning over a bush a block from home. Because I've barely eaten anything, it's basically another round of the dry heaves that've been plaguing my days and nights for weeks.

"Gross," a male voice behind me says. "That's my bush you're puking in."

I can't bring myself to look at the man. "I'm sorry. I tried to make it home."

"Have you been drinking?"

"Nope."

"Sure, you haven't. Move along, will you?"

I want to whirl around and tell him my husband was recently *murdered*, and he needs to be kinder to people because you never know what they're dealing with, but I don't waste the breath on someone who probably isn't worth the bother. Instead, I do as he asks and move along, half jogging the remaining block to my building and rushing up the stairs to my third-floor apartment full of memories of my late husband.

There's nowhere to hide from a loss of this magnitude. And now I'm doing weird shit like following men who remind me of Patrick from behind. I'm glad I never saw the guy's face. For now, I can hold on to the illusion that it could've been Patrick, even if I know that's not possible. Maybe me seeing someone who resembled him from behind was a message from him. Sometimes I feel like he's close by, but those moments are fleeting.

For the most part, I feel dreadfully alone even in a room full of people who love me. Bless them for trying to help, but there's nothing they can say or do to soothe the brutal ache that Patrick's death has left me with. I've read that the ache dulls over time, but part of me doesn't want it to. As long as I feel the loss so deeply, it's like he's still here with me in some weird way.

I'm aware that I probably need therapy and professional support of some kind, like what I got from Sam's group for victims of violent crime. It was helpful to know there're others like me whose lives were forever altered by a single second, but again, that support doesn't really change much of anything for me. Patrick is still gone.

Thinking of Sam reminds me I owe her a call to find out if she meant it when she asked me to be her communications director and spokesperson at the White House. A few months ago, a call from the first lady asking me to join her team would've been the biggest thing to ever happen to me. Now I have to remind myself that I owe her a call or a text or something, but that'll take more energy than I can muster right now.

I remove my coat, hat and gloves, toss them over a chair and head for the sofa where I've all but lived since Patrick died. As I stretch out and pull a blanket over myself, I feel sleepy for the first time in a few days. I hope Sam won't mind if I call her tomorrow. Or maybe the next day. She said she'd hold the job for me until I'm ready. What if I'm never ready? What would being ready for something like that even look like in the context of my tragic loss?

I'm so confused and lost and trying to figure out who I am without Patrick. That's not going to happen overnight. It'll probably take the rest of my life to figure that out.

My eyes close out of sheer exhaustion, and I'm shocked to wake up sometime later to realize I slept for a couple of hours, waking when my mom uses her key to let herself into my apartment.

"Oh, thank goodness you're all right." My mom, Justine, is tall and whip thin, with short gray hair and glasses. "I was worried when you didn't pick up."

While she gets busy in my kitchen making me food I won't eat, I check my phone to see I missed four calls from her. My family is worried about me taking my own life, even though I've promised them I wouldn't do that to them. Not that the temptation isn't tantalizing, because it is, but I love life too much to ever consider ending mine prematurely, even if it would mean

I could be back with my love sooner rather than decades from now.

Decades—five, six, seven of them. That's how long I'm probably going to have to live without Patrick. The thought of that is so overwhelming, I can't dwell too much on it or I won't be able to go on.

I never gave much thought to the concept of time when I thought there was plenty of it. Now I know that's not necessarily the case. Why would we think about such a thing when we're in our late twenties or early thirties and just starting our lives? It's not until disaster strikes that we understand that time is the most precious thing we have, and we don't know it until it's too late.

Time used to stretch out before me in an endless ribbon of possibility. Now it's a vast wasteland of nothingness that'll need to be filled with something until I run out of it.

I have no idea what that "something" will be.

Find out more about Roni's story at *marieforce.com/someonelikeyou*.

# ALSO BY MARIE FORCE

**Romantic Suspense Novels Available from Marie Force**

*The Fatal Series*

One Night With You, *A Fatal Series Prequel Novella*

Book 1: Fatal Affair

Book 2: Fatal Justice

Book 3: Fatal Consequences

Book 3.5: Fatal Destiny, *the Wedding Novella*

Book 4: Fatal Flaw

Book 5: Fatal Deception

Book 6: Fatal Mistake

Book 7: Fatal Jeopardy

Book 8: Fatal Scandal

Book 9: Fatal Frenzy

Book 10: Fatal Identity

Book 11: Fatal Threat

Book 12: Fatal Chaos

Book 13: Fatal Invasion

Book 14: Fatal Reckoning

Book 15: Fatal Accusation

Book 16: Fatal Fraud

**The First Family Series**

Book 1: State of Affairs

Book 2: State of Grace

Book 3: State of the Union

**Contemporary Romances Available from Marie Force**

*The Wild Widows Series—a Fatal Series Spin-Off*

Book 1: Someone Like You

*The Gansett Island Series*

Book 1: Maid for Love *(Mac & Maddie)*

Book 2: Fool for Love *(Joe & Janey)*

Book 3: Ready for Love *(Luke & Sydney)*

Book 4: Falling for Love *(Grant & Stephanie)*

Book 5: Hoping for Love *(Evan & Grace)*

Book 6: Season for Love *(Owen & Laura)*

Book 7: Longing for Love *(Blaine & Tiffany)*

Book 8: Waiting for Love *(Adam & Abby)*

Book 9: Time for Love *(David & Daisy)*

Book 10: Meant for Love *(Jenny & Alex)*

Book 10.5: Chance for Love, *A Gansett Island Novella (Jared & Lizzie)*

Book 11: Gansett After Dark *(Owen & Laura)*

Book 12: Kisses After Dark *(Shane & Katie)*

Book 13: Love After Dark *(Paul & Hope)*

Book 14: Celebration After Dark *(Big Mac & Linda)*

Book 15: Desire After Dark *(Slim & Erin)*

Book 16: Light After Dark *(Mallory & Quinn)*

Book 17: Victoria & Shannon (Episode 1)

Book 18: Kevin & Chelsea (Episode 2)

A Gansett Island Christmas Novella

Book 19: Mine After Dark *(Riley & Nikki)*

Book 20: Yours After Dark *(Finn & Chloe)*

Book 21: Trouble After Dark *(Deacon & Julia)*

Book 22: Rescue After Dark *(Mason & Jordan)*

Book 23: Blackout After Dark *(Full Cast)*

Book 24: Temptation After Dark *(Gigi & Cooper)*

Book 25: Resilience After Dark *(Jace & Cindy)*

***The Green Mountain Series***

Book 1: All You Need Is Love *(Will & Cameron)*

Book 2: I Want to Hold Your Hand *(Nolan & Hannah)*

Book 3: I Saw Her Standing There *(Colton & Lucy)*

Book 4: And I Love Her *(Hunter & Megan)*

Novella: You'll Be Mine *(Will & Cam's Wedding)*

Book 5: It's Only Love *(Gavin & Ella)*

Book 6: Ain't She Sweet *(Tyler & Charlotte)*

***The Butler, Vermont Series***

(Continuation of Green Mountain)

Book 1: Every Little Thing *(Grayson & Emma)*

Book 2: Can't Buy Me Love *(Mary & Patrick)*

Book 3: Here Comes the Sun (*Wade & Mia)*

Book 4: Till There Was You *(Lucas & Dani)*

Book 5: All My Loving *(Landon & Amanda)*

Book 6: Let It Be *(Lincoln & Molly)*

Book 7: Come Together *(Noah & Brianna)*

Book 8: Here, There & Everywhere *(Izzy & Cabot)*

***The Quantum Series***

Book 1: Virtuous *(Flynn & Natalie)*

Book 2: Valorous *(Flynn & Natalie)*

Book 3: Victorious *(Flynn & Natalie)*

Book 4: Rapturous *(Addie & Hayden)*

Book 5: Ravenous *(Jasper & Ellie)*

Book 6: Delirious *(Kristian & Aileen)*

Book 7: Outrageous *(Emmett & Leah)*

Book 8: Famous *(Marlowe & Sebastian)*

*The Treading Water Series*

Book 1: Treading Water

Book 2: Marking Time

Book 3: Starting Over

Book 4: Coming Home

Book 5: Finding Forever

*The Miami Nights Series*

Book 1: How Much I Feel *(Carmen & Jason)*

Book 2: How Much I Care *(Maria & Austin)*

Book 3: How Much I Love *(Dee & Wyatt)*

*Single Titles*

Five Years Gone

One Year Home

Sex Machine

Sex God

Georgia on My Mind

True North

The Fall

The Wreck

Love at First Flight

Everyone Loves a Hero

Line of Scrimmage

**Historical Romance Available from Marie Force**

*The Gilded Series*

Book 1: Duchess by Deception

Book 2: Deceived by Desire

# ABOUT THE AUTHOR

**Marie Force** is the *New York Times* bestselling author of contemporary romance, romantic suspense and erotic romance. Her series include Fatal, First Family, Gansett Island, Butler Vermont, Quantum, Treading Water, Miami Nights and Wild Widows.

Her books have sold more than 10 million copies worldwide, have been translated into more than a dozen languages and have appeared on the *New York Times* bestseller more than 30 times. She is also a *USA Today* and *Wall Street Journal* bestseller, as well as a Spiegel bestseller in Germany.

Her goals in life are simple—to finish raising two happy, healthy, productive young adults, to keep writing books for as long as she possibly can and to never be on a flight that makes the news.

Join Marie's mailing list on her website at marieforce.com for news about new books and upcoming appearances in your area. Follow her on Facebook at www.Facebook.com/MarieForceAuthor and on Instagram at *www.instagram.com/marieforceauthor/*. Contact Marie at *marie@marieforce.com*.

Made in United States
North Haven, CT
19 December 2021